Heart of a Gentleman

THE **HEARTS OF AMBERLEY** SERIES

The Vagabond Vicar
Gloved Heart
Heart of a Gentleman
The Doctor's Heart (coming soon)

Go to www.charlottebrentwood.com and sign up
to my email newsletter for book news!

PRAISE FOR CHARLOTTE BRENTWOOD

I am completely, unabashedly in love with this book. Many books claim "fans of Jane Austen will love this" - this one lives up to the claim. It's an enchanting read that pulls you into it and carries you happily along. It was so refreshing to read a high-quality book that was clean all the way through.
Heather from Word Menagerie on THE VAGABOND VICAR

This book is wonderful. It had me so involved that I could not put it down. What a great story, so well told. I loved it.
'Kindle Customer' on GLOVED HEART

I absolutely adored this novel. It's a beautiful, historical version of boy-meets-girl that manages to never fall into the dreaded classification of "cliché and predictable". The narrative is wonderfully written, with exquisite attention to detail.
Alexia Bullard for eBook Review Gal on THE VAGABOND VICAR

The author has written a delightful historical story that sees those times for what they were, not all wonderfully good people but also not all evil people. There is a very strong female lead … a sweet clean romance that made me fall in love with the characters and I was engaged throughout the story.
Sharon, a reader at Amazon.com on GLOVED HEART

One of my favorite things about The Vagabond Vicar was Brentwood's original story filled with interesting plot twists that kept me turning page after page. The suspense, action, and development of characters rose as the novel neared its close, bringing the ending to a touching conclusion. This is a Regency novel worth adding to your to-read list.
Katie Patchell at Austenprose on THE VAGABOND VICAR

Gloved Heart is a Regency romance complete with many swoon worthy moments. A delightful Regency romance with engaging characters.
Stephanie, a reader at Amazon.com on GLOVED HEART

There are no straight lines in this novel, and the story takes off in unexpected directions. It is a different approach to historical fiction and makes for interesting reading. Charlotte's prose is beautiful and so easy to read, like a river slowly flowing through the landscape. Gloved Heart with its secrets and mysteries, keeps you wondering until the very end. A most pleasant read.
Lisa - The Content Reader on GLOVED HEART

I loved this book. I find it extremely frustrating that there are so many historical romances which are merely fronts for endless, anachronistic sex scenes and so few genuinely affecting love stories like The Vagabond Vicar… the best book I have read in a long time. I couldn't put it down.
Carolyn Cooke, a reader at Amazon.co.uk on THE VAGABOND VICAR

Here is a tale that runs the gamut of emotions and gently brings along the reader for a heart touching and highly satisfying ride. An intricately woven tale with believable characters in a setting that is surely true to its era. The author's carefully constructed foreshadowing and descriptive technique provide a rich and enjoyable reading experience. I highly recommend this one!
Carpe Diem on GLOVED HEART

An unashamedly romantic novel, The Vagabond Vicar moves along at a great pace and is never boring. A lover of Georgian romance will enjoy this, particularly as it is not solely concerned with earls and dukes, but takes a wider view of the world. An indulgent read.
Nicky Galliers for the Historical Novel Society on THE VAGABOND VICAR

This is an adorable, heartwarming regency romance that will truly make you smile. I absolutely loved this book. Gloved Heart is such a lovely, charming and romantic novel. Although it does have its fair share of heartbreak (I cried on more than one occasion!), you will smile and feel warm inside when you read this. If you love historical fiction, romance, regency romance or just want something to warm your heart then you should definitely check this out!
Chelle - Curled Up with a Good Book on GLOVED HEART

HEARTS OF AMBERLEY
BOOK THREE

Heart of a Gentleman

CHARLOTTE BRENTWOOD

For my husband: my hero

Prologue

London, England

Spring 1800

"I love you, John."

It was the only time in his life he'd heard that sweet utterance. Those four little words were to be the making and undoing of John Barrington: the source of his greatest happiness and deepest sorrows.

Miss Julie Stone was his world, his everything. His first and only true love. From the moment he'd tenderly caressed her delicate hand, he couldn't see his future without her. His was entirely hers, and nothing else mattered.

After completing his education at Oxford he'd been whisked away to Europe for the obligatory Grand Tour. His elder brother George had certainly shown him the ways of the world, with endless nights, free flowing liquor, and women who were all too obliging.

On his return, and upon entering the London social whirl, Julie was the first woman he saw – really saw. Across the ballroom, a vision of dark hair and green eyes. When she had noticed him and smiled, it set his whole body on fire. But not a fire of lust – a pure flame which he had never known the like of before, nor since. He didn't even kiss her until they had promised themselves to each other.

She was his everything, and there was nothing he would not do for her. His every thought was occupied with her loveliness, and how he might make her happy. He wanted to give her his everything – which granted, wasn't that much. As the second son of an earl, he was not in line for a peerage. He lived on a tolerable allowance, but he hadn't used his time at university to develop any particular interests – except gaming and charming ladies.

The one ace he had up his sleeve was the property he was due to inherit on marriage. Consisting of a cottage ornée, a home farm, gardens, and some tenanted properties, he'd been told the estate would keep him comfortable – so there seemed little point in actively seeking a profession in the meantime. And with his mind (and heart) so well occupied with pleasing Julie, it hardly signified. She had her own generous dowry of some three thousand pounds. If well invested, it would give them security for the long term... for the family he longed to create with her. A house full of little Julies – what could be better?

After all, they didn't need all the superficial luxuries that life had to offer. Of what importance was it if they wouldn't be able to maintain their own London townhouse, or travel abroad? They had each other, and they had love. That was all that mattered.

After she'd given him those precious words, she took his arm, and he squeezed her hand tenderly. Gazing deeply into her eyes, he whispered, "And I adore you, my love. I will until my dying day."

He had never been surer of anything in his life.

PART ONE: THE ARRIVAL

Chapter One

Hampshire

June 1806

"Nearly there now, my girl."

Turn right at Willow Bridge, they'd said. After the sun dipped in the sky he came to a wide driveway with enormous gates, and there upon a huge stone plinth the word 'Willowbridge' was engraved. To the right there went a muddy lane. "I suppose that must be it, Thora."

Thora tossed her head a little and chuffed at him. He leaned down to give her strong neck an encouraging pat. She'd been with him for the three-day journey, tethered to the stagecoach and now hitched up to a hired cart which bore the load of his trunk and a few belongings. Indeed, he hardly went anywhere without her. She was his faithful companion, probably the only true friend he'd ever had. She'd been by his side for the last five years and he looked after her as if she were his child. It was unlikely he'd ever have children of his own. Except for... well, that did not signify.

He sat upright and toyed with a ring on his left hand.

"Off we go."

They started off down the road towards his inheritance, passing a handful of small cottages. "Those must be mine, too," he muttered to himself. As darkness descended, a fine mist began to swirl about the meadows, but John caught sight of his object as they rounded a bend.

His weary soul was encouraged by the light flickering in the windows of the little cottage ornée that was to be his home… for now, at least. They must have lit the fires to welcome him. His very bones ached from sitting in the saddle so long, but he'd wanted to bring his own mount with him – one trace of the better existence he had known until now.

As they approached the house, John dismounted. "Let's find you somewhere to rest," he said to Thora, and he led her around the house. Finding some small outbuildings, he called out in the hope that a stable hand would present himself. The only answer was cold, damp stillness.

He found the stable and unhitched the cart from Thora before leading her inside. He yawned and then shivered, his stomach growling. He longed to change into clean, dry clothes. But her needs came before his. The first stall was occupied by a donkey, which he surmised must be the servants' animal. He led Thora into the next stall and found her water and food. Unburdening her of her tack, he brushed her down and rubbed his hands over her tight muscles.

"There now, girl. Time for you to rest." He got her settled into the hay and, unable to find any other coverings, he retrieved a blanket from his trunk which his grandmother had made. He tickled her chin and bade her goodnight.

When he made his way back into the biting cold, it was pitch dark. He took some essential items from the saddle bags and made his way back to the front of the house. Trying the front door, he found it unlocked and pushed it open. The door shuddered inward, revealing a small entrance hall with steps leading up to the next floor. He turned into what must be the parlour, then stepped back in horror.

The fire was indeed roaring in the hearth, but the room was occupied. A man and woman were reclining in deep chairs, with their stocking-clad feet up on the small table in front of the fire. They each held a slice of bread on a long skewer, toasting them in the flames.

Recovering from his initial shock, his marched towards the pair in confusion. When they didn't stir, he cleared his throat loudly.

The man jumped up off his chair, dropping his skewer and causing his toast to fall into the fire.

"Who are you?" the man demanded, peering at him from beneath impossibly bushy eyebrows. He wasn't a tall man, but he had a stocky build and ruddy cheeks.

John straightened his shoulders. "Your master," he replied haughtily. "Assuming you are the help."

The woman also stood and turned to face him. "No, it can't be. Mr Barfoot?"

"Barrington," John corrected her through clenched teeth. "I am sure someone must have written with regards to my arrival."

"Well, Mr Wilson the bailiff did tell us someone would be coming to live here," the man said, "but we thought 'twould be another month or so before you actually turned up. We thought you'd spend Christmas with your family, at the very least."

John closed his eyes for a moment to gather himself. As far as his family were concerned, he was on his own. In point of fact, he'd always been on his own, really.

"As you see, that is not the case," he said coldly. "Here I am. Will you tell me who you are, please?"

"Oh yes, sir," the woman said, dropping into a wobbly curtsey. "I'm Betty Morgan, the housekeeper, and that's my husband Tom, who manages... well, tell him what you do, love."

Tom blinked at John. "All the odds and sods round the house and garden – you know, wood-chopping, tending to the animals and such."

"Right." John extended a hand to Tom, and the man stumbled forward to take it. His large, calloused hand squashed John's, and John tried to return the gesture with equal force.

"We'll be off, then," Betty said, looking at her husband pointedly. "If you need something to eat, there's some bread and cheese in the larder."

"Thank you, Mrs Morgan," John said, forcing his mouth into a smile. "I shall retire shortly. Could one of you show me to my room?"

The couple exchanged a glance.

"You might be more comfortable here, sir," Tom said slowly.

"What the devil do you mean? Sleep here, in the parlour?"

Betty nodded. "The fire's not lit in the main bedroom," she said solemnly.

"Can I ask that someone light it then, if you please?" What was wrong with these people?

"The thing is, sir, the fire's not fit to be used." Betty twiddled her apron between her hands. "The chimney's blocked and the sweep can't come 'til next week. We never thought you'd be here so soon."

John sighed. "And the other bedrooms?"

"No mattresses on the beds."

"I see." He'd had enough. One way or another, he'd have some peace and quiet – but there was no way he was sleeping in a public room, where anyone could barge in unannounced. "Thank you for that information. I should be grateful if you would show me the room all the same, so I might deposit my belongings."

"Very good, sir," Tom mumbled, sliding past John. "Follow me."

An hour later, John lay shivering under layers of thin blankets, the winter wind whistling through the room's windows. He wished he had his grandmother's blanket, which would at least provide some warmth. His teeth chattering, he cursed his parents for sending him here like this. But then, he cursed himself. He knew what he'd done… and he deserved much worse.

❧

A delicious warmth and enticing aromas encircled John when he awoke the following morning. A smile on his lips, he opened his eyes. Remembering where he was with a start, he bolted upright. "Oh yes," he murmured, "the couch. A gentleman does *not* sleep on a couch."

He recalled the moment the night before when his whole body had erupted into convulsions and he'd finally given in, heaving his blankets and pillow down to the parlour. The heat from the fire had slowly seeped into his bones, eventually lulling him into slumber.

Now observing the fire, he realised it had been replenished with more wood while he'd slept. First, he was mortified at the thought of a servant witnessing him sleeping there. But then, perhaps he'd been rude to the couple he'd surprised with his arrival. There was some sort of comfort in the knowledge they'd looked after him still.

There were whispers in the entryway, and when John turned toward the sound, he caught a flash of movement. A few moments later, he heard a clattering of dishes and then stood, stretching out his aching muscles. He caught sight of a clock on the mantlepiece. By gad, he'd slept until nearly noon. It had been a wearying few days of travel, to be sure. And well after midnight when he'd finally dropped off.

He ran a hand through his dark, curly hair, and found his way back to the bedroom. He performed his toilette quickly in the frigid air and dressed in the same clothes he had discarded the night before. He must fetch his trunk.

Back downstairs, he headed towards the smells of breakfast. On entering the dining room, he found Tom Morgan and a young girl laying out plates of food on the sideboard.

"Good morning," he said.

They both spun around to face him.

"Morning, Mr Barton." Tom nodded at him.

"It's Barrington."

"Ah, right-o. Sleep well, did you?" Tom grinned.

"Tolerably, thank you." John couldn't help smiling despite himself. He rubbed a knot in his shoulder. He raised his eyebrows towards the girl, then looked back at Tom.

"Oh yes, this is Rosie, our maid," said Tom. "She does all the jobs Betty and I can't manage, and she can be the one who fetches things for you and the like."

John turned his attention to the girl. She couldn't have been more than fifteen, and she twisted her hands nervously, unable to meet his eyes. "Hello, Rosie," he said.

She attempted a curtsey, and almost fell over.

Abandoning any attempt to converse with the girl, John turned back to Tom. "Does she live here too?"

Tom shook his head. "She lives with her family in one of the cottages on your land, down the lane." He yanked his thumb over his shoulder.

John nodded. "Very good. Well, Rosie, I won't keep you."

Tom gave her a little shove and she left.

John approached the sideboard and took in the little spread of toast, butter, jam, and ham. He poured himself some tea and then began to fill a plate. "Are there any other staff I should be aware of, Mr Morgan?"

Tom shook his head. "No, it's just the three of us. I suppose you'll be wanting to set about hiring more persons soon. A valet for yourself, for starters."

John surveyed his crumpled clothes and cringed inwardly. Was it that obvious that he was inexperienced at dressing himself? "Thank you, Mr Morgan," he said curtly. "I don't need your advice on such matters."

He took his cup, saucer, and plate to the table where some cutlery had been laid out. Taking a bite of his load, which he'd slathered liberally with the butter and jam, he sighed involuntarily. He'd feel better once he'd refuelled himself.

He addressed Tom again, who was hovering awkwardly. "My things are in a trunk around the back of the house."

Tom nodded. "Give us a shout when you're ready, and I can help you shift it up to your room."

"Thank you." John took a large sip of tea, but he had to stop himself from spitting it out. It was cold, and far from the fine blends he was used to drinking. He hastily took another bite of his toast to eradicate the bitter taste, then partook of some ham.

"This food is delicious, Mr Morgan," he said. "Please pass my compliments on to your wife." He thought the man might take this as a friendly hint to go.

"You can tell her yourself," came the reply. "She's still in the kitchen. And call me Tom."

John stared at him. He was supposed to be the one giving the orders. "All right," he said after a moment, "I will. But please don't think you need to attend on me like this." He was used to footmen being in attendance as he ate, but Tom was like a nervous cat.

The man was visibly relieved. "Oh, thank you, sir," he said, and dashed from the room.

John finished his breakfast in peace and then went into the kitchen.

Betty had her back to the door, kneading bread. John couldn't remember having ventured into a servant's domain for many years. Sometimes the female members of the family might consult with the cook directly, but he had always remained above-stairs. In such a small house, there were no such stairs to separate the master from his staff.

"Oh, Betty?"

The woman jumped with a scream and then whirled around, spraying flour across the room from her hands.

"Oh, do excuse me, I did not wish to startle you." This flustered John – he had never apologised to a servant either.

Recovering, she asked, "How can I help you, sir? Didn't you have enough breakfast?"

"No, it was plentiful, I assure you. In fact, I only came in here to tell you how much I enjoyed it. The jam, in particular."

She flushed with pride. "Thank you, sir. It's been only Tom, Rosie, and I for so long that I don't remember exactly what you toffs like to eat."

John stifled a laugh at the derogatory term and Betty flushed scarlet.

"I mean, what the master likes to eat. I'm sorry, I didn't mean –"

He rushed towards her, palms up. "Don't trouble yourself, Betty. I took no offense. How long *is* it since there was a master living in this house?"

She turned back to the bread and thought. "Well, it was when our girl Lizzie was still the maid – she's long since gotten married and moved to the village. It must be getting on for fifteen years ago that your cousin lived here."

"My mother's uncle."

"As I understand it. When he passed on, he said the house was to go to your mother or whoever she wished to take it over. We was just to wait until the person was ready." She smiled at him over her shoulder. "And now you're here, sir."

"Indeed I am," he murmured. Still parched, he procured some hot tea and gulped it down before heading outside.

The sky was smothered with heavy dark clouds, and he inhaled the chilly, damp air. It was really a day for staying inside, but he must see to Thora. If he was to hire staff, a stable boy would be ideal. But it hardly seemed fair to go to the trouble of giving people a place here when he'd probably need to let them go in a year's time.

Thora tossed her head and whinnied in obvious joy at seeing him. "Hello, my girl," he greeted her, nuzzling into her cheek. He made sure she had fresh food and water, and then set about grooming her properly. By the time he was finished, rain was pelting down on the stable's roof, which was not completely weathertight. "I hope you'll be warm and dry in here, Thora," he said, putting the blanket back on her. Water dripped on to the back of his head, dribbling down his neck and back. "You rest up, and we'll go exploring as soon as we can."

At the sound of a shout, he left the stable, and he found Tom waiting to move his trunk. Together they hefted it inside and up to his room. Then, John dried himself off and took a look around the house that was destined to be his home.

In his mind it had always been a sort of last resort, when the inevitable settling down had eventually transpired. However, recent events had catapulted him here rather sooner than he would have liked.

Some fifteen minutes later, his inspection of the house was complete, and he poured himself a cold coffee in the parlour for fortification. Mulberry Manor was a quaint little place, at best. The downstairs reception rooms consisted only of parlour, dining room and library –

hardly conducive for entertaining on the scale he was used to. The bedrooms above were pretty, he supposed, and afforded views of the thousand-odd acres he believed he owned, but only of such a number that a house party of all his London acquaintances would be impossible. At least he was not that far from town. Once he was able to come and go freely, he certainly would.

The house had possessed a grand ambience once, but now the paper on the walls was faded, the brass mouldings tarnished, and the rugs on the floors nearly threadbare. The question was – did he have the motivation to do anything about it? And would he have the funds? Still overwhelmed by recent events, he decided to leave those issues to another day. He glanced down at his hands and realised he was toying with his signet ring.

The front door opened and closed, and suddenly Tom appeared, clutching a newspaper.

"Mr Barnaby, would you care to…"

John snatched up the newspaper and growled, "Barrington." Then, taking a breath, "Thank you, Tom."

Tom eyed him for a moment and then left the room, muttering under his breath.

John took up the *Times* and greedily devoured it from cover to cover. He didn't actually care that much for the news of the world and Society, but the diversion was a tonic for his mind.

Resigned to sleeping in the parlour, he also took his dinner in front of the fire. After breakfast the following day, with the rain still set in, he began to unpack his belongings. The servants were all at church, leaving the house excruciatingly quiet.

The furniture in John's chamber was sparse compared to his mother's ostentatious décor, but functional. A wardrobe, a tallboy, and a dressing table with a chair and a mirror each took their place along the walls. He caught sight of himself in the mirror as he placed a pile of breeches in a drawer, and quickly looked away. When had his eyes become so sunken in, and his eyebrows knitted in a permanent frown?

He sighed as he withdrew some shirts from his trunk, then looked longingly at the bed. Hopefully the chimney sweep would come soon.

On the third day, being alone in the little house began to drive John mad. He had made an art of filling his life with distractions, and being alone with his thoughts was akin to torture. He must find some acceptable company.

Unbidden, his mother's farewell speech invaded his thoughts. "John, do try to settle into the community there. Perhaps you may find a suitable wife."

Ha! He had no intention whatsoever of endearing himself to the people here – not yet. And marrying was not on the cards for the time being, if ever. Women had ruined his life.

Truth be told, he had attempted to bring a wife to Mulberry, but she'd gone and married his nemesis instead.

A small, nagging voice inside him whispered: no one knew him here. He could start afresh. Be a new, better man. No one here had hurt him, or ever would. He would form no ties. Perhaps he could try living a life that would make his mother proud. Perhaps he could be the virtuous gentleman he was before. Before the "gentle" was well and truly dropped. He knew the exact moment it had happened.

Later that afternoon, the weather finally cleared as darkness fell. He readied Thora and used the light of the moon to guide them back to the village of Mulberry. Once there, he was drawn to the only building with lights burning inside.

John purchased a brandy from the publican and found a table in a far corner, aware of curious stares. As he sipped the liquor, its warmth spread from his throat throughout his body, until his brain was happily relieved of any reasonable thoughts. His gaze roved over the room lazily, until it came to rest on a female leaning against the far wall. Her dress exposed a little too much bosom, the rouge on her lips and cheeks a little too bright. He held her eyes for a little longer than was polite, then drained the last of his brandy.

"Can I help you, sir?" She propped herself up on the table, leaning in toward him with the merchandise clearly on view.

He put his glass down. "Yes, my dear, I think you can."

At least tonight he'd be in a warm bed… for a few hours.

⁊⁊

"It's not a pretty picture, Lady Helena, but I thought I should show it to you all the same."

Helena Davenport leaned over the desk in her study and studied the figures her steward had collated in his book of accounts. She ran her finger down to the bottom of the page, and gasped when she saw the final number. "Oh, my. Those repairs to the roof were a deal more than we expected, were they not?"

"Yes, my lady."

"And several tenants are behind with their rents. We cannot continue to sustain losses like this."

"Indeed. We may have to look at selling some decorative items if things do not improve in the short term."

Helena nodded gravely, then straightened and squared her shoulders. "At least once we sell our livestock next autumn, the situation will be much better."

Mr Privett smiled. "That is something we can be sure of. I shall see what I can make stretch in the meantime."

"Thank you, Privett. As always, your guidance is much appreciated." She took up a pen and paper and dipped her quill in the inkwell, beginning to take notes.

"You're quite welcome, my lady," Privett said, sitting back in his chair while he waited for her. "You know I promised your father I would look after you."

For a time, the only sound in the room was the scratching of Helena's pen against the page.

"Oh," Privett said after a while, "I heard the owner of the manor has suddenly taken up residence."

Helena was jotting down some figures. "Oh, really?" she murmured.

"Yes, my lady. The name of Barrington, if I remember right."

Helena finally looked up and nodded. "That sounds familiar, I think. Do we know anything about him? What has prompted his abrupt appearance? I suppose he must have taken a wife and decided to take up his inheritance in order to raise a family. I shall call on the lady when I have a free morning."

She closed the steward's book and handed it back to him before rising from her chair and moving around from behind the desk.

He also came to his feet. "From what I hear, my lady, he arrived alone."

Her steps towards the door halted. "Oh, did he?"

Privett nodded. "I'm led to believe the only locale he has visited thus far is the public house."

Helena raised an eyebrow. "Is that so? Well, perhaps he may deign to visit us in the near future."

She saw Privett out and then made her way to the drawing room, where she dropped into an armchair with a heavy sigh.

"What is troubling you, my dear?"

Helena met eyes with Miss Jane Godwin, the only other person in the lavish but old-fashioned room. "Trouble with finances."

"Ah." Jane picked up a teapot. "May I pour you a cup?"

"Please." Helena examined aspects of the room as the elder lady poured her tea just as she liked it. There was the painting of the third Marquess of Brackley, four generations ago. That should fetch a reasonable amount. Then there was the Chinese vase… but no, her mother had loved that. She couldn't possibly part with it. Perhaps the grandfather clock in the corner would be worth something?

"Here you are, Helena."

The kind crinkles at the edges of Jane's eyes soothed Helena's frazzled nerves. She accepted the cup and saucer with thanks and took a sip of the comforting brew. "What would I do without you?" she asked fondly.

Miss Godwin was Helena's friend and confidante, and along with Mr Privett, the only constant in her life since her childhood. Jane had been Helena's governess, and since the death of her father two and half years earlier, the woman had assumed the role of a companion and advisor. Helena's mother had passed when she was only five years old, having contracted a short and acute illness. Helena was an only child, and Jane had been the bright light of her existence as childhood friends came and went.

Helena had depended on her father, the seventh Marquess, and he seemed to depend upon her as well. He had involved her in estate management from an early age, improving her mathematics skills by showing her their incomings and outgoings, and having her accompany him on all his visits to their tenants. Her eyes settled on another portrait over the rim of her teacup. Her father, in his prime.

"I only hope he would not be disappointed in how I am managing things," she murmured. "He had such faith in me."

"It was faith well-deserved," said Jane reassuringly. "Everything will turn out for the best, you'll see."

Helena smiled at her. "I hope you are right."

There was more at stake than losing sentimental possessions. Helena's whole life depended on her keeping the estate afloat. She was the sole heir, but as she was a woman, there were conditions.

She drew a hand over her eyes, performing some mental calculations. She barely noticed when the door to the room opened. A polite throat-clearing dragged her from her contemplation. A footman stood before her with a letter on a salver.

"Just arrived for you, my lady."

"Thank you, Thompson," Helena said, recognising the handwriting on the letter as she picked it up. "Please be so kind as to let Andrews know I wish to see him."

"Very good, my lady." Thompson bowed and left the room, leaving Helena to stare at the letter.

"Are you going to open it?" Jane teased.

"I suppose I must."

She tore open the seal and read the dozen lines contained within. His usual blend of pomposity and disdain. "He's on his way here to spy on me again," she said.

Jane choked on her tea but recovered quickly. "Sinclair?"

"Indeed."

It was typical of her third cousin to show up when she was in dire straits. Extrapolating on her shortcomings was his specialty. Of course, he wanted her to fail. If she did, Willowbridge would be his, and he was sure to leave her in no doubt that he expected it would be. And as for that insufferable wife of his... Helena tried her best to be charitable to everyone, but some people seemed to be a lost cause.

Her butler came into the room. "You asked for me, my lady?"

"Yes, Andrews, thank you. Mr Sinclair is coming to visit. We should expect him in two days' time. Please ensure everything is in order should he show any... curiosity."

Andrews smothered a smile. "Yes, my lady. I shall ensure the usual rooms for Sinclair and his wife are prepared."

"Thank you, Andrews."

Once the butler had gone, Helena stood and went over to open a French door which led onto a small balcony. "I need some air," she said to Jane over her shoulder.

Once outside, she pressed her hands on the balcony railing and surveyed the majesty that was the Willowbridge estate, a vast parkland, farms, and the village of Mulberry. From her vantage point she could see the lake where her father had taught her to fish, the tree she fell out of causing her to break her wrist, and the rolling fields over which her gelding loved to gallop. She belonged here, and she would not let that man take it away from her.

She could secure the estate for herself through marriage. But she had absolutely no intention of letting a man waltz into her life and take over everything she had worked so hard for… and certainly no intention of ever falling victim to such a weakness as love. She'd watched her father spend the last decades of his life in desperate mourning for her mother. The only outcome of love was pain and suffering, and as a woman, giving up her own rights.

No, marriage was not for her. She would have to make things work or die trying.

Julie's laughter trilled through the trees as John chased her through the crowds of revellers at Vauxhall Gardens. It sounded as a symphony to John's ears. As fireworks burst into the sky, she dashed into a rotunda and let him catch her. He caught her elbows and drew her to him, watching the sparkling lights shine in her eyes.

"I've got you, my love," he said after the noise died down.

She nodded, smiling up at him and lifting her chin.

Smiling back, he lowered his mouth to hers and kissed her reverently. Pure love flooded through him and, he hoped, her as well. Drawing back, he tenderly caressed her cheek. "I hope your family will not come looking for you just yet."

She shook her head with another smile. "They are occupied with the orchestra. John…"

"Yes, my dear?"

"I have something I should like to give you."

"Oh?"

She reached into her reticule and drew out a small box, handing it to him.

His heart soared. "What is this?" He pried the box open, and saw within a large gold signet ring, set with a round black stone, likely onyx.

"It was my grandfather's ring. My grandmother gave it to him as a symbol of their love. He gave it to me when he was dying, with the hope that I might find true love one day." She looked him straight in the eyes. "And I want to give it to you."

"You do?" he gasped. He swept her up into his arms. "Are you sure, my darling? Such a meaningful treasure…" He could hardly believe it. He hadn't let himself dare to think that she was his forever. But now…

She nodded and took the ring from its box, before trying to put it on the fourth finger of his left hand. "You have large hands," she said with a giggle. She slipped it onto the smallest finger instead. "There. You can look upon it and think of me when we are apart."

He swallowed back tears. "I will, my sweet Julie. And I shall procure a ring for your finger which shows the world you will be mine forever. I only wait for the right time to ask for your father's blessing."

They soon returned to their respective family parties, but John cared little for where he was or who he was with. He had never felt more content, accepted – or so deserving of love. He must begin to get his affairs in order and rehearse what he would say to her father.

It was, however, before he addressed the man that he asked for Julie's hand in marriage. The proposal had slipped out before he could restrain his raging emotions. Assured as he was of her mutual affection and dedication, he could wait no longer.

It was the next time they contrived to be alone. During the intermission of a theatre performance, none of the swarming patrons seemed to notice when he pulled her into a little alcove behind the box office.

"Why, John," she laughed. "You are more shrewd than any of the actors!"

He shrugged, grinning at her, swimming in her sea-green eyes. "Who can keep one's mind on the play when such beauty is near? I must have you to myself."

She blushed charmingly. "And now that you have me, what do you have to say?"

He curled one of her russet tendrils around his fingers and leaned in closer. He brushed the lightest of kisses across her cheeks, thrilled when she shuddered.

He took both her hands in his. "My darling Julie, Miss Stone. I meant it when I said I must have you. I love you completely, as I have loved no other. Please say you will end my suffering and agree to marry me."

She gasped, her eyes widening. "Oh, John!"

It was a moment of perfect torture as he stood there waiting to see what she would say next.

Instead of speaking, she threw her arms around him, and he took a few moments to return the embrace. "Julie?" he whispered.

"Of course I will, you silly goose," she said, laughing at him. She pulled back and her eyes glistened as she gazed up at him. "Nothing would make me happier."

"You will? Oh, my sweet love. I shall make you happy for all eternity." He sealed his promise with a solemn kiss, which then began to betray some of the passion he felt.

She pushed him away gently, dabbing at the paint on her lips. "We must return to the theatre, John."

He nodded. "Yes. I shall go to your father immediately." He turned and took a step back towards the noise of the crowds.

She caught his arm. "Not yet, John. Let it be between us for now."

A pang of panic struck his heart. "Why?"

She squeezed his hand. "Once our understanding is public, my father will see no reason to keep me in town, and my season will be over. I was so looking forward to attending all the balls and entertainments with you."

He frowned. "But it is not a true understanding without your father's permission."

She took his other arm and drew him to her. "It is to me." She kissed him deeply.

John withdrew and smiled at her, a little light-headed. "Whatever you say, my darling."

Chapter Two

John awoke violently the morning following his escapade to the public house. His head was a screaming siren, and he had the extremely uncomfortable sensation of being poked by a large stick.

He forced one eye open, and to his immense consternation he was indeed being poked by a very large stick.

"Mr Barrington."

He bolted upright and pushed the heels of his hands into his eyelids before staring wide-eyed at his assailant. "Who the deuce are you?"

The man straightened. His attire was tidy, though by no means expensive. "I am Mr Wilson, sir. Your bailiff. I manage Mulberry Manor."

The world began to spin in increasingly tighter circles. John pressed one temple with his fingers. "I beg your pardon," he mumbled. "I manage Mulberry Manor. *I* own it."

The man had the audacity to laugh. "That may be so, sir… that you own it. But in your absence, I have kept your affairs in order. And now that you have settled in, I will show you what you are in charge of."

John sighed, and, locating a glass of water on the little table, reached for it. He only succeeded in pushing it over, and it crashed to the floor, splashing a good deal of water over Mr Wilson.

"Sorry," John said, his dry throat cracking on the word. "Hello there?" he called, hoping to summon one of his staff. He returned his attention to slight man in front of him. "While I would certainly like to see the extent of my landholdings, Mr Wilson, today is not the day. Be so good as to come back tomorrow."

Mr Wilson did not budge. "Sir, there are matters I wish to discuss with you today. We need to make some decisions."

We? Had he agreed to being in some sort of partnership? "My good fellow, I fail to see how my sudden presence has rendered you incapable of attending to your usual work. Go on as you normally would."

Rosie came scurrying in and curtsied with a gasp. She averted her eyes.

John regarded his attire, and realised he was shirtless. He shrugged and gave the maid what he hoped was a disarming smile. "Please bring in some coffee."

"Very good, sir," she said. Then on peeking up at him, a blush immediately crossed her cheeks. "Will that be all, sir? Will you have toasted bread, or ham?"

John's stomach churned and he grabbed the arm of the couch to steady himself. "No, just a proliferation of coffee. Thank you."

She curtsied again, and a smile rested on her lips as she turned and fled the room.

John turned back to Mr Wilson. "You're still here."

The man had the decency to pick up his hat and cane, but said, "I shall return to collect you this afternoon."

John flopped back onto the couch, awaiting his coffee. Hopefully Mr Wilson was as stern when collecting rents. His father had told him the bailiff would be paying him close attention to help him settle in – which really meant to keep an eye on him to ensure he didn't escape.

While awaiting the return of the bailiff some hours later, John surveyed the exterior of his house properly for the first time. The cottage ornée was pleasingly symmetrical. On either side of the entrance, there were large gables supporting bay windows which housed the dining room and parlour. Further rectangular windows above gave the bedrooms a view over what he acknowledged to be a pretty lawn and garden. A large tree stood on one side of the house, naturally devoid of any leaves in this season. A sloping thatched roof completed the cosy picture.

He wandered around the house, finding a kitchen garden, some fruit trees, and a barn close to the stables. Today Thora was grazing in a paddock a short distance away, near to the other animals which constituted his home farm.

He heard the arrival of a horse and found Mr Wilson out the front in a pony cart.

"Feeling better?" Mr Wilson enquired.

John stepped up into the cart with what he hoped was easy grace. "I assure you I have no idea of your meaning," he replied, stifling a grin.

Mr Wilson tittered to himself and urged the pony to a trot. "I'll not try to introduce you to all of your tenants today, but we'll cover the lion's share of your properties."

"Jolly good." John breathed deeply as they skirted around his gardens and through a stand of trees. He'd heard about this estate for most of his life, and it did feel good to be finally seeing what it was.

"I believe congratulations on your marriage are in order," Mr Wilson said.

"I beg your pardon?" John gaped at him.

There was a pause, and Mr Wilson pulled the cart to a stop. "You were to inherit the estate on your marriage, correct?"

John sighed and nodded. "That is true. My parents decided to, er, send me here now… but I am as yet unmarried." He met the other man's eyes unflinchingly. "That is all I will say on the matter."

Mr Wilson blew out a breath, taking this in. "You're on your own then? A pity. You'll find the nights here lonely without any company."

John was not going to admit he had already suffered this affliction. "It is of no consequence," he said testily. "I shall find some company soon enough." He considered. "This estate borders another named Willowbridge, does it not?"

"Aye, sir."

"And is that a considerable property?"

Mr Wilson laughed dryly. "Indeed, some twenty thousand acres. The largest estate for miles."

"One presumes the family must enjoy a range of entertainments when they're down from town."

The only response was a solid stare. "If you look about here," Mr Wilson said with a wave of his arm, "you'll see the majority of your lands."

They were positioned at the head of a valley, and the bailiff pointed out the boundaries of several farms among the rolling fields and a few hamlets nestled along a river. It was nothing compared to the thousands of acres his brother was to inherit, but it was his.

As inconvenient as his hasty removal here had been, at least he was away from reminders of what an ogre he was. He just needed to find something to do – someone to spend time with who wouldn't demand too much of him. He did not relish the thought of spending his days visiting his tenants and discussing drains and crops with Mr Wilson. The only acceptable company for a gentleman such as himself was another gentleman. There may be some tolerable folk among the local gentry, but he wasn't going to go knocking on every door just yet.

When introduced to the tenant farmer who leased the largest block of land on his estate, John was embarrassed by his complete lack of knowledge. He knew not what to ask the man about. How was he to be respected by these people when he knew nothing of their dealings? He hoped he hid his ignorance well. If he'd had some time to prepare, he could have learned a thing or two.

Perhaps Mr Wilson sensed how uncomfortable John was, as he drew their excursion to a close soon after this meeting.

As they drove back to the manor, John said, "Perhaps, another time, you could show me some of the estate records and such?"

"Certainly, sir," the bailiff said, betraying nothing.

As soon as they returned, John fetched Thora and prepared her for a ride. He needed to explore on his own terms and clear his head. "Come my friend," he said, mounting her, "let us explore."

He took her away from the house in the opposite direction to his tour with the bailiff, and into a wood beyond. He could feel Thora was itching to stretch her legs properly as usual, but he reined her in. "Woah there, girl, let's find our way first."

The wood was a promising location for future recreation, with many ancient trees soaring above the undergrowth. Before long, however, they passed a stone marker, which proclaimed they were now on the estate of Willowbridge.

Ah, he thought. *If only this wood was mine.* The small copse he'd seen earlier would never support game or deer. Shooting or hunting within the bounds of Mulberry Manor's land was out of the question.

At last, the trees began to grow further apart, and they rode into a vast manicured park. Thora cantered over lush undulating meadows, and he could almost sense her delight. A herd of deer startled as they came over the crest of a hill. Riding under the dappled light of more grand old trees, he was suddenly hit by blinding sunshine bouncing off a sizeable lake. On a little island near the centre of the lake, a folly was surrounded by a small stand of trees. On the other side of the water, a manicured lawn rose up, and up – and soaring above it all was a magnificent country house. Built of honey-coloured stone, the rear of the house featured a large central double-storied section, with rows of tall windows and a huge conservatory at one end.

Something stirred in John as he took in the façade. He felt at ease, almost at home. His place was within a residence such as this, not in a pokey little cottage. Unfortunately, his birth order had determined a different destiny. He was half tempted to ride around to the front and beg for admittance, but he knew it was not the done thing. He needed an introduction to the gentleman who presided over this magnificent property. He was probably an earl, perhaps even a duke. He would own the village, the parish, the hunting grounds. He would be master of his domain and determine his own future. John's ease descended into envy. Why must he have been a second son? Why did he not deserve this life for himself?

Some movement caught his eye. Someone, a lady, emerged onto a balcony and looked out over the grounds. A daughter of the lord's family, or perhaps a young wife? He'd discover all, soon enough.

He shivered and found himself broken out in gooseflesh. How odd. It was a strange sort of feeling, an almost certain feeling that this lady was to be of great import to him. He shook his head and reined Thora around. What nonsense. He hadn't had such an instinctive response to someone since…

As he returned to his modest abode, John imagined himself already acquainted with, nay friendly with, the lord of the estate. Before long they would be sharing a brandy and perhaps a cigar. Soon John would be a regular invitee to dinners and shooting parties, practically living in that grand mansion. It was only a matter of time. He could discover what the man liked and use his charm to become his friend, and there was sure to be other well-bred company to become acquainted with as well. Then the months would fly by, and he would be free to escape to Amberley or London or anywhere he damned well pleased. He could only but hope that the gentleman and his family did not leave for town for the season too early.

Helena accepted a piece of cake with a smile, cringing inwardly. As she bit down into the hard, dry, object and forced herself to chew, she said a hearty, "Mmm!", which satisfied her enthusiastic hostess.

The vicar's wife had many admirable qualities, bless her, but baking was not one of them. Despite having a maid to cook her meals, Mrs Powell insisted on making cakes for company, and presenting offerings which had apparently been enjoyed in her family for generations.

It probably didn't help that the lady's eyesight had been failing for many years, as she slipped further from middle age into the next. As she went to pick up the teapot, her frail hands shook, and tea splashed from the spout over the tea tray.

Helena immediately reached over and grasped the pot. "Please, allow me," she said gently.

"Thank you." Mrs Powell sat back in her chair with a sigh. "Bless you, dearie. What a treasure you are." She accepted her cup and saucer and then Helena poured her own.

"I received word that the new textbooks arrived at the village school this week," Helena said after she had washed down her cake. "I do hope they prove to be suitable."

"I'm sure they will be, dear. It was so generous of you to purchase them for our young ones."

"It seemed to be a necessity," Helena said with a rueful smile. "I was appalled when I discovered most of their existing books were almost fifty years old."

Mrs Powell nodded. "It is certainly not within the means of their parents to be buying their books." Children attending the school were mostly the offspring of tradespeople and labourers. Those with more funds would educate their children privately.

"I accompanied Mr Powell to the orphanage yesterday," Mrs Powell went on. "Those dear, poor little children."

"Oh, yes? I was planning to visit soon." The institution was about halfway between Mulberry and the neighbouring town, Walford. "Are they in need of anything in particular?"

"Why, yes indeed. There is a new foundling… I forget her name. She is twelve years of age, and already very tall."

"Twelve?" Helena repeated. "I wonder that she wasn't sent to a workhouse when she was found. I've never known a child of such an age to be taken in by the orphanage."

Mrs Powell nodded. "To be sure. She was spared that fate because it seems she is mute and it's not clear if she can hear. She was found in the churchyard in Walford, having fainted for lack of food. They didn't have the heart to turn her away."

Helena's heart squeezed. The poor dear. Of course they were right to take her in. "How can I help?"

"They have no clothes to fit her." Mrs Powell squinted at Helena. "She'd be about your size I think, though undoubtedly more slight."

Helena nodded. While she was not rotund, she had inherited generous curves from her mother. "I will certainly ensure she is taken care of." She sipped her tea thoughtfully and then set it back down on the table. "Are there any other needs in the village I can assist with presently?"

Mrs Powell chattered about all the local families and who was suffering from a malaise or who needed a strong man sent around to fix something.

Helena made mental notes, beginning to feel a little overwhelmed. As the vicar and his wife had begun to decline, increasingly Helena had accepted many of their duties. It had merely been the odd visit at first, but now Helena had taken charge of the distribution of food and clothing parcels to the needy, sometimes visiting the sick, and assisting with the village school. While she enjoyed helping people – and these people she counted as an extended family of sorts – her life had become unbearably busy. Not to mention the many small expenses which had begun to add up. All the little stresses of responsibility for this and that family, as well as her actual tenants and all the pressures of managing the estate… sometimes she just wished for a little peace and quiet.

She suddenly remembered something else. "Has Mr Powell had leave to visit with our new resident?" she asked.

Mrs Powell blinked. "Who?"

"Mr Barrington. He is now living at Mulberry Manor."

"Oh. I did not know that. I shall ensure Mr Powell goes to see him. I wonder he did not attend church on Sunday?"

"Yes," Helena said, "one would think he would be eager to meet his fellow parishioners."

She pursed her lips in spite of herself. She did not think herself a judgemental person. Indeed, she always tried to help everyone regardless of their situation. But there was something about the new arrival that rubbed her the wrong way even though she had not yet met him. Now, she thought as she kissed Mrs Powell goodbye, she could add heathen to his list of attributes as well as drunkard and loner.

Helena went directly to Allen's shop to procure fabric for the orphan's clothing. She would have to make a special order so there was no time to waste. Mrs Powell might assume she would have some of her own dresses taken in for the needy girl. But she would not simply find some hand-me-downs for the new orphan. She would get her measured by Mulberry's own seamstress and have some properly fitting gowns made. They would be simple, to be sure, but Helena's conscience would be soothed.

She seldom had any new clothes made for herself, due to the expense. She was skilled enough with a needle that she could repair or alter most of her garments if they grew damaged or worn. After all, there was no reason to keep up with the latest fashions. She was not trying to impress anyone.

She greeted the shopkeeper and asked for his fabric samples, carefully choosing those which would be durable yet comfortable. She also ordered the necessary linings and underclothes. She heard someone enter the shop, but she kept her focus on the task at hand until the shopkeeper had carefully noted down each of her items.

"I'll add these to your bill, Lady Davenport," he said, scratching away in his ledger.

"If you would, thank you," she replied, and she pushed away the rising panic from her gut. She couldn't let this account swell too much more. She must have a word to Privett. Surely they could find some funds somewhere to clear the debt.

Helena would have loved to browse around the shop for her own pleasure but there no was no point tempting herself when she had no intention of adding further to her account. As she turned to leave, she saw it had been a stranger who had come in just now.

From the cut of his green coat to the tie of his creamy cravat, and his black polished boots – this man was clearly a gentleman. One who took care in his appearance and wanted for nothing. Even his chestnut hair was arranged in a carefully haphazard fashion, the curls tumbling over his head like a turbulent ocean.

There was nothing particularly remarkable about him, she decided as she watched him wander down past the stationery items. He was perhaps a little taller than average, a little broader across the shoulders. But his eyes were exceptional, inciting a curiosity which halted her footsteps. They were such a dark brown as to almost be black, with a vivid intensity she had not seen the like of. Her heart seemed to stop beating, until he looked back at her. Then it began to race.

When his eyes met hers, she glimpsed something extraordinary in those shadowy depths… until they became guarded. He took in the measure of her and broke into a sly grin. Did he think she was admiring him? How irritating.

Her awe turned to repulsion. Helena had met enough men who thought they had something to offer her, when all they really wanted was to consume everything she had.

She withdrew behind a polished veneer and stepped toward him, extending a hand. "Mr Barrington, I presume?"

"The very one." She tried to ignore the spark she felt at the gentle pressure of his hand, undeniable even though they both wore gloves. He bowed down over her hand, and for an anxious moment she thought he might kiss it, though he did not.

When he straightened, his eyes were filled with playful interest. "As delighted as I am that you know who I am, I admit I cannot return the favour."

It would be rude of him to ask directly who she was – Society's rules of etiquette required that a lady introduce herself first. She was tempted to leave without giving him the satisfaction of knowing her identity, but she was above petty games, was she not?

She curtsied. "I am Lady Helena Davenport, of Willowbridge."

He smiled. "We are neighbours, and as such I hope we shall be on easy terms."

She did not smile, only nodding and gathering her shawl about her. "I should be going…"

"Preparing a sizeable wardrobe for the Season?"

What an impertinent question! Whatever would make him… of course. He had overheard her lengthy discussion with the shopkeeper. That this man would assume she was superficial and careless with money only served to reinforce her estimation of him.

Let him think what he may. She cared not for his good opinion.

"I have been ordering fabrics," she said tartly. "Not that it is any concern of yours."

His eyebrows raised, and as he opened his mouth to speak another man entered the shop.

"Good day, Doctor," Helena said to him, ducking past Mr Barrington and smiling to acknowledge the doctor's little bow before hurrying from the shop.

And so began the defining season of John's life. At first, it was just as Julie promised. They would bump into each other in Hyde Park, sit next to each other at musicales, and contrive to crave ices from Gunter's at the same hour. It was an enchanting little game, and John's heart soared.

As the weeks wore on, it became increasingly a challenge to secure a space on her dance card. Of course, he reasoned, she was in demand. She was beautiful, vivacious, and with a large dowry to boot. But none of her other suitors would love her like he did.

Each time he saw her laughing with a baron, eating supper with an earl, or – worst – dancing with a duke, he would look down at his signet ring and remind himself that she had chosen him.

As their meetings became few and far between, he grew restless. He would not allow himself to doubt Julie. He trusted her character, and it would almost be a betrayal of his own heart to think she could stray.

While at cards at Boodle's, one of his friends leaned over and said idly, "Barrington, why are you not at the musicale at the Stone apartments?"

"I beg your pardon?" John held his cards close to his chest instinctively.

"Oh, were you not invited?" The gentleman straightened. "The soprano Rosita Lovari is singing there this evening at a party. But perhaps I have the date wrong."

John's suspicions, which he hadn't let penetrate his heart, now spilled over. Her family were entertaining at their own residence, and she hadn't thought to invite him? How was he ever to gain her father's approval if the man never saw him, or said two words to him? It would have been the ideal opportunity to obtain his favour. Did their engagement mean nothing to her?

He laid his cards down on the table and stalked out of the room without another word. Half an hour later, he burst into the drawing room at the Stone's townhouse, knocking a servant out the way.

The soprano was in full flight, the accompanying music drowning out John's sudden entrance. The room had been organised into a theatre of sorts, with rows of chairs and sofas, and everyone had their backs to him. His eyes roved over the fine coiffures, until they came to rest on his beloved. She was seated, rather too close, to a broad-shouldered man with greying hair. The man's hand rested on Julie's shoulder, and as John watched, the man's thumb moved back and forth on her bare skin in a caressing gesture. Julie turned toward him and smiled, their heads drawing together in intimacy. He recognised the profile of Lord Bromley.

John lost the ability to breathe, grasping for the wall as the room spun. His whole reason for being was personified in that feminine form, and she was lapping up the attentions of another. The other man happened to have a prestigious title and extreme wealth. John had never felt the absence of both more keenly.

The soprano finished her aria, and there was a round of applause. Mr Stone stood to thank her, and then saw John.

But John was already advancing on Lord Bromley, murder in his heart. He leapt in front of Julie's father and addressed the man in front of the whole assembly.

"*What* are you doing with my fiancée?"

Lord Bromley's mouth dropped open in surprise, but then he laughed. "*Your* fiancée? Why, Miss Stone and I have become engaged this very night."

It was John's turn to be shocked. He gaped at Julie.

She looked upon him with compassion, but then schooled her features into cool indifference. Her voice, that beloved voice, only trembled slightly as she declared, "Lord Bromley has been courting me for almost the entire season. Perhaps you have not been fortunate enough as to witness it."

Her father advanced upon John and indicated the doorway. "Good night, Mr Barrington," he said pointedly. "How – interesting for you to have joined us in this manner. I trust there will not be a repeat performance."

John's heart was not ready to let go. "But I love her," he croaked.

"How sweet. But your love is of no worth to her whatsoever. Lord Bromley's affections are worth infinitely more."

John stiffened. His affections, or his bank account? Impulsively, he knelt down and grabbed Julie's hand. "Can we talk? Surely you have not agreed to this?"

She glared at him for a moment, then nodded. "Very well." She led him to a corner of the room. He had been hoping for another room altogether, away from this nightmare scene and Lord Bromley's keen gaze.

Julie wrenched her hand from his and took a deep breath, fixing her eyes on John's chin. "I have agreed to marry Lord Bromley. It is a most advantageous match."

Hearing the words from her own lips proved nothing but a dagger through his soul. "But you love me," he insisted. He held up his hand, the onyx on her ring shining in the firelight. "Do you not?"

She looked to the floor, and after a tortuous pause she finally met his eyes. Her beautiful emerald eyes shone. "Perhaps I did, once."

He stared, unblinking. "Perhaps," he whispered. And he held her eyes, so that she would fully behold the hurt she had caused him.
Then he turned on his heel and left the room, the house, and the city.

Chapter Three

She had to be the same lady he had seen on the balcony at the grand house. When they'd locked eyes, he'd had the same visceral reaction. Seeing her at close range had only intensified his sense that he had to know her. Something whispered to him that he needed to help her. How preposterous, when she was the usual highly-strung, conceited, materialistic woman he had met hundreds of times before. She was obviously comfortable in life. He'd happened upon her when she was in the midst of a large order of clothing items.

Even from behind, it was obvious from her clothing, hairstyle and posture that she was a lady. Face to face, she possessed the most natural beauty he had ever seen. Her hair seemed to be a hundred shades of blonde, arranged in an elegant yet simple style which framed her delicate features. Eyes of an icy blue seemed to pierce his, and her cheeks had coloured charmingly as he'd caught her gawking at him. With a quick glance at her hands, he noted she wore no rings of commitment. He'd been busying himself with appraising the shop's wares, but now he could see an item which held the most value. He instantly formed a plan, a kind of assault of congeniality, to gain her goodwill and then get an invitation to the house so he could meet the lord.

Annoyingly, when he opened his mouth to speak, he was assailed by nerves. He covered it over smoothly enough, but she seemed to have already formed a negative opinion of him. Just what had she learned when she discovered his name?

He tried to keep her talking, to get some information about the family and their plans, but to no avail. The conversation was over before it had really begun, leaving him seriously unfulfilled.

Perhaps she had taken his friendliness as flirtation, and she meant to put him off because she loved another. No matter, he'd find a way into the family. Even if it did mean submitting to a church service, and all of Mulberry's society eagerness to find out who he was and why he was here.

After she stormed past him and out of the shop, he turned his attention to the new arrival, who Lady Davenport had addressed as "doctor". He was probably at least ten years older than John, with greying hair around his temples and wrinkles indicating he was quick to laugh.

He shook hands with John. "Harding's the name. I'm the physician."

"John Barrington. Live locally, do you?"

"Aye, just outside the village. You're the chap newly installed at Mulberry Manor?"

"Indeed I am." Did everyone in the village already know who he was and where he lived?

"Well, I shall leave you to your business," said Dr Harding, and he turned turn look down another part of the shop.

John exhaled, relieved the man hadn't pried further into his circumstances. His opinion of Dr Harding grew positive. He admired those with intelligence and discretion. Above all, he hated someone poking their nose into his business.

He wandered about the shop, introducing himself to the shopkeeper and purchasing a few small items. Dr Harding concluded his own business at about the same time, and he smiled at John.

"Say, would you care to join me for a meal at the public house? I know all there is to know about Mulberry, and I can answer any questions you may have."

John returned the smile, although now he became concerned that perhaps Harding was more inquisitive than he had let on. His yearning desire for company prevailed. "Why yes, I thank you. I should be glad to join you."

He found, though, that once he was settled at a table by the window with a steaming plate of lamb and kidney pie in front of him, that Dr Harding was the sort of person who was comfortable with silence. Perhaps he was used to others bearing their burdens to him by giving them space to speak. John had no intention of bearing anything, and he asked the sort of questions he thought the doctor might expect, about the size of the village, the nearest militia, and the facilities and recreation available within riding distance.

"You'll find half a dozen or so families within the gentry which it may please you to associate with," said Dr Harding. "We may not have the numbers to justify any large or regular entertainments, but we are a merry bunch."

John nodded as he chewed and swallowed a delicious mouthful of pie. "I would very much like to be acquainted with the nobleman who owns the village. Davenport, isn't it?"

A peculiar expression crossed over Dr Harding's face as he also ate. Was he trying not to smile as he chewed? "Davenport, that's correct," he said finally.

"Do you know him well?"

"I am well acquainted with our patron, that is true." He broke out into a grin, his eyes sparkling.

"What is it? What's so amusing?" John did not like being ridiculed.

Dr Harding dabbed at his mouth with a napkin. "I feel I should let you know something about… er… Davenport."

John leaned forward. "Yes?"

The doors of the public house burst open, and two men came running in. "Harding, there you are. You must come at once!"

The doctor jumped to his feet. "My apologies, Mr Barrington. There must be some sort of medical emergency. Do give my regards at Willowbridge if you call. I wish you luck in your endeavours there!"

Casting his napkin and coins on the table, he rushed out with the two men, leaving John disappointed and perturbed that he was lacking some sort of intelligence. He had a funny feeling he was about to wander into some sort of social spider's web.

He settled the bill at the pub and led Thora back through the village. It was a bustling little place, appearing bigger than his quaint home of Amberley. The main thoroughfare was remarkable for its avenue of trees arching across the road. The spires of the church rose above them. The buildings lining either side of the road were a mixture of older half-timbered buildings and the newer style of white-washed shop with bay windows on the ground floor and inset rectangular windows above. He passed by many different types of people as he walked: ladies and gentlemen, farmers, and mothers with young children. Each observed him in their own way, from concealed curiosity to downright suspicion. John was not self-conscious under such scrutiny. He had long since stopped caring about what others thought.

❧☙

Helena dropped into the village tea rooms to regain her composure. Thankfully the place was quiet, and she secured a table on her own by the window.

When her tea arrived, she took a deep breath and inhaled the fragrant steam before drawing in a sip. *Ah, that's better.* Now she could reflect on what had just transpired at the shop.

She was usually a kind, charitable person, but she had behaved almost rudely. She was brusque, she ignored his friendly advances, and she didn't even say goodbye to him. In point of fact – it was definitely rudeness, which was so unlike her. Her father would have been shocked. Jane Godwin had taught her better manners than this. She would probably have to invite the man to dine at Willowbridge to remedy her behaviour.

The poor man had no idea that she had formed such an ill judgement of him before they had even met. He also did not help himself by grinning at her like that or asking a personal question. Even now she was so nettled by him she let out a cross little moan. Mortified, she glanced around to make sure no-one had heard. It appeared her neuroses were safe, for the moment. She had only grown more perturbed at the affect he had had on her. She should be above such trivialities. She had many other things – more important things – to occupy her attention.

She then thought about all the matters needing her consideration at the estate, as well as all the needs in their little society as reported by Mrs Powell. Forming a rough plan for her next few days made her feel a little organised, and when she finished her tea and biscuit she was fortified enough to proceed with the next task.

On exiting the shop, she looked up to check for passing traffic and found herself seeing none other than John Barrington, again. This time, he was seated at a table in the public house, raising a full glass of ale to his lips.

Drinking during the day... typical! All of Helena's prejudices reappeared and seemed justified. She would *not* invite him to dinner. A smug drunk was not the dinner companion for her.

Seemingly unable to look away from the man in the window, once again her pulse quickened. There was something compelling about that face, those features, those eyes. He had a kind of magnetism she had never experienced before, and she had to admit that it scared her. Perhaps that was the reason she had been so abrupt with him – to keep him at arm's length.

Gossip was already brewing about Mr Barrington, and about why he had suddenly decided to take up his inheritance before marriage. Some were speculating there was a rift with his family, but why was a mystery. Was he hiding a recent misdeed? With those enigmatic eyes, he probably left a trail of seduction and disruption in his wake. If he had done something to prompt a sort of banishment, it couldn't be that bad, could it?

She took a deep breath, again flummoxed as to how he agitated her so. Then she set off for the seamstress's cottage and made an appointment to visit the orphanage with her in order to obtain measurements of the new orphan. The woman was jolly and a gossip, and by the time Helena had left the cottage she was in much better spirits.

She made her way back to her carriage and looked forward to a lengthy conversation with Jane over dinner. Upon reaching her house, she was greeted by the sight of another carriage by the entrance. Her footmen were darting about with bags and cases.

As she alighted, a gloom settled over her. It was Sinclair and his wife. She had known their arrival was imminent, but she had rather hoped for tomorrow. She stomped up the steps to the front door and was met by Andrews, who seemed to be giving directions to three different servants at once.

"Ah, Lady Davenport, I need to inform you of–"

"Sinclair's arrival. Yes, yes. Please see that we are ready to serve cocktails in the drawing room at five o'clock, with dinner half an hour later. I have already agreed a suitable menu with Mrs Mead." She'd have enough time for a bath and then a chat with Jane before facing the familial onslaught.

On his return to the Barrington family apartments in London that cruel night, John flew up to his room and yanked the signet ring off his finger. He turned it over and over in his hands as he paced about the room in a fury.

He'd been nothing more than a conquest, and once she had nabbed him, she'd lost interest.

His heart was more than broken, it was vanquished. He resolved to never open it again, and it was a promise he was to keep. Female-kind was now his enemy. The only complication was the expectation that he marry before taking possession of his inheritance. Hurt drowned out any rational thinking with regards to that.

He marched over to the fire and raised his hand ready to throw the ring into the flames. But something stopped him.

Should he send the ring back to her, to remind her of her promise?

No. The thought of her then giving it to another man was unbearable.

What if she changed her mind, persuaded her family, and came back to him? How would he explain that he'd cast off this treasure?

He stopped, took a breath, and slid the ring back onto his finger.

There it stayed, as he went back to his family's estate in Shropshire and hid from the world. There it stayed, during the months that followed as he finally gave up on her. There it stayed, as he received news of her nuptials and then her first child – the child that was supposed to be his. He couldn't bring himself to take it off, let alone throw it away. It became a sort of talisman, a reminder of how he had been loved. But had he been, really?

Deep down, he knew his sister Catherine was the only one who really loved him. She was ten years his junior, but a sensitive creature with a wise soul. She could at once laugh at him and then censure him. He would only ever allow criticism from her – because she knew him intimately.

Catherine accompanied him on the journey from London to Amberley the morning after Julie's betrayal. When he'd instructed the carriage to be ready, she'd intercepted him and gently extracted the whole truth. He'd collapsed into her arms and wept.

She alone knew how completely he had loved, and how desperately he was wounded. They had never discussed it since, although he would sometimes glimpse pity in her eyes.

With all the full-bodied force, the all-consuming fire and devotion of his love for Julie, the same energy carried him away from any meaningful society. Away from companionship and love. Away from risk, hurt and self-sacrifice. Away, away, away… to the safe place of nothing.

As the years wore on, he withdrew into a shell of himself, subsisting on a diet of cards, fashion, libations, and country diversions. His social world depended almost upon the group of friends he'd made at Oxford. There were four other gentlemen who were determined bachelors, and they spent most of the summer rotating among each other's country houses for shooting, hunting, house parties, and the like. During the Season, they could be found together at almost any ball, soirée, or race meet. Many a debutante had tried to penetrate their circle and so far, all had failed. Conversation with them was easy, light. They asked nothing of him nor he of them. There was no knowledge of the hurts he carried, the reasons he kept his emotional distance. He could probably fade out of their circle without any of them noticing. He was like a shadow of a person, merely an image of himself, and it was an image he abhorred.

Chapter Four

One of the mortifications John must suffer due to his forced banishment was his immediate removal from the limited society he frequented. His friends would be expecting him at their respective estates, or in town for the spring at the very least. How was he to explain his disappearance? And how was he to get on without their camaraderie, superficial though it was? He even missed his older brother, and that was highly unusual.

Again, and again, he wished the deed undone.

He decided to give the family at Willowbridge a few days – no doubt Lady Helena would tell her parents about him, although he doubted her report would be positive based on her reaction to him. Surely they would extend some sort of invitation to him as a courtesy to a new neighbour?

While he waited, he occupied his mornings with correspondence. He wrote to each of his friends and let them know he wouldn't be in town for the Season, without revealing too much. Hopefully they wouldn't hint at a visit to Mulberry Manor – his little home was far beneath the standard they were used to.

After the humiliating circumstances of his departure, John was relieved to be free of his family for a while. But in the deafening silence, he swallowed his pride enough to pen a note to his parents, letting them know of his safe arrival and his good wishes for their health.

Then he wrote a separate letter to Catherine.

My dearest Catherine,

How I miss you already! I will not blame you if the sentiment is not returned. I hope you are well… do tell me all your news. It pains me to think of you in the world without me. I beg of you – please do not go and get married before I can meet the man!

He went on to describe his house and land, the village, and the few people of consequence he'd met thus far. Then he dipped his pen in the ink again and sighed deeply.

I do hope, one day, you may be able to forgive me.

With much love,
Your brother John

Still wrapped up in his thoughts, John found Tom Morgan eating with his wife at a table in the kitchen. He handed him the letters.

"See those get posted today, will you?"

Tom chewed, swallowed, and took the letters from John. "I wasn't going to go to the village today."

John stared at him. Of all the impudence… This man had had his run of this place for too long. Still, he supposed he had been a little terse. His parents had always told him to treat servants well, with politeness. He took a breath. "If you would be so kind as to have those sent today, I should be very grateful. Please." As he said the words, he couldn't help a tone of sarcasm creeping into his voice, but it did the trick.

The man grinned. "Certainly, Mr Barrows."

This was no case of forgetfulness, but a deliberate act to undermine him. He had to admire Tom's gumption, infuriating as it was. John glared at him and barked, "Barrington."

In the afternoons he continued to tour his property with Mr Wilson, meeting his tenants as they went about their work. Two days after meeting the lady Davenport, there was still nothing from Willowbridge. John decided to take matters into his own hands and visit them without being invited. His mother would shudder at the thought of him disobeying etiquette in this manner, but he was getting desperate. Besides, he had never let manners stand in the way of what he wanted.

He went by way of the main road this time, steering Thora in through the main gates. The sun was out at last, and it shone optimism into John's soul. He had a good feeling about this.

The driveway meandered through pastures and around bends, with no sign of the house at first. Then rounding a corner, John surveyed a delightful scene. He could see the house in the distance, every bit as grand as he remembered. A sparkling river threaded across the hills in front, and under a stone bridge with three arches. He rode over it, under a huge willow tree that must give the estate its name.

Guiding Thora to the front entrance, he dismounted and tethered her to a railing by the steps. Springing up them, he pounded on the door cheerily.

A butler opened the door and looked him up and down. "Yes?"

"Good morning. I am John Barrington, the owner of Mulberry Manor."

The butler nodded, unmoved. At least he didn't slam the door in John's face.

"How might I assist you, sir?"

"I wish to enquire after the master of Willowbridge. Is he at home?"

The butler arched an eyebrow. "You are meaning Lord Brackley, the seventh earl?"

John's heart beat a little faster. He nodded with excitement. "Yes, yes I am."

The butler frowned. "I regret to inform you that his lordship perished two and a half years ago."

John's mouth dropped open. Whatever could the man be about? "Then I am meaning the eighth earl, his heir – the current owner?"

"There is no such–"

"What is the matter, Andrews?" Helena Davenport appeared behind the butler, and John used the interruption to make his way inside the house.

"Salutations, my lady," he said with a bow. This morning she'd tied a green scarf about her hair, which tumbled from the fabric in golden waves.

"Mr Barrington," she said, with a little nod. "I'll take care of this, thank you, Andrews."

John swallowed his indignation at being referred to as "this".

"As you wish, my lady. This gentleman, from the manor, wishes to enquire for the master of Willowbridge."

Lady Davenport smiled at him askance. "Does he now?" She nodded at the butler, and he withdrew.

"Is the earl at home?" John asked her, trying to hide his impatience.

Her eyes flashed at him. He was baffled as to how he had caused offence.

She stepped closer and raised her chin. "I need to inform you, Mr Barrington, that I am mistress of Willowbridge. I inherited it from my father, and I own it in my own right."

John stared at her. She, alone? A female heiress was certainly uncommon, but not impossible. He was, for once in his life, speechless.

"I have guests, sir, and I would rather not keep them waiting." She looked over her shoulder, frowning. "You could join us, I suppose?"

It was the most noncommittal invitation he had ever received, but now that he was here there was no refusing. He watched her, caught off guard by the uncertain way she was chewing on her lip. She did not seem thrilled to be getting back to her guests. This was a different woman to the haughty young miss he'd encountered yesterday.

"If that would not inconvenience you, my lady, I should love to join you. But first, could I have someone see to my horse?"

She nodded. "Of course." She flagged down a passing footman and spoke to him quietly, then indicated John should follow her. "This way."

He followed her across a grand foyer, with a large central staircase leading up to the first floor. She opened the first door on the right, and they entered a grand drawing room with sunlight streaming through tall windows. There were three other people present, two ladies and a gentleman who stood on their entry.

"My apologies for the interruption," Lady Helena said. "May I present Mr John Barrington, who has taken up residence in Mulberry Manor. Mr Barrington, this is my cousin, Mr Sinclair, and his wife. They are staying here for a few weeks."

John bowed, and Sinclair returned the gesture. He was of small but stocky stature, dressed in bright shining fabrics which were a good deal too overbearing for this time of day. He had keen little eyes set in a ruddy face, and he wore a wig. His wife, similarly gaudy, dipped her head to acknowledge him.

Lady Helena extended her hand towards the other lady. "And this is my companion, Miss Jane Godwin."

"How do you do?" said John affably.

"Mr Barrington," said Miss Godwin, who seemed a good deal older than her mistress but with a vivacious glow about her. "It is a pleasure to see you here in Mulberry at last."

"Er, thank you," John replied, and he took the proffered seat next to Miss Godwin as Lady Helena also sat across the room.

"Mulberry Manor, eh?" Sinclair addressed him. "Is that the little cottage ornée?"

John nodded. "Indeed."

Sinclair smiled – at least, he stretched his lips. "How quaint."

John bristled. "And where do you reside, Mr Sinclair?"

"My wife and I live primarily in a London townhouse, although we get away to the country whenever we can."

John thought he could see Lady Helena go rigid out of the corner of his eye.

"And in the *near future*," Mr Sinclair went on, "we expect to take up residence in the country more *permanently*."

He fixed John with a meaningful stare, although John didn't know what it meant. He glanced at Lady Helena and was astounded to see she was shooting daggers at Mr Sinclair with her eyes.

"Mr Sinclair's expectations are likely to be unsubstantiated," she said with ice in her voice.

The gentleman shot her a smile from the corner of his mouth. "We shall see about that." He turned to John again. "Do you shoot?"

John nodded. "My father prides himself on his game."

"Capital. You'll find the pheasant here are plentiful. Assuming the weather holds – would you fancy a shoot on Tuesday morning?"

Something lifted inside John. With the news that Lady Helena was head of the household, his plans to become a regular at Willowbridge seemed dashed. But here was a welcome development. He held back a grin. "I would be happy to oblige you, sir."

"Ensure the gamekeeper is prepared, will you, Helena?" Mr Sinclair shot over his shoulder at her. She didn't respond, but John saw her knuckles turn white as she gripped a teapot handle.

"Will Lady Helena be joining us?" John couldn't resist asking.

"Ha!" Mr Sinclair chuckled. "I wouldn't trouble her with such trivial pursuits. She'll busy herself with some do-gooding somewhere, will you not, Helena?"

She finished pouring the tea and set down the pot firmly. "Charitable endeavours are all part and parcel of responsible estate management, Mr Sinclair. Something you know precious little about."

"If the estate is managed well," he shot back, "others should be looking after the poorer people."

"When one has spent one's entire life growing up in a community, one cares for those people as much as they were family. An outsider could never understand."

Mr Sinclair smiled at his wife, who was staring at a biscuit with malice. "It is the domain of sentimental females to have such feelings."

In this domestic spat, they seemed to have forgotten John was there. That was, until Lady Helena addressed him suddenly. "Tea?"

"Er, yes. Please." He rose and took the cup she offered. A thick silence descended on the room, punctuated by the occasional sip of tea or crunching of biscuit.

Thankfully, Mrs Sinclair filled the breach a few minutes later, beginning to chat about a shared relative and the goings-on of their many progeny.

Miss Godwin set her teacup down and turned to John. "I do hope you are all settled in," she said with a kindly twinkle in her eye. She had an almost motherly air about her.

"Tolerably," he replied, smiling. "Have you been companion to Lady Helena for long?"

"To be sure," she said, also smiling. "I have been in the employ of the Davenports for over fifteen years. I was first Helena's governess."

"Ah. Does she have any siblings?"

"No, I'm afraid. She is quite on her own. Her mother died when she was young, you know, and her father never re-married."

That explained a thing or two. She was neither daughter, nor wife, nor sister of the estate owner as he had assumed. She was a young woman out of her depth as the controller of a significant property.

A thought occurred to him suddenly, as he did not know if her surname matched her father's.

"She is not widowed, is she?"

"Good heavens, no. Lady Helena is not, at present, inclined to marry. With no near male relations, her father settled the estate on her entirely." She looked over at Helena. "Although there are conditions."

John swallowed a mouth of biscuit. "Oh?"

Miss Godwin eyed him, as if deciding how much to divulge. At that moment, Lady Helena addressed him instead. Her cheeks and neck appeared flushed.

"Will your affianced be joining you soon, Mr Barrington? I am so eager to meet the woman who agreed to take your hand in marriage."

This sudden challenge surprised and amused John. "I am sorry to disappoint you, madam, but I have no wife."

She raised her dainty eyebrows at him. "No wife? And no understanding with anyone?"

He puffed out a breath in indignation. "No. Not that it is any of your business."

"To be sure, it's none of my interest, either. I only made the assumption because you've chosen to reside at the manor so suddenly. What reason could you have except that you are setting up a house of your own due to matrimonial plans?"

John gritted his teeth. "I have my reasons," he ground out. There was an expectant pause, as if someone was waiting for him to outline what his reasons were. Instead, he gulped down the remainder of his tea and stood. "I must thank you for your hospitality, Lady Helena."

Sinclair jumped out of his seat. "Until Tuesday, then," he said, reaching for John's hand. "I'll have a gun prepared for you."

John shook the man's hand, his grip a good deal stronger than Sinclair's. He could not miss Lady Helena scowling at them. Her gave her a hasty bow on his way past.

His thoughts whirled as he rode Thora back home. Lady Helena had intrigued him. Her thinly veiled hatred towards her cousin surprised him. There was clearly some animosity between them, and she was no shrinking violet. What would she be like if she gave flight to her emotions, to that passion? Would she ever lose her self-control? He was tempted to provoke her himself, so curious was he. But then he reminded himself that lately he had played with the emotions of others and lost the game. He would have to rein his curiosity in, tempting though it was.

☙❧

Helena's usual annoyance toward her cousin had exploded into full-blown wrath. Not only had he descended on her house as if it were his own, but he had also engaged with her guest as if he was the head of the household and she his underling. He had embarrassed her and essentially informed a stranger that he had designs on the estate. She did not want to explain the finer points of her father's will to Mr Barrington. In fact, she wanted nothing to do with either man.

Her frustration was also inward. She'd done it again. She'd snapped at her new neighbour, albeit as a thinly veiled pleasantry. His visit hadn't started well – he had dropped in without an invitation, which was irritating enough… but then he boldly assumed she was merely the female attachment to the proper owner of her estate. He hadn't been the first, and wouldn't be the last, but she was already on edge due to Sinclair's presence.

Then, after Ruth Sinclair had prattled on at length about all the accomplishments of their relations, she was really too fed up with it all. They had only been here two days, and she had to withstand two weeks. She proceeded to turn her venom on the wrong man and had certainly offended him in the process by prying too close into his personal affairs.

She had been caught off guard for another reason, which she was trying rather unsuccessfully to repress and had therefore overcompensated for. Mr Barrington had appeared so suave, so effortlessly handsome when he strolled into her home, almost with an air of someone who expected to belong there. His presence fascinated her and irked her at the same time.

At least if the men went shooting, they would be out of her hair while she attended to more important matters. She had leftover food that must be delivered to needy folk that very afternoon.

She turned to her cousin, who was now lounging in a chair with one foot up on a low table.

"Mr Sinclair."

"Eh?" He lurched upright, as if he had been on the verge of slumber.

"I must insist that you speak to the gamekeeper yourself. I have a busy few days planned and I am not at leisure to supervise your recreation."

"I beg your pardon?" Sinclair leaned toward her, sneering. "My *dear* lady, have you forgotten that you oversee the workforce of Willowbridge? Who else could possibly execute my instructions?"

Helena clutched at her chest, gasping for air. "Have I *forgotten?*"

Jane came to her side and took up her hand. "Helena, my dear, you seem anxious. What can I do to help?"

Helena took her to a far corner of the room. "I had carefully organised my days this week and having to manage Sinclair's activities is the last thing I need."

"Consider it done, my love. I shall arrange it all." She paused. "I suppose that Mr Barrington will expect an invitation for dinner as well if they are successful."

Helena sighed. "Yes, I suppose so. Although my cousin is not a renowned sportsman, as you know." The ladies shared a smile. "If you have leave to arrange it with Mrs Mead, I should be ever so grateful."

"Of course." They had a quick conversation regarding Helena's preferences for the dinner, and Jane went directly to discuss it with the cook.

Helena left Sinclair to his own devices as much as she could during the following few days. When she came upon him carelessly rearranging the books in her library, or his wife carefully inspecting the silverware, she would take a steadying breath and try to put it out of her mind. She would not be intimidated.

The morning after Mr Barrington's visit, she took her lady's maid and the seamstress to the orphanage in her carriage. They carried various baskets filled with food, toys, and writing materials. The institution was a fifteen-minute carriage ride away from Mulberry on the road to Walford. It was in a large house which had fallen into disrepair when the owners had died. Her father, who loved children but of course only had the one, had taken it on as a passion project. He renovated it specifically to provide for needy children and Helena had spent her youth accompanying him on visits. It was her now a passion of hers as well – who was to say if she would ever have children of her own? And with no siblings or other close relatives, the little ones here had given her a window on youthful exuberance and some companionship. She took in a special interest in seeing them well-placed when they left the orphanage.

Their arrival was greeted with the usual enthusiasm, and Helena took time to speak with every child who wanted her. The new girl, tall and pale, was understandably timid and reluctant to be measured by a stranger. Helena spoke with her gently, and it became clear to her that there was nothing wrong with her hearing. With some love and attention, Helena hoped she may speak eventually. For now, she would ensure the girl was warm and comfortable with new clothes. It became apparent that some of the other children had worn out their clothes or shoes as well. Helena would not personally undertake the task of outfitting all of them, but she made a note to speak to Mr Powell about any available tithes, and she would ask Privett to send along some extra funds as well.

As usual, she was reluctant to leave, but leave she must. It may be a trial being female a great deal of the time, especially when it came to exerting authority over men. But she revelled in the nurturing aspects of her duties – she was really at her most content when she had made a material difference in the lives of others, even if that was just with a kind word or acts. It was something her mother, God rest her soul, had instilled in her.

Without this sort of work, what would she have? She wouldn't let that odious man Sinclair take it all away from her. And she had much rather be playing games with the children at the orphanage than taking shots at partridges like the men. Many of her deeds may go unnoticed, but they filled her heart and that was all that mattered. It was enough to stop her from dwelling on any other wishes her heart might make.

Catherine was barely out, and certainly not wise to the ways of the world. John took it upon himself to protect her from any dangers, any unwholesome advances. Only the best, worthiest suitor would do for his beloved sister.

While at a ball at Almack's, a notorious cad charmed Catherine during a dance and then led her from the room. John missed nothing and was after them.

When he found them in an alcove, the blackguard already had her in an embrace, with Catherine's protests clear.

He wrenched the man off her. "Weston! You go too far!"

Weston met John's murderous glare and his eyed widened in terror. He struggled under John's grip. "Barrington, now see here…"

John pushed him away and snarled, "Pistols at dawn."

Then he reached for Catherine's trembling hand and gently escorted her to a quiet corner, staying with her until she regained her composure.

He also needed to calm his boiling rage. The man had taken advantage of his sister's innocence – or would have, had he not intervened. Apart from any mortification or injury she could have suffered, if they had been discovered by anyone else her reputation would have been ruined forever, meaning her chances for a respectable marriage would be doomed before they even began.

John had no choice but to call the man out. Perhaps George should have been the one to do it, but he had the annoying habit of letting things slide that were too difficult. John was a man of strong passions, and once his sense of injustice or revenge was in play, there was no going back. He would see through whatever it was, whatever it took.

Mist swirled through Hyde Park the following morning. His foe's hand shook as he took his weapon from the box. John's hand was steady as always. He knew what he had to do. He looked Mr Weston right in the eye and smiled at him confidently. Mr Weston's eyes were wild and bloodshot, and he uttered a sort of squeak. Had John's reputation preceded him?

They stepped back the required number of paces and turned on the command. John, being the excellent marksman he was, could have easily killed the man. But it wasn't the done thing. When the roar of gunfire exploded from either end of the clearing, John heard a bullet whizz by his ears, and then the cry of his opponent as a bullet went into his right leg, just below the knee.

John nodded in satisfaction as he handed the gun back to his second and then strode back to where his horse was tethered.

Weston would know never to trifle with Catherine – or John Barrington – ever again.

Chapter Five

Say what you would about John Barrington, there was no denying he was a crack shot. Partridge after partridge fell from the sky.

Mr Sinclair on the other hand, was far too busy recounting his list of grievances against the Davenport family to focus on his gun. Each time he missed a bird, he would utter some kind of excuse – the light, the wind, his gout – and quickly pass his gun back to his man before launching into his next tirade.

"Do you know what it means to be denied something that's owed to you? I am the next male in line, Willowbridge should be mine!"

"Yes, sir," John said mildly. "I do have a notion of what that is like."

He did his best to remain polite with his quasi-host, without agreeing outright with the man's sentiments. As a second son, he was all too familiar with feeling deprived and hard-done-by, but there was something about this man's attitude he did not like. Perhaps it was the ungentlemanlike way he discussed the ladies of the household, both present and deceased. John may have committed sins against the fairer sex, but he knew better than to openly insult his hostess or speak ill of the dead. He'd never been fond of whining to others either, preferring to take action instead.

As he took up his gun again, he cast a sidelong glance at his companion. "Would that I could be of assistance, sir," he murmured, as a way to stop the man's flow.

"Funny you should say that." Mr Sinclair grinned. "You may be the only one who can help us."

"Pardon me?" John shivered in the frosty morning air.

Mr Sinclair fixed him with a steady stare and licked his lips. "Are you familiar with the terms of her inheritance?"

"Do you refer to Lady Helena? No, sir, I am not." He had to admit that the subject had interested him ever since Miss Godwin had alluded to complications therein.

Beaters began to flush out birds afresh, and Mr Sinclair indicated he would wait for John to take his shot. The gun's report cracked through the crisp air, and another bird was won.

"I say, bravo," Mr Sinclair said, clapping John on the shoulder.

He shuddered involuntarily. "Terms, you say?"

"Quite. In order to ensure future solvency, her father settled the estate irrevocably on Lady Helena with the provision that there must be over three thousand pounds of profit in the third year following his death."

John considered this. "That hardly seems unachievable, given the size of Willowbridge and the diverse nature of its tenants."

"Indeed. However, Helena's father was a man far too generous, and there have been major expenses since his death."

John directed him a sly smile. "How did you discover that?" He doubted Lady Helena would have divulged such information.

"I have my sources," Mr Sinclair said, with a grin that could only be described as ugly.

"And pray tell, what will happen if Lady Helena fails to meet the conditions of the entail?"

Mr Sinclair's chest puffed up visibly. "The estate passes to me."

"I see." John did see. Now the dynamic at play between the heiress and her rival was all too comprehensible. His mind began to bubble with questions. "Are there any other terms?"

Mr Sinclair paused as he took up his gun again. "If she marries before she is one-and-twenty she will keep the estate regardless of the profits."

John's eyebrows shot up. "Indeed?"

"Yes." Mr Sinclair looked down the barrel of the gun and chuckled. "But that's unlikely." He fired and caught only the wing of a bird. "Capital!" he cried, as if the job was done.

John had been about to enquire as to why Lady Helena, with her obvious beauty, intelligence, and fortune, should end a spinster, but his attention was pulled to the bird Mr Sinclair had injured. John couldn't help but think of the bird's suffering, and although it might offend his host, he went to finish the job.

Handing the bird to the gamekeeper, he turned back to Mr Sinclair. "Enough, wouldn't you say?"

Mr Sinclair nodded. "Jolly good."

They strolled back to the house. "You must join us for dinner tonight," Mr Sinclair declared. "We'll be enjoying these birds for days in some form or other. And I should be grateful to have another man across the table." He grimaced. "As it is I dine with three women every night."

John grinned back at him. Despite his misgivings about the man's character, that did sound like something akin to torture. "I should love to accept the invitation," he replied. "But pray tell, what did you mean when you said I can help you? What do you want me to do?"

Mr Sinclair shrugged. "I don't want you to *do* anything. What I want is *information*. Just tell me what she's about, with regards to the estate. Any little tidbits may prove helpful."

John regarded his companion thoughtfully. His puffy countenance reeked of desperation. It was almost a little sad. And what the man was asking of him seemed a lot like espionage.

"Of course, my good man, when I am installed at Willowbridge, you can frequent it as much as you like, hunt and shoot as you please… You can even entertain your friends if you wish. I'd be glad of some refined company." He looked meaningfully at John to ensure he was sensible of the compliment. "Don't think our Lady Helena will be that kind to you."

Barrington grunted in spite of himself. Kind? She was frosty at best. And the offer of free rein at the estate was incredibly tempting. It was what he had desired from the moment he'd caught sight of it. Still…

Mr Sinclair had stopped moving and was gazing at him beseechingly. It was pathetic, and John couldn't stomach it anymore.

"Well, sir, I'll see what I can do," he said, if only to stop the man from begging. It was no guarantee of any effort on his part.

"That's the spirit!" Mr Sinclair clapped him on the back and resumed walking. "Remember, we need to look out for ourselves. I know *she* will. And if she marries one day, the new lord of the estate won't want you on his turf."

That was an unfounded assumption, but John had had enough of postulating. He increased his gait, and Mr Sinclair started to pant in his efforts to keep up. That kept him from talking.

Helena knocked on the door of a local gentry family that same morning. The visit, prompted by Mrs Powell, was to a widow who had recently come to live in Mulberry with her brother. Helen had met her briefly after church the preceding Sunday.

A maid showed her through to the drawing room, where she came upon the lady and her two children at lessons.

"Mrs Kendall, is it not?" Helena said as they exchanged curtsies.

"Yes, my lady. Alice Kendall. And these are my two little ones, Bertie and Lottie. Robert and Charlotte, I should say. They are eight and six."

The children, rather adorably, attempted to bow and curtsey to her, before their mother instructed them to continue with their reading and writing while she talked to "the lady".

Helena studied Mrs Kendall as they sat opposite each other. The woman was probably no more than five years her senior, but she had a tired, sorrowful air about her which negated any impression of youthful vivacity. Her hazel eyes were sunken into dark circles, and her tawny hair fell in scraps around her face. She was a picture of grief, though she obviously had to hide it from her children, and Helena's heart ached for her.

She said quietly, "You are recently widowed, I understand."

Mrs Kendall nodded. "Only last month," she said, with a quiver in her voice. "At Trafalgar."

"Oh, my dear." Helena reached out and took the lady's hand. A few moments later, Mrs Kendall curled her own fingers around Helena's, and they sat in silence while she gathered her emotions.

The maid came in with tea, and Mrs Kendall cleared her throat, beginning to pour with a trembling hand. "I still have the use of our cottage," she said, "but I couldn't bear to be there anymore. My brother has been so good as to extend the invitation for us to stay for as long as we need. I cannot think that I can ever return home again."

Helena nodded, accepting a cup. "I have observed Mr Pike to always be a kind and generous man." She indicated the children. "You teach them yourself?"

"I do, for now. I hope they will go to the village school if we stay into the new year."

"I am sure they would find some friends there," Helena said

reassuringly. "And you will find Mulberry is a delightful place to live."

Mrs Kendall smiled. "Thank you, my lady. You are very good."

Helena smiled back. "If there is anything you need, you have only to ask. In point of fact, I was going to invite Mr Pike to have Christmas dinner at Willowbridge as I know he has no relations nearby. Perhaps you would be so kind as to do this on my behalf – and I hope to see you, Bertie and Lottie there as well."

"How lovely. I should love to have Christmas in a grand house."

"We are quite informal, I assure you. I should love to have you."

Helena made her way back home with a full heart. She went to the kitchen to see what menu Jane had agreed on with Mrs Mead. To her surprise, the staff were busy with plucking and preparing game birds. She had thought they were having trout.

"A bountiful shoot today," said the cheery, rotund woman in response to Helena's enquiry. "I'll make a stew and pies as well as the roasted birds you'll have for your supper."

"Wonderful. Thank you." They discussed the other courses and Helena picked up an apple, cheese, and bread to see her through until dinner. She wandered to her study, where she found Privett at her desk.

"Good day," she said, swallowing down the last of her apple. "I was not expecting you today. Is everything in order?"

He looked up with kindly eyes. "I have been thinking of ways we might shore things up a little." He rose and insisted she take his place. Seating himself opposite, he tucked his ledger under his arm. "Really, my lady, we ought to be raising our rents. They haven't been changed since your father's passing, and with inflation the way it is…"

Her heart started to pound. "With inflation the way it is, our tenants can barely afford the necessities of life."

He blinked, frowning.

"I'm sorry," Helena said, shaking her head. "I did not intend to snap at you. I value your advice, really, I do." She rubbed her hands over her eyes. "Perhaps we could look at a small increase, if it really will make a significant difference to the estate's viability."

"I'll draft up a proposal, my lady. You do not have to take any action right away."

She held his sympathetic eyes. "Thank you, Privett. I really do not know what I would do without you."

Helena sat in the study by herself for a long while after her steward left. It felt as if they were on a knife edge, and if anything went wrong, they would tumble off the precipice and into the gloom. Willowbridge could slip through her fingers at any moment.

Enough. She was never one to dwell on problems.

She went to the drawing room, which was thankfully free of the Sinclairs. Jane was occupied in darning stockings, and Helena dropped down beside her, finding one of her dresses to re-hem.

"I've hardly seen you today, my dear," Jane said.

Helena nodded wearily as she threaded a needle, too tired to summon words.

Jane reached over and placed a hand on Helena's arm. "It pains me to see you like this," she said. "Will you not go to town for the next season? Surely the time has come to get a husband, to share your burdens. You cannot carry on like this, working yourself into the ground."

Helena took a breath, steadying her resolve. "No," she said firmly. "I must do this on my own. I will not have a man assume ownership of my lands." She began to pull stitches through her gown, although they were a little wobbly.

"But my love," Jane persisted, "if you were to find a man who adored you and made you contented, who owns what would not matter."

Helena shook her head. "It's not worth the risk."

"I only wish to see you happy. My heart despairs of you living your life alone."

"I am not alone." She winced as the needle went into her finger.

"I am sure you know my meaning." Jane sighed. "There is a depth to romantic love that can be found nowhere else. I would hate to have you end up like…"

Their eyes met. Helena dropped the dress into her lap. "Please, Jane, are you so very miserable?"

Helena had counted her friend as a woman who seemed satisfied with life without a man.

"I am very fortunate" Jane said earnestly. "I would never wish you to think me ungrateful for all your kindnesses."

Helena frowned. "Hush, Jane, you know I love you dearly."

"Thank you, my dear. I value my place with you deeply. However, especially as I grow older, I do wonder what it would be like to have the company, support, and love of a good man."

They continued with their work, a heavy silence between them.

Helena had not ever thought that Jane was lonely, but now she began to wonder if she had been selfish, keeping Jane with her constantly. She hadn't considered what life would be like for the two of them in the future. She had barely considered anything past the deadline set out in her father's will.

❧

John had a spring in his step as he led Thora back to her stable stall. A morning in the crisp air, free to wander about in expansive English countryside, and practising a skill he excelled at – he felt more like himself than he had since coming to Mulberry. It was just the tonic he'd needed.

Entering through the front door, he found some letters on the bureau. He snatched them up and went into the parlour, sinking into an armchair by the fire.

The first letter, from his mother, was a perfunctory acknowledgement of his own message. It concluded with a reminder that Mr Wilson would let them know if he tried to leave Mulberry or got into any trouble. He crushed the letter in his hand and threw it into the fire.

The other letter was in the hand of his beloved sister. He tore the seal open eagerly and began to read. Her words lacked her usual affection, which stung, but he understood her reserve.

Dear John,

Thank you for your letter. We are all well. There have been a few developments in Amberley which will be of interest to you. A dean came from London to see about the business with our vicar, which I believe you had a hand in. The woman at the centre of the scandal presented herself and cleared Mr Brook of any inappropriate behaviour, and the dean declared him innocent.

Thus, Mr Brook has decided to remain in Amberley and is now betrothed to Cecilia Grant. We are all very glad and look forward to celebrating their nuptials.

The other result of Mr Brook's trial was that the Fortescues have decided to give shelter to Amy Miller and her child, so she will also be able to stay in our village with her friends. I think our mother is much relieved.

Louisa and I have been decorating the house for the Christmas and it is beginning to look very festive. Perhaps we may get some snow before yuletide.

Wishing you a happy festive season, and all the best for the year ahead.

Yours,
Catherine

John sat back and took a deep breath. Developments, indeed. He'd spent his last several months waging an unholy war against the vicar after the man meddled in his affairs. But the better man had won, fair and square. All of John's attempts to get rid of him had been in vain. Instead of forcing Mr Brook to leave, John had been exiled instead. Brook's exoneration was the final humiliation. He was utterly defeated. To think that the vicar, who had been a pompous newcomer, had ousted him – he who had been born in Amberley, who was the second son of the earl who ruled over it. It was too much.

John rubbed his hand over his face and stood. What he needed was a bath. He wanted to be well presented for his dinner at Willowbridge tonight, so a wash and a shave were in order. He poked his head into the foyer.

"Hello there?"

Tom Morgan appeared. "Yes, sir?"

"Draw me a bath, there's a good chap."

Tom drew himself up to his full five foot, five inches, and spat out, "I'm not your chap, and I ain't your valet, neither. You can fill your own bath."

John gaped at him. "Of all the impertinence!" Was he drunk? "What about Rosie?"

"She's far too wee to be lugging pots of water around. I'll get my missus to put a pot on the boil for you. Then you can fetch the water y'self." He turned on his heel.

"With what?" John called after the man as he disappeared down the hallway. The only reply was the slamming of a door. John stared at it in shock and wonder. Draw his own bath? Was he a peasant?

He'd be damned if he was going to haul his own water up and down the stairs. He stomped up to his bedroom and shrugged out of his shirt, then shivered. When was that chimney sweep going to come? He went to his washbasin and soaked a cloth in water. He brought it to the back of his neck and gasped as the icy water dripped down his back. "This won't do," he muttered.

With a sigh he left the room and stalked down to the kitchen. Betty gasped at the sight of his bare chest and abandoned her vegetable preparations in favour of dashing into the larder.

John noted that the heavy cauldron was indeed alight on the hearth, and he located a smaller tub on a shelf to one side. Grumbling, he went to the pot and filled the tub, trudging upstairs with it several times. Then, once the pot was boiling, he poured the hot water into his tub and made four return journeys with that too. The tub was heavy, and while he traipsed up the stairs, he endured the indignity of the scalding water splashing out onto him. He was strong and could bear the weight, but he felt some sympathy for the little maids who had performed this duty for him his whole life.

At last, his travails complete, he stripped down and dipped a toe into the bath, which was decidedly less full than he would have liked. It wasn't as hot as he preferred, but it would have to do.

As he lowered himself down into the water and laid his head back on the bath with a sigh, he ruminated on how low he was in many ways. If he was an heir, he'd be properly waited on for the rest of his life. His thoughts drifted back to Willowbridge.

Now, John's goal might be not to cosy up to the lord – or lady in this case – of the estate, but to her second cousin. Sinclair seemed to believe beyond a shadow of a doubt that he would inherit Willowbridge, not Lady Helena. He only wanted a little help, he said, and if John was to provide this, his reward could be enjoying the hospitality of his neighbour whenever he pleased. Of course, it was easier to get on with a man than a woman – far less complicated, so this was really preferable.

Something nagged at his conscience, though. Something about the man's ambitions seemed so underhanded. John was no saint, of course, but he had no reason to wrong Lady Helena herself. And where would she go once Sinclair became the owner of her estate?

He decided he must find out more, if only to ease his own mind, before aiding Sinclair's cause.

Five years after they parted ways, John saw Julie Stone again. She was in his country home, standing there talking to his sister as if nothing had happened. But what was she doing in that shabby dress? Had she been abandoned by Lord Bromley? He could only see part of her profile, but it was the same chocolate-coloured hair, the same emerald eyes, the same slight figure. For a moment or two, he forgot how to breathe.

He'd thought he might be over her. But seeing her was like ripping the wound open, and he knew the shadow that was constantly over his heart was her. He'd never known such a love, before or since.

Finally forcing in some air, he cleared his throat and approached. What was she doing here?

Catherine heard him and turned with a smile. Did she not realise how this would torment him? "Dearest John, come and meet my new lady's maid. This is Amy Miller."

"Your new…" John's eyes flew to the young woman again and took in the details as she curtsied to him unsteadily. Yes, the nose was less pert, the chin was pointier, and her face in general was more oval than Julie's. She was probably taller, too. And yet, he could not look upon her without seeing his former love.

"John?" Catherine prompted him.

"Er, yes. Hello, Miss… Miller?"

The girl nodded. A little smile caught about her lips, and as she looked up at him, a blush crossed her cheeks charmingly. "I'm pleased to meet you, Mr Barrington," she said.

He couldn't help but be flattered; she obviously found him attractive. But he had never dallied with a servant, and he wasn't about to start now. And being with her was all too confusing given every time he looked at her, he would be reminded of his heartache.

Miss Miller helped Catherine prepare for her first season in London, and John couldn't help but be in her presence as he preferred his sister's company above any other family member. She appeared to enjoy his wit, and he found it easy to be around her, given she would never aspire to anything serious with him. He basked in her starry-eyed admiration. He found himself engineering ways to speak with her. He lapped up the attention, without any risk of a relationship.

Amy was the spitting image of Julie, not only with her hair and eyes – she also had the same lively countenance, the same ready laugh and fierce stubbornness. She'd also had a beguiling innocence that he'd deceived himself into thinking that Julie had. It was altogether bewitching - a combination of all his past hopes and desires in live, breathing, and kissable form. As the months passed, he broke his resolve not to fraternise with servants. If John caught her alone in a passageway or on the stair, he would catch her in an embrace or steal a kiss. Her enthusiasm only stoked his.

He'd admit to himself that he made her love him, and unlike Julie, her esteem seemed loyal and steadfast. All the while, Mrs Grant had been throwing her daughter at him, and he'd enjoyed flirting with her every now and then. But he had no serious intentions there either: Cecilia Grant had none of the attractions he would want in a wife – if he wanted a wife. That was until the vicar discovered what he was about and made himself an enemy. Then John pursued a different path, bent on revenge.

Chapter Six

Helena's heart was heavy, her faculties drained. The last thing she wanted to do was host a dinner, but she couldn't very well have the meal in her bedroom and leave Mr Barrington to the Sinclairs. Alas, she was too honest to feign a headache or another malady.

It was twilight when Mr Barrington arrived; Helena saw him draw up on his horse from her bedroom window. Before dismounting, he leaned forward and hugged the horse around its neck, saying something to it with his head to one side. Then, after his feet were on the ground, Mr Barrington gently caressed the horse's face and patted the hair between her ears, all the while whispering something to her. The tenderness in his featherlight touch was mesmerising, and Helena watched in awe until one of her grooms came to take the horse. Then she checked her appearance, smoothing down her green silk dress, tucking away a stray curl, and pinching her cheeks for good measure.

Almost as an afterthought, she took up a bottle of perfume from her dressing table and sprayed it into the air, stepping into the fragrance. She closed her eyes and inhaled deeply, enveloped in her mother's memory. The scent of gardenias had been her mother's favourite, and it was the only fragrance Helena had ever worn. She dabbed a little on her wrists and behind her ears and left the room.

She descended the main staircase as Andrews let their guest in. As her eyes met Mr Barrington's, all her fatigue and worries seemed to vanish, and something else entirely fluttered in her stomach. He removed a greatcoat to reveal a striking green coat, which almost matched the colour of her gown. It seemed to have been stitched onto him, so snugly did it fit across his broad shoulders.

"Good evening, my lady," he said, taking her hand and bowing over it. His eyes never left her face, and she couldn't look away, somehow transfixed. What was it about those dark orbs that held her spellbound?

"Good evening, Mr Barrington," she replied, curtseying. "Would you like to follow me?" She turned towards the drawing room.

"Certainly, I would." Was there something suggestive in his tone?

She looked back over her shoulder at him and found his expression all innocence. But then he winked… or was it just a blink? She sighed and walked on, finding their three dinner companions already assembled in the room. Her nerves were jittery, and she had no idea why. It must be because she'd had a taxing day… although that was not unusual.

"Ah, there you are, Helena." Jane regarded her with what appeared to be relief, clearly cutting off Mrs Sinclair in verbal flow.

Sinclair himself was seated on a couch with a newspaper, which he lowered slightly on their arrival. On seeing her guest, he brightened, and he invited Mr Barrington to share his thoughts on a political development. The gentleman duly sat beside him and peered at the relevant article.

Helena was free to rescue Jane from the clutches of her cousin's wife. "Good evening, ladies. I shall order some drinks. What would you like?"

She navigated the choppy waters of small talk until it was time to go to the dining room. The gentlemen emerged from the newspaper, and Mr Barrington offered an arm each to Helena and Jane.

"I must apologise," Helena said as she placed her hand on his sleeve. "We have uneven numbers."

"Not to worry," he said jovially. "It is a pleasure to escort in two esteemed ladies rather than only one."

Even through his clothes, Helena was sensible of the strength of Mr Barrington's forearm. It was calming, somehow.

The dinner courses were served, and it was in the second course that the partridges were laid out before them.

Helena looked to Sinclair, trying to keep her expression neutral. "You shot these birds, cousin?"

He squirmed in his seat. "I, uh…" He cleared his throat.

Helena couldn't help exchanging a smile with Jane. "I thought not."

Sinclair narrowed his eyes at her. "Our guest is an accomplished marksman," he told her, with some malice.

She turned her smile to Mr Barrington and rose her glass to him. "My thanks, sir."

He likewise tilted his glass to her. "Happy to oblige, my lady." He smiled warmly. "Any time. I thank you for the other delicious dishes. You have an excellent cook."

She nodded an acknowledgement, unable to hold back her own smile. Then she quickly returned her attention to her plate.

A few minutes later, she was obliged to glance up again when Mr Barrington asked, "Will there be some fox hunting over the winter?" He had directed the question at Sinclair, which irked her.

"Sadly, no," her cousin replied. "Helena objects to the hunters 'trampling' over her fields and forests."

Mr Barrington raised an eyebrow. "Ah."

When Sinclair shot her a sardonic look, it was too much. How dare he embarrass her in her own home? It was for her to decide what sport was to be had. He was privileged to be her guest.

"There are those among us who are not of a disposition for fox hunting," she said archly, "due to being unable to keep a good seat." The truth was, Sinclair was overweight and not at all athletic. She had only seen him on a horse once, and she pitied the poor beast.

Sinclair only huffed in response, but his wife filled the breach. "If one is provided with an appropriate mount by one's host – or hostess – one would have more success in the endeavour."

Helena took a breath to defend her provision of horses, but she was hushed by a warning look from Jane. She closed her mouth, and an uncomfortable silence followed. She was ashamed of herself. She should know better than to sink to Sinclair's level.

Unexpectedly, it was Mr Barrington who stepped in to break the awkwardness.

"Do you ride, Lady Helena?" he asked.

"I do indeed." She wished she could gallop away from this dinner.

"Then you must keep a good stable."

She nodded. Was he coming to her defence? "We keep the horses necessary for the carriage, and the farm, as well as for riding."

He smiled. "And no doubt you included a riding habit in the large order you made at Allen's shop the other day. I know how you ladies love to keep up with the latest styles. It is my observation that the appearance of the female rider is generally a greater priority than the horsemanship."

Sinclair snorted approvingly.

Helena stared at him. He dared to insult her horsemanship?

"Helena, was that order not for the –"

But Helena would not let Jane clarify her actions. Why should she favour Mr Barrington with an explanation? Her original estimations of him now rang true.

"At least I keep my wits about me," she retorted, "which cannot be said about those who addle their brains with too much drink."

He swallowed his mouthful of wine and then gaped at her. "I am sure I do not know what you mean."

❧

John's birds were duly roasted, carved, and presented on the table in the elegant, tasteful dining room. He had dressed with care for dinner, though he hardly knew why. As Lady Helena descended the stairs in the foyer, his breath caught. She seemed to float across to him in clouds of green, her hair piled on her head in luscious curls. And when she bid him follow her, he was enveloped in a heavenly scent of beauty and innocence. He was grateful to be snaffled by her cousin soon afterwards, so he could rein in his appreciation.

He was seated between Lady Helena, at the head of the table, and Miss Godwin at his left. Mr Sinclair sat across the table. He was enjoying a delicious assortment of dishes and beginning to enjoy himself. He watched the verbal volleys between Lady Helena and Sinclair with interest.

Now he was somehow in a war of words with his hostess. Unfortunately, her observation was more astute than she knew. While he would never ride while inebriated – he could not risk injuring Thora – he had come to lean on alcohol to dim his regrets.

His comment about females and horses was perhaps overstepping the mark, but he had yet to meet a woman who took riding seriously – except as a means to parade about in front of the opposite sex.

He observed Lady Helena as she picked the pheasant meat off the bone meticulously. Did the woman ever relax? She seemed somehow bound up in knots. Once again, John wondered how he might break through that veneer.

Lady Helena laid down her knife and fork and excused herself, mumbling about needing to check on something. John turned to Miss Godwin and smiled politely. The terse exchange of a few minutes earlier still seemed to be hanging in the air.

Miss Godwin swallowed her mouthful and then smiled back. "Lady Helena has had quite a trying day," she said quietly. "Her nerves are on edge."

John nodded, understanding. She meant to explain why his hostess had been sharp with her words. He chose not to reveal that he admired her boldness, even as he had been a little embarrassed by her accusation. She seemed remarkably sure of her own mind for someone of relative youth.

"If you do not mind me asking, of what age is Lady Helena?"

She eyed him keenly. "She will soon be turning twenty. And you, sir?"

"I am eight-and-twenty."

Miss Godwin went on to enquire about the ages of his siblings and where his family seat was situated. As he was concluding his replies, Lady Helena reappeared.

"My apologies," she said with poise, smiling at each person in turn. "The dessert courses will be served shortly."

The provision in her father's will weighed on his mind as he watched her now entertain with aplomb. The candlelight danced in her eyes... but she was clearly tired.

She caught him looking at her, and she frowned, then raised her eyebrows at him.

He turned to Sinclair. "How long do you mean to remain in Mulberry on this visit, sir?"

"Oh... another week or two. We'll go up to London for Christmas as most of the family gathers there."

Family. A pang hit John's heart. He'd never had Christmas away from his family.

Lady Helena cleared her throat. "You would of course be, er... welcome, to dine here on Christmas Day," she said to John. "I am entertaining a party of friends for the occasion."

He couldn't bear anyone's pity. He was not her friend, and he'd feel very awkward imposing on a cosy gathering.

"No," he croaked, then he cleared his throat. "My thanks, my lady, but

I of course have another engagement on such a special day."

"Yes, of course," she said, and she snatched up a macaroon from a platter, taking a large bite.

Shortly thereafter, the ladies withdrew. Sinclair poured the port and toasted John's health. They relived some of the moments from the morning's shoot.

"I've always had more success with partridges, myself," said Sinclair with a sniff. He drained his glass of port and poured himself another, topping up John's glass as well. "Not much partridge to be had around here, though."

"A pity," John said amiably. "Excellent stuff, this," he said, indicating his glass.

"Oh yes. Helena's father always ensured the wine cellar was stocked with the finest. But I do not think his daughter sees to it that the vintages are replenished, on account of the fact that she imbibes rarely. Got her mind set on other things."

"I see," John said. When it was clear Sinclair expected more commiseration, he added, "Also a pity."

Sinclair leaned forward, his beady eyes locked on John. "I think we are of the same mind. Let's face it, Lady Righteous here" – he jerked his thumb towards the drawing room – "will never take you into her fold. When I become the heir, as I always should have been, we'll be allies. I will see to it that we both enjoy the lifestyle we deserve."

Growing increasingly uncomfortable, John squirmed in his seat. How could he change the subject diplomatically, without actually promising anything?

Sinclair lurched further towards John. "If you help me," he said thickly, his voice coated in port, "we both prosper."

John's main goal now was to disengage the man, whose odour was less than savoury. "Well," he said with a smile, "when you put it like that..."

They clinked glasses and Sinclair sat back with a satisfied smirk.

John let out a breath. "Shall we join the ladies?" he suggested.

The drawing room was deathly quiet when they entered. Mrs Sinclair was writing a letter, Miss Godwin was reading a book, and Lady Helena was jamming a needle into some fabric, as if the cloth itself was responsible for all her worldly worries.

He seated himself next to her, and a quick glance was her only acknowledgement. She yanked her needle through the garment, and the thread broke. She muttered something caustic under her breath and sighed deeply, her eyes closed. When she opened them again, it seemed as if every muscle in her face was taut with tension.

"Why, Lady Helena," he said softly, causing her to jump. "I have never seen a woman wound up so tight!"

"How dare –" she began, and then she sighed again, her expression changing from exasperation to plain weariness. She regarded him as if weighing up how much to tell him. "I have responsibilities," she said finally. "To all the people of Mulberry."

"Well, not all of them." He smiled. "I do own some properties."

Her eyes narrowed, and then she smiled in spite of herself.

"I do not doubt that you have a lot on your plate," he went on gently. "It is clear to me that you need some respite. A holiday, perhaps. Could you not go up to London for Christmas?"

Her smiled vanished. "Why does everyone want me to go to London?" she snapped.

John stared at her. How could his attempt at mending things have backfired? The woman was an enigma. Didn't every lady long for London?

Everyone else stared at her, too, and she dropped her eyes to her sewing, which she then cast aside angrily.

An awkward silence filled the room.

Miss Godwin suddenly stood. "Shall we have some music?"

Sinclair, who was now on the wrong side of merry, cried, "Aye! And make it amusing, if you please!"

Miss Godwin cocked her head at him in a placatory gesture and took her place at the pianoforte. She selected a piece from among the sheet music on the stand and began to play. The music was dulcet, tranquil, like a glistening river slowly meandering down a wooded valley. He saw Lady Helena's shoulders slump as she relaxed a little. Some of her curls had escaped from the ribbon atop her head, and they fell about her neck in soft, tempting tendrils. With her eyes downcast, her long lashes brushed against her shapely cheeks, and when she caught him looking at her those same cheeks turned a rosy shade of pink. Something stirred within him.

He was in danger. Sweet, beautiful danger.

Helena willed her heartbeat to slow down. The look in John Barrington's eyes had sent her pulse racing. She took a deep breath in an attempt to quell the colour rising in her cheeks. Why was he staring at her that way?

No doubt he thought her out of her senses, as she'd been snapping at him all evening with sometimes only the slightest provocation. She rubbed her temples and was overcome with a need for her bed. Perhaps Mr Barrington had been right – at least, partially. She probably did need to get some rest if she was to carry on managing Willowbridge efficiently. The quieter winter months would afford some more peaceful moments, would they not? That is, if the citizens of Mulberry didn't demand as much attention as usual…

Jane finished playing the first piece and caught Helena's eye. She frowned and then raised her eyebrows, questioning if Helena was out of sorts. Helena shook her head and smiled to ease Jane's mind. Involuntarily, a yawn overcame her, and Jane grinned at her sleepy shrug. Then her fingers began to race across the keyboard in a lively reel.

There was a shout of delight from Sinclair, who began to clap along. A moment later, to Helena's mortification, he started flinging his wife around the room. Mrs Sinclair shrieked in apparent glee as she was twirled and twirled again.

Helena buried her face in her hands. The man was drunk, and beyond any sense of decorum. At the sound of laughter, she emerged from behind her fingers and met eyes with Mr Barrington, who was lost in mirth. The hilarity was contagious, and she found herself grinning back at him.

Then, in one graceful movement, Mr Barrington rose from the couch and reached for her hand.

"Oh, I really do not think…" she began.

"It will do you good," he said, laughing again, and this time he took her hand and pulled her to him.

"Well, I never!" she exclaimed. The nerve of him, to assume he knew what was good for her.

He led her away from the Sinclairs, to a space over by the window. A lump caught in her throat. The last time she had danced a reel, it had been with her father. Indeed, there had never been another man she had enjoyed dancing with.

As Jane began a new phrase on the piano, Mr Barrington broke into the most popular reel dance steps. It was clear he was not rhythmically gifted, but his enthusiasm was admirable, and his eyes never left hers. After several bars, he paused, and held his palm out in an invitation for her to reciprocate.

His eyes were so kind, so encouraging, that she forgot her bones were weary and her feet began to move almost of their own volition. She didn't remember all the steps, but Mr Barrington's face lit up in such a way that any self-consciousness melted away and she smiled back at him.

He reached for her again and began to twirl her around and around, and she threw her head back and laughed, caught up in the delightful dizzy whirl.

He was laughing too, a joyful low rumble which roused her heart. The music came to an end, and he gave her one last spirited spin before catching her in his arms. Their laughter died down and they were left panting in an embrace, his arms strong around her back and shoulders. Their faces were inches apart as he smiled down at her. She forgot there was anyone else in the room as he drew her into the depths of his eyes, making her feel as if she, too, was his entire world.

"A tonic for your spirits, I think?" he whispered, breaking the spell.

She nodded. "Yes. Thank you."

He released her, and she went to sit down next to Jane, who raised her eyebrows most disconcertingly. She ignored her companion's curiosity and picked up a book, pretending to be engrossed. It was several minutes before she could calm the frenzied beating of her heart. Could she convince herself it was only because of the dancing, and not due to her charismatic partner?

Soon afterward, as yawns threatened to overtake her, Mr Barrington rose to leave. Helena summoned a groom to bring his horse, and she saw him to the door.

"I thank you for a pleasant evening," he said, his eyes twinkling at her.

Helena took a depth breath, steadying herself. "You are most welcome, sir," she replied. "I do hope the moon gives you enough light to guide you home safely."

They heard the crunching of his horse's hooves on the gravel, and he shrugged into his greatcoat.

He reached for her hand and bowed over it. "Goodnight, my lady."

"Goodnight."

Still holding her hand, he gave her fingers a little squeeze and one corner of his mouth curved into a lopsided smile. She gulped in a breath and snatched her hand back.

As the door closed behind Mr Barrington, a shiver ran down Helena's spine. That smile – it was unnerving. It told her he had some sort of wicked plans which would likely become apparent at the least convenient moment. His eyes had danced with some sort of calculated amusement. That look stayed with her as she readied herself for bed, and as she willed sleep to come in the thick blackness of night. There was a measure of intelligence and wit lurking within those eyes, which sparked her interest. Would he use his powers for good or evil?

It was the night of the Ashworth summer ball, an annual event which celebrated his family's return to the country each year. It was a particularly sultry night, and John was in a mood to make merry. There was little entertainment to be had among the local villagers, but he was in good spirits and determined to enjoy the evening.

As their invited guests began to arrive, the family made a receiving line in order of seniority. The Fortescues were the first to be greeted by his parents, and before his turn John leaned forward to wink at Catherine. She grinned back – his darling sister. She was in her full bloom, her confidence buoyed by the wonders of her first season in town. To his relief, she had not yet accepted any proposals of marriage. She would remain with him for a little longer yet.

He bade good evening to each of their guests, as he had done a hundred times before.

"Don't you look lovely, my dear," he heard his mother say. "A vision."

John glanced over to see the slight form of Cecilia Grant, a local gentry girl, now greeting his brother. She was maturing into what he had to admit was an attractive young lady. And it was no secret that her parents had John himself in their sights. From what he knew of her, she was far too scatty for his tastes… but he acknowledged she was the most appealing female he'd met so far that evening, and dancing with her could be diverting.

Miss Grant was now curtseying before him, and he reached for her hand, pressing a kiss on her gloved fingers. "A vision from heaven," he said with a smile, and the lady turned a fetching shade of scarlet. He released her hand. "May I claim you for the minuet?"

She raised her enormous blue eyes to his and hesitated for the barest moment before replying, "Of course, sir."

Conversation with Miss Grant during the dance was scant at best, painfully awkward at worst. He withdrew from her company as the music ended, lest she be erroneously encouraged. He sought out a drink from the far end of the room. He was then approached by a footman, who handed him a letter.

"This came in the late post, sir."

John murmured his thanks and frowned as he scrutinised the handwriting on the missive. It was unfamiliar, and something made the hair on the back of his neck stand on end. Without a word to anyone he made his way to the library and sank into an armchair, placing his drink down on the adjacent table. He tore the seal and angled the paper toward the nearest candlelight. It read:

Mr Barrington,

I write to you in the capacity as solicitor for Lord and Lady Bromley. The latter has, I regret to inform you, recently perished due to consumption.

John's heart stopped beating. *Perished…*

It was a dying wish that you be sent the enclosed letter, written in her own hand not one month ago. On her request, its contents have been sealed and remained private, even from her husband.
Should you have a need to reply, my address is…

John hastily discarded the page and took up the second letter, breaking an identical seal. And there was the hand of his beloved, although it was shakier than he'd known, as if somehow broken.

Dearest John,

I write this to you from my bed, as I no longer possess the strength to leave it. I know I am not long for this world. As one does when one's days are numbered, I have reflected upon my life and the decisions I have made.
My greatest sadness is that I will not see my children grow. My greatest regret is losing you.
It was naïve of me to think I could ever be content with another, when there was such a man as you in my heart… the kindest, gentlest, sweetest man in the world. My husband has not been unkind, but there is no love between us. I was a fool to think his money would make me happy.
Not a day goes by when I do not think of you fondly, and hope that you have found your own joy. I have been careful to avoid such gatherings in London where I suspected you would be present, as I did not want to cause you further pain. That I

caused you any pain at all is something I have never forgiven myself for.

I know not if you have cherished my memory to the same degree. I have hoped you would forget me and yet that thought is unbearable. I never stopped loving you. I could not pass away without letting you know – that I adored the man I knew you were. And you loved me without question. I have never been accepted so wholly, so graciously, so wonderfully. I am haunted by my words to you that night, when I told you I no longer loved you. It was a hideous lie meant to stop you from embarrassing us both. I can still see the desolate hurt on your face. I am sorry.

I know not what has become of you, but I like to imagine you settled at your country manor with a darling little family and a wife who admires you. Despite everything, I cannot help but feel jealous. No one could love you like I have. My heart will be yours always.

Yours ever,
Julie

The letter fell from John's hand as a guttural cry emanated from him – from his soul. His breathing became shallow and laboured as long-buried feelings came flooding back. After all this time, this was a glimpse of the delicate creature he has cherished… who he cherished still. And now she was gone. The grief was still fresh, and now doubly acute.

He would not have the luxury of public grief. This was a burden he must bear alone, and it would eat up his heart, his very soul, until there was precious little left.

He ran to his father's study and closed and locked the door behind him, taking the solitary candle over to a bottle of brandy. He poured himself a glass and drained it in one gulp, then downed another. And another.

Then he collapsed into his father's chair and wept. He tried to read Julie's words again through a veil of tears. *Never stopped loving you… heart will be yours always… my greatest regret…*

He cried for the pain she must have suffered in her final days. He cried for the years she had been married to a virtual stranger. But most of all, he cried for the life they could have had together. If he had known she still loved him, he could have fought harder for her. During those months when he waited for her to come to her senses, he should have sought her out and reminded her of their love. Would she then have lived? He had failed her.

The hurt penetrated to his core… what might have been - the man he might have been, the family they could have raised together. Instead, he was a pathetic loner without any hope of real happiness.

Sighing heavily, he tucked the letters into an internal pocket in his jacket and dispatched one more brandy. Now considerably unsteady on his feet, he groped for the door and lurched into the hallway, figuring he should return to the ball. He needed distraction. He needed to not feel anymore.

But just before he re-entered the ballroom, he encountered Julie – no, it was Amy. Those damnable green eyes, that coffee-coloured hair – it was torture of the bitterest kind. In his incoherent mind, they were one and the same. And he wanted her desperately.

She beamed at him adoringly, and it was almost too much for his besieged heart to bear. "Good evening, my sweet," he murmured. "Will you join the party?"

She shook her head, eyes lowered. "You know full well that is not my place."

"Oh, that I wish it were," he said, and her eyes flashed back to his.

"John…" she whispered, colouring.

What was he doing? He knew not. John had never before given Amy any hope of his affection. His mind swirled with a concoction of regrets, grief, and a sore need to be wanted. And she wanted him; there was no denying it.

He leaned over and spoke into her ear. "You look beautiful tonight. The loveliest lady here."

"Oh!" Amy giggled and pushed a hand to his chest in protest. "I think you are in… very high spirits, sir, and you know not what you say."

How true those words were. He was acting on pure instinct, pure need, without any rational thought whatsoever. He reached for her hand, and she gasped. Their eyes locked for a moment before she pulled free and ran off towards the servants' stairs.

He would not be so easily discouraged, not tonight. His entire body pulsated with the raw emotion of losing Julie once again, and it was as if

Amy was her shadow. When he was speaking to Amy, his heart had been addressing his beloved.

When he caught up with Amy and coaxed her outside with kisses, he continued to whisper words that he'd only ever said to Julie. She seemed entranced, and eager to return his passionate embraces at length. He was now so possessed of love and desire, that he finally took what he had craved with Julie. And with it, the innocence of Amy Miller.

Any satisfaction was short-lived. He had only a dim recollection of events the following morning. His memories were a haze of lust and brandy, but he soon realised what he'd done. He'd gone too far – taken more than she wanted to give. It surprised even him that he could have overstepped the mark without any premeditation. He'd probably never been that intoxicated in his whole life, his judgement so horribly forsaken.

He wasn't the first gentleman to take advantage of a servant, and he certainly wouldn't be the last… but that didn't make it any less of a crime, a heinous sin against someone who trusted him. He knew it, deep down, in the places in his heart he never visited.

Chapter Seven

As John travelled back to Mulberry Manor after the dinner party, he found himself whistling the cheerful reel he and Lady Helena had danced to. Its joyful rhythm matched the gait of Thora's steps. There was but one image in his mind's eye: that of Lady Helena twirling around him, laughing with free abandon. How her countenance had changed when she was relaxed and seemingly happy. Her blue eyes sparkled, her cheeks glowed in a becoming flush, and the trill of her laughter had made his heart soar. It was a stark contrast to the woman who had seemed agitated for most of the evening.

And when he'd said goodnight to her, she'd regarding him with a new sort of vulnerability which told him he had succeeded in breaking down a little of her façade. Her openness had made her even more beautiful, and he was captivated. He may have then been a trifle too familiar with his gestures as he took his leave, and she immediately retreated behind her emotional wall again. No matter, that was probably for the best. Then they were both safe.

Making his way up to his room, the chimney freshly swept, he remembered something he'd said to the lady and her cousin. He'd positively scoffed at her invitation to Willowbridge for Christmas Day, embarrassed at his situation and the isolation it brought. Surely his family would miss him during the festive season, too? If only a little? He readied a pen and paper and sat at his dressing table. Taking a breath to steady his thoughts, he wrote a short note begging to be allowed admittance to Ashworth Hall for even a few days over Christmas. He promised to remain within the house lest his presence among the village people should provoke hostility toward the family. Sealing the letter, he began to undress and wondered what Lady Helena was doing. Then he shook his head – whatever had made him think that? Still, the thought remained. Was she likewise dressing in her nightclothes, her hair now cascading down her back? He shivered. It was all too alluring a mental picture, and one he best not dwell on.

❦

At the sound of a tuneless whistling two days later, John looked out of his bedroom window. A man was striding towards the house clad in a broad hat and dark clothing, with a remarkably pious air… It could only be the vicar.

John bounded down to the kitchen and inhaled the rich aromas of a bubbling soup and proving bread.

"Betty?"

The woman turned to him, her hands remaining busy on the bench. "Aye, Mr Barrington?"

At least she *knows my name.* "I'm going out. If anyone should call, tell them I should be gone a while."

She regarded him with suspicion. It was indeed the first time he'd seen fit to inform her of his comings and goings. "Right you are," she said with a nod, before returning to her work.

John dashed out the kitchen door and to the stables. A solid knock resounded from the house. Was the man trying to force godliness on his very abode?

He ran his hands over his mare soothingly before picking up his tack. "There now, girl, we're just going for a little ride," he murmured to her as he fastened the girth.

He directed Thora directly to the copse on the eastern boundary, towards Willowbridge. He brought her back her to a trot as they wove through the trees. As his thoughts likewise slowed, he asked himself why he desperately wanted to avoid the vicar.

He'd never been afraid of conversing with anyone… with one notable exception. He lived his life free from obligation and fear. Until now. He knew exactly why he had flown from his own home.

It wasn't just a dreary conversation he wanted to avoid, or the usual attempts to recover his soul. He was afraid of being discovered for just how lost he'd become. How wicked, how depraved. John was so traumatised by what he'd done that he was afraid of being made to face it.

While he hadn't the least intention of ever revealing why he'd been forced to come to Mulberry, he feared that if a man of God was perceptive and clever, he might be able to tease some of the truth out of John. And the truth wasn't something he was willing to part with. He didn't even want to admit to himself how low he'd fallen.

He'd also tangled with another clever vicar recently, and that had *not* ended well. In fact, it was in part the reason why he found himself here, alone.

He pulled Thora up to a stop by a stream and dismounted to let her drink. Willows overhung the flowing water, and their reflections turned the rushing water a glossy green. The stillness and tranquillity only served to underline the torment in his soul. How ridiculous he was, that he had to avoid a man of the cloth who was probably harmless. The man was only doing his duty in visiting a new parishioner, after all. After some tea and biscuits and pleasantries, it probably would have been over with no harm done.

But now, with his fear now trespassing into his new life, he knew. He was a coward. He hated it, but it was true. He supposed he'd been a coward ever since Julie Stone abandoned him. He'd thought that avoiding real human contact was admirable, in a way. Now he saw that he'd been hiding all along. Even now, he hid his face in his hands, wishing he could disappear altogether.

"Mr Barrington, are you quite well?"

The sudden sound of a voice in the present lurched him from his ruminations. It was a female voice. With a gasp he wrenched his hands from his face and stood from where he'd been sprawled on the riverbank. "I beg your pardon," he sputtered.

He blinked and took in the sight before him. Was it an angel? She was a vision of light, her cerulean coat and blonde hair glowing in the sun at her back. As he focused on her face, he recognised Helena Davenport, and the pure beauty of her features took his breath away.

Her brow, though, was creased with concern, and he recalled her question. Suddenly flustered, he replied, "Er, yes... quite well, I assure you, my lady."

Then he remembered his manners, and bent into a lopsided bow, almost losing his balance.

She reached out a hand to steady him, grasping his forearm with a giggle. "All evidence to the contrary," she said, her clear blue eyes smiling into his.

He broke into a grin and glanced down at her hand. Her gentle pressure made his pulse quicken. "I do hope *you* are in good health?"

She hastily removed her hand, her cheeks a little flushed. "Indeed, I am out riding my gelding, Cornelius." She gestured to the horse tethered to a nearby tree. That explained her colouring; it was merely from the exercise. "I see you have your mare."

"Yes, this is Thora." He moved to give the horse a pat on the flank.

"A heroic name, to be sure."

He nodded. "She has a strong spirit."

"You are well suited, then, I think," she said with a smile. Before he could ask as to her meaning, she went on, "I lately had a visit from Mr Powell, the vicar. He said he would go over to the manor to introduce himself to you."

John hitched in a breath, and then tried to assume a casual air. "Oh, did he? A shame I missed him."

Her eyes narrowed. "Why do you not go to church?"

He gave a shout of mirthless laughter. "My soul is beyond redemption."

She regarded him seriously. "No one is beyond redemption. That is the entire point of the scriptures, which you would find out if you attended to the teachings."

He could not mock her earnestness. He could see in her eyes a genuine concern for him, not just condescension. "If it will please you, madam," he said evenly, "I shall make an effort to attend from time to time and therefore partake in trivial chatter with the villagers. But please do not raise your hopes for some kind of conversion."

She smiled again. "Very well."

He looked about them for her companion, but in vain. "You are without a groom, my lady?"

She nodded, her smile fading and her chin raising. "I am."

He remounted Thora with ease. "That is highly improper, is it not? What if you should need to dismount, or should find yourself in trouble?"

She shrugged, stepping up onto a tree stump next to Cornelius. "I concede dismounting can be an inconvenience. If needed, I will simply stay mounted until I return to the stables. I will not, however, find myself in trouble. I have been riding almost since I could walk. And there is no question of my getting lost on my own lands." She then mounted the gelding with impressive grace.

Her confidence was unusual, and intriguing. He'd never seen a woman riding alone. His senses piqued, he was in the mood for a little mischief. He nudged Thora and they came alongside Lady Helena. "Ah, but perhaps the danger would come in the form of an unscrupulous gentleman."

She raised an eyebrow. "Are you such a man, sir?"

"Perhaps."

She returned his smile, her eyes telling him she was up to any challenge he offered. It was more than he could resist. "I do apologise for not seeking permission prior to trespassing on your property."

"Not at all. As my neighbour you are welcome to exercise Thora on the Willowbridge estate whenever you please."

Something about her tone indicated a type of condescension, as if she was making sure he knew her lands were superior to her own. That raised his heckles, only fuelling his competitive inclinations.

"Thank you, my lady. I shall take up the offer and give Thora her head for a while."

She gave him a polite nod. "Good day to you, then." She brought her mount to a walk, beginning to move away from John.

But he brought Thora around beside her and said, "Join me, won't you?"

She head whipped around to him. "I hardly think..." she began hesitantly.

"I haven't had the pleasure of a friendly race for months. You've mentioned you're a confident rider, and there must be some open fields nearby where we can give them full rein."

"Well, yes, of course..."

"I am sure you couldn't beat *me*, though."

She gasped, pulling Cornelius to a halt and glaring at John.

"I hate to contradict a guest, Mr Barrington, but if I were you, I shouldn't be so sure about anything."

This time the assurance in her voice excited him. Thora felt the energy and began to walk faster. "Is that so?" he said with a grin.

She gestured over the rise of the hill. "I'll take you over to the home farm. There are some lovely rolling pastures there." And with a quick backward glance, she spurred her horse into action.

He shouted a laugh and took off after her at the gallop.

⁂

Helena grinned in spite of herself as she heard the thundering of hooves coming up behind her. She was enjoying this too much. She couldn't remember the last time she'd raced Cornelius against a creditable competitor… if ever. Her gelding was up to the challenge. Keeping him ahead of Mr Barrington and his mare was exhilarating. Every nerve in her body seemed to tingle as she guided Cornelius over hedgerows and across fields. One of her cows gave a startled moo as she passed by. "Morning!" she called back gaily.

Mr Barrington began to draw up beside her, and stealing a glimpse at him, she saw he was equally thrilled by the chase. His countenance was alert, open and joyous. It was the first time she'd seen him so at ease, and the same could be said of herself.

She was never more content than when on her horse, so relaxed and carefree. It was her father who had taught her to ride. She could feel his easy, comforting presence with her whenever she mounted.

"That was an unfair starting advantage, Lady Helena," her opponent called, panting.

"Surely you would expect a mere female to need a head start, Mr Barrington?" she shouted back, returning her attention to their course. She pointed ahead. "See that barn over there? First to arrive is the victor."

He laughed. "Jolly good, my lady." Then as he spurred Thora on, she also nudged Cornelius to greater speed.

The horses were fairly evenly matched, although Thora did have a strikingly muscular frame. If it were a case of brute strength Mr Barrington would likely win. But she knew this land like it were an extension of her own body, and she knew this paddock undulated suddenly and irregularly. As they came to the first depression, she heard Mr Barrington exclaim, then pull Thora back. She guided Cornelius down and up with ease, darting a look over her shoulder to make sure the other horse hadn't faltered. They were safe, but considerably slower.

She smiled again and made the dash to the barn, pulling Cornelius to a walk by the time Mr Barrington arrived.

"A home advantage this time," he said, also coming to a walk beside her. "I should love to compete with you both on neutral territory."

She laughed. "I am not in the habit of racing in public, Mr Barrington. I am not in the habit of racing at all."

"Yes, I suppose a lady taking up such a dangerous sport would be frowned upon. Pity," he went on, almost to himself, "I could have made it interesting with a wager."

She pulled Cornelius to a stop abruptly, disgusted. Gambling must be one of his vices, of which there were many. It was a timely reminder. She had been liking his company more than she should.

He also pulled up, regarding her with surprise.

"Mr Barrington," she said sharply. "I have no intention of becoming an object of sport for you or anyone else."

His mouth dropped open for a moment. "Lady Helena, I assure you I did not mean…"

"I am sure there are already enough people speculating on whether I will succeed or fail." She clamped her mouth shut. He'd hit a nerve. She hadn't meant to say such a thing to him.

His eyebrows flicked up. "What is your meaning, my lady?"

She had no intention of elaborating. Her struggles were her own, and she did not trust this man nearly enough to reveal any more. She passed a hand over her eyes, suddenly weary.

Being young and female complicated Helena's position as the ruler of Mulberry society. She had the reflected respect of her father, but she sensed there was a great deal of doubt concerning her ability to manage the estate. It was more obvious in her father's peers, who owned other estates near and far. Ties which had been close had withered since his passing. Instead of extending a hand to help her, they had suddenly become very busy with their own affairs. It only made her all the more determined to succeed without outside help. Her only dilemma, as she was determined to remain a spinster, was that the estate would pass out of her immediate family on her own death.

"Will you assist me to dismount?" she asked abruptly, desperate to distract Mr Barrington from her outburst. "I shall show you some of the new initiatives on the farm."

"Certainly," he replied, before slipping down from his own saddle.

It was only as he approached, his eyes locked on hers, that she realised the folly of her request. While she could slip down from Cornelius on her own, if necessary, it was safer to have the help of a block or her groom. She was so used to her groom that being in close quarters with him was commonplace.

Mr Barrington was no groom. She had not failed to notice the strength and grace of his physique as they'd galloped across the terrain together. His synergy with Thora made him doubly attractive. And now, as he gazed up at her with his arms outstretched, something in his countenance made her feel secure, yet excited. The warmth in his eyes, set in the handsome angular features of his face, set her insides leaping.

Helena took a deep breath as she unhooked her right leg, then took her left foot out of the stirrup. She fell rather heavily onto him, her hands on his shoulders, but he caught her smoothly around the small of her back, his hands coming to rest around her waist.

"I have you," he said, smiling into her eyes kindly.

She could not help smiling back, as she forced breath into her lungs. Her traitorous feelings whispered, *I wish you did.* It was the first time she had had an inkling of wanting to belong to a man, and it terrified her. And yet, as his gentle pressure on her hips sent shockwaves throughout her body, she didn't want him to let her go.

The world began to spin as she became lost in his eyes, and she wondered how she would stand, let alone walk.

He frowned a little. "Are you quite steady, my lady?"

She cleared her throat, lowered her eyes and breathed, "Yes, thank you."

John spurred Thora to greater speed, and she responded brilliantly. They both began to sweat from the exertion. But even his horse's swift and steady gait couldn't distract or soothe John. It was two days since the ball and his indiscretion. He'd behaved badly, and he knew he couldn't dally with Miss Miller any longer. To hurt her had not been his intention. He couldn't recall every moment, but he could hear her screams. He would hear them every night.

His shame was already so acute that he couldn't bear to come face to face with her. His training as an English gentleman had developed an upper-lip so stiff that apologising was out of the question. Like the coward he was, he'd mostly remained in his room or out of doors since the ball. He told himself it was to spare her the pain of any further embarrassment. He hoped that, one way or another, it would all blow over and they both could forget it ever happened. Life could go back to being how it was before, except he wouldn't dare a similar level of familiarity with a servant, or any lady for that matter, ever again.

He was in this heady mix of guilt and denial when the new vicar, William Brook, chose to confront him regarding the appropriate treatment of servants. As he handed Thora to a groom at the end of his ride, the self-righteous man dared to challenge John's behaviour, beginning with seemingly innocuous, although unnecessary questions.

He tried to answer the man's queries as to his inheritance with nonchalance or at least aplomb, but his façade broke when Brook all but ordered him to stay away from the staff. "Direct your desires to their proper place," he'd said. The vicar's words struck him at his worst ebb, their pinpoint accuracy like an arrow to his soul.

A vicar's place was to sermonise and help the poor, not to meddle in private affairs. His feelings towards Mr Brook, which had been indifferent at best, were now transformed into dislike and suspicion. How much did he know?

It added a sort of paranoia to the growing emotions clawing at his gut. No one else could suspect. Not that he thought the girl would dare to bring proceedings against him, and if he were to end up charged with something the law hardly ever sided against a peer. Regardless, he would continue to stay away from Amy Miller, to avoid anyone speculating about what he'd been up to. And the cleaner the break was, the sooner her feelings, whatever they were, would subside. He convinced himself he was doing her a kindness by keeping his distance. He only wished he could erase her memory of what he had done... no, he wished the act itself could be undone.

When Cecilia Grant crashed into him after church that week (he was an irregular worshipper, at best), he noticed Brook regarding them with what could only be described as jealousy. So, at a little card party, he flirted with her when he knew the man was watching. A little gentle ribbing about the lady when Brook joined the family for a shoot completed his assault on the other man's ego. Perhaps now the vicar would keep his opinions to himself.

Chapter Eight

John tried to appear engaged in what Lady Helena was telling him about her estate. But his attention was mainly rapt on how elegantly she walked, the tendrils of hair that wafted about her lovely face, and the soft timbre of her voice. Her hips swayed gently with each step – the very hips he had held not ten minutes earlier. The blood still pulsed rapidly around his body as he recalled the feel of her slender curves. But the sensation was more than just attraction, it had been as if he held a precious jewel in his arms. He had such a protective instinct towards her; it was quite overpowering.

Even with his attention divided, he could not mistake the enthusiasm – nay, passion – with which she talked about her endeavours since taking over management of her lands. He had never heard a lady talk about soils, types of feed, animal breeds and by-products before… and he had certainly never been so captivated to hear about such subjects. She really cared about looking after her lands and animals – more than any gentleman he knew.

"Do you not have a steward to manage all this for you?" he enquired incredulously.

She nodded. "Of course. But I have a vested interest in making a good profit from the estate, and there is so much to do that I feel it is my duty to assist as much as I can."

Duty: something John knew little of prior to coming to Mulberry. It was the first time he saw someone who appeared to enjoy giving of themselves to these types of activities, that the work was its own reward. Except… she also mentioned a vested interest. What was it Sinclair had said about the conditions of her inheritance?

As they led their horses back towards her house, Lady Helena explained it was the home farm that she took an active interest in. These lands were not tenanted out and they supplied most of the food for her household, as well as income from the sale of corn, wheat, and livestock. It was on this land that Helena's shepherds were nurturing a new high-quality sheep, the Southdown. As they walked among the woolly animals in question, she talked about their various attributes and how they had increased the herd.

"We are relying on a good lambing season this spring," she concluded.

He nodded, still in awe of her knowledge and dedication. "To what end?" he enquired.

She eyed him warily, as if weighing up how much truth to dispense to him. She heaved a sigh, then said, "We intend to sell off the entire flock in the autumn. It will provide us with the surety we need to keep the estate afloat this year."

He stopped in his tracks, shocked. "To keep it afloat? Are you in such dire circumstances?"

She glanced at him, then away, shrugging. It seemed this was all the answer she was to give. She began to walk again, this time more slowly, her shoulders slumped as if in defeat.

"I am sorry to hear that," he said, falling into step beside her again. "If I can be of any –"

She held up a hand to cut him off. "Thank you, no." Then she motioned in front of them. "It is not far to the house; we'll see it once we ascend this crest."

Was that a hint that she was eager to be rid of him? Should he offer to leave her to her solitude? John wasn't used to navigating the waters of politeness like this, and it unsettled him that he cared not to offend her. Even so, his curiosity got the better of him when he asked her, a few minutes later, "Does, er… Sinclair know the estate is hanging in the balance?"

Her eyes flashed to him. "No, of course not. I do not want him meddling."

"Quite. And your sheep breeding programme…"

She shook her head. "He knows nothing about the farm, nor does he ask."

"I see."

She raised an eyebrow. "Why do *you* ask?"

Why, indeed. He knew it was unfair that he knew more than he was letting on. But revealing Sinclair's scheming would only upset her and cause more familial unrest.

Instead, he chose to answer her question with one of his own. "I don't suppose you have a dowry sitting idle somewhere?"

She frowned. "In point of fact, I do. It would easily clear my debts and allow me to make all the improvements I need to Willowbridge and my other properties… theoretically."

Of course, she would need a theoretical husband. Despite what Sinclair said, she would be an attractive catch in the marriage mart. "All you have to do is er… get married," he said lightly.

She gave him a level stare. "Yes, that is all."

Clearly it was not a prospect she found appealing. He kept his tone mild. "Have you never been tempted?"

"By the money?" She laughed bitterly, shaking her head. "When not only my dowry, but all my property, would be signed over to my husband? Willowbridge is mine. I have no intention of allowing some man to come in and do with it as they wish. Or to do with me as they wish," she added in an undertone.

Then she looked up, as if remembering he was there. "No – I have not been tempted," she said.

He took a moment to absorb this speech. Her point of view made perfect sense, of course, but it was completely at odds with the ways of their patriarchal society.

He knew not how to respond but was sensible of refraining from further prying into her private affairs. As they came over the hill and Willowbridge house came into view, in all its magnificence, he sought to lighten the subject.

"You will head up to London in the spring, I take it? Your new fashions will need an airing." He smiled, assuming he had mentioned something which would animate her as it did most females.

"And miss the flowering of the mulberry trees?" she replied, almost dreamily. Then she met his gaze and frowned. "No, I never go to town, unless I have unavoidable business there."

He stared at her. "But surely you have a residence there?"

"Oh yes, there is a family townhouse in Mayfair. My cousin holds court there frequently."

"And the season is no draw to you?"

She shook her head. "We have our own little merriments in Mulberry society. There is certainly enough to keep me occupied here – more than enough."

"Really?" He could not fathom what could possibly keep a young lady from the entertainments of the glittering city.

She sighed. "I expect you could not understand as you have not managed a large estate. An entire village."

This stung him to the bone, although he tried to keep his expression neutral. He had lived his whole life knowing that privilege fell to his brother. "No, I have not," he said quietly.

"I take an interest in my tenants' affairs," she went on staunchly, "and do whatever is necessary to service their needs. It is all in the interest of keeping the wider estate profitable, of course. But I grew up with these people – they are my community. I care about them. I could not abandon them just to parade about in Hyde Park and spend my nights dancing at crowded balls."

Had she just lectured him, demeaning his way of life? He was not used to a lady speaking so frankly, and he began to wonder what kind of man would suit such an outspoken woman.

He studied her for a moment, as they approached the house. He accepted that she thought she did not need a husband, but did she not crave some attention or merriment? Would she let her lovely bloom go to waste without any admiration at all?

"I have company enough," she said firmly, putting an end to the conversation as if she had heard his unspoken questions.

What an odd woman! How entirely opposite to him. He craved the diversions of London, as a means to escape his loneliness and distract him from his failings. She spurned them entirely. He was sure he could never be happy if he was forever isolated here in the country.

They went around the back of the house, towards the stable block.

"Why are you here?" she asked suddenly. "'Tis obvious how tedious this is for you."

Had she read his thoughts? He hesitated while he formulated a response. "I thought it was high time I surveyed my inheritance," he said evenly.

"That is fair," she said as a groom came running out to take Cornelius from her. "*You* shall go to London for the Season, though."

It was an assumption, not a question. How the devil was he going to respond to all and sundry asking him about this as the Season neared?

He took a breath and waited until the groom was out of earshot. "Are you trying to get rid of me?" he asked finally.

"Perhaps." In her eyes there was a delightful sparkle, which hinted at a capability for wit and perhaps flirtation. She seemed pleased to have the upper hand again, to be in control.

He smiled back at her, but inwardly he sighed with relief that he had sidestepped that line of questioning.

❧

Helena was a whirl of emotions as she changed out of her riding habit and fixed her hair. She had gone out riding for some much-needed peace and solitude, but the sight of a figure lying next to a horse by the stream had drawn her in. She could not have imagined the gamut of experiences that would result from their accidental meeting.

Feeling overwrought and overwhelmed, she was glad to find Jane in the drawing room, darning stockings by the fire.

Her companion looked up and smiled as she sat down opposite. There passed some comfortable moments of silence while Helena found some work of her own, only the occasional crackling of the fire punctuating the air.

"Did I see you riding with someone, my dear?" Jane then asked idly, her eyes not leaving her needle.

Helena willed herself not to blush, her mind's eye suddenly occupied by Mr Barrington's face as he held her in his arms. "Why yes, I happened upon Mr Barrington down by the willows and he, er, challenged me to a ride."

At this her eyes raised. "Challenged you?"

"In a manner of speaking." Helena tried to shrug away any significance. Then after mulling on their time together some more, she spoke again. "Do you not think it odd, Jane, that after not coming here his entire life, Mr Barrington suddenly turns up without so much as a valet, let alone a family for company? And not just for a visit, but ostensibly to live here without any apparent regard for estate management?"

Jane considered. "He must have his reasons. Why do you not ask him why he came?"

"I did."

"And?"

"He said he wanted to see his property."

"Well, then." Jane went back to her stitching.

"There is something else," Helena went on. "He does not seem to want to be here."

"What is it? Do you suspect something underhanded?"

"I cannot say." She paused. "Is it not odd that when I mentioned Mr Powell was on the way to see him, that Mr Barrington did not immediately turn for home to meet him?"

"Mmm," Jane said, "mayhap he was more interested in the company before him."

At that Helena did blush, and she hastily resumed her own sewing.

But she knew better than to be flattered by Mr Barrington's company. His apparent rudeness towards the vicar likely had more to do with his state of mind that morning. When she'd come across the gentleman he'd been in a posture of despair, almost desolation. Of course, she did not know him well enough to ask about what had happened to make him so upset. She doubted she would ever be on close terms with him – why would she?

And yet… she had been freer with her words with Mr Barrington than she had been with any other gentleman, excepting Privett. That worried her. What if she had revealed too much? *Ah well,* she reasoned, *there wasn't anything he could do to hurt her… was there?*

She instantly regretted telling him the estate was in trouble – she abhorred the pity in his eyes. His offer to help was embarrassing. A man she hardly knew, with a questionable reputation, in a cottage ornée which was once owned by her family… Insulting, that's what it was. She knew he meant well. But she should be above such help.

As for Mr Barrington, despite their lengthy discussion, she had more questions than answers. The man was inscrutable, phlegmatic – intriguing.

There was something about those dark, intense eyes, his roguish lopsided smile, the way he carried himself with such ease and yet such mystery… Something about him drew her in, even though she was sure she was playing games with the devil. Although she knew she would lose some part of her soul in the bargain, something about him made her desperate to play… and win.

At their parting, he'd given her one of those crooked smiles and her stomach flipped over, with a sense of both fun and danger. Perhaps the danger only lay with keeping her heart in check?

Was she trying to be rid of him? Well, maybe that would be for the best.

❧❧

At four o'clock four days later, it was already dark. Rosie came into the parlour, where John was, to draw the curtains and stoke the fire.

"'Evening," he greeted her.

She curtsied to him. "Sir."

"Has the afternoon post come yet, do you know?"

"I believe our Tom is collecting it and is due home at any minute."

John began to thank her, but his voice was drowned out by a crack of thunder. A few moments later, rain began to drive against the windows.

It was a decidedly soggy Tom Morgan who stomped into the room and handed him a letter from beneath his greatcoat.

"Thank you, Tom," John said. The reply was a grunt, at which John couldn't help but add, "A little damp, are we?"

Daggers shot from Tom's eyes as he removed his greatcoat and shook it out. Water sprayed across the room, with a good deal landing on John.

"Oh," Tom said with mock regret, "a little damp?"

John burst into laughter, and after a few seconds Tom joined him.

"Aye," Tom said. "Raining cats and dogs out there. Looks like a proper storm is blowing in. Hope Betty's got something warm for dinner." He left the room, and his heavy boots could be heard clomping towards the kitchen.

Now alone, John tore open the letter from Ashworth Hall, and then heaved a sigh.

No, John may not visit for Christmas. But they sent their best wishes for a joyful festive season.

John snorted. "Wishes, indeed," he muttered.

That night, he sat again in the parlour with a glass of port in front of the fire. The wind whistled through the windows, the rain was incessant, and a freezing draught stole in under the door and whipped around his ankles. His staff were long in bed.

He had never felt more alone. His very flesh and blood didn't want him. Was this horrid solitude destined to be his future forever?

As the port warmed his insides, his mind conjured up an impossible life. A loving voice spoke tenderly in his ear, and soft warm arms wrapped around him. The shouts and squeals of children echoed around the room. He relaxed and melted into the sensation of love, acceptance, happiness.

I love you, John.

His eyes flashed open. The memory was as clear to him as though the lady was in the room with him, despite the words having been uttered five years earlier. And the resulting pain, like the memory, was sharp and clear. He shook his head, trying to purge it, but he remembered where he was, who he was – what he was. He looked down and discovered he was squeezing his signet ring. The stone was black and cold like his heart. He shivered violently.

John cursed his treacherous mind for taunting him with the possibility of hearing those words again, of someone who could see him for who he truly was and would take him into her heart forever. He did not even know who he was anymore. He had buried any truth, any conscience, long ago, when he had been hurt more than he could bear. He could not risk letting anyone in, not again. His silly imaginings were nothing more than a fantasy which would never be real.

Later in bed, in a stupor of sweat and delirium, different images took hold of his brain. Screams, fear, betrayal, hate. All of his own causing, in a moment which proved just how weak he was.

He gasped in a breath, suddenly awake. He pushed away the curls which clung to his forehead and sat up, reminding himself of the truth. It was better for him to be alone – then he couldn't hurt anyone else.

The wind now blew with such ferocity it too sounded as a scream. John stumbled out of bed and found his dressing gown. He'd have a glass of water, and then he had best check on Thora.

When he opened the back door, umbrella in hand, the freezing rain immediately splattered in his face and penetrated his gown. He sheltered his eyes and peered at the deluge, which drove across the yard in nearly horizontal torrents.

He threw the umbrella to the floor and stalked into the storm. *Bloody hell.*

It was the night of the annual harvest fair, and all of Amberley's populace were out making merry on Ashworth land. John kept up his jovial façade, but it felt as if he was rotting inside. He was careful to keep track of Amy Miller's presence wherever he went, so as to keep his distance. It had been hard to completely avoid seeing her as they went about their lives, and he couldn't fail to notice her pitiful attempts to talk to him. Hopefully she would desist soon. He'd escape to a friend's estate soon enough.

As his family prepared to return to their house and let the villagers enjoy the festivities without them, John noticed Amy eating supper on a hay bale with her friend, Miss Grant. The very same Cecilia Grant who was angling, somewhat awkwardly, for his hand.

He knew Amy was on intimate terms with Miss Grant, so if she had revealed his wrongdoing to anyone, it would have been Cecilia. He debated internally whether to approach them for quite some time, before finally gathering up his courage. He must know if Amy intended to reveal what he'd done. He pushed down the feelings of remorse and approached them.

When Miss Grant greeted him cordially, it was apparent she knew none of what had transpired. He whisked Cecilia away before Amy had a chance to reckon with him in front of her. Then he cursed himself, again, for his cowardice.

Miss Grant was in lovely looks that evening, and she flattered him with smiles and blushes. He enjoyed watching her movements as they danced in the firelight, and he bathed in her simple innocence. If only he could have some of that for himself.

In fact, she'd been so entrancing during the dance, he decided he'd try to kiss her. If she did fancy him, she should be delighted. After all, it was common for courting couples to indulge in a little affectionate behaviour before they were wed. He had it in his mind that she would be wanting – nay, expecting – advances from him.

Perhaps he hoped that some of her goodness would rub off on him, would somehow erase some of the evil in his heart. It might show him what it would be like if he did give in and offer for her. Though he had absolutely no intention of ruining her. A little kiss where they would not be discovered was safe enough.

But the suggestion of the kiss spooked her, and not into a demure refusal. She verily screamed, "No, Mr Barrington, I will not!"

She was afraid of him. And little did she know, she had every reason to be. Poor thing. Guilt over his actions flooded back. He was someone to be feared. How low had he become?

Humiliated, he wished her well and turned to go. Was he really so grotesque, so unlikable, so horrible an ogre that even a simple gentry girl like Miss Grant didn't want his affection? Confusion and hurt ripped at him. She had been encouraging him, had she not? But perhaps that was only to appease her parents' wishes. Perhaps she really thought him hideous, and her inviting behaviour was just an act. Her family only wanted him because of the Ashworth status at any rate.

The rejection struck him to the core, stirring up his old wound and making the pain ache anew.

"Damnable females," he muttered. They could make you suffer for even the smallest lapse of vulnerability.

There was something fundamentally wrong with him, a quality that made him unlovable. He knew enough to be charming to mere acquaintances, but he completely lacked the ability to form a true bond with the fairer sex – with anyone, if truth be told. He had told himself it was because he wanted to keep himself safe from further hurt, but now the realisation hit him that no one had tried to get close to *him*.

He was a second son, his looks had been called striking but were no means classically handsome, and he hadn't gone out of his way to cultivate gentleness which would make him more amiable with the opposite sex. There was never any danger of more heartbreak after all – Julie had discovered his deficiencies before shackling herself to him.

As he stalked away, he heard Miss Grant bid his goodbye and he turned back. He tipped his hat to her but was in too much agony to speak. He could not hide the raw emotion in his expression.

Then he ran back to where Thora was tethered, cursing himself for his transparency. He was falling apart... but he must not let them see. Instead, he immediately began building up his walls of protection again. Upon waking in the morning, he was back to his lackadaisical self, ready to spar with the world. *Damn them all.*

Chapter Nine

T he wind blew with such force that it roared in Helena's ears as she lay in bed, and the house groaned, creaked, and whistled as if it were a large animal straining to break free from chains. It had rained constantly for hours on end. The roads would be impassable for days. At least she knew the animals on the home farm were safe in their barns. Her sodden farmer had called in to reassure her of this before retiring for the night.

Suddenly there was an almighty bang, and Helena leapt out of bed with a scream. She clutched at her chest, her heartbeat racing. "What was that?" she whispered into the gloom.

She sighed and reached for her dressing gown. Sleep was impossible now. She dragged a chair over to the smouldering fireplace and curled up in it, watching the glowing embers. Would John Barrington sleep through the storm?

Helena! she scolded herself. There was no reason to be thinking of that man – of any man. She wondered again why he would come to settle here without a family or even a wife. He certainly had the sort of charms that could captivate a woman. Was he nursing a heartbreak? Helena was no stranger to heartbreak, even though she had no experience with romantic love.

She gasped at an abrupt pounding on her door. She stumbled out of the chair and rushed across the room, before opening the door only wide enough to see who it was on the other side. "Yes?" she croaked.

It was the same farmer from earlier, with his hair plastered to his head and his clothes drenched. "I'm so very sorry, my lady, but I need help."

"Adams, what is it?" Helena said, opening the door all the way. "Let me get you a blanket; you must be freezing."

He shook his head. "There isn't time. The storm has blown the barn door open, and all the sheep have got out. They have wandered to a flooded field and the water is rising. I need help to get them out!"

"Heavens!" Helena grasped her head in both hands, trying to think. Who could she call on at this hour? She could hardly ride to Privett's house in these conditions. She took a deep breath. "We'll need to wake the servants," she said, trying to sound calm. "The footmen should be able to assist you. Give me a moment."

"Thank you, my lady." Adams stepped back into the hallway.

Helena quickly shrugged out of her nightrail and pulled on a dress and cloak. Then as an afterthought, she found her sturdiest boots and put them on. She rushed to meet Adams in the hallway and began to lead him towards the servants' stairs.

Sinclair burst into the hallway, his nightcap askew on his head and his candle casting angry shadows on his face. "What the devil is all this noise? It is hard enough to sleep with –"

"The animals are at risk of drowning, and we need to get them to safety. Will you help, Sinclair?"

"And risk catching my death?" he scoffed. "No, thank you. Don't you have people for this sort of thing?"

"I'll help, if I can."

Helena turned to find Jane behind her. "Oh, dearest," she said, clutching her hand. "Could you please find as many towels and blankets as you can to help the men when they get back. I'll meet you downstairs when we have roused them."

Jane nodded and squeezed her hand. "Of course." She ran down the hallway in the other direction.

Ten minutes later, Helena and some very grumpy footmen, along with the groom and driver, assembled in the foyer with Adams and Jane.

"We need two groups of people," Adams instructed. "One to search for any stray animals, and one to help drive the main group away from the flood." They quickly agreed that two footmen would go with the groom and driver to search, and the others would follow Adams to the help herd the flock.

"I shall go too, of course," Helena said, grabbing her sturdiest bonnet.

"But my lady –" The farmer began to protest.

"Only if I can go with you," Jane said firmly.

Helena hesitated only briefly. She didn't want to risk Jane's health, as she was twenty years Helena's senior. But she knew the resolute look in her eye wasn't to be countered. "Very well," she said, and the two women linked arms, following the men from the house and into the torrents of rain and wind.

Their task took nearly two hours by the time Adams was reasonably confident all the sheep were safe. The rain had turned to sleet, the icy drops stinging their faces. Helena worked in desperation, knowing losing these sheep might lose her the property. Working as a human chain in the dark, they drove the panicked sheep back to the barn where they barricaded the door with tree trunks.

Once they were all back safely in the house, and wrapped in blankets, they lit candles and Jane made hot cocoa for everyone. Now in fairly good spirits, they toasted Helena's health. She thanked them tearily, toasting Adams for checking on the animals during the night.

Helena overslept the following morning, and by the time she rose and opened her curtains, the sun was breaking through the clouds.

"My goodness," she whispered as she surveyed the landscape. There were branches strewn everywhere, and a few trees downed. The river was still flooded, the bridge almost completely under water.

There was a gentle rapping on her door, and Helena opened it with trepidation. There she found Privett, his brow creased in concern.

"My lady," he said with a quick bow, "good morning. I am sorry to disturb you like this, but we really do need to see about the damage the storm has caused. In a quick survey I have already noted several houses impacted."

Helena nodded wearily. "Yes, I shall come down directly. Please help yourself to coffee while I breakfast, and I will ask for Cornelius to be brought around."

Privett smiled and gave her shoulder a little pat. "Very good, my lady."

꙳

John, almost as weary, was likewise employed with his bailiff, on his way to Longdale Farm to see the weather's destruction. On his arrival, the problem was plain to see. A large tree had been completely uprooted and had crashed down onto the house's thatched roof.

"It is very bad," Mr Wilson said as if that were not obvious.

"To be sure," John agreed sombrely. He'd met the farmer, Mr Granger, on a few occasions now, and felt they were on friendly terms. He was sure he could be of some help in determining their immediate needs before work on removing the tree and repairing the roof could begin.

"I do hope they are not too distressed," John murmured, before knocking on the cottage's door.

He braced himself for a hysterical wife, blustering husband, and shivering children.

Granger threw open the door and smiled at John. "Mr Barrington, sir, good of you to come." He stood aside, and John entered the house marvelling at the man's composure.

He quickly realised he was not the first to greet the family. His mouth dropped open, and he stared at none other than Lady Helena Davenport as she embraced one of the children while wrapping him in a blanket. Miss Godwin gave a basket to Mrs Granger, which looked to be stuffed with food.

His shock spilled out of his mouth. "What are *you* doing here?" he demanded.

Lady Helena whirled around to face him. "Why Mr Barrington, are you addressing *me* thus?"

"Certainly I am. Pray tell, of what concern are my tenants to you?"

Her eyebrows raised, and she took a slow breath in and out before replying to him. "Did you think I exaggerated when I said I care about the needs of my neighbours? The Davenports have lived with these families for generations." She stepped over to Mrs Granger and took the woman's hand. "We grew up together. How could I ignore them at a time such as this?"

He was flabbergasted. It was one thing for a local lady to be showing charity to her neighbours. It was quite another for the largest landowner in the district to be trampling all over his affairs. It could not be borne. And such an angelic picture she had painted of herself, how could he possibly dismiss her without seeming like a monster?

He took a breath and folded his arms across his chest against the chill blowing in from above. Looking up, he saw branches poking through the thatch, and the hole they had created. Then he became again cognisant of the attention of everyone in the room.

"That is all very well. I… thank you for your exertions. But I am here now. You may go."

She gave some sort of cough. "May I, indeed? Well." She let go of Mrs Granger's hand, smiling at her. "I'll check on you again tomorrow," she said, before glaring at John as she swept past him.

Miss Godwin gathered up some things, nodded at John on her way past him, and followed Lady Helena from the house.

John cleared his throat and looked to Mr Granger. "A fine state of affairs you have here, Granger."

"Aye, sir, that gave us the fright of our lives, it did," he replied, gesturing to the tree.

"I'll wager it did," John said, smiling at him.

Some fifteen minutes later, with the family in relative comfort, John and Mr Wilson left the Grangers with promises of the supplies and assistance to come. At the sight of Lady Helena and Miss Godwin standing at the far end of the yard, John came to a sudden halt.

"What the deuce is she doing?" he muttered. Then he turned to his bailiff. "She has a steward, does she not? Why does she take the trouble to poke her nose in where it's not wanted?"

Mr Wilson glanced over to Lady Helena, and then studied John. "Helena Davenport is the glue that holds our society together," he said quietly. "Even before her father's death, there were many who would have been lost without her."

John frowned at him. It was as if the woman had everyone under her spell. He'd best do his best to resist the magic.

"Oh, Mr Barrington, a word with you?" The object of his thoughts called out to him, and he steeled himself as he strode over to her.

He bowed quickly, intending to keep things civil. "My lady?"

She was clearly not of the same mind. "How dare you speak to me like that, in front of the Grangers?"

Such was the vitriol in her words, he involuntarily stepped backward as if from a physical blow. She was flushed, her slim nostrils flaring and her fists clenched. Her visible anger did nothing to intimidate him, however: he was always one to rise to a challenge.

"I beg your pardon, my lady," he said mildly. "As this is my property, not yours, I fail to see why you should deem it your responsibility."

"Humph! Who do you think has been seeing to their necessities in your absence?"

"Why, Mr Wilson, of course."

"That gentleman has been collecting rents and discussing business with Mr Granger, naturally. But who has provided the children with the winter clothes they need, or paid for a doctor when they are sick, or kept Mrs Granger company when Mr Granger drives the animals to the saleyards?"

John considered. "Why, the vicar, or his wife or other parish members."

She nodded. "That is so, but we are only few and the Powells are no longer capable of performing many tasks. And who do you think they look to for guidance, decision-making and financial assistance?"

Her passion and contempt made him extremely uncomfortable. He swallowed and held up a hand. "I take your point, my lady. You may desist from further explanations."

At this, her eyes widened and she pursed her lips. She opened her mouth, but Miss Godwin put a hand on her arm and whispered something in her ear. A few moments later, she spoke again, keeping her voice measured. "I await your apology, Mr Barrington. I am entitled to respect, as the major landowner of Mulberry, as your peer, and as a lady. And some thanks would not go amiss, for helping to look after your tenants while you have neglected your duties."

He gaped at her. This was too much. How dare she reprimand him thus, with no knowledge of his reasons? Why did she think she could assert authority over him in such a way? He could not spend the remainder of his days being lorded over by a such a female. It was unsupportable. Let her reign over her own sizable property and leave him to have dominion over the little he had.

He bowed again. "I will offer whatever you *think* is due, Lady Helena, with my best compliments. And now I should be getting on to see to the repairs."

He turned, but she caught his arm.

"Do you think you have a large problem here, with this farm? Imagine that multiplied many times, and you may be scratching at the surface of what I am facing with my properties in Mulberry."

He met her eyes, and something within him shifted. This close, he could see the worry lines on her brow, and the tired smudges under her eyes. She looked exhausted, spent. He examined her hand on his jacket, and noticed her nails were ragged, her skin dry. Could it be she was actually doing *work* for the sake of her tenants? She snatched her hand back, her cheeks colouring further.

And then, the enormity of what she had on her shoulders – or what she had assumed – became more real to him. She had the financial and functional responsibility as the estate owner, but she also possessed the nurturing heart of a woman. To his mind, it was impossible to be both to all people. Something had to give.

"Can I help?" The question left his lips before he could consider it.

She frowned. "I beg your pardon?" she whispered.

"As you have pointed out, my tenants have benefitted from your assistance. Am I able to return the favour and help with some of the issues you are now facing?"

She stepped back, seeming confused. "I know not what… that is, I am not in the habit of…"

Miss Godwin put an arm around her shoulders. "Thank you, Mr Barrington," she said to him. "And good day." She led Lady Helena away, speaking to her. After a minute, the younger woman rested her head on Miss Godwin's shoulder while they walked… almost as if she was too tired to hold it up herself.

๛

The following day, Helena gazed out of her study window as she awaited Privett. She drummed her fingers on the windowsill absentmindedly. Through all the many problems and desperate people they had come across the day before, the one thing that stuck in her mind was her confrontation with Mr Barrington. Perhaps it was because he'd succeeded in ruffling her feathers, and she hadn't been able to brush it off. She still seethed over his treatment of her, as if she were a mere nuisance and not actively helping his tenants. Had he actually thanked her? The man was as slippery as a snake.

Her reaction to him perturbed her. Jane had warned her not to provoke him, had coaxed her to return to Willowbridge directly. But she'd been so incensed she didn't listen.

It hadn't helped that he'd surprised her at the farmhouse like that, and immediately gone on the offensive, challenging what she knew to be the natural order of Mulberry. Her worry and exhaustion from the previous night and her surveyance of all the property damage she needed to put to rights certainly added fuel to her fire. She had a particular abhorrence for male egos getting in her way. He'd behaved like a tomcat with a rival in his territory. Perhaps she had behaved a little like a female cat, hissing and spitting at an unwanted suitor. It was not a flattering picture. She shouldn't care… so why did she? It was maddening.

She'd been sensible of his scrutiny of her when they were in close quarters, and knew she'd been found wanting. She was not a polished, delicate lady. Her looks were simply not her priority. Even if she did want to marry, she was hardly in a state fit for the marriage mart. It was irksome in the extreme that his assessment embarrassed her. Why should she desire his good opinion? Perhaps because being near to him made her breath catch, and her heart race? She shuddered with the memory.

His offer of help was… befuddling. She'd never admitted her strife to a peer, to someone who might be able to assist her. Was his offer financial or otherwise? She would not take the time to find out. She did not know him well enough to let him intrude into her affairs.

Half an hour later, she had agreed with Privett on the works they needed to commission to fix all the properties affected by the storm.

"I wish I had been able to help with rescuing the stock, my lady," Privett said over his glasses, his benevolent countenance a balm to her heart.

"I thank you, but it is really just as well that you were well-rested to help me visit all the households yesterday."

He smiled at her briefly, and then closed his notebook. "We really need to look at installing drainage on the home farm, my lady. This problem has been left too long unchecked – we can't afford to lose the land for cropping and grazing."

Helena's heart began to pound. "My goodness, how much is a system of drainage?"

"I will need to look into it, my lady," he replied. "I shall present all the relevant figures to you together with the estimates for the storm repairs."

She nodded. "Thank you."

A heavy sense of dread settled in the pit of Helena's stomach. There had been no spare money before this, and now she needed to find some huge sum just to bring her properties back to satisfactory order. Privett was right about the drainage; they could not risk losing that land. They'd come very close to losing her precious livestock.

Once they had all the estimates, she would need to give up precious family heirlooms and goodness knows what else to keep them afloat. A lot of her furnishings were showing their age and were worth next to nothing. The obvious answer would be cutting the number of staff she employed, but she couldn't bear to plunge someone else into hardship.

She instinctively knew it would be a choice. Between securing the profits she needed to keep Willowbridge and ensuring the comfort and health of her tenants.

If they could just hold on until the end of the year…

John was doing a reasonable job of occupying himself in order to suppress his feelings of guilt and avoiding their object. That was until one morning, ten days after the harvest festival, when there was a soft rapping on his chamber door.

"Yes, what is it?" he called. It was perhaps his valet, come to help him with his cravat. There was no reply, and the door did not open.

Then there was the same tapping on the other side of the door. He jumped up from his desk and stalked over, muttering under his breath about the quality of the help.

He threw the door open, censure ready on his tongue. When he saw Amy Miller standing meekly on the other side, he recoiled. The power of speech promptly abandoned him.

"G-good morning," Amy said, her voice thin.

He opened his mouth, but nothing issued forth. Fear paralysed his every muscle.

"May I come in, please?" She looked up at him with huge, pleading eyes, and he found himself standing aside to let her enter. How he missed the days when she had regarded him with adoration instead of trepidation. They were simpler days.

John quickly peeked into the hallway, to ensure no one was watching. Then as he closed the door behind himself, his mind began to race with possible reasons for her presence with him. None of them were agreeable.

She did not keep him in suspense.

Standing in front of the window and twisting her fingers together, she kept her eyes on the floor and said, "Mr Barrington, I feel I must inform you that I am with child. Your child."

His clutched at the bedframe to keep from toppling over. Blinking hard, he rasped, "You are sure?"

She nodded. "Quite sure."

"And you are sure it is – mine?"

At this she met his eyes with a furious glare. "*Yes.*"

He swallowed, averting his own eyes to avoid her justified ferocity. An apology sprang up inside him. He desperately wanted her to know he *was* sorry, that he wished things were different, undone. That he wanted a different life for both of them. When he took a breath, he choked on his emotions, and instead found himself saying, "Will you deal with it?"

She gasped. "If you mean… will I have myself butchered… no, I will not."

He gaped at her, and a bitter laugh escaped his lips. "Then you are a stupid girl." Did she not want to save herself from a life of judgement and peril?

There was a horrible silence, his words seeming to echo mercilessly around the room. Then Amy burst into tears, and he cursed himself for heaping insult on insult. Why couldn't he tell her of his regrets?

A moment later, she fled from the room, sobbing. He heard footsteps on the servants' stairs, and a door slamming.

Heaving a sigh, he sat down on the bed and buried his face in his hands. *A child. Your child.* His folly was even greater than he'd imagined, and now there would be physical proof of it. Not that anyone would know it was his. And surely she'd be sent away for her confinement. Far away.

When he began to think clearly, he went to his mother. She would make it all go away. Even though she seemed to have a soft spot for Amy, clearly she could not keep a pregnant – and unmarried – servant under her employ.

"Yes, John, what is it?" Lady Ashworth laid her reading eyeglasses in her lap atop the letter she was reading. She was seated in her parlour with her lady's maid.

"May I have an audience with you… in private?"

Her eyebrows raised a trifle. "Indeed, you may."

The maid needed no further instructions. She quickly and quietly withdrew.

Lady Ashworth gestured towards the other sofa and John perched on it, frightfully nervous. A cad he may be, but he had never intentionally lied to his mother.

"I have come into some knowledge which I think it would be pertinent to inform you of," he began.

"Come into some knowledge?"

"Yes." John clasped his hands together tightly, the band of his signet ring cutting into the adjacent fingers. "I heard a servant talking, and I have every reason to think they were being truthful."

Lady Ashworth sighed. "Speak plainly, John. You know I abhor gossip. What is it?"

John's mouth went dry, his tongue seeming swollen and his throat thick. He must plough on. He cleared his throat. "Catherine's maid, the Miller girl, is expecting a child."

"Oh!" One of Lady Ashworth's hands flew to her mouth, and then she stared at him for some moments. "That is no small matter. You are sure of the source of this information? I will need to speak to Amy, of course, and I have no wish to distress her for no reason."

John blew out a breath. "I am certain," he said, then he searched the room for a diversion. "Any news of interest?" he inquired, indicating the letter she held.

Later that afternoon, John was trying to read in the drawing room, when the door burst open and his sister ran in, clearly distraught.

He jumped up from his chair and went to her, taking her hands in his. "My dear Catherine, what can be the matter?"

He steered her to a sofa and sat down with her.

She gulped in a breath. "It's Amy. I still cannot fathom… she's gone and got herself pregnant. I had no idea she even had a sweetheart!"

As tears gathered in his adored sibling's eyes, John began to panic anew. His own heart would always ache when hers did. "Please, Catherine, don't cry," he begged.

"Mama told me today, though she does not know who the man is. I wish him to hell! Amy says he is not sympathetic to her situation."

"Well…" John shifted uncomfortably. "We do not know the specifics." He squeezed his eyes shut for a moment. He'd never lied to Catherine, either.

Her tears now flowed down her cheeks. "She will have to leave us."

"Dear Catherine, worry not. We will get you another lady's maid."

"John! Don't you see? I do not care if I have a maid. I worry for poor Amy. She has no one. Nowhere to go. She will be quite desperate."

John frowned. "Nowhere?" he whispered. There must be places for women in trouble. And she must have some family, somewhere.

"And I will miss her," Catherine wailed against his shoulder. "I was quite fond of her, and I know you were, too."

At this, John froze. How much did Catherine know about Amy's infatuation with him? And would Amy take Catherine into her confidence?

"Is she… has Miss Miller left Ashworth yet?"

"Left? Goodness me, no. Mama will let her stay another month or two, until her pregnancy is obvious. We are to keep the knowledge to ourselves."

"I see." *Two months?* Two more months to be confronted with the image of his folly, with the risk of his misconduct being discovered?

As he stroked Catherine's head and her weeping subsided, a renewed sense of dread came over John. *She will be quite desperate.* Desperate people took desperate action. No one knew that better than he.

Should he bribe Amy to keep her quiet? It was a tempting notion, but with what funds could he do such a thing? He was down to his last few coins, and he wasn't due his next allowance from his father until Christmas.

He decided to take a few days to consider his position, but to his utter disbelief, that very Sunday his private bubble of guilt was well and truly burst.

Chapter Ten

Meanwhile, the drained, anxious look in Lady Helena's eyes haunted John. As usual, his emotions had run away with him, and he had addressed a lady with anger instead of respect. She was quite right; he had spoken out of turn. Still, would it have been too much to ask for her to seek his permission – or even just notify him – before she entered his property? Then at least he wouldn't be surprised by encountering her. It stung that he had been expecting to meet the Grangers as a saviour of sorts, but he had been usurped by someone who was more skilled in the arts of offering comfort than he.

There was something about her situation which didn't make sense to him. If she had no intention of travelling to London or anywhere else, and her finances were desperate, why had she been making a large clothes order when first they met? Knowing now a little more of her character, she did not seem the type to fritter away money on superficial indulgences. He supposed everyone had their weaknesses though, and who was he to judge?

While, as Lady Helena had taken pains to point out, he was not experienced in estate management, he did have a good head for figures. Would she allow him access to her accounts, to see where savings or efficiencies might be made?

He shook his head as he polished off the final bite of the excellent beef and ale pie Betty had cooked. Lady Helena had a steward to assist her, and hopefully he was doing a satisfactory job. There was no reason for

John to meddle in her affairs. None whatsoever. But when he saw such a beautiful woman so haggard, how could he remain idle? For some unknown reason, her distress, whatever the cause, tugged at his heart. She was getting under his skin, and he was spending entirely too much time thinking about her.

Mr Wilson was a welcome distraction when he arrived, clutching a wad of papers. However, John's relief soon turned to despair when his true circumstances were finally made clear to him.

His bailiff took the proffered seat at the dining table. "Good afternoon. I have taken the liberty this morning of having a tradesman assess the damages at the farmhouse."

John sat up straighter. "Yes? What sort of figure are we talking?"

Mr Wilson pointed at a figure on the paper before him. "About two hundred pounds."

John flinched. "Likely more than we'll see from them in rent per annum."

"Aye. But if it is not fixed, the house will have to be condemned and the long-term rent will be forfeited."

John rubbed his temples. "Indeed. And how much, er… do we make per annum?" It was a topic he had been reluctant to address directly, and he'd been taught to discuss such things was vulgar – but his bailiff had not been yet forthcoming with the information, either. He could not be ignorant any longer.

Mr Wilson fussed with his papers. "It is a perhaps a question of how little. Your lands are picturesque, to be sure, but not very productive."

John sighed. "Do not keep me in suspense, man. How much?"

"In the region of one thousand pounds. Certainly enough to live on, but perhaps not as much as a worldly gentleman like you would expect."

It was a far cry from the eight thousand his brother would have at his disposal once he inherited Ashworth Hall in Shropshire. Not to mention the opportunity to influence others politically and socially. When Markham inherited his father's title, he would also gain respect, worth, and honour. Qualities John could only dream of at present.

"One thousand pounds?" He drained the last of his coffee. "I could not keep a carriage on such funds."

As Mr Wilson had said, a thousand pounds would comfortably enable the necessaries such as food, clothing, heating, Thora's expenses, and the servants' wages. But not much else. Certainly not travel or any other little luxuries. He had always intended to live here eventually, when his family's support and company grew tiresome, but now the prospect of renting it out while he remained in his family's London townhouse sounded much more appealing. After all, once this year was over and he was free to leave Mulberry, surely he'd start collecting his allowance again and that would give him freedom of movement among other things.

His bailiff seemed determined to cheer him up. "You could hire more staff, Mr Barrington. I am sure you must be used to having the services of a valet, for example."

"Oh yes," John said. "And a butler, footmen, house maids, and stable hands, too. But what would be the point in employing such people when…" He trailed off.

Mr Wilson eyed him expectantly. "When?"

When I am going to be leaving in under a year. He may have had more than his fair share of transgressions, but he still had his conscience, and he could not bear to hire several staff knowing full well they would be redundant when he left to pursue his usual interests.

He avoided the question, indicating the other man's calculations. "This is the full extent of the costs arising from that weather?"

"Aye, sir. But there's a lot more to do besides, if you wanted to examine your declining assets…"

"Steady on," John said, holding up a palm. "One disaster at a time, if you please."

The men agreed on beginning the repairs, and Mr Wilson departed soon afterwards.

John retired to the parlour to consider what he had learned. With his allowance cut off, he'd been depending on the income from this estate to give him a tolerable existence. It would be ample if he planned to spend all his days rotting here like a country squire. What would life be like without escaping to the company of his friends in London or at their estates?

He'd always assumed he would be self-sufficient eventually because he had Mulberry Manor in his back pocket. Now he began to question some of his choices. Perhaps he should have joined the army after all. Was it too late to take a different course?

With his spirits dampened, recurrent feelings of insignificance and shame resurfaced. His family didn't want him, and his friends were out of reach. He went to the liquor cabinet, considering drinking himself into a stupor. But he'd already drained the last of the brandy, and the only other options were some sort of fortified wines which were not of good enough quality to recognise.

As the sky darkened, he considered braving the cold to go to the tavern. He'd just selected a jacket when there was a knock at the door. It was Sinclair, bearing a bottle of fine brandy. John welcomed the man in enthusiastically.

"I do apologise for barging in without an invitation," Sinclair said as John showed him to a chair in the parlour.

"Not at all," John said, eyeing up the bottle. "Looks to be a fine vintage."

Sinclair grinned at him greasily. "To be sure. Gentlemen of our class cannot drink anything substandard now, can we?"

John shook his head with a smile, procuring glasses. "What brings you here this evening?" he asked, taking his own seat as Sinclair poured the dark amber liquid into each vessel.

"I am shortly to leave the county, so I thought I should pay my respects to my future neighbour. Here's to your health."

They clinked glasses and both drained the brandy in one or two gulps. John asked Sinclair about his engagements in London over the Christmas period and deflected enquiries as to his own plans. Before long, John had lost track of how many glasses he'd downed. He was vaguely aware that Sinclair wasn't filling his own glass as regularly, but he didn't care. Now that he knew he had to conserve his own funds, he would make the most of any alcohol provided free of charge.

When they had exhausted discussion on mutual acquaintances, the most desirable neighbourhoods, current fashions, and which politicians would be up in London, even the brandy could not make Sinclair less dull. John was sure the man would be leaving soon, but then the conversation took a familiar turn.

"This time next year, I should be installed as the rightful owner of Willowbridge, and we can enjoy a snifter of brandy in the drawing room without my niece putting a dampener on things."

"Jolly good," John said cheerfully, polishing off another glass. "Capital stuff, this."

Sinclair smiled, offering a top up. "I am so delighted to know I can rely on you."

John paused before raising the glass to his lips again. "Rely on me?"

What was it he was supposed to do again?

"Yes, my good man. Have you found out anything about Helena's plans for the estate?"

Even in his inebriated state, John hesitated. Something nagged at him, prompting him to be loyal to Lady Helena.

Sinclair leaned forward. "Remember, you will be spending eternity under her thumb if she succeeds.

Have you already had a taste of her medicine?"

John stiffened, remembering how she had assumed authority over his territory, and the sound telling off she gave him afterwards. "I believe I have," he slurred.

"Well, then, if you know something, it would be in *your* best interest to let me know."

John couldn't think straight. The man had a point. If Lady Helena were to fail, which she might, it would stand him in good stead to be on friendly terms with the new owner, would it not? He would still help the lady if it were in his power to, but having an oar on both sides of the boat could surely do no harm.

But what information could he share with Sinclair? If he'd only known the man was coming, he could have thought of something before his brain was addled with drink. He was about to ask for the man's address in London when a memory dropped into his mind.

He put down his glass and rested one elbow on a knee. "D'you know," he garbled, "there is the sheep."

Sinclair blinked. "The sheep."

"Just so. Her ladyship said they were rare, and she would sell them to save the estate."

Sinclair's eyes glinted. "Did she now?"

John nodded and slumped back into his chair. A delightful fog settled about him, and he began to drift off into a brandy-tinged slumber.

When he woke, parched and nauseous, the fire was nearly out and he was alone. Only the bottle and glasses on the table signalled to him that he'd had a companion. For the life of him he couldn't remember who it was.

He recalled what had happened about a week later, when he received a case of that same brandy delivered from Mr Sinclair in London. He grinned as he lifted each bottle from the case. Perhaps a little "intelligence" here and there could be just what the doctor ordered.

Helena inhaled the heavenly scents of cinnamon, orange, clove, and fig as she entered the kitchen at Willowbridge. "Well, Mrs Mead, it certainly smells like Christmas in here!"

The rotund, good-humoured lady looked up from a bowl of pudding dough. "Just so, your ladyship. We should have more than enough for everyone in Mulberry!"

It was an annual tradition Helena loved – on Christmas Eve the Davenports would bring a Christmas pudding and other seasonal treats to each of their tenants. Then on St Stephen's Day, the leftovers from the celebratory meal and some knitted garments were shared amongst as many needy families as possible.

"Here," Mrs Mead said, handing Helena a spoon. "Try some of the fruit mixture." She had a mischievous gleam in her eyes.

Helena gave her a sideways glance before digging into the appropriate bowl with a smile. After tasting the soft, tender fruit, she exclaimed, "Dear me, Mrs Mead! Is that truly the correct quantity of brandy?"

Mrs Mead chuckled, taking the spoon back from her. "To be sure, it is, my lady. Quite the right amount to ensure a merry Christmas."

Helena joined her laughter. They were soon joined by Jane.

"The evergreens are ready for hanging, my lady," she said.

Helena turned to her. "Thank you, Jane." She exchanged another smile with Mrs Mead before following Jane to the drawing room where they would begin hanging the decorations.

The fire roared in the grate, amplifying the aromas of holly, rosemary, ivy, and bay leaves. The small tables around the room were covered with twine, silks, and paper, as well as sweetmeats and warm spiced wine. Most of Helena's maids and footmen were engaged in cutting and tying, eating and laughing. Was that the first flakes of snow falling beyond the window?

These were the sights and smells she'd known every year of her life. But now they were accompanied by an unwelcome pang of loneliness. She sat down at a table in the far corner and began to string holly and ivy together, hoping to conceal her emotions.

Sinclair came strolling through, whistling a cheery tune. He actually smiled at Helena as he stopped to inspect her work. "Capital, capital," he said.

She gaped at him in horror. Who was this man, and why was he so happy? If it was purely because he was due to leave for London within the hour, and if so, why had he not left sooner?

"Allow me to help you with that," he said as some holly fell off her table.

"Er… thank you," Helena said, her eyes narrowing as he sat in the chair next to her and gathered up some sprigs of rosemary and bay.

"Not at all, my dear cousin."

Now she was very suspicious. He'd only ever said such words in sarcastically. She reached for some mistletoe. "Pray tell me, dear Sinclair, where did you go to yesterday evening?"

"Why, to see John Barrington, my lady."

She rocked on her chair, nearly falling off. "Mr Barrington? He is still here? I thought he would have left to visit his family by now."

Sinclair shrugged. "I imagine he'll depart today also."

"What was the purpose of your visit?" Sinclair had shown very little interest in Barrington during his stay.

He raised an eyebrow. "I am sure it is not your business, my lady, but I merely visited to wish him farewell and give him my best wishes for a happy festive season."

Not one of his words rang true. Why did he look even more smug than usual? It was clear she wasn't going to get any further information from him.

She turned back to the task at hand. "I do wish you a safe journey," she said evenly.

"And a happy Christmas to you, Helena."

He took the hint and dropped the greenery in a messy heap on the table, before scraping his chair back and going over to speak to one of the footmen. Before long he departed the room, and Helena knew it was the last she would see of him for a few months at least.

She sighed. Even to the last, his tone hinted at his dislike of her. Apart from his inherent jealousy, she knew he thought her too serious, that her management of Willowbridge was too austere for his liking. If only he knew the true depth of her troubles. And even though he was a blood relative, using her name without the proper address grated on her, almost as if it was an insult. He knew her less well than most of Mulberry. She did not feel as though they should be on intimate terms.

The manner of his leaving would haunt her for days afterwards. He must be scheming to have her fail to retain ownership of Willowbridge. That he seemed so content, so self-satisfied, made her worry that one of his schemes could somehow derail everything she had worked so hard for. And there was no way of finding out what he was up to… unless it had something to do with Mr Barrington?

She wondered how long that gentleman would spend in Shropshire. She was relieved to have him away for a time, to give her confused feelings a chance to subside. She couldn't deny she was attracted to him, and he made her feel something she'd never felt before – a kind of lightness mixed with a spark of intrigue. But she still had doubts about his lifestyle and questions about his past. Something made her wary. She'd probably never known anyone as complex.

Helena cringed thinking of the way she spoke to him at Longdale Farm, almost like a school matron correcting a naughty child. It was this side of her that likely irked Sinclair the most, but when she felt an injustice had been done, she could never rest until she confronted it.

She may have overdone it with her resolve to keep Mr Barrington at arm's length, at least until she knew more about him. Instead of aloof, she may have appeared frosty, haughty, patronising. She buried her face in her hands. Maybe the man was right. Perhaps she could benefit from some time away, or some sort of break. She didn't like who she was at present.

Sometimes she wished she could have the kind of pampered, carefree lifestyle that Sinclair assumed the owner of Willowbridge would enjoy. Would she return to London once the estate was secure? Perhaps - she did miss several old friends. But many were now married and occupied with their own families.

Helena turned to watch the happy activity in the room. Most of these people would be at home with their families tomorrow. She would be with those she considered her dear friends, but it wasn't the same. Taking a breath, she rose from her chair and went into her study before she embarrassed herself in front of her staff.

Christmas was a particularly sensitive time for her. She didn't miss her mother as such – her memory was now only a fragrant idea. She missed the idea of having a mother, but she was fortunate to have such a kindred spirit in dear Jane. Instead, her heart ached for her father, who had been such a cornerstone in her life. His warmth, his generosity, his gentle authority – these were all the things she aspired to the most. Did she ever really appreciate all he had done for her while he lived? Guilt plagued her – that she hadn't said enough or done enough to please him. And now, would she ultimately fail him?

She closed her eyes, and his loving voice returned to her. *My dear little Nelly, have you been out riding again? Come here, Nelly, and let me tell you a story. Oh, my dear, I fear I will leave you sooner than I had hoped...*

As with most English aristocrats, he hadn't been one to lavish physical affection on her. But she could still feel his quiet strength as she sat on his lap, engrossed in one of his tall tales. She'd rested her head on his soft whiskers and laid a palm on his chest to feel the sure beating of his heart.

A portrait of her father hung on the wall next to the desk. "I miss you, Papa," she whispered, and a lone tear slid down one cheek. "I will do my best to make you proud."

"There you are, Helena. Are you quite all right?" Jane came into the room bearing a glass of wine, which she laid on the desk as she took in Helena's expression. "Oh, my dear girl," she said, coming around to take Helena in her arms. "I know you still grieve."

Helena allowed herself to cry in Jane's embrace for a time. "You shall be without your family on Christmas Day as well," she sniffed. Jane's family lived in Cumbria, and she only saw them once or twice a year.

"Oh yes, but you know I abhor travelling in winter. I shall look forward to visiting with them in the spring when the roads are drier." She pulled back and dabbed at Helena's face with a handkerchief. "There, now," she said soothingly, with a bright smile. "We shall be very merry tomorrow, you shall see."

Helena nodded, managing a tremulous smile in return. She accepted the glass Jane gave her and availed herself of several restoring mouthfuls. The spices in the wine warmed her inside.

"I think it is time to go and choose the yule log?" Jane suggested. "I do believe the gardeners are ready."

Helena stood and wiped the remaining moisture from her cheeks. "Yes, do let's." She linked arms with Jane, and they put on their coats and gloves. There was indeed a light snowfall, and the flakes tingled on their faces as they headed to the nearest grove.

Once the log was safely burning, they would take a carriage loaded with puddings around the village, spreading warmth in all hearts – especially their own.

Recently back from a ride, John washed and changed his dress. He had hoped the exercise would lighten his spirits, but these days he was under a permanent cloud of regret and guilt. Even Thora seemed to eye him with distaste.

As he dismissed his valet from his chamber, he saw the family carriage pulling up, and watched his mother step out. March out, more precisely. Her steps seemed to set the ground on fire. Unease seized his stomach in a vicelike grip. Something had been awry since the church service that morning, when the irritatingly pious vicar had dared to allude to Amy Miller's condition and the wrongdoing that had caused it. *Insufferable man.* It was as if Mr Brook himself were John's conscience.

Toying with his signet ring, he turned and slowly made his way from the room, along the corridor and to the landing. From the top of the stairs, he could hear his mother's raised voice intermingled with his father's. It seemed they were in Lord Ashworth's study. He took a deep breath and descended the steps.

Just as he reached the entrance hall, the door to the study burst open, and Lady Ashworth stormed out. "You!" she cried, stalking towards him.

John jumped and then shrank under the fierceness of her stare. "Mama?"

"I despair of you," she spat out. "You will have an audience with myself and his Lordship immediately."

His Lordship? He really was in trouble. He nodded and followed her back into the study. A wave of nausea washed over him as he closed the door behind himself.

Lord Ashworth sat in his chair behind the large desk, leaning forward on his elbows and pinning John to the door with a hard, unflinching gaze. Lady Ashworth stood beside him with a hand on his shoulder, her lips pursed in a kind of resignation.

John had been admonished by his parents before, for the likes of spending all night gaming, or missing important family gatherings. Now and then he'd offended one of their friends by refusing to submit to expected niceties or speak to their daughters. He could sense this was different.

He swallowed hard. "Yes?"

What followed was a shock, even for his jaded soul.

His relationship with his parents was a distant one. From a parade of nannies, to boarding at Eton and then Oxford, his authority figures had been mainly elsewhere. But he had always come home to Amberley or the London townhouse and felt at his ease. Although they didn't share any real truths between them, he had felt a degree of acceptance, if not love.

But now, the steely looks from both mother and father told him he'd gone too far. He was no longer welcome in their home, in their family.

At the completion of the interview some twenty minutes later, John fled to the garden, running until he began to stumble on the frigid ground. Then he slumped against a huge oak tree and hid his face in his fingers as tears finally began to cascade down his cheeks.

Banished. I am to be banished from my own village, my own home. And to stay in that little corner of Hampshire for an entire year without venturing forth. There would be no London, no Season, no visiting friends or family. Nothing to distract him from his own wretchedness.

"You are to take an active interest in matters of that estate," his father had said. "It's time you assumed some responsibility."

John had accepted this meekly, but there was worse to come.

Lady Ashworth had come around from behind the desk to look him squarely in the eye, only inches away. "John, I have never been so disappointed. So appallingly sad. To think you have sunk so low. Well, I wash my hands of you!"

John's insides twisted and turned uncomfortably. "Mama, I did not mean –"

"Hush!" She pushed her palm at him, then continued at a whisper. "I have always loved you and indulged you too much. Not anymore." She stepped back. "You are no longer my son."

Now, clutching at the tree trunk, he choked on his grief at her words. Of course, he loved his mother, whether he wanted to or not. Her admission of her affection, so many years craved by him, now came too late. He no longer deserved her love.

When the cold rendered his limbs numb, he hobbled back towards the house, a new plan forming in his mind. His disgrace complete, he redirected all his shame and remorse into a need for retribution against the vicar, whether that be stealing his beloved Cecilia from under his nose, or worse. He was sure it was Brook who had tipped his mother off.

Now, it would be warfare.

Chapter Eleven

Christmas Day dawned crisp and white. John woke early but stayed wrapped up tight in the covers until a stripe of sun shone brightly through the gap in his curtains. What would he do with himself today?

He'd bade farewell to the Morgans the afternoon before: they were gone to stay with Betty's sister for a few days. He was completely alone, and the silence was unbearable.

With no one to start his fire, John stumbled about in the freezing air, finding kindling, paper, and matches. The water for his toilette was icy cold, and to expedite the process he didn't bother to shave. What was the point?

He couldn't bear to attend the Christmas Day church service – after all, he'd brashly asserted his intention to be installed at Ashworth House instead. No, he must remain ensconced in his little house, and keep out of sight. He'd unknowingly become his own jailor this time.

Ripping chunks from one of the loaves of bread Betty had baked for him, he read the newspaper from beginning to end and then started on one of the few volumes from the library. He shivered, having not lit the fire in the dining room. How he wished he was in the drawing room at home with his family, sharing gifts and warm wine.

At ten o'clock he grew restless and set out for a walk. All the shops and establishments in the village were closed today, so there was nothing to divert him even if he wasn't pretending to be in Shropshire.

He stayed close to the house to start with, trudging through the snow in his boots. A robin sang a merry tune high above him. John huffed out a steamy breath and quickened his steps, stalking into the woods.

There was really nowhere else to go but Willowbridge. The place drew him with magnetic force. He was determined to remain concealed, but before he knew it the glow of candles in the windows and the strains of music playing had pulled him right up to the formal garden to the west of the house.

He paused, hiding behind a hedge, and gazed longingly through the glass. Would he catch a glimpse of…

"Why, Mr Barrington, what are *you* doing out here?"

John jumped, and fell into the bush, scratching his face. "Ow! I, uh…"

The man, who must be a groundskeeper, offered his arm to help John right himself.

He tutted as John brushed leaves from his coat. "I'm sure Lady Davenport wouldn't approve of you lurking in the shrubbery." He smiled. "Come into the house, where it's warm. There'll be plenty of food to go around."

John's heartbeat quickened, and the fog of his breathing intensified. He was not here – he was with his family at Ashworth… as far as anyone knew.

"No, thank you," he said hastily. "I must be going."

But the man had taken his arm again and was leading John firmly towards the house. He was so cold and hungry he didn't have the energy to refuse further. He would have to endure the embarrassment of his failure to remove from Mulberry. As the grand front door opened, the smell of Christmas meats and spices overpowered him. He'd think of a plausible explanation.

The man told John to remain in the foyer and disappeared further into the house.

John rubbed his icy face, which was surely scarlet from the cold, and shrugged out of his greatcoat before taking in the scene about him.

The grand house was charmingly decorated with ivy and mistletoe, and the scent of pine made him miss home so badly the pain was palpable. As female laughter floated on the air from a neighbouring room, he swallowed hard. Had Catherine missed him at all, as she'd likewise strung together sprigs of holly?

Suddenly a door was flung open, and the social cacophony grew louder. Out came the butler, with Lady Helena close on his heels. She was a vision in a cream gown trimmed with red, her hair a mass of shining curls. Her face glowed gorgeously with a radiant smile, and his heart began to race as he met her sparkling eyes.

She stopped in her tracks and her mouth dropped open. Any trace of the smile vanished.

"Why is *he* here?" she sputtered.

The butler turned to her and said dourly, "He was found in the garden."

She stared at the man with a frown. "In the…" Then she shook her head in what looked like disbelief, and then dismissed the servant, who slid silently away. Lady Helena then regarded him with a mix of bewilderment and suspicion.

John stepped forward and bowed low. "Merry Christmas, Lady Helena."

She did not curtsey. "Mr Barrington. As I understood it, you had somewhere better to be."

Sweat broke out on his brow as he straightened. "I, uh, thought you might need me here, my lady." He smiled, hoping he appeared gallant instead of sheepish.

She gaped at him. "Need you?"

He met her incredulous eyes. Even though his comment had been mostly in jest, her response stung. Did she think him that useless?

He took a breath, and another step closer. "I did not intend to impose on you," he said quietly.

Her eyebrows flitted up. "And yet, you have."

"I… yes." He knew the rules of society – though he often bent them – and turning up for a party without an invitation, a Christmas party no less, was the height of rudeness. There was, however, something more than disapprobation of breached etiquette in her countenance. Some deeper acrimony lay within. He was thoroughly unwelcome, a sensation that was agonisingly familiar.

He bowed again. "You are quite right, my lady. I do recall the suggestion of a space at your table some weeks ago, but I am sure you will have filled that vacancy by now. I really only came to give you my best wishes." He bowed again and turned back towards the door.

"Who will you share Christmas dinner with?" she called after him, the sound of her slippers tapping on the floor tiles in his direction.

He picked up his greatcoat, and glanced at her briefly, summoning the best smile he could. "It is of no consequence."

She closed the distance between them and took the coat from his hands. "I shall have Andrews air this out for you and set a place for you at my table."

He met her eyes in surprise. They held a note of compassion, and perhaps something else.

"Your presence will even up the number of ladies and gentlemen," she explained. "Do follow me."

John's frosted insides began to thaw. Her gracious nature must have overwhelmed her affronted feelings. He so appreciated her gesture in creating the illusion that it was in fact he who was doing her a favour.

"My humble thanks," he said, and this time his smile was genuine. He offered his arm, and she placed her hand on it lightly. He inhaled her sweet aroma and admired the graceful arm which extended from her shawl. Oh, to be able to tenderly stroke that arm, and feel her quiver.

Good grief, John, pull yourself together.

His reverie was broken when they entered the drawing room, and found a jolly party of about a dozen, assembling around the piano.

He leaned down toward her ear. "Are these people your family?"

She shook her head, a low laugh escaping her lips. "Heavens, no. They are my neighbours and dearest friends."

Come to think of it, he did recognise some faces. There was the vicar and his wife, the doctor, Miss Godwin and…

"Why, Lady Helena, your steward is here."

They advanced upon the group. "Of course he is," she replied blithely. "I invited him."

"To eat alongside you?" It was his turn to be surprised. "But he is under your employ."

She turned to him with a dark expression. "And he is also the nearest thing I have to a father these days." She lifted her hand off his arm and he felt its absence keenly.

He'd offended her, again. He could not ever recall causing so much umbrage without meaning to.

As Lady Helena rejoined the group, most of them looked in his direction, and he endured a barrage of incredulity.

"Are you quite well?"

"Is your family in good health?"

"Why have we not seen you the last few days?"

He smiled as convincingly as he could, and waved away their queries with a simple, "How could I bear to leave my new neighbours?"

There were still puzzled looks, but no one bothered to question him further.

He inwardly breathed a sigh of relief, but then was immediately set upon by the vicar and his wife.

"Greeting to you, Mr Barrington," the aging man said, offering a frail hand for shaking. "I do not recall seeing you at our Christmas service?"

Helena was still in disbelief. The very man she'd been determined not to think on had somehow made his way into their cosy Christmas circle. Why had he not returned to his family? Was it merely a case of bad roads? Why had he not said as much?

She had been, initially, determined to refuse him entry – as any lady of the house should when intruded upon in such a manner. Did the man not have any pride? Could he not have called some days earlier to beg for an invitation?

Perhaps, she reasoned as she accepted a posset drink from Jane, it had been his pride that had kept him away. She shrugged in answer to her friend's questioning look.

When she'd scolded Mr Barrington for imposing on her, she'd never seen someone so crestfallen. He was disappointment personified, and her heart immediately flipped from injured to sympathetic. With his dark eyes a mix of shock and sadness, she saw a glimpse of the true man beneath the bravado. He had never looked so handsome.

She choked on the thought, and then smiled away the resulting looks of concern. She was letting her emotions get the better of her.

Jane sat at the piano and began to play Christmas hymns. Helena mouthed along to the words, willing herself not to cry. She had already been feeling vulnerable, her feelings close to the surface. Now an impossible mix of excitement, curiosity, and apprehension coursed through her. She must *not* betray herself. Though she had a strange notion she would be strongly tempted to reveal her innermost thoughts.

She attempted to divert her thoughts by taking in the joy in the faces around her. She was next to Mrs Privett, who linked arms with her, while her other hand was clasped in her husband's. There was Mr Harding, who gave her a friendly wink, and the Powells, who were engaged in enthusiastic, though tuneless singing. Also assembled were the widow Mrs Kendall and her two children. The little boy and girl were turned out beautifully with pure delight written on their faces. Helena swallowed a lump in her throat, before nodding acknowledgement to Mrs Kendall's brother, Mr Pike.

And Mr Barrington… where was he? She turned to look over her shoulder, and there he was. Standing behind her, a little distance away from everyone… and not singing. He nodded to her but made no attempt to join the group.

He was an odd man, to be sure. She chewed her lip thoughtfully. Was he accustomed to being the outsider?

Focussing back on the piano, her mind remained on the man. She recalled why his presence made her uneasy. Sinclair had alluded to a conversation between them, and it was somehow linked to his newfound confidence.

As she joined a rousing last chorus of "The First Noel", she resolved to find out more about Mr Barrington's dealings with Sinclair. If there were devious plans afoot, she must thwart them. The complication lay in needing to have a private discussion with Mr Barrington without seeming improper. She must choose her moment with care.

Smothering a sigh, she joined in the spirited clapping which marked the conclusion of the carols. Shouts of "Capital!" and "Jolly good!" rang in the air, and it did Helena's heart good to feel the cheer of her guests.

Andrews appeared and announced Christmas dinner was ready. The natural partnerships of ladies and gentlemen formed to go in to dinner, and Mr Harding offered his arm to Jane as he often did in such circumstances.

All that was left was for Helena to accept the escort of Mr Barrington. He noticed the pairings and approached her solemnly.

"My lady?"

She eyed his proffered arm before accepting it. Being so close to him could be regrettable, but this could be her only chance to speak her mind. She was unable to stop herself from inhaling deeply as they began to walk. His earthy, masculine scent overpowered her, wreaking havoc on her defences. She closed her eyes against the sensation, against the warmth that threatened to derail her.

"Are you quite all right, Lady Helena?"

The quiet, concerned tones uttered near her ear did nothing to help. She forced her eyes open. "Yes, of course," she said quickly, although she heard the breathlessness in her voice. *Ridiculous.*

She allowed him to lead her to the front of the group and she inclined her head to indicate the direction they should go.

Glancing behind to check Harding and Jane were not too close, she began her inquiries. "I hear from Sinclair that you lately hosted him at the manor."

She heard his intake of breath, and saw his head turn towards her, though she kept her eyes focussed ahead. "He has put a different light on the visit," he replied. "Sinclair called upon me, and it would have been impolite to refuse him admission."

Her mouth dropped open and she locked eyes with him involuntarily. "He visited you? In the evening? Uninvited?"

He nodded.

Her stomach began to swirl with anxiety. They must be on very familiar terms for Sinclair to assume so much. How often had they been meeting? And how much information had they shared?

"Bosom buddies, are you?" she spat out.

He frowned. "I would hardly say –"

"Have you two been conspiring against me?" She checked her tone, with another furtive glance to ensure no one had heard her. She seemed safe.

In terms of Mr Barrington though, she felt anything but safe. She felt his arm tense underneath her hand, as taut as marble. Had she invited the enemy into her house?

He cleared his throat as they entered the dining room. "Nothing of the sort, I assure you. We drank to his health in advance of his leaving the county."

She scrutinised his countenance. He was now the one avoiding her gaze. Any fledging trust or budding feeling for him went suddenly cold within her. Could she believe anything he said? What was he really about?

They had paused by her place at the head of the table, and the other couples were filing in.

As she smiled at each person, she whispered tersely, "I do hope you realise that everyone in the village is on my side. If you were to go against me, you would do well not to show your face here again."

He laughed and gave her hand a little pat as if she'd told him a joke. She wrenched her hand free immediately, a gesture which was not lost on Jane, taking her place at Helena's left.

He turned and looked down at her, keeping his smile in place. "Come now, my lady," he said in an undertone, "it is Christmas Day. Shall we call a truce?"

Confound the man. He was the one who may have transgressed, and now he was making her look like the aggressor. It would not do to lose her temper in front of those present, especially not today.

She took a deep breath. "You are right, Mr Barrington. This is not a day for quarrels. Come, and let me introduce you to the guests I do not think you have met."

He bowed in acknowledgement and followed her to Mr Pike and Mrs Kendall. She went through the motions of social niceties, her insides churning. She deposited him at his assigned seat and fairly fled to the other end of the table.

Jane turned to her as she sat down. "Is everything in order, my dear?"

Helena smiled at her and nodded. "To be sure."

She welcomed the distance she had from Mr Barrington at the far end of the table. It would not be possible for him to speak with her during the meal, and she could attempt to continue on as she normally would.

But, rather inconveniently, he was in her direct line of sight – and she in his.

In the following days, it became clear that many in the village suspected him of ruining Amy. He once again cursed the name of Brook, and he made his feelings very clear when he next saw the rogue.

What really bothered him, more than the man's betrayal, was the exposure. Now everyone knew how low he had sunk. Even those beneath his notice would look upon him with disgust. The shame of it, once hidden and quietly eating away at him, now would follow him wherever he went. And would it send him to a magistrate? Would Amy Miller's extended family combine their resources to mount a trial?

It didn't bear thinking about. Indeed, all he could think about was retaliating against Brook. Stealing the Grant chit from under his nose would be the perfect revenge. She was below his station, to be sure, but she was a gentleman's daughter. He needn't worry about obtaining the approval of her parents. They had pushed her at him, rather obviously.

Her affection for Brook may be a barrier, but he was confident in his ability to charm her. She'd always become delightfully flustered in his company. It would only take a little nudge.

He certainly did not expect such a forceful, single-minded refusal, and a critique of his behaviour towards Amy, to boot. The two ladies did seem to be on very friendly terms, so it shouldn't have surprised him that she knew so much.

The bluntness of her rejection stung. "There is nothing in the world that would convince me to marry you. You are not worthy to be called a gentleman."

His incredulous protests proved futile. She'd probably go running to Brook with the news of the sorry scene, heaping more embarrassment upon John. It could not be borne. His rage only intensified. The expanding ramifications of his despicable behaviour only seemed to spur him to other unscrupulous acts.

John's next opportunity to confront the vicar was when he happened upon the man on the road near the Ashworth estate. John had been intending to ride to the village to purchase new shoes for Thora, but when he saw Brook hurrying along, he couldn't resist pulling his horse up directly in front of him. And then, the reason for Brook's haste became clear. John glanced over his shoulder and saw Miss Grant, laden with her satchel, and heading into the woods. He laughed. This was a gift. He would unhinge Brook, and expose him as the ordinary, imperfect man he was. He dismounted and did his worst.

First, he threatened to publicly reveal the couple's indecent intention to meet privately. Brook explained that away. Then, he insulted Miss Grant for refusing his offer of marriage. John saw the fury in his enemy's eyes and saw his chance to fracture the man's relentless righteousness.

It only took a little more goading, a little allusion to his marital plans for Miss Grant, to unleash a little violence.

The vicar's punch was admirably strong, and it took a few moments before John was able to respond in kind. He heaped vitriol on Brook with his fist and his words. When it seemed as if the vicar would leave with a little dignity intact, John dealt the final blow. His gut twisted as he lied and told Brook he might take advantage of Miss Grant, using the most vulgar terms he could think of.

It worked. Brook roared at John and launched a powerful right hook.

It was the last thing John remembered. He awoke with a pounding head and a blood-soaked shirt some time later.

Any satisfaction on account of breaking through his adversary's defences now paled in comparison to the humiliation of having been thrashed by a vicar – the very one who had outed him and paved the way for his downfall.

Chapter Twelve

A fire roared in the grate, but it was not his proximity to the flames that had John sweating. The effect of Lady Helena's verbal assault was akin to a physical blow. His blood pulsed madly, yet he felt strangely numb. The worst of it was that he could not, with any surety, answer her questions.

Something about the manner of Sinclair's visit to Mulberry Manor had petrified her. She had the look of a wounded animal, snarling and suspicious. She had all but threatened him with a mob of angry villagers.

The night in question was but a blur of brandy and boorish company. What had he said to the man? He couldn't summon the memory, but he knew he'd divulged something important because of the amber bottles that now occupied his liquor cabinet.

The fact that he could not recall exactly what happened had set him to panicking when the lady made her inquiries. Surely nothing he'd told Sinclair could influence Lady Helena's inheritance?

A footman placed a silver plate on the table in front of John, and his mouth watered as he took in the sight and smell of thick slices of ham, golden potatoes, and a pile of diminutive carrots.

"Gravy, sir?"

John glanced up at the footman, who bore a gleaming gravy boat. He nodded, and all but licked his lips as the servant poured a generous serving of the rich liquid over his food. Gratitude flooded through him as he was finally sensible of his good fortune. His neighbour was so kind as to set a place at her table for a man she was wary of, who had barged in uninvited at the last moment. She was mercy and manners personified… except for the part when she threatened him, of course. He chuckled to himself. She was a riddle – and that made her all the more fascinating to him.

Thanking the footman, John looked over across to table to his hostess. Her eyes were already upon him, and she tilted her head with a curious expression. She must have noticed his mirth.

He shook his head to signal it was nothing of consequence, and then he hastily picked up his glass of wine.

"Thank you," he mouthed as he rose the glass to her.

Her brows lifted briefly in apparent surprise, then she lowered her eyes. Appearing to think for a moment, she then reached for her own glass and returned the gesture with an exquisite smile. Her lips were barely parted, but her eyes shone so warmly he felt she was pouring light into his tattered soul.

She returned her glass to the table and turned to address Mr Powell. Was that a blush creeping up her chest? He dare not flatter himself.

He returned his attention to his food and sliced through a carrot. But he could not keep his gaze away from Lady Helena for long. He was transfixed.

It was something about the way the candlelight caressed her hair, her collarbone, her arms… and the pure grace of her movements. The way she delicately ate her dinner, and chatted with her friends, was so beautiful to him it was almost like watching the ethereal dance of an angel.

He made himself look away from her in an attempt to keep his feelings hidden. He instead admired the candelabras set on the table and took in the scene around it. The people gathered all seemed to know one another very well, so at ease were they in their conversations. The lady to his left, Mrs Kendall, was preoccupied with tending to her two children, and so didn't have the leisure to converse with John.

The doctor, Mr Harding, was to his right, and he kept up small talk with John when not laughing with the Privetts about the outrageous exploits of a mutual acquaintance.

Did these people know how lucky they were, to belong to such a merry group? They appeared so relaxed and happy. John didn't know the last time he'd felt either sensation, or such an air of unconditional acceptance. When had he last shown someone his true self? Not since *her*. He'd hidden himself so far behind a protective wall he barely knew how to live without pretence. The weight of the signet ring on his finger seemed to intensify with the heaviness of an invisible, insufferable burden.

John's heart burned with envy, struck with a sudden desperation to belong, to be accepted for who he really was… to be loved.

He blinked, suddenly sensible of tears pooling his vision. He hastily dragged his sleeve across his face. *Pull yourself together, John.* He had made a point of never revealing his true feelings in company, and this was not the time or place to expose what must remain hidden.

At the conclusion of the dinner and dessert courses, the party were invited to return to the drawing room for games and more music. Lady Helena smiled at each guest in turn as they filed past her, until at last it only remained for John to be her escort again.

But instead of taking his arm, she gasped and gaped at his neck.

"Goodness me," she cried, glancing up at him with wide eyes. "Who tied this cravat for you?"

He touched the offending item with a defensive hand. "I did it myself, my lady, but I was not expecting to be in the company of others."

"Indeed. It was remiss of me not to notice before. You are not fit to be seen like that."

John expected her to summon the butler or some other man, but instead she began to yank off her gloves.

"Come closer," she commanded.

A spark ricocheted around John's body. "Yes, my lady," he said submissively, and when her eyes met his again, he winked at her.

Her mouth twitched in what must have been amusement, but she shook her head at him in an attempt at rebuke. Then she reached up and pulled the knots of his cravat free with her bare hands. It clearly was not the first time she'd performed such an action. Why should she have any experience in removing a man's neckcloth? A heady mix of intrigue and jealousy took him over.

Lady Helena frowned as she worked on re-tying his cravat and ran her teeth over her bottom lip once and again. He watched, riveted. Would that he was the one gnawing on that lip, and he found himself running his tongue over his own.

His eyes dropped to the neckline of her dress. But instead of allowing himself to drink in her charms, he noticed the edge of the fabric had been patched up. It was expertly done, but still noticeable. The cloth of the gown was a lovely shade, but it had obviously been well worn. She was not buying new clothes for herself.

Good Lord. He resisted the urge to gasp as she grazed the skin on his neck with her nails. The sensation sent a rush of fire over his entire body.

"There you are," she said, giving the cravat a final pat as she stepped back.

"Thank you," he said huskily.

She hesitated. "Shall I procure a mirror, so you can ensure it meets your expectations?"

He shook his head and smiled. "I would not dream of altering your work."

Her eyes flitted to his as she pulled her gloves back on. She returned his smile briefly before reaching for his arm.

"How did you learn to do that?" he asked, purposely taking up a slow pace towards the drawing room.

"My father didn't have a valet in his final years," she replied. "I learned."

"No valet? Whyever not?"

She shrugged. "He'd had the same man for decades. Couldn't bear the thought of someone else."

This was the first time she'd mentioned her father to him, and he could sense some emotion in the tightening of her hand around his forearm. He did not want to offend her, but he burned with curiosity to know more of her.

In a low voice he enquired, "How old was he…?"

"Five and forty," came her choked reply. The man had been in the prime of his life.

He halted their progress in the hall outside the drawing room and turned to her. "How long ago?" He sought her eyes, but she kept them downcast.

"Two years," she said softly.

He placed his hand on top of hers lightly. "Was it expected?"

She shook her head and blinked a tear from each eye. It was as if they were falling on his own cheeks, so acutely did he feel her pain. Even though he'd never lost anyone close to him, except–

"Sudden," she whispered.

"I am sorry," he whispered back, his heart breaking for hers. How well she bore her grief, likely burying it under her sense of duty. She was clearly made of stern stuff, but surely she needed some tenderness?

She allowed him to lift her hand from his arm, her eyes meeting his as he withdrew his handkerchief. She did not object when he kept her hand in his. As he carefully wiped her tears, she regarded him with an apparent mix of wariness and wonderment. He hoped she could see guileless empathy reflected back in his.

Repocketing his handkerchief, he dared to place his other hand on her back as an expression of comfort.

While her brows raised at his touch, she did not withdraw. Instead, she leaned toward him further, allowing his hand to slide about her waist. It was a small movement, but it was monumental for John.

She was beginning to trust him. Should she?

⌘

Helena sighed into John Barrington's hold, encircled in a tender connection that began with his gentle grasp of her hand, and ended with his arm supporting her back. She should have seen his actions as in intrusion, but he exuded such kindness and sensitivity. She had never known such serenity at the touch of man, or such ready acceptance of her raw emotions.

She'd been held by several other men before - but only brief hugs with her father, and the holds needed for dancing. It had never been like this. Even with the lightest of embraces, she felt as if she was floating above her sorrows, her worries, her cares. There was a sweetness in his manner that drew her in. And in his eyes, she saw a man who didn't want to take from her, only to give. In this moment, she wanted his all.

The sound of laughter from the room within brought her back to reality.

"My guests! Do excuse me." She stumbled backwards, out of his grasp. "I – please –"

Catching his bereft expression, words failed her. *I don't want to leave your arms, either. I apologise for letting my emotions get the better of me... but I am glad I did.*

As she turned to the door, her usual reservations began to return. A short time ago she had been peppering him with questions, suspicious of his motives. And now, she had allowed herself to be completely in his spell. Could he somehow turn her vulnerability against her?

She fairly ran into the drawing room, hoping he would not betray the closeness they had just shared. It would be too much to be embarrassed in front of her closest friends.

She took in the scene of the Kendall children playing happily by the fire, and Privett nearby debating something with Harding, likely the war with France. She went over to the others, who were in a group near the windows, being served wassail by Jane. The delicious aromas of apple and spices rose from the steaming bowl on the side table.

"Oh dear, I am neglecting my duties!" Helena exclaimed as she joined their circle, her attempt at cheeriness sounding shrill even to her ears. "Dear Jane, do allow me to fill the remaining glasses." She reached for the ladle and smiled determinedly at Mr Pike as he handed her his cup.

When she gave it back to him, out of the corner of her eye she spotted Mr Barrington enter the room, and inwardly sighed with relief when he joined Privett and Harding.

She filled a glass for herself and then fixed an attentive expression on her face as Mrs Powell related an anecdote. But her mind was on the man across the room with his broad back to her.

Her resolve, her self-control, her good sense had been eroded by repeated assaults on her senses. His silent thanks from across the dinner table had touched her more deeply than it should have. It was those dashed eyes of his, so expressive and penetrating. And there had been something else in his gaze... a sort of admiration that went beyond neighbourly respect. Beyond anything she was prepared to entertain.

Then there was her ridiculous urge to fix his cravat. It was more than a desire to show her skill. Before her was the picture of masculine perfection, except for that one little detail. Once remedied, the image would be complete.

Except she hadn't anticipated how close she would come to him, the large presence of his body, the distracting fragrance of sandalwood, the feel of the little hairs on his neck when she brushed them with her bare fingertips. The gesture had acquired an air of intimacy – to herself, at least. It was a service a wife might provide her husband if he became dishevelled while from home.

She reminded herself: he was the man who had been so disrespectful at Longdale, who had been entertaining Sinclair, who had suddenly appeared to claim his inheritance without any explanation.

Why did he have no visitors – no friends or family? There was definitely something odd about John Barrington, and yet… he had shown genuine sympathy towards her father's demise. The soothing way he had taken her hand, had dabbed at her tears, had supported her with a strong yet soft hand at her back. It had awakened such a strong need it scared her.

How readily the tears had come. They belied her intentions to always appear as a capable heiress. But she was tired of the performance, and she admitted it to herself: she wanted to trust Mr Barrington, desperately.

She was entirely too weary of navigating trying situations on her own. That is, without allowing herself free expression in the company of others. There was dear Jane, entirely devoted, but Helena didn't want to cause her distress. She divulged some details of her difficulties, to be sure, but none of how scared, or worried, or despairing she was. Some days, she wanted to be the child again going to her governess for comfort. She would give anything to crawl into Jane's lap again, taking solace from her loving arms.

But she was not a child anymore, and her troubles were far greater than a skinned knee or a churlish boy. She would not heap the real burdens on Jane. No, she needed to prove she was above the care of a governess.

Then there was Privett. She didn't want to expose him to her feminine emotions, or any notion of incompetence. If he didn't think she could manage the estate, she would lose her most important ally in business. She'd already been more vulnerable in his presence than she would like.

A female friend of her age could be a suitable sounding board, but she had no close friends who were in a similar situation. Her peers were well-married, in comfortable situations with only domestic and social concerns – and far from Mulberry.

No, what she craved was an equal in close proximity. Someone who could share in her strife and her joys, who she could be entirely herself with. But the very real threat remained – if that someone was a man, if things took their inevitable course… he would own her. And Willowbridge. Would the solace of trust and love be worth the potential sacrifices she would have to make? In the face of Mr Barrington's caring, unguarded countenance, she had begun to wonder as she'd never wondered before.

John tried to listen to the discourse of his peers concerning Napoleon's Ulm Campaign in the Rhine, but his contributions were limited to the odd "quite right" or "certainly not". His tête-à-tête with Lady Helena remained at the forefront of his thoughts, his feelings.

Miss Godwin appeared at his side to offer hot drinks and he saw an opportunity. He waited while Harding and Privett accepted their glasses, and then he fell into step with the lady.

"Mr Barrington." She smiled. "Your company tonight is… an unexpected pleasure."

He returned her smile, not sure if her comment was complementary. He didn't delay in pursuing his object. "Miss Godwin, you may think me impertinent…"

Her steps halted and she raised an eyebrow. "Go on."

"There is something about our lovely hostess which I cannot seem to make sense of. Before we first met, I overheard her ordering a large quantity of clothes and other necessaries at the shop – as any lady might. But it has since become apparent that she is of a… thrifty nature."

Miss Godwin stared at him levelly, giving away nothing.

"I wondered if you might perhaps know how she could countenance extravagance given the, er, circumstances?"

The lady smiled again. "Mr Barrington, I do know why Helena made that order – but perhaps you should ask her about it yourself?"

He stiffened. "I would rather not cause offence. I am only trying to make out her character, you see."

She placed kindly fingers on his sleeve, her eyes beseeching. "Is it really so difficult to imagine why she would be purchasing a new wardrobe?"

"Pity me, Miss Godwin, for I am but a simple creature."

She waved away his words impatiently. "Consider her nature," she implored. "Her love for Mulberry and its people drives everything she does."

John stared at her for just a moment before he realised her meaning. "Of course!" It was obvious now. He really did look like a simpleton – and Lady Helena like an angel.

Miss Godwin nodded. "Did you know, sir, that during that damaging storm our Lady Helena took it upon herself to join a rescue party in the middle of the night? That she herself pulled stranded animals to safety?"

John gaped at her. "She could have caught her death."

The lady nodded. "The thought never occurred to her. That's her way. She never thinks of herself. I sometimes think she will end up in an early grave, so determined she is to sacrifice everything for this property."

John shook his head. "Why?"

"Well, to make her father proud. And to continue to serve our little community."

John nodded. "Her father…" The pain in Lady Helena's eyes was fresh in his mind and he glanced over at the lady.

"Willowbridge is the only home she has ever known and has been in her family for generations."

John kept his gaze on Helena as he asked, "And where would she go, if it were to fall out of her hands?"

Miss Godwin sighed. "She would be entirely at the mercy of her cousin, Mr Sinclair."

John whipped his head back to her. "Entirely?"

She nodded sadly. "Indeed." She stepped back. "I will return to the pianoforte now. Please enjoy your evening, sir."

He bowed to her and returned his attention to their hostess. There she was, surrounded by cheery people, but none that she could count as a blood relative. Was she really all alone in the world, save for Sinclair? Was that why she had hidden herself away in Mulberry?

The whole party gathered around the piano again. He advanced upon the group slowly, his eyes locked on her.

She glanced over her shoulder briefly as if she could feel his scrutiny. Then she took a second look, eyeing him with an apparent mix of curiosity and suspicion before resolutely turning away.

He came around to stand just behind her and whispered in her ear. "May I have a word with you, my lady?"

She quivered. A tiny movement that no one else would have noticed, but it sent a spark of satisfaction through John. He held his breath.

She tilted her head towards him ever so slightly and gave one small nod as Jane began to play a festive tune and the children joined hands to dance.

John smiled to himself and withdrew quietly, moving to sit in a winged chair by the fire.

Lady Helena settled herself likewise. "What is it, Mr Barrington?"

John, if you please. He cleared his throat. Would she ever allow him to address her as Helena? It was incredibly unlikely, though he wished it could be. He drank in the vision of the flames reflected in her large clear eyes, her lips parted with expectation.

"I have been thinking on that time we, er, spoke," he said finally. "At Longdale Farm."

"Oh, that," she said, dropping her gaze to her hands. Was she still angry with him?

"Yes," he went on. "I do not think that scene painted either of us in a favourable light –"

Her eyes flashed to his. "I beg your –"

"And I should like to apologise sincerely for embarrassing you in front of your friends."

She stared at him. "Oh."

"I thank you for your efforts in giving the Grangers comfort." He smiled at her. "You seem to have quite the talent for anticipating the needs of others, which is something I, sadly, cannot claim."

She appeared to be considering her response, and he waited anxiously.

"All it takes is practise," she said, with a hint of a smile at the corners of her mouth.

He let out a breath, and then asked impulsively, "Might you be willing to teach me?" She would think he was flirting; she would probably retreat into herself or become defensive. But he could not take the words back in, and he couldn't help leaning forward, to see what she would say.

Catherine Barrington tended to her brother's wounds following her altercation with the vicar. It wasn't the first time she'd performed such an office. But on this occasion, her normally steady hands shook, and she was silent instead of chatting in her usual way.

Something was afoot.

"Catherine?" He sat up on his bed and took the bloody cloth from her hands. "What is the matter?"

She lifted her eyes to his, and in them he found an irretrievable sadness. Of course: she knew. It was only a matter of time after that ugly scene with his parents. He should have been the one to tell her, but how could he?

After what seemed like an age, she spoke. "It could have been me."

He laid the cloth to one side and laid his hands over hers. "Whatever do you mean, my dear?"

She took her hands away and got up from the bed. "Imagine, brother John, if it were I who was… sullied. Attacked."

The darkness in her eyes spooked him. He tried to laugh, but it sounded as a bark. "Do not be ridiculous, Catherine. You are a lady. You are protected. It could never happen."

"That may be. I am also a woman, just like Amy. She has no family, no brother to protect her." She stepped closer to stare straight into his eyes. "How much worse it is that you took advantage of someone who could not protect herself. From *you*."

Her words held an unmistakable note of disappointment… and disgust. His own sister hated him, and of course, he deserved no less.

"I am sorry, Catherine," he said brokenly.

She blinked and tears ran down her cheeks. "How could you, John? How could you do that to Amy – against her will?"

He would never forget the hurt in her eyes. "My dear," he attempted to take her hand, but she pulled it away. "I know it was wrong. I *feel* how wrong it was. I wish I could erase it." He paused. "But Catherine, you must understand – I was… inebriated, at the time."

She gasped. "You were what?"

"It was during the ball that I found out that… that Julie had died. It brought all the old hurts back afresh. I must have downed nigh on a whole bottle of brandy before I crossed paths with Amy again."

Catherine stared at him.

He ploughed on. "So, when she let me kiss her the way I used to kiss

Julie, I was so hurt and confused I must have…"

She shook her head. "That does not excuse it, John. If anything, it makes it worse. That when your senses were impaired you committed such a vile and horrific act. Is that really the man you instinctually are?"

"No!"

She stood. "Well, I am sorry for Julie. Sorry for Amy. Sorry for you. And sorry for myself, to be losing my favourite brother."

He took her head in his hands. "No, Catherine, you are not losing me. I must only be away for a year."

She shook her head to free herself from his soft grasp. "No, John." She began to sob. "I have already lost you. I know not if I ever knew you at all."

She went to the door, and he chased after her. "Catherine, please! You know how I adore you."

She turned to face him, her face drenched in tears. "I hope this time away teaches you something, dearest. I hope you can somehow return a better man. Although at this point, I honestly doubt you can."

Her words stung him to the core. He let her go.

He was up all night, mourning his close friendship with his sister. He had thought theirs a bond that would never be broken. He had taken it for granted.

At the dawning of the day, his heart was filled with anger instead of remorse. If that confounded vicar hadn't tipped off his mother, this wouldn't have happened.

He dressed with cold determination. He had lost too much. He would have his revenge. He would go to London directly and find the chink in the man's armour. Everyone had a little scandal hidden somewhere.

The clergymen were tight lipped at first, naturally suspicious of his motives. But his coins were enough to make one church warden, apparently feeling slighted in favour of Mr Brook, speak freely. Just as well it was only a few coins, as he didn't have many.

The intelligence provided to him was saucier than he could have hoped. It mattered little whether the story was true, as long as it was true enough that Brook could not deny it. The time had come to get rid of the man, once and for all. By the time John was finished, Brook wouldn't be able to preach anywhere in England.

Pushing his guilt aside as he rode back to Amberley, he revelled in the knowledge that retribution would soon be his.

Chapter Thirteen

Helena took in the sight of Mr Barrington, his lithe figure sprawled in the chair, the firelight dancing across the curves and angles of his face, and an enticing spark in his eyes. She was attracted to him beyond measure, and it was unquestionably all his fault. He couldn't help being so handsome, of course, but did he have to look at her that way?

He was staring at her lips as if he meant to devour her. And did she want to be devoured? The thought was beyond reason.

His compliment regarding her talent for serving others had lit her up inside. Hearing those words from him truly meant something. It was gratifying to have him recognise this about her, rather than just seeing her as a busybody like Sinclair did.

She had dismissed him as a man ruled by his ego. But he had put that aside just now to apologise to her. She felt the gravity, the honesty behind his words. They lifted her spirits at just such a time as they needed lifting.

And then there was his request to speak to her just now. Who did he think he was, breathing words into her ear like that? The sensation had been shocking, overpowering, alluring, distracting… positively sinful.

He was apparently sincere one moment, mischievous the next. Whatever was she to do about him?

She chose not to rise to his suggestive comment, instead saying, "I too have considered that day with regret. It must have been disheartening to arrive at your property and find another trespassing. In future I shall seek your approval in all matters concerning your tenants."

He sat back in his chair, the light in his eyes dimmed somewhat. "I thank you," he said quietly. "There are of course no restrictions on your visiting whomever you wish."

Her disappointment at the change in his demeanour was palpable. She wanted that light in his eyes again.

"There is a way you can learn more about helping those about you," she said archly.

He sat forward, all anticipation again. Did he imagine she was about to flirt with him? Did he not know that she was a woman of substance?

She smiled. "The vestry."

He blinked. "I beg your pardon?"

She laughed. "The parish vestry, of course."

There was a lengthy pause. Then, "What did you have in mind, Lady Helena?"

"Why, that you take your place at our parish vestry meetings and undertake any duties arising. I have been remiss in not inviting you earlier."

Her proposal was clearly not met with unbridled enthusiasm. Instead, she was met with a steely glare. This confused her. She was offering him a chance to become involved with his community, in a place where he would surely see out his days… and also the opportunity to spend more time with her. The vestry provided Helena with vital information and influence in the running of the village. She wouldn't be without it and could not understand why he wouldn't jump at the prospect of being included. It was an offer of acceptance to their small circle. He should be grateful.

When he did not respond, she leapt into the breach. "Did you ever attend the vestry in… er…"

"Amberley? Yes, on the odd occasion."

He did not elaborate. "So, you are familiar with how they operate."

He nodded.

Unfamiliarity was not an excuse, then. It was only… distaste? She ploughed on. "We meet on the first Monday of the month, in the office at the rear of the church."

"I shall consider it, thank you," he said finally, parting his lips. It was hardly a promise. There was something empty in his smile.

She decided on a different tack, a sense of unease beginning to stir within.

"Well, then. What charitable endeavours do you like to undertake?"

The perfunctory smile faded. "I, er…"

"Now, do not be modest," she said, shaking her head. "Tell me what causes you have supported in the past."

She leaned toward him, desperate for some sort of reassurance that he loved his local people the same way she did. Surely he could not be so superficial as to ignore those less privileged than himself?

❦

John took a long breath. He didn't want to disappoint her, especially not with the burgeoning trust building between them. The problem was the chasm between their natures: she was a saint and he a sinner. Could he ever hope to bridge the divide?

Charitable endeavours… well, there has been… He wracked his brain for something that might have been mentioned in church or by his mother or sisters. But his mind was blank.

John had reluctantly attended parish vestry meetings in Amberley on a handful of occasions, and found them to be dry, pointless affairs. A waste of his time. He was not the type to be getting involved with running the affairs of a village. He frankly did not care about church maintenance, or town beautification, or organising amusements for the lower classes.

"I make a point of attending my family's annual harvest fair," he said at last.

She nodded eagerly. "Such a rewarding occasion for your labourers and their friends. What else do you take an interest in?"

John squirmed in his seat, and studied his hands, which were clenched on his lap. He should have paid more attention to his mother's causes. Why could he not summon one thing?

He could not bring himself to stretch the truth, not when she was so virtuous. He threw up his hands in a helpless gesture.

Her brow furrowed and she looked away. "No interest in…"

He could think of no more to say but was determined not to escape the conversation. Meanwhile, piano music issued forth with relentless gaiety.

After what seemed like an eternity, she abruptly sat up straighter, and her eyes narrowed. "Could it be, Mr Barrington, that you do not care to better the lot of those who are less fortunate than yourself? Is your world centred only around your own pleasures?"

He had expected a negative response, but this cut him to the quick. He swallowed hard but didn't demur from her accusatory gaze. "I would not put it quite that way, Lady Helena," he replied. The world afforded him few pleasures.

"Then how, sir, would you put it?"

He blew out a slow breath. "I have had… other priorities."

"I see." She stood. "Please excuse me."

He rose as well, as was courteous, and decided it would be best for him to slip out unnoticed after she had re-joined the group.

She did not, however, go towards the pianoforte. She went in the opposite direction, and into an adjoining antechamber. He went across the room hesitantly, unsure what he should do. She wanted privacy, so he should go.

But when he took one last look in that direction, he caught sight of her skirts. She was pacing up and down, clearly agitated. It pained him that he, and his lack of purpose in life, had caused her distress. Did this mean she cared for him, even a little? If she did not, why would his deficiencies upset her?

He made a decision, and advanced upon that room. His presence might incite further friction, but he could not leave her in such a state.

When he entered the antechamber, she was not within. Instead, she was in the larger hall it led to – a picture gallery. Now, it appeared all of her ancestors looked down upon him in judgement. He wished there was time to discover which one was her father.

She turned at the sound of his footsteps and winced on regarding him, almost as if he had struck her.

"I do beg your pardon, Lady Helena," he began. "May I escort you back to the party?"

She hesitated, and then marched straight up to him, addressing him in a quiet, cold voice. "Do you mean to tell me you have no intention to participate in village life?"

"My lady. I could hardly be expected to undertake duties and such when I know next to nothing of the local environs or the people that inhabit them."

She raised her eyebrows. "But how do you expect to learn if you do not take an active interest?"

John sighed heavily. "As yet, I do not wish to form these sorts of ties in Mulberry."

"Whyever not?"

It was a fair question. The manor was after all his inheritance and where it was expected he would spend the majority of his time in the future. It was reasonable to assume he would want to utilise whatever talents he had to contribute to the village and surrounds. But while he was under this wretched cloud of guilt and serving his equivalent of a sentence, he would rather not have anyone getting too close or prying into his affairs. Especially one Lady Helena Davenport, who would no doubt spread word of his deeds to everyone in the county and ruin any chance of future peace here for him.

That all made perfect sense, but his heart pulled him toward her with undeniable force, especially as she stood there looking up at him with her eyes lost and pleading.

"You mean to leave." She spoke before he could find any more words. "You mean to go to London, to determine your future?"

"I –"

"Why don't you leave now, and spare us the trouble of furthering your acquaintance?"

He took in a breath and closed his eyes for a moment as he said, "I cannot."

☙❧

"Cannot?" This answer Helena had not expected. Mr Barrington said it as if he were not master of his own will. The unexpected nature of this response caught her off guard and dissipated some of her anger and anxiety.

After a pause, he answered. "My family wish me to remain here for the time being… to learn about my property."

She studied him. That was obviously not the whole story but there was no reason why she should press him further on that score. "You will go to London for the Season, though? Your family must expect you to find a…" She willed herself to say the word. "…wife."

He shook his head. "I am to remain here."

This was puzzling in the extreme, but then movement caught her attention. He was fidgeting with a ring on his right hand, which was remarkable for the deep, dark black of the stone. It was the kind of ring one was given as a keepsake or an heirloom.

"Your ring," she said, nodding toward it. "What is the meaning of it?"

He looked down at his fingers, as if unaware he had been touching the ring, and then yanked his hands apart. His eyes flashed to hers, and within them there was so much pain and desolation her heart constricted. The muscles in his jaw clenched, and she saw him swallow hard. Was he holding back tears?

"Mr Barrington," she said softly, and she reached out to him on impulse. Whatever memories or secrets were tied to that ring, Helena had a feeling it was the answer to many of her questions about this man.

"I do not wish to discuss it," he said, as he stepped back a fraction.

His small movement was a rejection, and she instantly regretted expressing any sympathy towards him. Embarrassment and hurt mingled into resentment.

Placing her arms back firmly at her sides, she said, "I see." His statement served to remind her they were virtual strangers, who knew precious little about each other.

He owed her nothing. But he surely did owe something to the people who lived and worked on his lands, especially if he were to stay here for the time being.

He bowed suddenly. "I shall take my leave. I thank you again for admitting me today."

She caught his sleeve. "One more moment, if you please."

He turned back to her. "Yes, my lady?"

The man's true character had been made clear to her once again when he admitted having no interests beyond his own life. "Other priorities," he had said. She could guess what those were, based on the male acquaintances she had made while in town: gaming, sporting pursuits, drinking, and finding willing females. He was as shallow as the rest of them.

He was a sycophant, who had sailed through life by saying the right words in the right ears at the right time. And now, through a show of kindness and flattery, he was attempting to gain her good opinion. Just like all the men in town who had chased her for her supposed fortune. He was only trying to get close to her for his own gain. She didn't know what he wanted from her, what his object was, but it could not be genuine. It was lies, all of it. He would not have it, whatever it was. He would not have *her*.

He was exactly the kind of man she despised. But he was worse than the others because he had nearly succeeded in making her vulnerable. He'd made her desire closeness with him – but this was where it ended. She *would* cast him out of her house, but not before she had given him the setting-down he deserved.

Her voice shook with emotion as she began to speak. "To my mind, the very definition of a gentleman is one who puts others before himself. *You* only look for what you can take, not what you can give. You, sir, are no gentleman."

She folded her arms over her stomach, hoping she appeared defiant and strong, but it was in fact a sort of self-embrace to keep her hands from trembling.

Mr Barrington stared at her open mouthed for a moment, then he inhaled and exhaled slowly as his eyes roved about the room, apparently considering how to respond to her accusation.

"Don't be absurd," he sputtered. "I'm the son of an earl. My aristocratic breeding is obvious in my style of dress, the manner of my speech, by my tastes and pursuits. My deportment. I am a gentleman, through and through."

She shook her head. "You are a gentleman by birth and breeding, to be sure. But by character? Heavens, no. I am convinced you know not the meaning of the word. A gentleman earns his authority over others; he does not impose it."

Anger sparked from his eyes now, and a flush spread from his neck – from that perfectly tied cravat – to his cheekbones. "How dare you question my gentility?" he demanded with quiet force. "You, who have all but shunned polite society?"

What did that have to do with anything? "I hardly think –"

"Why do you hide yourself away in Mulberry when you could be enjoying the delights of London, or even Bath? There you could use your charms and intelligence to secure…"

"A husband?" she interjected, spitting out the word.

He nodded. "Yes. A partner, if you will."

She would not, could not. Breathing heavily, she issued a challenge to him instead. "I might ask the same of you, sir: why have you come to Mulberry without a family? Why have you had no visitors? What are you hiding? Or *who* are you hiding from?"

He placed his hands on his hips, looming over her. "That, madam, is none of your affair."

"Oh, but my maidenhood is a concern of yours?"

"Helena!"

The combatants turned to see Jane striding toward them.

"My dear, you can be heard from the drawing room. Whatever is the matter?"

Helena stepped away from Mr Barrington and took up the hand Jane offered. "Nothing of significance," she said, not daring to look at him.

"No indeed," he returned, his voice icy cold. There was a pause, and the movement of the candlelight shadows told her he had bowed. "I bid you good night."

"Good night," Jane replied, and she squeezed Helena's hand as he marched past them and from the room.

As soon as he was gone, Helena's defences crumbled, and she burst into tears.

"Oh, dear Helena." Jane led her to a pair of chairs and helped her sit. "What did he do to you? Was he cruel?"

"Yes... no. I don't know." She buried her face in her hands in confusion. It seemed nothing was in her control anymore. She was perilously close to saying something – or doing something – that she might regret for the rest of her life. And the trouble was, the potential pleasure of doing so terrified her. The problem was she didn't know if her next transgression would be one of love or hate – passion or fury. Passionate fury? It was unsupportable.

She finally acknowledged that her exhaustion had her emotions sitting too close to the surface. She had to get away, to get herself back to an equilibrium.

She took a breath, wiped her eyes, and took both of Jane's hands. "Let us go to London."

John could not help feeling a trifle smug in his triumph. He'd told the parish vestry members all about Brook's indiscretions, and the revelation had had the desired effect. To see that man finally at a loss for words, and down from his pious horse, was satisfying indeed.

His gratification was short lived, however. Not long after returning to the house, there was a gentle rap at his chamber door.

"Come in?"

The door opened slowly, and the face of Amy Miller appeared. He swallowed a gasp at how pale and drawn she was. His own battered heart turned over. He may not have loved her, but he had cared about her. Of course, she would despise him now. But she had never said a bad word to his face.

There was so much he should say to her, but it was impossible to begin.

"Yes, you may enter," he said softly, and she came in with careful steps.

Her body was beginning its bloom into motherhood, and it suited her. She must be in her last days at Ashworth Hall, in accordance with his mother's terms.

He gestured to a chair, but she shook her head. He waited to see what she would say, a sweat breaking out on his top lip.

"I – I have come to ask you something," she began, staring resolutely at his waistcoat.

He had half expected this. She would likely be in need of funds. And the stark truth was, he had none to offer. He now had no cash available to him, and no idea when more would materialise... perhaps after Christmas, when the rents at Mulberry would be next collected. His parents had made it clear that he would only be given what was necessary to live on by the bailiff who managed the place.

"You liked me once," she said, in a pragmatic manner. "I would not object to... that is..."

She began to blush. John rubbed his signet ring in agitation. What the deuce was she saying?

"I have come to beg you to set me up with a... situation."

He frowned. "A situation?"

She twisted her fingers. "A house. I mean, a little flat, or something. I am, for now, without a place to go."

She dropped her gaze to the floor, and suddenly realisation dawned.

"You are offering to be my mistress?" John whispered.

She nodded, wincing.

"I see," he said dumbly.

It was, in point of fact, the perfect solution. He could assuage his guilt by making sure she was comfortable, and he could make sure she was hidden away where he wouldn't be constantly reminded of his folly. Of course, he would never ask her to see him, let alone do anything else. She needed no reminder of his horrid touch.

"You – you need not see the child." Her voice broke on the final word, and John's throat clogged up as he had an infinitesimal insight into all that she was feeling.

"Amy," he said, his own voice cracking. "I –"

"Please."

Her eyes met his, beseeching. For a horrifying moment, he thought she might drop to her knees in front of him.

Any platitudes he could have offered, any regrets he could have expressed – would never be enough. At this moment, she had summoned tremendous courage to come to him and plead for his assistance. With all that she must hate him, she would still submit to his desires in order to secure a roof over her head? Her situation must be desperate indeed.

As much as he wanted to assist, his lack of funds made paying for her lodgings impossible. There was no point asking his parents for the money to pay for a mistress… even though she wouldn't be performing any mistress-like duties.

He must refuse her offer. But his pride would not allow him to admit the truth… or perhaps it was his innate resentment toward being the poorer second son. Cursing himself, he forced out a hideous remark about not wanting to lie with a mother.

Pain sprang into her eyes, as if she'd been dealt a physical blow.

Another one.

He instantly wished he could take the words back. But he could not.

Amy nodded, her chin wobbling. Then she fled the room.

John stared at the doorway blindly for several moments, then staggered over and pushed the door shut. He poured himself a brandy with shaking hands and sank into an armchair. Who had he become?

It was the final despicable act in a long line of despicable acts. With that damage done, it was time to go. Setting his glass down, he packed the final belongings he could fit into his trunk and sent word to the stable hand to have Thora ready at dawn.

Shaving and dressing in the dark and cold of morning, John prepared to leave his home without any goodbyes. His heart ached, wondering if his beloved sister would even miss him when he was gone. He must prove to Catherine that he was the man she had thought he was. He knew not where or how to start. But first, he had to get through this wretched year away in the middle of nowhere… with little to do except ruminate on his shortcomings. He'd filled his life with distractions, but now there would be none.

At least in Mulberry he'd be an unknown, untainted by any of this. Perhaps there he could pretend he was a decent human being, keeping his secret crime hidden for as long as possible.

PART TWO: THE CHALLENGE

Chapter Fourteen

John had another few days on his own at the manor before his staff returned from visiting with their respective families. Thankfully the days were fine, and he spent many hours riding aimlessly on Thora, roaming a little further from home each time.

There was a lot of time to think. Too much time.

You, sir, are no gentleman.

Her barb burned a hole in his chest, where conflicting emotions churned.

John supposed his definition of a gentleman was one who was free from burdens, who took leisure to spend time with his friends and enjoy the charms of women. But that was mainly the domain of the eldest son, and bitterness about that had long fuelled his insolence.

To have Lady Helena Davenport illustrate *her* standards for a man of good breeding had been humbling to say the least. Her shock at his lack of altruism sparked extreme mortification in him, which was then veiled in indignation. Was it not enough that he had to look after his tenants, animals, and other business matters? Did he have to aspire to save the world, too?

Now, it took him back to the time when he had tried to be the model of everything good and worthy. He'd have moved heaven and earth to impress Miss Stone and her family. But giving his all in order to prove his worth still hadn't been good enough. He had vowed to never exert himself again for a woman. Why would he, when pain and suffering was

153

the only payment?

Something about Lady Helena had him questioning everything. It was folly to dwell on it, on her.

Happy was the day when his staff returned. He awoke to the sounds of clanging and conversation in the kitchen and sprang out of bed. He quickly performed his toilette and dressed in wrinkled clothing from the day before, pathetically desperate for company.

He strode into the kitchen and found the Morgans and Rosie assembled, eating their breakfast. His bailiff was also seated around the table, with a cup of coffee in his hand.

"Tom, Betty, Rosie, Wilson – good morning!"

Shocked faces swung to him, and they all struggled to their feet accompanied by a strained chorus of scraping chairs. "G'morning, sir," Tom greeted him, as Betty and Rosie bobbed curtsies and Mr Wilson put his cup down to shake John's hand.

"Sit, sit, do," John said, and rather impulsively, he drew out a chair for himself and dropped into it.

His staff stared at him, and then at each other, as if they'd seen a ghoul.

"Sit!" John said, with rather more force than he'd intended, and they all scrambled to obey. "How are you all this fine morning?"

"I'm very well, Mr Barrington," Mr Wilson replied.

"And your family?"

"Very well, too. I thank you."

"What is it we can do for you, sir?" Tom asked. "You'll be wanting sommat to eat?"

Betty nodded, her eyes flitting to the larder.

"Only when it suits you," John said, waving a casual hand. "I only came in to say hello."

Still they eyed him warily. Had he never done this before?

Perhaps he hadn't.

He turned to the maid. "Did you have a good Christmas, Rosie?"

She nodded on a mouthful of toast. "Yes, sir. We went up to my cousin's farm. There was a big mob of us. It was ever so merry. What about you, sir?"

Tom sent her a reproachful glance for her bold enquiry, but John wasn't in a mood to stand on formalities. The question did, however, make him uncomfortable given all that had transpired. All four pairs of eyes were on him again.

He forced a smile. "Er, yes. Very merry too. Quite the spectacle, in fact."

He cleared his throat, stopping himself from saying anything further to arose curiosity. Instead, he considered what Rosie had said, and realised he knew nothing of her situation. Did he even know her surname?

"Er, how many in your family, Rosie?"

"In our cottage? Nine, sir."

"*Nine?*"

"Yes, if you're counting m'self as well."

John had been past that cottage. How could nine people fit in there, let alone find place to sleep?

"And how are you placed, in the order of things?"

"Second, sir. I have one older brother."

John nodded, considering. "And what does your father do?"

Her brow furrowed. His questions must be bothering her. "He labours on the local farms, and we've a few animals to care for as well. Why is it you need to know, sir?"

He smiled. "There's no need, Rosie. Don't be troubled."

He glanced around the table. There were all staring at him, perhaps wondering who he would interrogate next. This would not do. He pushed his chair out and stood. "Well, I shall leave you to your meal. I'll find something in the larder myself, Betty."

Aware of the woman gaping at him, he went to the cupboard and helped himself to bread and butter, before pouring himself a coffee.

"Good day," he said to his staff as he hastily left the room, feeling like an outsider in his own home. Of course, he'd never desired conviviality with servants before. It *was* quite unlike him to seek the company of the lower orders. Indeed, most of his class would consider it quite unnatural. He must make an effort to find some other companionship among Mulberry's gentry. He was clearly in want of it. A pity that he had alienated the one person whose company he desired the most.

His conversation with Rosie remained in his mind as he partook of his simple breakfast in the dining room. His object had been to ascertain how the family was supported financially, and now he was fairly certain that Rosie's wage would be critical to their survival. It was quite a burden for one so young, although it must be a common one. He had never considered the lot of the scullery maids or stable hands at Ashworth House… but perhaps he should have.

"Nine people in that tiny cottage…" John murmured to himself as he sipped his coffee. Their way of life was beyond his comprehension, and yet, within his realm.

∾

Helena braced herself against the side of the carriage as its wheels bumped and bounced over ruts in the road. Her one remaining vehicle was now hardly fit for travel, but it wasn't that far to London. She hoped it would stay in one piece until they arrived.

It seemed a folly to retain a carriage in order to travel to a townhouse she couldn't afford to keep, but such was the way of things. Her father's will decreed that all the Davenport property should be kept intact if she were to inherit. So, the London house must remain in her possession for now.

She could have cut costs by trimming the staff at the townhouse – or indeed at Willowbridge – but she wouldn't be able to live with herself if she caused anyone to be without the means of supporting themselves or their family. As it was the London staff were slowly reducing, as those who moved away or retired were not replaced. Sinclair was sure to tell her how displeased he was with the reduced level of service.

Helena turned to Jane. "Are you quite sure Sinclair is gone?"

Jane nodded. "The housekeeper confirmed it by letter this morning. He is gone to stay with his mother's family for the new year."

Helena let out a breath. "Thank you, dear Jane."

On Boxing Day, Jane had sprung into action, rapidly assembling the necessary staff members to make arrangements for their departure. They left three days later, accompanied by two footmen (now riding alongside the carriage as guards), Andrews, and Helena's maid. It had been nearly two years since Helena had travelled anywhere, not least because she wanted to avoid the expense.

The carriage began to slow as they neared London and traffic increased. Helena peered out the window at the clammer of horses, carts and pedestrians all making their way to the great capital. She wondered who each had left behind at their respective homes, and what business pulled them away. The city seemed to be a disparate mingling of success and squalor, with each man drawn to the promise of a better life amongst its crowds and avenues.

As the carriage rolled its way nearer to her residence in Kensington, fog still clung to dark corners and alleyways. Helena fairly felt her lungs constrict with the chimney smoke which permeated the air. Houses gave way to six-storey apartments sandwiched together in neat rows and squares, barely allowing sunlight to break through.

"I do hope this is for the best," Helena muttered, mainly to herself.

Jane placed a hand on hers. "The change will do you good," she said reassuringly.

Helena turned to meet her eyes. "I'm sure you are right," she said, smiling. "And it is my wish that the diversion will suit you, as well."

"You are very good," Jane said, squeezing her hand.

It was but a moment later when the driver gave a shout to indicate their arrival, and once the carriage pulled to a stop there was a flurry of activity before their door was opened. Helena took in the familiar exterior of the townhouse as she stepped down to the street.

The black front door was framed by a pair of white columns, and the white brick walls on either side supported tall windows segmented into six panes. A row of windows above were framed by a long black balcony. These two floors housed the formal and informal living rooms, and the floor above were the bedrooms. Finally, within the roof attic space, dormer windows housed the servants' quarters. It seemed entirely excessive for her needs. It should belong to a family who would enjoy all it could offer… much as she had in her youth.

The memories came flooding back as soon as she stepped into the entrance hall. As she hung up her coat on a hook, she remembered her father lifting her so she could reach her bonnet before they went to the park. Up in the elegant drawing room, she could almost hear the sound of her mother playing the piano. It was in her mother's bedroom that the memory was particularly strong. She was sure she could still smell her fragrance on the air of the lavender-coloured room – the décor unchanged since her death. In fact, not much about the house had changed at all since then. Helena clung to a post on the bed and choked on tears, trying to cling to any kind of memory.

Her mother had loved London. Helena had faint recollections of watching her being fitted for clothes, and going to have ices together at Gunther's. The city had seemed like a beautiful fairy land of surprises and delights. But when Helena grew up, the grim realities of the marriage mart were all too clear.

During her first and only season, her was father proud of her but increasingly hopeless, knowing he was out of his depth. Helena also keenly felt the absence of her mother at all the assemblies. Jane was already her guide, but it wasn't the same for her as all the other young ladies. The mothers formed groups of connections which were impenetrable to the Davenports.

What her father gave her instead was a love for the country, and their family seat of Willowbridge. They had both been relieved to return, and no more was said on the matter of matrimony. Father and daughter enjoyed an all too brief time of peace and tranquillity together before Lord Davenport became ill.

Helena visited her father's bedroom as well to ensure everything was in order, before finally going to her own chamber, where her maid and the housekeeper were beginning to unpack her belongings. She went to the window and took in the bustling street below, hoping all the noise had not unsettled Cornelius. It was, of course, nothing compared to the frantic activity that would still come to town with the height of the social season, from Easter until July. She would be back home well before then. But now, the thought of her cherished Mulberry was somewhat complicated by the presence of a tall, dark gentleman with piercing eyes.

⤜⚬⤛

It was New Year's Day, and John's chagrin over the Christmas night altercation had subsided somewhat. He had no idea how their discussion had turned so heated, but he knew his reluctance to join the vestry and his lack of philanthropic history had deeply offended Lady Helena.

He knew the lady's haughtiness was rooted not in arrogance, but in fear. She was afraid of losing her home, her property, her security. Her heritage. She seemed worn out with the effort of making it work. Just as John was beginning to break down her walls, she'd identified one of his weaknesses, one that hit to the core of her existence. She'd struck out with words in defence, as a soldier strikes out with his sword. In her mind, she likely *was* in a war of sorts.

Was he to be her ally, or her hidden enemy? In his heart, he knew the answer. He wanted to help her… Whether he would be around to see her triumph, it mattered not. He had never met her equal, and if anyone deserved his assistance it was Lady Helena Davenport. But what could he do? If nothing else, he would try to share in her burdens.

His thoughts strayed to earlier that evening, when she'd confided in him about her father, and allowed him to comfort her in his arms. How good and right it had been. If only he was a better man, he could look forward to more such moments.

He must see her. To smooth over the ructions of their last encounter, and to pledge his loyalty. To take on whatever he could. He would do whatever she needed. Having her accept his help would be the first hurdle to overcome.

Riding over to the great house, his nerves crept in. Would she even admit him? Her opinion of him was now sunk so low that she might refuse him entry. He could only but try.

He ensured Thora's comfort in the Willowbridge stables and returned to rap on the front door. When it opened, it was not the face of the familiar butler, but another manservant who greeted him.

"Good morning, sir. How may I help you?"

"Good morning. I have come to speak with Lady Helena. Is she within? Perhaps with her companion?" It would not do for the servants to gossip about him wanting a private audience.

The man shook his head. "I'm sorry, sir. She is not at home."

"But you have not checked…" John was familiar with the "not at home" excuse, usually given by a lady after the servant had informed her who was calling. Perhaps in this case, it really was the truth. "Will you tell her I called when she returns? Perhaps I may write her a brief note?"

"I'm afraid that won't be possible, sir. She will not be returning today. She is gone."

John stared at him. "Gone?"

"To London, sir."

"What? Oh, er, London, you say?" That certainly hadn't been her design when they had last discussed it. Had he angered her so much that she felt the need to escape him? "Do you know the intended duration of her stay in town?"

The man shook his head. "Several weeks, I believe. Perhaps months."

Months.

"I thank you," John said. "Good day." He pivoted and descended the steps to the gravel path, his thoughts churning as he made his way back to the stables. What a mess he'd made of things.

He took Thora on a long route back to the manor even though the icy air pricked at his lungs. Why did her assessment of him matter so much?

A short while later, he found Betty in the kitchen and consulted with her on the evening's supper. Requesting his luncheon be brought to the parlour so he could remain by the fire, he turned to leave.

Before he advanced more than two steps, Farmer Carter strode into the kitchen and slapped a huge boar down onto the kitchen table. "There y'are, Betty."

"That's a fine beast, Carter. The lord be thanked."

It was indeed a huge animal. John also thanked the farmer before he went on his way.

"Whatever will we do with it all, Betty?" he asked. It seemed somewhat wasteful to kill such an animal when his household were so small in number.

"Oh, I'll make use of it, don't you worry y'self. Tom'll help me with the butchering."

John's mind was working in ways it never had before. "Tell me, do we ever give any of our meat to others in the village?"

"Yes sir, we share the offcuts with some of the widows and sometimes to the orphanage. Offal and the like."

He nodded. "I see."

The very definition of a gentleman is one who puts others before himself.

John set his jaw in determination. "With your blessing, Betty, I should like to do something different this time."

She laughed. "You don't need my blessing, sir!"

And so it was, that John Barrington walked down the lane that afternoon with a boar slung across his shoulders. He would not give only offal or off cuts this time. No, he would bestow the whole animal.

The sky was already darkening as he approached Rosie's cottage. From within the sounds of conversation, laughter, and a baby's cry issuing forth. He shifted his weight and knocked on the door.

There was a shout of consternation, and the door was thrown open to reveal a short but stocky man, with bright eyes inset in a ruddy face. "What do you think –" he began angrily, but then he took in the sight of John from head to foot. "Who are you?"

"Er, good evening," John said. "I am Mr John Barrington, your daughter's employer."

The man's bushy eyebrows shot up. "Oh. You better come in, then."

He stood back to allow John's entry.

"If you'll allow me a moment," John said, laying the animal down in front of the house.

"What the devil is that?"

"A boar."

"Well, I can see that, but why is it there?"

John scratched his head, and indicated he would go inside. "I'll explain, Mr… er…" Heavens, he really didn't know Rosie's last name. He felt his oversight acutely.

"Denby," the man said, as John stopped to enter the cottage. "And here is Mrs Denby, and all our brood."

The interior of the cottage was dark and smoky, and it took John several moments to identify anyone. The room reeked with the stench of cheap tallow candles, and wood fire smoke stung his eyes. As he began to acclimatise, he saw that the building was only one space, with sleeping quarters around the walls only cordoned off with sheets.

"Hello there!" he greeted Mrs Denby, hoping he sounded cheery and not appalled. The woman was jiggling the baby on her hips while stirring a large pot over the fire. Some of the children were playing some sort of game at a small table up against the far wall, while the remainder were huddled together on the floor. Most were without shoes, and clearly bathing was not a regular habit.

Rosie sprang up from the group on the floor, still dressed in her maid's clothing. "Mr Barrington! Why are you here? Have I done something wrong?"

"No, no, Rosie. Don't be alarmed. As to the reason for my visit, I should like to make a gift of an animal from my home farm to your family."

"You should what?" Mr Denby cried. "You mean that huge boar outside? For us?"

John smiled. "Yes. I know winter can be a hard time for everyone, and I hope this will make it easier to feed your family for a week or two."

Mrs Denby left her place on the opposite wall and came to his side. "Oh, sir, are you sure? We'd be ever so grateful. But we must give you something in return. I'm afraid" – she exchanged a glance with her husband – "we can't pay you for it."

"I have no expectation of payment," John said gruffly. "And I cannot accept anything from you."

"Well, then, stay for dinner," Mr Denby said, giving him a hearty slap on the back.

John held back a cough. The smoke was now making his eyes run. "I couldn't possibly impose," he said, heading back to the door. "But thank you all the same."

"But…"

Mrs Denby gave the baby to one of her other children, and hastily grabbed a jar from a shelf. "Here you are," she said. "It's elderflower jelly. Take it, please."

John took the jar from her with a smile. "My thanks, Mrs Denby. I'll see you tomorrow, Rosie."

He ducked from the house and hurried back towards his own home. He heard the sounds of Mr Denby and one of his sons moving the boar somewhere, and something inside him lifted as he made out the incredulous tone in their voices. His gift would mean his own household would need to eat more simply for the time being, but it was a small sacrifice for a hopefully more substantial gain.

Perhaps there was something in this charity lark after all.

Chapter Fifteen

As Helena set out for her first ride with Cornelius in London, tiny flakes of snow began to descend from the heavens. She lifted her face to the sky and revelled in the sensation of the flakes settling on her face like frozen sparks. Was it snowing in Mulberry?

It was still early morning. Jane hadn't emerged for breakfast when Helena and her groom departed the townhouse. They entered Hyde Park near Kensington Palace, just as the first rays of sunshine began to filter through the bare oak and chestnut trees in the avenue. Crossing the Broad Walk, she urged Cornelius on and was soon at a canter through the wooded parkland. She took in gulps of crisp air as they passed the round pond. Cornelius tossed his head happily and she patted his neck, echoing his contentment. It wasn't the country, but it would do for now.

Helena had no intention of riding along Rotten Row, where the social elite paraded up and down on mounts or in carriages. It was notorious as *the* place to encounter gossip – or perhaps a future husband. It was unlikely to be crowded at such an hour, but why take the risk? Unlike all the other ladies her age, her purpose in London was not to ensnare an eligible bachelor.

In point of fact, she wasn't quite sure what her purpose was, only that she needed to be away from home for a while.

She brought Cornelius down to a trot and lead her groom along Budge's Walk. Though she hadn't been here of late, Helena remembered the paths clearly. Her father loved to bring her to the park because her mother had loved socialising here. They were actually not too far from the spot where Lord and Lady Davenport had first met. A shiver ran down Helena's spine at the thought, and she wondered if it were possible that her parents might be watching her at this very moment. Theirs had been a true romance.

She pulled Cornelius to a halt, wiping at her eyes. "I miss you," she whispered. "I wish I had your happiness, brief those it was."

Her groom came alongside. "Lady Helena? Is something the matter?"

Helena cleared her throat, shaking her head. "No, indeed. Isn't the park lovely at this hour? Let us ride over to the Long Water and then skirt the perimeter back to the house."

He tipped his hat. "Very good, my lady." Her let her ride in front several yards, before following behind again.

Not long after returning to the townhouse, a slow, steady rain began to fall. In the afternoon, Helena sat in the window seat in the drawing room and watched the water form rivulets on the window. It muted the greens and browns of the square opposite.

She held a cup of tea in her lap but had yet to take a sip.

She rested her head on the window and closed her eyes. Unbidden, the sensation of John Barrington's arms about her waist came back to her, and with it a feeling of warmth and security… and longing. She allowed herself to bask in that glow for a minute or two, in the fantasy that she could grasp support and affection from someone strong and loving.

Helena jerked upright and opened her eyes with a start. Mr Barrington did not love others above himself. He'd admitted as much.

And yet, when he looked into her eyes, he'd convinced her that he sensed her need for comfort, and he wanted to be the one to give it to her.

"He doesn't know what he wants," Helena murmured to herself.

She had very nearly allowed her heart to be touched by him. Now, she had removed herself from the threat… for a time, at least. She would remain here while she renewed her strength.

"A penny for your thoughts?"

Helena jumped, and some tea splashed into her saucer. It would be cold by now. "Nothing of consequence," she replied to Jane. She stood and took her tea over to the low table. "Shall I order some more refreshments?"

Jane joined her and they sat on the sofa together. "If you wish." She smiled at Helena, a knowing smile. It was the kind of smile that made Helena wonder if her companion could read her mind.

She hoped not. What a treacherous mind it was.

❧⊷❦

As winter closed in further, John began to fall into something of a routine. He groomed Thora daily, even when conditions did not permit riding. Especially then. When the weather allowed, he made an inspection of his lands.

He read and re-read the newspapers. When he'd exhausted every book in the house's small collection, he turned to studying the previous accounts and records of the estate.

He'd never been enclosed like this over winter. Usually, he'd be on a hunting and shooting tour of sorts, staying with various friends and having them visit him at Ashworth in turn. As he didn't know where any of his acquaintance would be at present, there was no point in writing to them.

Instead, he took to writing to Catherine at least twice a week. He described his surroundings and apprised her of all he'd experienced thus far… well, not *all*. There were some things he was reluctant to admit even to himself.

There was no reply. Perhaps the family was travelling, or she and Louisa had gone to stay with friends or family. Or perhaps… she had refused to read his letters. His dear sister. John's last memory of her was that haunted look in her eyes, a silent promise she would never forgive him.

After some weeks, there was finally some mail – a thick dispatch from Amberley. He snatched it up eagerly and ran up to his bed chamber to break open the seal. Contained within was a bundle of letters from his friends, who assumed he still resided at Ashworth. Impatient for news from Catherine, he turned over every sheet in anticipation. But there was nothing from his family, not a single note enclosed. The snub cut him deeply.

He pored over the letters, which were all similar in nature. How did John get on, why had he not been in touch, could he come to their estates for sport?

He set about deflecting them as best as he could, hoping not to cause offence. He explained he was in Hampshire, on urgent business relating to his inheritance. He regretted he could not issue a reciprocal invitation. His accommodation was too basic in comparison to theirs. There was only one spare room of a decent size, and he lacked the personnel and hunting animals to make sport possible.

He knew not how much the party gathered at Willowbridge for Christmas had heard some of his altercation with Lady Helena, but the abrupt manner of his leaving was enough to make him reluctant to engage with any of them. There would be questions asked, and they would undoubtedly side with their patroness.

In the long winter nights, he had only his conscience for company, and it made for a tortuous bedfellow. Regret and guilt weighed heavy on his soul in the dark and deathly quiet. His deficiencies and longings wound tighter and tighter in his chest until he trembled violently, sweat drenching his sheets. He would usually wake with a parched throat and an aching body.

He could not remain a recluse forever. He needed to go to the village when Thora needed new shoes, to procure more paper and ink, or to have his coat mended. On one such occasion, he happened upon Mr Harding in the shop.

"Good day, Mr Barrington."

John jumped at the sound of his name. "How do you do, Mr Harding?"

They shook hands, and both men went about concluding their transactions with the shopkeeper, remarking on the weather and the state of the roads.

Harding turned to John as they left the shop. "Care to join me for some luncheon at the public house? I've a craving for one of the cook's mutton pies."

John's need for company outweighed his uneasiness. "Yes, I shall. My thanks."

Once they were settled in at the establishment, and their meals served, Harding wasted no time in giving voice to the awkward subject.

He swallowed a mouthful of pie and cast a bemused smile at John. "Well, young Barrington, I have rarely seen Lady Helena so heated as at the Christmas party. I would love to know what provoked such emotion, although of course I am far too polite to pry."

John broke into a smile in spite of himself as he met the doctor's kindly eyes. "I do apologise for my conduct, sir. I assure you had no intention of provoking her. She is… an interesting woman."

"Indeed, and usually quite rational. I do not think I've heard her shout at anyone before. It caused quite a stir."

John reddened, pulling at his cravat. "Was she, er, in good spirits, afterwards?"

Harding considered this. "I could not say. She was with Miss Godwin for a time, and then on her return to the party she announced her intention to prepare for a removal to London. Quite unusual."

John knew not how to respond, giving his attention to his stew. In his mind, he recounted the words that had passed between himself and his blonde accuser. He remembered the fire in her beautiful blue eyes.

Harding did not press him further, but after a lengthy silence, John was somehow compelled to explain.

"Lady Helena has views – strong views – on my lack of participation in local offices."

The doctor nodded. "Does she, indeed?" He ruminated a moment before continuing, seeming to choose his words with care. "You are not long resident here, so it is reasonable for you to take some time to find your feet."

"Thank you, sir –"

"However, when you have become more familiar, you will see that our patroness is extremely devoted to her service of Mulberry, to an extent that she may work herself into an early grave. She takes on far more than she ought. So… if she should offer to have someone else assist, I should think that person should be gratified."

John stared at him, feeling much like he would after his father had given him a dressing down. Harding went on.

"It also rather speaks of her estimation of your talents. She would not ask for help from anyone she thinks unworthy."

"Is that so?" said John, trying to quell the hope rising within him. "You know Lady Helena quite well."

Harding nodded. "Practically all her life."

"And you have never considered helping her… by asking for her hand?"

The doctor's eyebrows flitted up, and then he laughed. "Goodness me, no! I'm old enough to be her father. Lord Davenport was a great friend of mine; God rest his soul. I am, in point of fact, her godfather."

"Ah, I see. Jolly good."

"Besides, Lady Helena once told me she has no intention to marry." He regarded John thoughtfully. "Of course, I wonder if she is yet to meet the right man."

Colour began rising up John's neck, and he hastily cleared his throat. "Perhaps I might join a parish meeting at some stage, as a beginning."

Harding nodded approvingly. "Just so. I knew you were a reasonable kind of chap."

John smothered a laugh. Why would he think that?

"Naturally, the parish vestry will not meet again until Lady Helena's return."

He smiled and returned to his luncheon. The remainder of the meal passed pleasantly enough.

When they exited to the street and shook hands, Harding kept hold of John's hand for a moment longer.

"I know not of your struggles, my boy, but sometimes the best way to ease our mind is to put our energies into others."

John's breath caught in his throat. There was something so genuine, and yet so knowing, in the man's gaze. It was as if Harding could see right through him... or would, soon enough.

He gently pulled free from the man's grasp. "You are too kind," he uttered, before fixing his hat on his head and dropping into a hasty bow. "Good day."

❧

Helena had no intention of widely socialising while she was in London, but she could not refuse an invitation from her mother's friend, Lady Lockhart. It was for a soirée at her house, which would include entertainment and dancing.

It had been quite some time since Helena had readied herself for an event with people of Quality. She surveyed her worn dresses anxiously. "I'm afraid none of these will pass muster," she said to Jane.

"I'm sure we could work wonders with a lovely shawl and some pretty jewellery," Jane said encouragingly. "Unless..."

Helena turned to her. "Unless?"

Jane drew in a breath and took Helena's hand. "Your mother's gowns. I am sure she would have wanted you to have them."

Helena gripped tight to Jane's hand as the room seemed to spin.

"Mama's?" she whispered.

Jane nodded. "Why not give them a purpose? It would not dishonour her memory."

The late Lady Davenport's room had been left exactly as it was when she lived. There had been no discussion of Helena using her gowns during her season – she would do nothing that might cause her father pain. And now he was gone, and she could not obtain his permission, wouldn't it be wrong?

"Come, my dear." Jane gently guided her from the room. "Both your parents would have wanted you to look your best, do you not think? Your mother had dresses she hardly wore." They walked down the hallway towards her parents' suites. "Granted, they would not be the height of fashion these days, but she had impeccable taste."

Tears welled in Helena's eyes as they came to the door of her mother's chamber. "Yes," she said thickly. "She chose my father."

And so it was that Helena was announced into the party at Lockhart House in a dazzling gown of the palest blue, and a soft grey stole embellished with fine embroidery. Jane had added a few hasty stitches here and there where the fit of the dress was not quite so, but in general it complimented Helena's figure perfectly.

And instead of the notion that she was trespassing somehow by wearing it, Helena felt she was embraced in her Mama's care. It was as if her mother's strength was present in the fibres of the fabric, and Helena entered the room with confidence, poise, and serenity.

"Oh, Helena, my dear!" Lady Lockhart crossed the room to greet her, taking her hands and dropping a kiss on each cheek. "How lovely you look."

She took Helena about the room, reminding her of those she had previously met, and introducing her to several new people. There were a few gentlemen who took up her hand as they bowed, and she braced herself for an evening of potentially tedious overtures.

Thankfully, her hostess ended her tour with a group of young ladies, her daughter among them. They chatted excitedly about the season ahead: the new fashions, which high-ranking gentlemen were still unmarried, and the date of the first ball at Almack's.

Helena smiled and nodded, adding an "indeed?" or a "to be sure," when required. She was relieved when it was time to go through to the ballroom for the musical entertainment.

A string quartet played Haydn and Beethoven for nearly an hour, during which time Helena was able to relax and lose herself in the music. She acknowledged that town did have its share of delights if one were willing to play along with society's games.

She remained near young Lady Lockhart when it was time to seek refreshments, but she was approached by some gentlemen asking for a place on her dance card. She had no card, but politely agreed to dance with each of them in turn. Her only alternative would be to sit with the gossiping matrons at the side of the ballroom while her female acquaintances were claimed by their suitors. She had no wish to submit to well-meaning interrogations regarding her marital intentions or lack thereof. She only hoped she could remember the dances well enough.

As the string quartet returned, the first gentleman came to claim his dance. She held no illusion of her beauty or charms having enticed him to her side. The other young ladies gathered were in the flush of youthful blooms, and far more inclined to flirt. No, it was her status as an heiress that would have been spread about the drawing room from the moment she had set foot in it.

The man was of average height and looks, and his top lip glistened with sweat when he rose from his opening bow. He was young, perhaps only five-and-twenty, and previously unknown to her. His conversation was nervous and sparse, and the two dances would have passed by easily, had he not been inclined to step upon her feet.

Helena remembered her next dance partner from her previous season. He raised an eyebrow at her from where he stood across from her in a line of gentleman.

"Still unmarried, Lady Helena?"

She blinked, her mouth open in shock. Was this his idea of flirtation? While the manners of her country friends may be simple, they at least had tact and decency.

As they began to step through the figures, she retorted, "I may well ask the same of you, Sir Peter."

He guffawed. "Ah, there's that independent spirit. I recollect it well."

Independence and frankness were not among the desired feminine graces, and well Helena knew it. Sir Peter's dance steps were faultless, showing off his lithe figure handsomely, and Helena was aware they probably made an attractive couple as she had been told in the past. For many young ladies desperate to secure such a husband, that would be enough to have them hanging on his every word.

But not for her.

Helena honoured promised dances with three further gentlemen, and then asked for the use of a carriage to take her home.

Lady Lockhart embraced her regally. "Dear Helena, must you leave so soon?"

Helena smiled at her gratefully. "I have had a wonderful evening, my lady, but I am not used to keeping late hours."

Lying in her bed a while later, sleep was elusive. Her head thrummed with the rhythms of the music she'd moved to, and her spirits sagged from the effort of maintaining social appearances.

But more than that, there was a nagging feeling, which embraced the edges of her heart and persistently begged her to take notice.

It was the sensations of joyful abandon, delicious freedom and, yes, thrilling infatuation she'd experienced the last time she'd danced in Mulberry, with John Barrington. How much of a contrast that was to the emotions, or lack thereof, she'd suffered through when she danced tonight.

She recalled that dinner with the Sinclairs, how her cousin had provoked her and how weary she'd been. Then, for no apparent reason other than to buoy her spirits, Mr Barrington had insisted she dance with him… and his efforts had succeeded. Perhaps there was some good in him after all? Unless it was all a ruse in order to somehow take advantage of her good will.

She sighed and rolled over in her bed. She was supposed to be here to forget about him, and the weight of her responsibilities. Why could she not keep him from her mind?

Their last encounter on Christmas night plagued her thoughts. Her righteous anger had almost subsided, replaced with a good deal of embarrassment. In accusing him of amorality, it was she who had spoken unkindly. She supposed her ridiculous challenge of his gentility was a vain attempt to push him away, to fight her growing attraction to him.

She rolled over the other way, groaning. How was she to exist alongside him now with any degree of dignity?

She'd behaved badly. In the morning, she would try to put things right.

Chapter Sixteen

John mulled over his conversation with Harding as he ate his dinner alone. The doctor's view was an interesting one: that Lady Helena had been asking for his help – whether consciously or not. And that he should take it as a compliment rather than a criticism. Still, her words rattled around in his brain.

Your ring... What is the meaning of it?

He observed the object in question, the way the candle's flame set the onyx alight. It had been a gift so precious – but was it now holding him captive in the past?

In some ways it was a ring around his heart: stopping love from getting in or out. Squeezing it unbearably, reminding him of his unworthiness. Yet, he couldn't bear to take it off, because it also told him that he was, perhaps, loved once.

He ached with a desire for human connection, for acceptance. He still burned with the humiliation and agony of his rejection. Above all, he wanted to be loved for who he was – but he didn't even know who that was anymore. He didn't like himself, so how could he expect anyone else to? He wasn't worthy of love... certainly not worthy of someone like Lady Helena. He was a failure as a man, as a human being.

His thoughts were interrupted by the sound of the Morgans chatting away in the kitchen as they ate their dinner. Their conversation with punctured with exclamations and laughter. John had never been jealous of servants, but now his heart was tinged with that uncomfortable emotion. Oh, to have some company.

After many weeks of silence, John at last received a letter from Catherine. He ran up to his bed chamber and carefully broke the seal.

My John,

He broke into a grin at the familiar greeting, his muscles relaxing somewhat. It wasn't "my *dear* John", but it was an acknowledgement of their previous closeness.

I have so enjoyed reading your epistles. I was reluctant to receive them at first, but in my heart I knew I could not ignore you forever. I wish that dreadful episode had never occurred, so we could go on as we always did. I miss you so.

"And I miss you, dear sister," John murmured as he sank into his chair. She had been the one constant through everything, and now, the deprivation of her company was the worse punishment of all.

Catherine went on to describe how the family had spent their Christmas and the weeks that followed. Several relatives had come to visit, but she was already fatigued by the cold, damp weather.

Would she benefit from a change of scene? The idea dropped into his head, and he latched on to it. He couldn't leave Mulberry, but surely she could visit?

He immediately penned a letter. It was selfish, perhaps, to beg her to come to ease his loneliness, but he'd take good care of her. He would prove himself a good brother after all.

He responded to each point in her letter and concluded with his invitation.

Do ask Papa if you may visit, my darling sister.

That Sunday, his wretched solitude finally got the better of him. He dressed with care, and made his way to Mulberry's church service. Many eyes were on him as he entered the quaint building and made his way up the centre aisle. Finding a seat next to Mr Pike, he ignored the stares, assuming his practised air of refined indifference.

The service itself was fairly typical, and John went through the motions. The vicar spoke kindly, as a doting grandfather might. His style was in stark contrast to the impassioned teaching of Mr Brook in Amberley. That man was too astute for his own good.

Mr Powell rested his weight on a cane as he bid farewell to the parishioners at the rear of the church.

"Good day to you, Mr Barrington."

John shook his proffered hand. "And to you, Mr Powell. I do hope you are in good health?"

"Aye, I thank you." He exchanged a glance with his wife. "But we do miss our benefactress dearly. Mrs Powell and I are simply not up to the task of caring for our flock these days."

"Oh?" John had not expected to be on the receiving end of a confessional. "Well… why do you not hire a curate?"

Mr Powell shook his head. "We are but a small parish, sir. The tithes…"

"Ah." John considered, and opened his mouth to speak again, but was intercepted by the woman behind him, who was impatient to confer with the vicar.

John moved away, a little relieved he had been stopped from making any commitments he may regret later. Making his way out into the churchyard, he prepared to exchange pleasantries with Mulberry's gentry.

As John attended to the little trivialities arising from managing his tenants that week, he was reminded of how Lady Helena took a deep interest in her tenants' lives. He didn't know the first thing about the circumstances of the Ashworth tenants in Amberley. It had never occurred to him to wonder about it. Why should he when it would never be his lot to manage them? But now, he could conceive of how Lady Helena derived satisfaction from looking after her community, almost as a shepherd tends his flock.

At his next meeting with Mr Wilson, he abruptly asked, "What do my tenants need?"

The bailiff regarded him over his glasses. "Mr Barrington, we've already discussed the state of your finances. There is precious little to spare…"

John shook his head. "No, I don't mean money. I mean help. What about the man who looks after the home farm?"

"Carter?"

"Yes, Carter. Has he a family?"

"Aye, sir. A wife and four wee ones."

"Do they need anything?"

Bailiff regarded him, dumbfounded. Finally, he said, "I shall enquire with Farmer Carter on your behalf."

John nodded. "Very good. Thank you."

⌘

Helena's next invitation was from a dear friend, Laura Montgomery, with whom she had played often in her youth. Laura's family was long connected to the Davenports, and they frequently visited with each other. Helena and Laura had a kind of bond where upon they could tell each other secrets, be their honest selves, and never stand upon ceremony.

They had made their debut into Society together, and by the end of the season Laura was betrothed to a man who suited her in temperament and breeding. And then, the friends' lives began to diverge.

They had written to each other often, and Laura had visited Willowbridge as a newlywed. This was the first time they had seen each other since then – and Laura had become a mother in the meantime. The frequency of her letters had subsequently decreased.

A butler showed Helena into an elegant sitting room, and there was Laura with a baby playing about her feet. The room was tastefully furnished in the modern style, and the draperies coordinated perfectly. Laura did always have an eye for colour, and here she'd had the resources to use her talent.

"Lady Helena Davenport," the butler announced, and when Laura rose and turned to greet her, it became obvious she was with child again.

"My dear," exclaimed Helena, "you didn't tell me you are expecting another!"

They embraced tenderly.

"No dearest, I know how busy you are, how many demands you have." She gestured towards the sofa. "I didn't want to bother you."

"Nonsense! I have few friends like you. I desire more than anything to be your confidant and support."

Laura scooped up her baby girl and then settled next to Helena.

Helena smiled as huge round eyes found hers. The little face was framed with wispy hair, and a sweet little nose emerged from two impossibly pudgy cheeks. Her arms and legs practically demanded to be squished.

"Hello, Agnes," Helena said softly. "How old is she now?"

"Fourteen months. We expect she'll walk any day now."

"Oh, my." Helena pulled her attention away from the child and back to her mother. "Has it been terribly hard?"

"In the early days, certainly. I wanted to nurse her myself, you know, and that has meant precious little sleep at times."

Helena nodded. "And now?"

"I have a night nurse and my mother visits frequently. Rex's mother too. Oh Helena, I shouldn't say such things. I am sorry."

Helena swallowed back the lump in her throat and shook her head to dismiss the apology. "Are they doting grandparents?" she managed to inquire with a smile.

"Oh, yes. In fact, I have never felt closer to Mama as I do now." She paused and reached over to take her friend's hand.

Helena gazed down at their hands and willed herself not to cry. It was just one of the many joys she would never know.

She knew her father would have loved to see a little child in the house again. He always made a fuss of any small visitors. Had she disappointed him with her choices?

Laura was living the life Helena should have been destined for, if she had had a brother to inherit Willowbridge. Now seeing her comfort in person, it would have been easy to envy her friend for the relative ease and happiness of her situation. Of course, what she did envy was her living parents.

If she *had* wanted to experience motherhood, would it not be less meaningful without her own mother to guide her? That could be a reason why the idea had never appealed. Perhaps she was afraid of venturing into unknown territory without a maternal mentor.

There was also the estate's precarious position. Would it be right to bring children into such a circumstance? It was all theoretical in any case – the main barrier to becoming a mother was of course the requirement to have a man take dominion over her. *No.*

"Would you be a dear and ring for tea?" Laura asked.

"Certainly." Helena complied with the request. "Is there anything else I can do for you?"

Laura smiled bashfully. "Would you take her, while I relieve myself?"

Helena laughed. "Why, of course! You should have said earlier." She sat back down, and Agnes was placed in her lap. Helena cradled her awkwardly at first, but then as Laura left the room the little girl wriggled closer against her and burrowed her face into Helena's chest.

Something shifted in her heart. Instinctively she bowed her head and inhaled Agnes's scent, her eyes closing at the unique and wonderous smell.

Then she tentatively put a finger on one of the chubby little arms, before gently stroking it. The delicate skin was so soft and silky it took her breath away.

Suddenly, Agnes began to whimper. Alarmed, Helena wondered how to soothe her. She stood and began to bounce her, but the cries only worsened until Laura burst back into the room.

She rushed over, her arms outstretched. "Shh, shh, shh, come to Mama." There was pure love in her eyes as she took Agnes into her embrace.

The loss of the child's warmth left Helena feeling strangely bereft.

Agnes's cries subsided as her mother caressed her tenderly. She stretched up to press a wet kiss to Laura's cheek.

The gesture was Helena's undoing. It could no longer be denied. She wanted to know that love for herself. More than wanted… *craved.* She turned away as the tea service arrived, swiping at the tears gathering in her eyes.

The friends settled into conversation as if they'd never been apart. It was three hours later when Helena rose to take her leave.

Laura saw her to the front door. "Will you not come and visit us in the country, my dear? Are you simply too occupied at home in the autumn?"

Helena opened her mouth, and then closed it again. Yes, she was well-occupied in Mulberry. But spending time with such a dear friend had soothed her soul. "This year," she said slowly, "I need to ensure things are right with the estate."

Laura nodded. "But next year?"

Helena smiled. "I would love to receive an invitation."

❧❦

On a bright March morning, John was surprised to find Mr Privett, Lady Helena's steward, on his doorstep. He ushered the man into the parlour and begged him to sit down.

"That will not be necessary, I thank you. My business will be brief."

"Very well." John waited with some trepidation.

Privett reached inside his coat and withdrew a letter. "I have this for you, from my lady. I do not know what it contains."

John's pulse jumped, and he reached for the missive.

But Privett withheld it, his eyes narrowing. "I want to ask something of you."

This was quite irregular. John straightened and folded his arms. "What is it?"

Privett looked him dead in the eye. "Give our mistress the respect she deserves."

John's eyebrows shot up, but he could see kindly affection for Lady Helena in the man's eyes. What did the steward know? Why should he issue a warning like this? It must be because of the Christmas affair.

He nodded, his hands falling to his sides. "I will do my utmost," he promised, and meant it.

The letter was duly handed over, and Privett saw himself out.

John closed the parlour door and sat in front of the fire, staring at his name on the outside of the letter, written in Lady Helena's elegant hand. Mrs *John Barrington*. He imagined the small but significant word in front of his name, and then scolded himself for conjuring up such a ridiculous notion. He broke the seal and began to read.

> Mr Barrington,
>
> I hope you will forgive me the liberty of sending you this letter. Even I, who have shunned polite society, am aware of the breach of propriety.

John smiled. His words; her wit.

> I shall not bother with needless pleasantries. I would rather come directly to my object. I am sure you have long forgotten our discussion on Christmas evening.

Forgotten their discussion? It was constantly in his thoughts!

> I know not of your past, of what you have endured. I know not why your priorities have been so different from my own. Nor is

it my right to know what has brought you to Mulberry, alone, at this point in time. And thus, it is not my right to question your actions or your motivations – and certainly not your character. For that, I offer my sincere apologies. I like to think of myself as charitable, and yet my manner towards you has been far from that.

John shook his head. Did she forget how she set a place for him at her festive table, uninvited?

I do not wish to behave in such an unladylike manner again, and thus I am taking some time to return to an equilibrium. As you have observed, I have lately been overwhelmed by the monumental task before me, as well as the proliferation of little tasks. Indeed, you seem to have discerned more than I have myself. I remember you once offered me help, and I did not know how to receive it. Perhaps, in the future, I shall set my pride aside. I am sure you have much to offer.
I do hope to obtain your good opinion. Can we be congenial neighbours in the future? Please accept my best wishes for the health of yourself and your family.

Yours,
Lady Helena Davenport

John fell back into his chair, closing his eyes against a rising tide of emotion. She was everything good and generous. His heart turned over, and he knew he was in danger. Not close to, or within sight of – but in real danger… of falling in love with her. He, who was so undeserving.

He was sure he had seen admiration in her eyes, too. Even if he were able to romance her, she would abandon him the moment she learned the truth.

Little did she know, her original instinct to distrust him was correct. He possessed a heart so dark it would overshadow her bright one. She wanted to gain his good opinion? He laughed bitterly. It was he who would need to do the earning. And by God, he yearned to do just that.

He'd vowed to never change himself for a lady. In fact, he'd been determined to avoid them altogether. What was happening to him?

She was right: she knew almost nothing about him. And yet, her letter was the epitome of honesty and candour. Did he deserve her confidences? And what could he give her in return? Surely anything he could tell her would only lower her opinion of him.

Against his better judgement, he sat down at a little desk in the corner and found a sheet of paper. It would be rude not to reply, would it not? But how much of his feelings to put on the page? A myriad of phrases passed through his mind as he re-cut his quill pen. How could he even send her a letter, when he was not acquainted with anyone in the household save for two unmarried women? Just before his nib touched the paper, a solution came to him.

As John poured wax on the joins of the paper an hour later, he made a decision. He very much doubted her assertion that he had a lot to offer – but he would help her, and her Mulberry, as much as he could. And if that meant reaching out to those whom he would previously consider below his notice, then so be it. The time had come to look beyond himself. He was sick of his own company, his own needs, his own desires, his own thoughts. With Lady Helena as his inspiration, he would take steps toward giving of himself.

Maybe if he did something good here, it could atone for some of his mistakes. Well, not his biggest mistake. That could not be undone. He knew it would haunt him and especially his victim forever.

He pressed his stamp into the wax with determination. He would not wait a moment longer to begin.

❦

It was not long before Helena tired of the London lifestyle. Indulgence and self-absorption were unnatural to her. She jumped at the chance to attend a charity function in aid of accommodation for disabled returning soldiers. There must be something she could do to help.

The event was at a fashionable tea salon in Knightsbridge. Helena and Jane were shown to an elaborately decorated banquet room with a small stage, rows of chairs, and tables laden with a variety of food and beverages. The chatter of those already gathered filled the air. There was no outward sign of the cause they were supporting.

The ladies found a registration desk, and Helena enquired, "Where do we learn of what we can do?"

"Do?" the woman replied with a laugh. "Why, you must bid on one –

at least – of our delightful items in the auction. Here you are." She handed them a printed list. "You'll find the objects on display at the back of the room."

Helena nodded slowly. "Thank you."

As she and Jane moved away, she whispered to her, "Money. That is all they want?"

"That seems to be the case," Jane said with a smile. "And there is nothing wrong with that."

"No… but the true joy of charity work is in the work itself, would you not agree?"

"Certainly. And many of these ladies likely do engage with the work. Only not today."

Helena smiled back at her. "You are too good, my dear friend." They strolled to the large display of available items. "I daresay buying lovely things is the preferred method of contribution."

It was a good thing Helena had no desire to purchase a new vase, or chair, or painting, for she had no money to buy them with. She observed each object with disinterest. That is, until she came to a beautiful evening dress. In the softest shade of pink, it was overlaid in sheer gauze netting, which was itself embroidered in delicate silver thread. She gasped as she ran her fingers over the exquisite lace which framed the bodice. She'd never seen such quality. It was so fine it might float away on the wind.

She was suddenly aware of Jane staring at her, and she dropped her hands to her sides with a sheepish smile. "Exceptional, is it not? I would never have occasion to wear such a dress!" She glanced down at the suggested auction bid, and hastily moved on.

They settled themselves at a table, and were soon joined by other ladies, whose ages looked to range from Helena's to Jane's. Helena fingered the patched-up neckline of her day dress as she gazed at the refined fashion of the other ladies. Did they think her inferior?

The women all seemed to know each other, and after they had politely introduced themselves, became absorbed with talk of their husbands and children. Jane poured Helena a cup of tea and they sipped as silent observers.

That is, until the lady next to Helena addressed her. "What of you, Lady Helen? Who is your husband?"

Helena cleared her throat, returning a slice of cake to her plate. "I have no husband."

"Oh." Looks of confusion and pity were directed at her from around the table.

Jane spoke up. "Lady Helena is heiress to the Willowbridge estate in Hampshire," she said with pride.

"I see!" said the adjacent woman. "How fortunate you are."

There was a brief silence, and then the conversations of domestic bliss resumed. Helena jammed the cake into her mouth and wished for the event to be over. Could she slip out before the auction?

After what seemed like an appropriate duration, Helena rose, dabbing at the corners of her mouth with a napkin. "Jane, shall we –"

"Come, come, ladies. It is time for the auction to begin." The lady from the registration desk had appeared at that precise moment and began ushering Helena and Jane to the chairs in front of the stage. Rather fortuitously, Helena found herself sitting next to Lady Lockhart. At least she wouldn't have to explain her situation again.

There was a short talk on the plight of the returning soldiers before the auction commenced. Object after object were brought to the stage and bids flew around the room. When the evening dress appeared, the last item, Helena bit her lip. She shouldn't want something so frivolous, and yet she did. She'd get over it soon enough. Lady Lockhart was of the same taste it seemed, as it was one of the items she won.

As the applause died down and ladies began to mill about again, Lady Lockhart turned to Helena with a smile. "Nothing to tempt you, my dear?"

Helena gave a little shrug. "I do not have cash in my possession," she said, feigning ignorance of the clearly displayed auction terms. Winners were to be issued with an account to settle later.

Lady Lockhart regarded Helena kindly. "I perfectly understand. I was not always so comfortable. Were it not for my marriage, heaven knows what would have become of me. I had a good name, but little else."

From her other side, Jane whispered that she would seek further refreshment. Helena nodded and returned her attention to Lady Lockhart, desperate for something like maternal advice.

"I do not mean to pry…"

"Nonsense, Helena." Lady Lockhart patted Helena's hand. "You may ask me anything."

"Thank you. Is yours, er, a happy marriage?"

Lady Lockhart's eyebrows rose a fraction. "We did not marry for love, if that is your meaning. But we have come to a mutual admiration and fondness. Now I miss Lord Lockhart if we are parted. He gave me my precious children and has always taken good care of me."

Helena considered this, wondering if the care was related to financial needs or otherwise.

"Did you have to give him much property?"

Lady Lockhart studied her. "I see what is troubling you, my dear. I was not an heiress like you, so my dowry was the only asset my husband could take. It must pain you to think of legally giving up Willowbridge. Of course, had you a brother, the situation would be quite different."

She squeezed Helena's hand. "I think it will be a long and lonely road if you do *not* have someone to share it with. Your Mama would have wanted you to be happy. You need to examine your life and be honest with yourself – will keeping a tight grip on Willowbridge keep you content in all the years to come? Or is there a deeper felicity to be found?"

Tears pricked at Helena's eyes, and she embraced Lady Lockhart on impulse. "How kind you are, and how wise. Thank you."

They both rose. "If you need assistance, dear girl, do let me know. Write to me and tell me what you decide."

Helena smiled. "I shall." She found Jane and they were soon walking back home. Her thoughts turned to Mulberry, and the charity needed there. "I do worry that the vulnerable are not being well looked after in my absence," she said to Jane.

Little did she know, help was at hand from the most unlikely of sources.

Chapter Seventeen

"What am I doing here?" John muttered to himself as he arrived at the vicarage.

He rapped on the front door, and upon opening it, the vicar's bushy white eyebrows fairly hit the top of his head.

"What are *you* doing here?" the man sputtered. Then, remembering himself, "How can I be of service?"

John cleared his throat. "It is I who should like to serve."

"Serve?"

The man had a point. How could someone as depraved as John be of any help to a man of the cloth? Well, he could only but try.

"I'm aware Lady Helena would usually perform a good many services to assist you in your charitable endeavours about Mulberry. May I be permitted to fill the breach?"

"Oh, I see." Mr Powell stepped back and held the door open wide. "You had better come in, then."

John stooped to enter the house, being a good foot taller than the diminutive vicar. He could not remember having willingly entered a holy house such as this before. He held his breath as he crossed the threshold, but the sky didn't darken, and the ground didn't quake. In fact, the cottage appeared quite normal as he was shown into the parlour. Comfortable, even.

"I shall ask Mrs Powell to make some tea," the vicar said. "Do be seated."

"Oh, no, please do not trouble her," John begged. "If she is able to join us, I should like to know about any needs she oversees."

And so it was that the following day, John set out for the orphanage, laden with the week's leftovers from the village bakery. His nerves were on edge. He'd seen his fair share of poverty – in London it was rather hard to avoid it – but this was new territory. His conscience also nagged at him, that his own child brought about by his folly could well have been in such a place. But he pushed the thought down, not wanting to make the child real in his mind.

The baked goods were gratefully received, and his presence scrutinised with understandable curiosity. A swarm of children touched his clothes, and he tried his best not to shrink.

"This is Mr Barrington, of Mulberry Manor," the matron announced.

"Good morning, Mr Barrington," the children duly intoned.

"Er, good morning," he replied, making himself look at each little urchin. Their clothes were a hodgepodge of patched-up garments, but their hands and faces looked clean and their eyes bright. They were a variety of ages, most seeming to be less than ten years, and more girls than boys.

"The boys tend to find positions more easily," the matron explained.

Then, an older girl appeared, probably about thirteen. "That's Grace," the woman advised. "We normally wouldn't take one of her age, but her parents…" She gave a heavy sigh. "Their demise was quite unfortunate. The poor thing was in a desperate state."

He watched as the other children gathered around Grace, and she gave them all an affectionate cuddle in turn.

"Lady Helena was so generous as to provide for her."

He turned back to the matron. "What do you mean?"

"I only asked for a few old dresses and such – as they seem to be about the same size. But our kind patroness supplied her with everything she will need for a good year or two, from undergarments to coats."

John let out a breath as he realised *this* was charitable order Helena had transacted at Allen's that day. "I see. Lady Helena is very kind."

"Oh, yes. Such a blessing! She truly wants the best for each child. It saddens me to think she may never have her own…"

This comment had a surprisingly emotional effect on John. He swallowed. "The girl," he said, nodding towards Grace. "What will become of her?"

The matron shrugged sadly. "For now, she helps with teaching the children," she replied. "We are trying to find a position for her."

John considered this. "And if you do not?"

Her eyes met his gravely. "The workhouse, of course."

He nodded. John had never set foot in such an institution, but even he knew they were regarded as worse than a prison.

"What skills does she possess?"

"Her parents were in trade in Walford, milliners. She's a dab hand with a needle, and of course she can trim a hat splendidly."

A thought dropped into John's head. "Is she well spoken?"

The matron cocked her head. "As well as any country girl with a basic education. She can read and write and add numbers. She used to work in the shop, you know, so she needed to present herself tidily and serve the ladies."

Serve the ladies. "Indeed?"

John's head was full as he rode back to the manor. He whooped with joy when he saw a letter from Catherine on the side table in the hall.

Angling the page toward the light, he skimmed through her descriptions of visiting with friends and family, shopping trips and dancing lessons. Then, he found what he was looking for.

> Papa does not think it wise for me to visit you. The first objection is of course that a condition of your exile was no family contact. Secondly, he does not wish me to be away in a year which may determine my matrimonial fortune. He also assumes you do not have the staff to look after me properly.

John's heart sank to the floor. He quickly flipped the paper over to read the next line.

> I have, however, made a good case, telling him I will report back regarding your activities and the health of your estate. He has finally relented. I am allowed to visit after we return to Amberley from London.

"Hallelujah!" John fell to his knees, overcome with joy. She would be here, with him. A connection to his world, a sparkling jewel in the family crown. That is, if she was not engaged and occupied with wedding planning. Perhaps that was what Lord A assumed, and his permission was no more than a placation.

His mood darkened as he pictured admirers pursuing Catherine. No man was good enough for her. He'd had to deflect several unsuitable would-be suitors during her first season. Of course, he acknowledged that she should set up her own household one day. But the thought of her in a loveless marriage, or worse, pained him to his core. She must be happy. He must see her happy. But this year, she would be in town without him to protect her… a notion which distressed him greatly.

Above all things, he wanted to save his beloved sister from the same suffering he had endured.

❧❦

Helena returned from her morning ride and was greeted in the vestibule by the townhouse butler.

He received her hat and gloves, and then said, "Begging your pardon, ma'am, there is a man waiting for you in the drawing room."

Helena blinked. "A man?"

"Yes, my lady. A gentleman. Shall I tell him you are from home all day?"

"No, no, that shan't be necessary. I shall go up to change. Is Miss Godwin with him?"

The man nodded. "Yes. She ordered tea when he arrived twenty minutes ago."

"Very good. Thank you." Helena rushed up to her room, tugging at the buttons on her riding habit. Had she accidentally charmed a gentleman during one of her outings? She didn't recall doing so.

Ten minutes later, still fussing with a comb in her hair, she entered the drawing room to find a tall, handsome gentleman engaged in conversation with Jane. They both stood on her arrival, and the man bowed deeply.

Helena curtsied and introduced herself.

"Lady Helena, may I present Viscount Thorpe."

Helena indicated they should both sit. "How do you do, Lord Thorpe?"

"I am quite well, my lady, I thank you."

Helena took her place on the sofa next to Jane, a bundle of nerves.

"How may I be of assistance?"

"Fear not, my lady," said Lord Thorpe with a grin. "I have no designs on you. For that you need to look closer to home, I think."

Helena frowned. What impertinence was this? "Whatever can you mean?"

"Forgive me." He held up an appeasing hand. "Here you are. With his best compliments."

He reached over and handed Helena a letter. Her heart began to pound. Could it be…

"Thank you," she said, glancing down and turning the letter over to see the return address. "Ah. How came you…?"

"Barrington is a good friend of mine. He sent this missive to me, knowing I would be in town. He impressed upon me that everything is above board, and I need not worry for your reputation."

"I see." And yet there was his comment about having designs… What had Mr Barrington put in his accompanying letter to Lord Thorpe?

"Well," began the viscount, moving forward in his seat as if he meant to leave.

"Lord Thorpe, may I ask you a question?" Helena blurted out.

He sat back again. "Anything, my lady."

"You say you are a good friend of Mr Barrington?"

Lord Thorpe nodded and smiled. "Indeed, my lady. I have known him since our days at Oxford."

Helena hesitated, but then could not resist. "Mr Barrington wears a ring with a black stone. Who gave it to him?"

Lord Thorpe's obliging countenance immediately clouded over, and he shifted in his seat.

Helena waited.

"Well." The viscount met her eyes again. "It was an important person from his past. More than that I cannot say."

Helena nodded. "Thank you, sir. I greatly appreciate your kindness."

She rose and summoned the butler to show him out. She mulled over his answer as she resumed her seat.

It *was* an important person? Had the person died, or were they simply no longer important? It could not be the latter – Mr Barrington seemed to have an intangible bond with the ring, with whomever it was. It was obvious that the object was no mere trinket he toyed with idly. It meant something to him – the giver meant something to him.

Her curiosity was disconcerting. His past shouldn't matter to her in the least. And yet it did.

"I think I shall check on the dinner plans with Mrs Mead," Jane said, laying her embroidery down. "Do seek me out if you need me." She squeezed Helena's shoulder affectionately before leaving the room.

Helena took a deep breath and poured herself a cup of tea. His hand on the page was boldly done, but with care.

Lady Helena Davenport, of Willowbridge, Mulberry

She gazed at her name, the pen strokes almost a caress on the paper. Then she shook her head at her own stupidity and opened the letter.

Dear Lady Helena,

Please accept my deepest thanks for your letter. Under the circumstances I shall forgive your breach of propriety and now engage in my own subterfuge. You need not worry about Thorpe, tease though he might. I can vouch for his discretion.
It pains me to think that anything which has passed between us has caused you to be uneasy. I accept the apology you were so kind as to offer, but you were not the only one to speak brazenly that night. I too regret what transpired between us, and I am sorry to have provoked you so. We seem to be in the habit of causing each other offense. But as you have extended the proverbial olive branch, I am hopeful we can henceforth be at peace.

A great weight lifted from Helena's shoulders. She took a sip of tea and settled back onto the sofa.

No matter what I have been through, there is no excuse for disrespecting a lady, or for selfish behaviour. You were right to challenge me. Your words have caused me to evaluate my choices – to realise there has been choices.
You must know you are much admired in Mulberry for your goodness of heart, strength of character, and generosity of spirit. How could I think ill of you in the light of such

veneration?

It is I who have imposed; it is I who have fallen short. And it is I who must earn the honour of your good opinion. I may never be the perfect gentleman, but will you accept my commitment to try?

Yours, etc
John Barrington

Helena dropped her head back against the cushions and exhaled, closing her eyes. She'd been nervously waiting, hoping, for a reply from Mr Barrington, all the while telling herself it may never come. She knew not what she had expected his sentiments to be, but his words exceeded anything she could have hoped for. It seemed her harsh words, rather than causing him to despise her, had instead had a positive effect on his point of view towards her *and* himself. His change in attitude, a sense of pride falling away, could only but raise him in her esteem.

No matter what I have been through…

The words took Helena back to the day she'd been out riding and happened upon Mr Barrington by the stream, his head in his hands and shoulders slumped – a picture of desolation and defeat. And then he'd said, "my soul is beyond redemption". At the time the comment appeared to be merely an excuse as to why he didn't need to attend church, but now she recalled a haze of darkness in his eyes. "Good lord," she whispered, "what has he done?"

Shaking her head to free the unpleasant conjecture, she recalled instead the thrilling race on horseback which had then transpired. Not to mention the closeness of Mr Barrington when he had helped her dismount. Thrilling, indeed.

"Goodness gracious, Helena, pull yourself together." She drained the last of her tea and folded up the letter, slipping it into the pocket of her dress as she stood. There were more important matters to attend to, such as business arising from Privett's latest missive.

Despite this, it was not the steward's letter which she read over and over, and over again, before the dimming of the day.

⮞◆⮜

A week later, John received a letter from Viscount Thorpe.

There were the usual comments on the goings on at parliament, and the politics within his own family. Then just before closing off, he added in this note.

> You have chosen well, my friend. If you fail, may I be permitted to try?

John laughed, pleased with the former sentiment and amused by the latter attempt to rankle him. It was in a spirit of goodwill, the jocular spirit shared by all the bachelors he usually spent his time with.

Reading the line again, his mirth faded. Had he chosen Lady Helena? In the sense of choosing the one he wanted above all others? He could not say, but if he were to then he was almost guaranteed to fail. There would be another man, like Thorpe, who could love her with a clear conscience.

And yet, hope sprang up inside him. Her confidence in him spurred him on. Perhaps she'd seen something in him that no one else could.

Now that John had had his eyes opened to the needs of those around him, he could not stop. He tackled the requests of the Powells efficiently, and surprised himself when he enjoyed doing so. How had he not looked beyond his own privilege before? Why had no one told him the gratification of helping other people? They probably had, but it had fallen on unhearing ears.

He went back to Longdale Farm to check the repairs to the roof were still in order and see if they needed anything further. Mrs Granger opened the door of their cottage, her babe about her in a sling, and her mouth dropped open.

"Oh, it's you, sir! Is anything amiss? Jim's out planting grain with the lads and won't be back for hours yet. Oh! Bless me, are you wanting to come in?"

"Thank you, Mrs Granger, I shall."

John stepped inside the dim house, and once his eyes adjusted, he discovered three girls sitting at the table, two sewing and one churning butter. Four sets of eyes now regarded him with something like awe and fear.

"I've just come to check on the roof," he said as kindly as he could manage.

"Oh, it's just grand!" Mrs Granger said.

"See?" The eldest girl pointed above her head, and John observed that the roof was indeed holding firm. Then he was subjected to the same scrutiny as before.

He turned back to the mother. "I, er, thought to ask if I might, er, do something for you."

"Like what?"

"Well…"

"Could you check on our Bart?"

"Bart? One of your sons?"

"Aye. He's too young to help in the fields, but he doesn't want to stay here with his sisters. He should be about somewhere."

"Oh. Certainly."

John exited the house, frowning. His mission was to locate a small child. What if he couldn't be found? And what if he could? What was he to do with him?

He tied his scarf tighter about him as a blast of cold wind struck him. The sun barely shone in a dull, murky sky. And yet this boy had chosen to play outside. He could be anywhere.

There was no sign of him in the fields immediately beyond the cottage, and so John began to search in the assortment of outbuildings to the side and rear of the house. He poked about in the barn, the stables, a shed, and even the privy. Nothing. Concern began to flicker inside him.

"Bart? Where are you, Bart?"

There was a lull in the wind, and John discerned a sort of banging, tapping sound. He went towards it, around to the back of the barn. And there he happened upon a small boy, waiflike and barefoot, kicking a large stone around.

"Bart?"

The boy looked up and cowered on the sight of John.

He slowly approached. "No need to be afraid, boy. Your mama asked me to find you."

Huge brown eyes still regarded him suspiciously.

"My name's John. I live over the hill there." He pointed, then smiled. "I heard you don't like playing with your sisters."

"No!" Bart shouted. "They do silly things. I want to help Papa like my brothers."

John nodded. "I'm sure you will, one day soon. For now, how about you kick that to me?"

Bart looked at John, and at the stone, then grinned and nodded. He drew back a little leg and shoved the rock at John with all his might.

John ran forward to intercept it with his foot and sent it back again. The game continued until John noticed a long, straight stick nearby. "Toss it to me, will you?"

"Yes, sir!" Bart threw the stone with admirable force and John side stepped quickly to hit it with the stick. The boy giggled as he ran off to retrieve it.

The scene took John back to his school days, playing cricket in the summer. He couldn't remember his father ever playing with him in this manner, but if he ever had a son, he would. It had never occurred to him that he might have the chance to be a father.

Awareness hit John like a bullet. He did have a child. But he wouldn't have the chance to father them.

"Zounds!" John leapt aside at the last second as the rock came hurtling at his face.

"Sorry, mister!"

John retrieved the 'ball'. "Not to worry; try again."

After they each had a few turns with the stick, another was procured, and a raucous sword fight broke out. At length, John feigned an injury to his chest and fell back to the ground.

"You have me! You have me! I surrender!"

Bart pounced on top of him, kneeling on his chest and pinning him down with his stick. "I am victorious! King Bartholomew reigns!"

John laughed, truly laughed, with childlike joy. Was this the sort of thing that fathers would feel?

He decided the only proper way to remove said child from his person was to tickle him. Before long, Bart was writing on the ground and shrieking with glee. It was a wondrous sound, piercing to the centre of John's heart.

Collecting himself, John sprang to his feet and helped Bart do the same.

"Come on, lad. Let's take you back to your mother."

Shortly thereafter, he was thanked profusely by Mrs Granger for entertaining the boy.

He found himself saying, without any hint of irony, "I am happy to help."

His guilelessness shocked him. Had he ever been truly genuine with anyone, save for Catherine and Julie? Could it be he was starting to care about his new neighbours?

Ruminating on this as he rode home, he was surprised to discover that caring did not simultaneously mean some sort of pain. In fact, it was oddly freeing.

Chapter Eighteen

Helena and Jane strolled arm and arm in St James' Park, admiring a sea of daffodils. The sky was overcast, but winter's chill was fast fading. Many others were out enjoying the earliest signs of spring. They passed a large woman walking an impossibly small dog, a couple of advanced age shuffling among the flowers, and a pair of lovers on a bench, staring into each other's eyes.

"My dear?"

Helena pulled her eyes away from the serene twosome. "Yes, Jane?"

"Are you intending to remain in London over Easter? Shall I ask Cook to buy some lamb for the Sunday dinner?"

"Easter…" The time in London had fairly flown by. How could it be nearly April already? There was really nothing to be gained by staying longer. The change of perspective, and variation of company, had worked a restorative effect.

But now, in her mind's eye, Helena yearned for the sight of the daffodils which would be adorning the pastures of Willowbridge. She belonged there; she was needed. London had its diversions, but she longed for the serenity of Mulberry… for her friends and loved ones… for a certain pair of dark eyes.

"No." She turned to Jane. "No, we shall not stay. Pray enquire as to the state of the roads. I need to go home."

Two days later, the ladies were on their way back to Hampshire. They broke the journey to Mulberry with a night at a coaching inn in

Basingstoke. The following morning, as the carriage rumbled its way along the roads in the rain, Helena withdrew a small likeness of her father from her reticule.

She closed her eyes, and remembered the way he held her as a child on long journeys. She would sit on his lap and burrow into his chest, with his arms strong about her. He would often hum a gentle tune, and more often than not, she would be lulled into slumber.

Now, as she opened her eyes, tears rolled down her cheeks.

Jane reached over and took her hand, silently offering a handkerchief.

Helena gave in to her sorrow for a minute or two, before blowing her nose and taking in a deep breath.

"Jane, do you think he wanted me to have Willowbridge?"

Jane squeezed her hand before releasing it. "Of course, dear child. Why would you question it?"

Helena sighed. "Why did he make the terms so difficult?"

"I rather think he didn't want you to struggle and be burdened with a hard life on your own."

She nodded, the logic not helping with the anxiety she felt. "I miss him so."

"I know, my dear. I do too. He was a man without parallel. He would be so very proud of you."

Helena's eyes misted up again. "If I fail…"

"We will find a way to go on," Jane said quickly. "Precious though Willowbridge is, there must – there *will* be other parts of your life that will provide more fulfilment."

Helena didn't want to consider it. The last thing she wanted was to be a burden on someone else.

She must not fail.

❦

As John rose to greet the morning each day, he found himself with more motivation to breakfast quickly and set out from the manor. Without time to dwell on his insufficiencies, and with an increasing number of connections in the village, his general contentment improved markedly. He caught himself whistling cheerily on more than one occasion. He no longer suffered through appointments with Mr Wilson, instead taking a genuine interest in all the goings on and work to be done. The season's warmer temperatures only added to his gusto.

It began to feel like another life, far removed from his other one away from Mulberry. He was without his family, his friends, his usual amusements, but somehow, his resentment of that removal had faded. His acquaintances here were ignorant of his past, and that granted him a sort of freedom. He knew this would be temporary, that the worlds would collide at some point, but for now the distinction allowed him a measure of ease.

But something was missing… or rather, some*one*. His lovely neighbour was never far from his thoughts, or his feelings. He was certain his appreciation for her had increased during her absence, and he was unsure of how to behave around her, nervous to betray himself and embarrass her.

The suspense of how things would be between them increased as the days passed. How long did she intend to be away? Surely not for the whole season? Mulberry was not the same without her presence: gentle, yet strong. A lady of quality and beauty, whose main concern was the betterment of the lives around her.

She'd exposed him for the superficial cad that he was. He wanted to prove he could be more than he'd been, to make himself better for her. Even if she never saw him as more than a friend, the effort to show her his potential would be worth it. *She* was worth it. He was surprised to realise that now her opinion was the one that mattered the most, next to Catherine.

As he readied himself for church on Easter Sunday, he let his emotions carry him into flights of fancy. Would Lady Helena allow him to prove that he could be the one to support and help her? To love her? He adjusted his cravat and met his own eyes in the mirror. Hope and desire changed at once to conscience and unworthiness.

"You," he spat out, as if the very word was an insult. "You are not worthy of her."

As his state of mind continued to plummet, he considered not attending the service. Just then, Tom called out, inviting him to walk to the church with him.

He blinked hard, trying to bring himself back to the present. "Jolly good," he shouted back, reaching for his coat and hat as he left his bedchamber.

Half an hour later, he settled into his usual pew in the nave, with the widow Kendall adjacent. They entered into a typical conversation about the weather and the change of seasons, before John was suddenly rendered mute.

There, entering the pew on the opposite side of the aisle, was Lady Helena Davenport and Miss Jane Godwin. A tide of well-wishes flowed around them as they took their seats.

"Oh, it's Lady Helena," Mrs Kendall said, following John's gaze. "Her return will be celebrated by many."

"Indeed," John said. Miss Godwin sat almost directly in his line of vision to her employer, preventing John from really seeing her during the service. The last thing he wanted to do was expose himself by leaning in such a way…

He really did try to concentrate on the Easter message, but it was nigh impossible. As the various parts of the service proceeded, such as kneeling for prayer, standing for song, and taking communion, he glimpsed a blonde curl, or a slender hand, or the arch of her back. He could be in no doubt as to his infatuation with her. It was overpowering, exciting, enthralling… distracting.

At the conclusion of the service, he joined the orderly queue of parishioners making their way back down the aisle to greet the vicar and leave the church. He didn't dally with the Powells, eager to get outside and find her ladyship.

It was easy to spot her, as she was like a queen bee surrounded by her loyal workers. Clearly it would be a long wait before he could talk to her, but that afforded him time to admire her from afar.

She wore a dress of the palest yellow, akin to the shining hair which framed her face in soft ringlets. Her sea green spencer jacket brought out the matching shade of her eyes. Today, there was a radiance about her he hadn't seen before.

A glow emanated from those eyes, her smile, her very essence. She seemed relaxed and happy as she curtsied to some and embraced others. Her merry countenance brought a smile to his own lips.

She was so beautiful, and yet without any apparent awareness of it. She was perfection.

John politely deflected greetings from other parishioners as he drew nearer to her. After what felt like years, he was finally at her side. She turned to see who it was, her ringlets swinging with the motion.

On seeing him, her eyes widened and her mouth dropped open. "Mr Barrington! You're at church!"

He grinned at her reaction. No 'hello' or 'how do you do'. He waved his arm around at their surroundings. "So it would seem. Welcome home, Lady Helena." He bowed.

"Oh! Yes, um, thank you." She dropped into a curtsey, wobbling as she rose again.

He caught her elbow to steady her, a warmth beginning to circle around his heart.

"Are you pleased to be back?" he asked, his breath hitching when her eyes met his. He reluctantly released her arm.

She beamed. "More than pleased. Delighted."

"I must thank you," he said quietly, "for the honour of your correspondence."

Her cheeks coloured charmingly. "And the same to you," she said. The conspiratorial glint in her eyes set his pulse to racing. A secret with Lady Helena. How delicious.

He cleared his throat, eager to keep her talking. "How did you find London?"

A hundred emotions seemed to flash across her face. "It was precisely what I needed," she said at last.

He smiled. "I am glad. Although, you were missed."

❦

The power of intelligent speech completely abandoned Helena the moment she beheld John Barrington in the churchyard. Could it be that he was *more* handsome than when she'd last seen him? The curl of his hair, the breadth of his shoulders, and of course the intensity of his eyes caught her off guard. Would that she could read his thoughts.

She'd been overjoyed to see all her Mulberry friends again. But on seeing him, her world seemed to tilt on its axis, and she was off balance, but wonderfully so. She'd completely forgotten her manners, exclaiming in surprise at seeing him in this place for the first time. What had changed?

Then her curtsey, an abomination. The touch of his hand at her elbow, transfixing. Their eyes meeting, spellbinding. Sparks radiated through her whole being.

His mention of their letters had set her to blushing, infuriatingly. His words were now etched on her heart, so often had she read them. His praise, his humility, his promise to show her more depth to him. She wanted to begin that journey now, *now*. At this moment, she was consumed by his presence, and everyone milling about the yard seemed to fade away.

And now, he told her she'd been missed. She'd heard the same sentiment from most of those who had greeted her thus far, but from him, she hoped it was different. *By whom was I missed? You?*

"By anyone in particular?" she asked, and instantly regretted the words. He would assume she was flirting. Was she?

"By most, if not all, I am sure," he replied, and her heart sank. Perhaps she had made an error of judgement. Was her attraction unrequited?

She forced a smile and nodded, then cast her eyes to the ground, her skin colouring a deeper shade.

"The many you care for will have felt your absence most keenly." She wished he would stop speaking on the subject. It was clear he was not going to appease her ego. She looked past him, to where Mrs Kendall stood with her children. She should greet them and so excuse herself from further chagrin.

"And as for myself…" Helena held her breath as he paused. His words were soft, the deep timbre of his voice enveloping her. "I have never felt so closely connected to anyone after such a short time. I would have scarcely believed it possible, but my life here was not the same without you."

Her eyes flew to his and found no trace of irony, only admiration. She'd heard pretty words during her season and been untouched. But now she bathed in his sentiments as if they were the summer sunshine.

She took a breath, smiling shyly at him. "I too have –"

"Lady Helena! Oh." It was Mrs Kendall, and it was apparent that she'd belatedly noticed the intimate moment passing between Helena and Mr Barrington.

"How do you do, Mrs Kendall?" Helena greeted her, with only a slight tremor in her voice. "I hope you fared the winter well?"

Mr Barrington bowed to them both and took his leave. He seemed to take a degree of warmth with him, and Helena shivered.

She hoped he might return to escort her and Jane back to their chaise, but when she had at least concluded civilities with all her acquaintance, he was gone.

She began to slip back into her usual routines. On Monday she went to her regular meeting with Mrs Powell, preparing for a long list of unfulfilled duties.

"I do hope my absence was not too taxing for you," she said as she accepted a cup of tea.

"Not at all," Mrs Powell replied with a smile. "You may rest easy on that score."

"Oh?" Helena's teacup clattered down on to her saucer. "Who came to your aid?"

"Various members of the congregation came forward, notably Mr Pike and Mrs Kendall, and Mr Barrington, of course."

Of course? "Mr Barrington?"

"Oh yes, he was the first, and the most frequent. Such delightful young man – I wondered at his shyness to begin with."

Helena concealed a smile, knowing that Mr Barrington was not at all shy. He had some other reasons for avoiding contact with the clergy and its flock. And now, were those reasons no longer valid?

"Are you quite well, my dear?"

Helena blinked. She must have been frowning. "Quite well. Thank you, Mrs Powell."

Practically everywhere she went in the days following, she kept hearing about John Barrington's selfless deeds. He even appeared at the first vestry meeting, making it almost impossible for her to concentrate on the business at hand. Although he retained an apparent air of modesty, the other vestry members chipped in further evidence of his endeavours.

Who was this man, and where was John Barrington? Was he, somehow, suddenly – a gentleman? She stared at him in wonder as the meeting concluded. He caught her gaze and sent her a lopsided smile with a wink.

The gestures warmed her inside, making her feel inexplicably special. They also reassured her that he wasn't pretending to be someone he wasn't – at least, not completely.

She smiled and shook her head while gathering up her papers. There was still some mischief lurking beneath the façade of goodness… and he was still as complex as ever.

Walking home, she began to wonder if his recent actions were all a big joke at her expense. Why, the man admitted to not doing a single charitable act in his life. Was this all a charade to gain her favour?

The truth would come out, sooner or later.

❧

The land was coming alive again as John perused his estate. New life was emerging everywhere, from the butterflies in the air to the beasts in the fields. More flowers opened every day, and John even found himself whistling a merry tune as he led Thora through a carpet of bluebells in the woods one day. Had he ever really noticed the beauty of spring before?

More often than not, he'd stray over to the pastures of Willowbridge, and there was no point in trying to delude himself as to his motives for dallying there.

It was on the fourth or fifth day of meandering that he finally saw her as he approached the lake on foot. Lady Helena had her back to him, leaning up against a large chestnut tree. As he came around to face her, he saw she had both palms resting on the trunk, her head also tilted toward the bark. She did not register his presence at first, her expression seeming content and melancholy at the same time.

"Good day, Lady Helena." He bowed.

"Oh, hello," she said softly, as if she were somewhere else in her mind. Then she straightened, and then dipped into a curtsey. "What brings you to my gardens, Mr Barrington?"

"Oh! I, um…" He could not bring himself to invent a falsehood, nor to risk embarrassment with the truth. He pointed to the tree. "Does this specimen hold significance for you?"

Lady Helena gazed at the tree, her countenance becoming misty again. "My father adored this tree," she said. "When I was a girl, a swing hung from this branch." She looked to the bough above them, its new bright green leaves shining in the sun. "My father would push me higher and higher until I squealed." She smiled, then looked back to John. "I feel closer to him here."

John nodded, longing to bring her into his arms and take some of the burden of her grief. "Thank you for the honour of your confidence," he said finally, and he extended his arm to her.

She took it, and they began to walk towards the lake. "How has the winter treated you, Mr Barrington?" she asked.

"Tolerably," he replied, unable just yet to put words to how transformative the season had been. "It appears the frost is gone for good."

202

"Yes, and there's more baby animals by the day."

He looked over at her. "Your sheep?"

She grinned and nodded, an excited sparkle in her eyes.

"How is your lambing rate?"

"Most satisfactory."

"Capital! That is good news." Perhaps the estate would be safe in her hands, after all.

John paused at the edge of the lake. He gazed across the rippling waters to the island in the centre, then at a little boat tied up at the small jetty in front of them. He smiled as he decided it was the perfect plan.

"What is it?" she enquired.

John turned to her and gestured toward the boat. "This a golden opportunity to show you how gentlemanly I can be, Lady Helena."

She glanced at the boat and then back at him, rather dubiously. "Are you asking me to get in the boat with you?"

He grinned. "But of course. Is it seaworthy?"

She hesitated, beginning to regard him as if he were dicked in the nob. "I believe so. But –"

"Well, then." He stepped on to the jetty and reached for her.

She remained where she was and chewed on her lip.

He took a step back toward her. "I'm not going to drown you, my lady. I am a competent rower. And we are in full view of your house." He pointed. "Surely at least one pair of eyes will be upon us, should you be worrying your honour will be compromised."

At this she gave a little squeak, presumably of indignation. Perhaps it hadn't been gentlemanly to allude to such a thing. He turned back to the water. "When was the last time you visited the little island?"

She came to stand beside him, but it was some moments before she spoke.

"Not since I was a girl." A mistiness drew over her eyes as she regarded it. "Not since…" She faltered, and he realised he'd stumbled into another sensitive area from her past.

"Forgive me, my lady. I shall leave you to your solitude."

He bowed and took a breath to wish her good day.

"No," she interjected.

He waited.

"No, do not leave. I think I should like to go to the island again. And to show it to you." She stepped past him on to the jetty. "And I'll have you know, Mr Barrington, I am a competent swimmer." She turned back to him with an impish smile. "If you so much as put a toe out of line, I shall take myself back to shore."

Chapter Nineteen

Mr Barrington's laughter echoed around the woods. She glowed inside, pleased she'd amused him.

With quick strides he bounded onto the jetty and settled one foot inside the small vessel, steadying himself before extending his arm to her.

"My lady."

She placed her gloved hand in his, and then allowed him to grasp both her elbows while he settled her down onto the wooden plank toward the rear of the boat which served as a seat. He shrugged out of his coat, untied the mooring line, and took his place at the bow. Then he took up the oars and guided them into the crutches.

He grinned at her boyishly. "Shall we?"

She could not help returning the smile, nodding. While she'd been rowed about on the lake by her father as a girl, he was not so inclined to do so after her mother's passing. The island was a sacred place for both of them, often viewed from the shore. It was only the gardener who used the boat to get to it. She hadn't intended to visit it at this juncture, but she instinctually knew it would be easier with Mr Barrington by her side.

He pushed the boat through the water with broad strokes. While Helena was cognisant of the sun on her face and the water lapping at the hull, she was far more aware of the muscles of her companion's neck, arms, and shoulders as they tensed and flexed under the fabric of his white shirt. Heat began to crawl up her neck.

She chastised herself. This would not do. She looked away, focusing on a willow overhanging the lake. Gaining some more clarity, she realised this was the perfect time to quiz him about his apparent change in behaviour.

"Now, sir," she began, "you have some explaining to do."

Panic crossed his countenance, swiftly replaced by a nonchalant curiosity. "Indeed, madam?"

His troubled expression worried her. What was he afraid she would discover? There were so many things she didn't know. For now, she had to start somewhere. She looked upon him again, trying to ignore the way the dark curls of his hair shone in the sun's rays.

"I wish to discover why you have suddenly become a beacon of charity, after admitting you care not for helping those in need."

His arms ceased their movement, and he regarded her in such a way that reminded her of a nervous child at the orphanage.

"When I wrote to you," he said at last, "I said I wanted to prove myself to you."

She looked beyond her flattered feelings. "Could this all be an act to prove a point?"

"No indeed, my lady." His eyes flashed with indignance. "I shall admit the dressing down you gave me injured my pride. But your subsequent confidence in me, your encouragement to look beyond myself, and your example, spurred me on. I… have begun to change – for the better, I hope."

His countenance was free of guile, and he also seemed hurt or confused by her words. She wished them unsaid.

Mr Barrington looked over his shoulder and noticed they were drifting very close to the island. He manoeuvred the boat around, then leaned over to grab the rope hanging off the small landing platform. All the while, his expression remained miserable.

Helena felt something was slipping from her grasp. "I am sorry if I insulted you or misjudged your intentions."

He avoided her eyes as he helped her alight from the boat. She waited for him to join her on the platform and then continued, "You must acknowledge that it is astonishing for me to see such an abrupt change in your attitude."

He took a step on to the grassy verge of the island and slipped back into his coat. "Yes, and I think your rebuke was just what I needed to begin. In your letter, you said you thought I had something to offer, and I hoped that might be true."

She bounded in front of him. "Of course it's true."

"But it never occurred to me before. I have always considered myself somewhat… worthless."

She smothered a gasp, shocked at this admission from a man she had once thought arrogant. Could it be true?

Her heart ached for him as he stood there, downcast. She had the distinct impression they had just broken through an important wall.

She reached out a tentative hand and curled her fingers around his. "Why would you feel that way?"

He took in a ragged breath, and gently squeezed her fingers. He looked about them. "Is there somewhere we can sit?"

"Yes. I'll show you."

Low shrubs and carpet roses formed the island's perimeter. From the landing, they followed a path of grass and moss hedged with lavender on either side. It led to the main clearing in the centre, where blackthorn and cherry trees, thick with masses of white and pink blossoms, gave shelter to the folly. Rising from a circular base, six Romanesque pillars supported a dome. In the centre of the structure was a sculpture on a plinth – the bust of a woman. On either side of the clearing were curved stone bench seats, scattered with lichen. She led him to the nearest one and together they sat. Helena kept her hand in his.

Then he held his other hand before her, and she saw he wore the dark stoned ring over his glove on the little finger.

He turned to her. "You asked me who this is from. Was from."

His eyes flitted to hers and she nodded, half dreading the answer. Then she watched as the rise and fall of his chest accelerated.

"I did love once," he said thickly. "But she died twice: once for me and then again from this world." Tears emerged from the corners of his eyes.

Helena swallowed back her own. "Oh my, I am sorry. Was it… recent?"

He shrugged. "Oh… we courted about five years ago. She died last year. Just before…" He broke off, his face contorted with pain.

"Please do not speak more if it brings you grief. I had no business in prying."

He gazed down at their entwined hands. "I feel it is only right to tell you. My life began with a great deal of promise, of dreams. But when she abandoned me, I lost myself. I have been a shadow of a man ever since. But now…"

He met her eyes, his so filled with emotion that all breath left her lungs.

It became clear he could not give voice to these feelings. At last, she stepped into the breach. "Could there be some hope?"

He smiled tremulously, and another tear ran down his cheek. "My dear lady, if there was it would be due to none but you. Whatever happens, I am in your debt."

Whatever happens… What did he want to happen? What was the worst that could happen? She tried in vain to search his face as he looked about them, apparently taking in their surroundings for the first time.

"This is a very serene place," he said. "What is it?"

She took a deep breath and looked upon the statue fondly.

"This… monument… is my mother's final resting place," she whispered.

∽∘∾

John followed Lady Helena's gaze to a sculpted bust, the centrepiece of the folly. Except it wasn't just a folly. It was a memorial, to the very person who should have been this lady's guide and comfort.

He frowned, angry with himself. He had chosen that moment to heap his burden onto her, when he should have been sensitive to the weight of emotion she must be feeling in this place. Why hadn't he noticed the significance at first, or at the very least, asked?

He returned his attention to Lady Helena's profile. She still held his hand, and she knew not how much courage her touch had given him. It had allowed him to speak of the secrets of his heart. But now, he needed to be the one to provide comfort and care.

He placed his other hand on top of hers, as if embracing it in both his own. She turned back to him, her exquisite clear eyes etched with sorrow and vulnerability. How could he show her that she could trust him? Why should she?

He pushed his insecurities aside and rubbed the back of her hand with his thumb. "Do you visit often?" he asked softly.

She shook her head. "No, indeed. I have not been here since she was interred."

He began to sweat. Had he blundered into sacred territory, all in the name of getting closer to her? "What a clod I am, trespassing like this. Did you mind me bringing you?"

"No." She smiled; a placid, peaceful smile. "It is good to come again. My father couldn't bear it. He took such great care to enshrine her so beautifully, but his pain was too great to look upon it ever again."

He looked over to the monument. "Do I have your permission to approach it?"

She nodded, and he relinquished her hand as he let her lead the way. The delicate blossoms in the trees above formed a floral canopy to the structure, and those that had fallen made an ethereal carpet in and around it.

Lady Helena took hold of one of the pillars, as if not strong enough to hold up her own emotion. John wished he could be her strength. He examined the bust, and marvelled at how like her mother Lady Helena was. Even in marble, Lady Davenport was clearly a beauty. She held herself with dignity and grace... much like her daughter. How would John have fared if this formidable lady had been alive today?

"Do you remember much of her?" he asked gently.

She shook her head. "Not much at all. Although, when I was in London, I was reminded of being there with her."

He watched in silence as she took tentative steps inside the folly, right up to the sculpture. Her hand shook as she extended it to the face, and then she tenderly caressed the cheek.

She was still for a long moment, and then her shoulders slumped as she gulped in a breath.

She must be crying. John's heart reached for her, willing her to return to him so she would not have to bear this alone.

As if her heart had heard his call, she turned back around and closed the gap between them, her cheeks indeed stained with tears.

He opened his arms, and she hesitated for only a second before accepting his invitation. She slid her arms around his middle, pressing the weight of her sorrow against his chest and abdomen. He laid one hand on her back, just above her waist, and the other in the centre of her shoulders. His hand was on the bare skin below her neck, and as he gently rubbed his fingers across her spine, he wished he could touch her without being sheathed in the glove. Surely his warmth would soothe her more.

As she nestled into his chest with a hiccup and a sigh, he instinctively lowered his head to her, letting his cheek rest on the side of her neck. "She must have loved you very much," he whispered. "So very great a loss. Is there anything I can do?"

She shook her head, then tightened her hold. "Only this."

John's breath caught. She must mean he was helping in some small way. His embrace, their closeness, provided her with a measure of solace. The knowledge was enough to make his own eyes prick with emotion. What a privilege, to be given the honour of her confidence and her trust. And with the feel of her body fitting so perfectly with his own, it felt as if a kind of union was already taking place – that she was softening his heart, little by little.

And to his immense surprise, he had no selfish urges even though a beautiful woman had wrapped herself around him. It would be so easy to take advantage of her, but the very idea was repulsive to him in the purity of this moment. There was instead an unfamiliar and lovely surge of protectiveness, of wanting to stop her crying and somehow meet her needs.

She cared so much for others, and so little for herself. He had spent so long being an island, only tending to his own needs and desires, that seeing the world through her eyes was completely the opposite. He was wholly sensible of the treasure she was and, suddenly, aware of how undeserving he was to hold her.

He drew back sharply, and she stumbled, her eyes round with surprise.

"Forgive me," he said hastily. "I fear we are not in view of the house, and I have taken liberties."

"No," she said, frowning, "I –"

"Are you ready to go back?"

She stared at him, her eyes searching. Finally, she simply said, "Yes."

They returned to the boat in silence, and as John rowed his spirit was in turmoil. Had he now gone and closed the door she'd opened? If he had, it was probably for the best. But he was desperate to keep the tenuous connection alive. He thought back to their earlier conversation and her suspicion about his motives for being charitable.

He cleared his throat, and his heart skipped a beat as she looked into his eyes. "I am happy to admit that giving one's time in the service of others is quite gratifying."

She smiled. "Do you really think so?"

He smiled back. "I do."

"There, now. Do you see? Once you start helping others, there is no turning back."

"To be sure." He paused. "Will *you* accept some help?"

Her brows raised, but her smile remained while she tilted her head to the side. "Perhaps," she said, and to him it sounded something like a promise.

When they reached the jetty, John moored the boat and assisted Lady Helena ashore. Lest she think his recent withdrawal was a rejection, on impulse he reached for her hand and drew it to his lips, keeping his eyes fixed on hers. He paused while dropping the kiss onto her glove, giving her his own promise with his eyes. If she wanted him, he was here for her.

"Goodbye, my lady," he said at last, before he began the walk back to the manor. *Oh, that you were* my *lady.*

His mind and heart were in a whirl as he made his way through the darkening woods. A chill settled about him, a distinct contrast to the warmth of the sun, and Lady Helena, a short time before.

He could still feel the wonderful way her figure had melded into his, as if they'd been cast from the same mould. Even now, the force of the affection he felt for her startled him. Could he open his heart again, at the risk of its very destruction? Was it already opening?

More than anything he didn't want to risk hurting her. She may be beginning to trust him, but he couldn't trust himself. He was nothing more than a heathen, falling for a paragon of virtue. He was making a genuine effort to better himself, but could he ever be enough?

When he was nearly at the house, he was met by Farmer Carter mounted on his horse. The man nodded to John in an agitated manner.

"Is all in order, Carter?" enquired John.

"Aye, for now," Carter replied. "But d'you think you could help with gathering the stock? There's a storm on the way and we've new lambs in the fields."

"Of course, Carter. I'll return with Thora directly."

The man nodded an acknowledgement and then raised his eyes skyward. "They look like snow clouds to me."

❧

There was no wind at all; it was deathly silent. Thick snowflakes drifted down in eerie silence, engulfing the ground in soft yet freezing carpet. It was not yet wholly night, but now the impenetrable snow drifts made it almost impossible to see.

Snow in April was not unheard of, but Helena didn't remember it ever coming so suddenly and so violently. It had begun not more than half an hour after she returned home from the lake. Beginning to change for dinner in her bedroom, it was her maid that had observed the first drifts of snow passing by the window. Panic stabbed her heart. She knew the home farm, her future, was at risk. She turned to her maid and told her that her evening gown would not be required. Instead, she dressed as warmly as she could, donning her heaviest boots. All she would do was check all was in order so she could relax. She'd been full of emotions from the afternoon with John Barrington, but now all of that was pushed aside.

An hour later, she raised her lantern and peered into the descending gloom. She'd helped Adams escort the rare lambs and their mothers into the barn, and they both kept a tally. There were some missing, and no explanation for their absence. They would need to start again, scouring every square foot of territory. Adams went to get more help, telling Helena to remain where she was in the safety of the barn. But of course, that was impossible.

She searched about for a long stick, and once she located one, she moved slowly forward through the deepening snow, gently sweeping the stick over the ground. If there was something lost beneath the drifts, it should become apparent. With each step, the more her stomach churned with dread.

Another hour later, and her worst fears were confirmed. There was no sign of life in the paddocks the sheep had been in. In the pitch black, Adams called Helena to the fence line at the crest of the hill, and there he showed her the source of their trouble. The weight of the snow had caused a fence post to fail, taking down several palings with it. The resulting breach was wide enough to allow the stock to escape. The neighbouring field was vast, steep, uneven terrain – inhospitable even for animals.

Helena stared in horror. "They could be anywhere!"

There was a pause. "We'll find them, my lady. But I don't pretend they will survive long in these conditions."

Helena fought the urge to retch. "No, I don't suppose they will."

"May I suggest it is too dangerous for my lady to continue on?"

She took a breath, and asked herself what her father would do. "No, Adams, you may not."

"I thought that would be the case."

Some time later, Helena began to tremor involuntarily with the cold. She had rolled her ankle on rough ground, and her arm ached from holding the lantern aloft. She knew it would not have much more fuel left to burn. Tears had turned into ice on her cheeks. They would need to turn back.

"My lady?" At the sound of Adams' voice, she turned and followed his line of sight. Two bobbing sparks of light seemed to be approaching in the darkness.

"Lanterns?"

"Looks like it."

In spite of everything, Helena rushed forward towards the lights, stumbling and tripping as she went. As she came nearer, she made out the shapes of two horses and their riders. She waved her free arm frantically, praying they would see her through the white haze.

Mercifully, they came straight toward her, and when they came into clear sight before her, she recognised none other than Mr Barrington and Farmer Carter.

"John!" she cried, her mouth nearly numb with the cold. "What… why?"

"Lady Helena. I wanted to make sure your dear flock were all safe. And I have something for you."

She stared at him helplessly, then watched as he opened his great coat. Nestled within was not one, but two little lambs.

Helena gasped. "Are they alive?"

"Yes. They were in poor condition when I found them, but I think they will pull through."

"Oh, thank God! Did you see the mother?"

Mr Barrington nodded. "Carter has her."

Helena looked to Carter and saw him cradling the ewe. "My lady, we can't be certain she will live."

"Are the others all accounted for?" Mr Barrington asked.

She shook her head. "I think we have… lost… four."

By this time, Farmer Adams had caught up. "We'll keep searching for them on our return, my lady."

"We shall follow," Mr Barrington said.

"Thank you," Helena said to them both, which seemed wholly inadequate. She shifted her weight and her ankle failed, causing her to fall to her knees.

"You're hurt?" The sharpness of Mr Barrington's voice cut through the snow. She heard his concern.

"Just my ankle," she said, pushing back up to her feet.

"You must ride with me."

She stared at him. "But you have the lambs."

"Here." He wriggled forward in the saddle and offered a hand up.

Resigning herself to his protection, she let him take her weight, and in no time at all she was sitting astride behind him. She adjusted her skirts and shifted against him, the saddle pushing them tight together.

"Are you comfortable?" he asked over his shoulder.

"Yes," she replied, unsure of where to put her hands.

"Hold on to me with your arms and keep the lambs secure."

She threaded her arms under his and then clasped her hands around the bundles at his front. "Ready."

He nudged Thora forward, and she navigated the hill at a steady walk. Once they were over the crest and could make out the glow of the house, they moved through a trot to a canter. Helena squeezed her arms about Mr Barrington's torso, pressing herself tighter against him as he rose in the saddle. Even through his layers she could feel his strength and his warmth. Their bodies moved as one in rhythmic motion as he guided them to her home. Her ankle throbbed as it bounced against Thora's flank, and she could feel his sense of urgency as he navigated around and over the obstacles in their path.

They stopped at the barn where the lambs and their mother were given to a farmhand.

"I thank you both," Helena called to both men. "The snow is so deep now. You must stay at Willowbridge tonight."

She wrapped her arms around Mr Barrington's middle and gave him a grateful squeeze, his torso firm under her hold.

"That would be sensible," he said. "Thank you, my lady." He slid his free arm around hers and squeezed her back. And he kept her in this embrace as he urged Thora onwards through the thick drifts to safety.

On their arrival, a flurry of servants arrived to assist them. Her groom appeared to help her dismount and take the horses. Andrews was on the threshold and, after enquiring after her health, he sent footmen off to order food and a hot bath. Then he took her hat and coat, handing her a steaming cup. She drew from it deeply, then turned to Mr Barrington and Carter, who were awkwardly loitering in the doorway.

"Come in, gentlemen, and close the door!" she commanded. "Andrews, Mr Barrington and Mr Carter will need to stay with us tonight."

Andrews' eyebrows fairly hit the top of his forehead before he assumed his usual neutral expression. "Yes, my lady. I'll have rooms prepared for them at once."

"And once they are settled, please send up supper trays and have their baths filled, as well."

"Of course."

Jane appeared and enveloped her in an embrace of affection and relief. "Thank goodness you are home, my dear. Is all well? Oh." As she pulled back, she noticed their guests over Helena's shoulder.

Helena turned back to the men, wincing as pain shot up through her leg. She longed for her bed, and when she looked up, she caught the concern in Mr Barrington's eyes. She took a breath. "Is there anything else I can –"

"Lady Helena's ankle needs attention," he said to Jane directly, urgently. "In case she doesn't mention it."

Jane nodded, immediately taking Helena's arm. "Thank you, Mr Barrington."

He shook his head, smiling, and his eyes locked back on Helena's. All pain and discomfort left her as she drank in their tenderness. He spoke to her with equal sensitivity. "Please go now and get warm – and rest."

She should have been affronted by having someone give her orders in her own house. But instead, she felt protected and cared for. She nodded, weariness overcoming her. "I bid you sleep well," she said, returning his smile.

Chapter Twenty

The fire had begun to take the chill off the room, and John finally divested himself of his jacket and boots. A footman delivered a dinner tray, and while he tucked into pork, potatoes, cauliflower and parsnip, a couple of maids made a repeat pilgrimage with steaming water to fill the bath in the far corner. One blushed and dipped into a curtsey when John's eyes happened to meet hers on her way past. His lack of cravat and partially unbuttoned shirt was no doubt the cause of her embarrassment. In the past, he probably would have winked at her. But now, he had no inclination to tease. Now, his mind was only on one woman.

Half an hour later, he lowered himself into the hot water and rested his head back with a sigh. What an eventful day, and what a turn of events. When he'd persuaded Farmer Carter to come with him to offer assistance to their neighbours, encountering Lady Helena was the last thing he'd expected. What had she been doing out in that knee deep snow, halfway down a steep bluff? She was lucky to have escaped with only a slight injury. Were the blessed sheep worth her life?

The force of his protectiveness surprised him. How could he have only known her for five months? He would be bereft should anything tragic happen to her. But did he have the right to ensure she was safe?

It was Miss Godwin's role as Lady Helena's companion to give her comfort and company. He was envious of that intimacy. Why couldn't he be the one to take her weight as she went upstairs? Couldn't he be the one

216

to untie her stocking, and bind her wound? He could distract her with trivialities while they partook of their supper. Then he would lay her in her bed gently, and settle her within the covers, holding her hand and caressing her head until she fell asleep.

He sighed deeply and began to wash himself. His limbs were heavy and sore from the day's exertions, and by the time he hefted his shirt back over his head and slipped into bed he was very nearly asleep.

When he awoke later it was pitch black. He sat up, a strong wind whistling through his windows. The fire in his grate was reduced to smoking embers. One of the windows began to rattle and bang, and he rose to see to it. To his surprise, half of its surface was covered in windblown snow. It was a mighty spring storm indeed.

He managed to tighten the catch on the window, but the gusts still broke through like hideous shrieking. He went back to the bed and sat on the edge, drumming his fingers on top of the covers. A few moments later he was up again, pacing about the room. He went to the mantlepiece and squinted at the clock in the centre. It was nearly half past three.

He muttered a curse, knowing falling back to sleep was nearly impossible. He began to walk about the room again, and the walls seemed to get closer and closer with every step. Before he knew what he was doing, he opened the door and stepped into the hallway. He sucked in a breath as the chilled air pricked his skin.

He looked down the hall, at the rows of closed doors. Which room was Lady Helena's? He wouldn't dream of disturbing her, but it was agony being so near and yet so far, unable to check she was well. She'd shouted his given name as he'd approached her on horseback in the snow. That knowledge warmed his heart, even as he shivered.

He crept along to the landing, and rested his elbows on the balustrade that overlooked the entrance hall. Would she ever call him "John" again?

At the sound of a click, he whipped around, sensing movement further down the hall. A figure approached with a candlestick, slowing when its head tilted in his direction. When he could clearly identify the person, his skin tingled all over. It was Lady Helena, with a blanket wrapped around her, and her hair in a long plait over her shoulder. Her gait was still hindered by her injury.

"I couldn't sleep," he said, somewhat apologetically. There he was, in nothing but his shirt and stockings. "The storm."

She nodded as she came to within a foot of where he stood and set her candle down on a console table. "Nor could I."

He should excuse himself immediately and return to his room. He should. But she stood there, gazing up at him with searching eyes. What was she looking for, and could he give it to her? Taking in the loveliness of the ringlets framing her face, and the way the candlelight defined her cheekbones, her nose, her lips, he broke into a smile. He would not be anywhere else in the world.

She returned the smile, and he imagined she might be blushing. "Is your room comfortable?" she asked.

He nodded. "Quite comfortable, I thank you, my lady. How is your ankle?"

"A sprain, I am told. It is bound up now and I suppose I shouldn't be walking on it."

He chuckled and couldn't help inching towards her, as a moth to a flame. "No, I expect you shouldn't."

To his immense surprise, she also shuffled closer. "You cannot imagine my relief when I saw it was you in the snow," she said. "I was quite despairing of ever making it back to the house tonight. And the precious few you saved… I am so very grateful."

Then, almost in the same breath, she stretched up and grazed his cheek with a kiss.

Time seemed to stand still as she slowly withdrew. Wanting her to know how much more he wished to be of use to her, how precious she was to him, he grasped her free hand and set his other about her shoulders in a gesture of affection and protection. Then he dipped his head and set his forehead against hers, their breath now as one. "It was my honour to be of service to you," he whispered.

Her lips parted into a smile, and beneath the blanket he caught a glimpse of her nightrail. Her hand under his on his chest, she rubbed her thumb over his shirt and sent sparks shooting through his body. It was folly to linger any longer.

"May I assist you to your chamber?" he asked, straightening reluctantly.

She nodded and reached for her candlestick. She accepted his outstretched arm and leaned on him as she stepped forward with the offending foot. Oh, to have her lean on him forever.

She came to a stop three doors down, grasping the door handle. "Here we are."

John stood as still as a statue, lest she think for a moment that he would behave improperly. "I do hope you can fall back to sleep erelong."

She opened the door. "Goodnight, Mr Barrington." And then, she was gone.

❧

Some days later, Helena sat hunched over at the dining table, poring over figures. She'd intended to do a quick reconciliation over breakfast, but that had been over an hour ago.

"Why will you not balance?" she muttered to the numbers on the page. Laying her pen down, she gazed out of the windows, and her mind wandered to an increasingly familiar subject.

What an extraordinary day she had endured last week, and what an extraordinary gentleman Mr Barrington… John… was turning out to be.

Letting him take her to her mother's island had been like letting him into the secret, scarred places of her heart. He'd offered the comfort she so badly needed. And he'd said "My dear lady…" How dear was she to him? His subsequent actions seemed to provide an answer. Surely his new enthusiasm for altruistic endeavours could not explain it all.

When she found him on the landing in the dead of night, he'd again rescued her, unknowingly, in an hour of need. Sleep had evaded her due to the throbbing of her ankle and the stresses of searching in the snowstorm. And there he was, with warm arms and kind words. Could she fool herself into believing that her kiss had been only in gratitude?

No, she could not. With him standing there in nothing but his shirt, she could feel the heat and tautness of his skin through the fabric. As he'd helped her back to her room, she'd found herself longing to be wrapped up in his arms until the morning.

Her building feelings had kept her awake in a state of heavenly agitation. Just before dawn, she'd finally collapsed into sleep. By the time she woke, breakfasted, dressed, and came downstairs, Mr Barrington had already left for the manor.

The only occasion she'd been able to see him since then had been the vestry meeting. But she was suddenly overcome by disabling shyness and could not even look upon him. She could barely concentrate on the matters at hand. Was she turning into one of those flighty women she despised?

She forced herself to focus again on the numbers and letters in front of her and sighed heavily. She stretched her arms above her head then winced, rubbing at her stiff shoulders and rolling her head from one side to the other.

Something closed around her hands, and she shrieked, recoiling. Pulling her hands free, she twisted around to see who her assailant was… and met with a pair of chestnut brown eyes. She momentarily forgot how to breathe.

"It's only me," Mr Barrington said with a gentle smile. He set his thumbs into the tender spots of her shoulders and began to rub little circles around her knotted muscles. "Will you allow me?"

She stared straight ahead again, in shock, but was soon placated by the delicious sensations he was creating: a heady mix of relief and pain. "Mmm-hmm," she squeaked her permission.

He had removed his gloves, so his fingers worked both heat and pressure into her tissue. Before long, he was using every part of his hands on her neck, shoulders, and upper back. No one had ever touched her in this manner. A little moan escaped her as he worked a particularly sore area. His hands stilled briefly at the sound, and her skin began to flame in embarrassment. But the exquisite marvel of his touch continued, and her eyes fluttered shut as she fully relaxed against the back of the chair, giving herself over to his treatment.

And then it was over. He removed his hands, and her neck and shoulders were instantly cold – bereft.

She opened her eyes, blinking, and turned to gaze up at him. There was an unmistakable ardour in his eyes. "I, er, thank you," she stuttered. She did not trust her legs to stand. "Will you sit down? Would you like some coffee?"

He shook his head in response to her offer, but pulled out the dining chair next to her and flicked the tails of his coat over it as he sat. "How are you today, Lady Helena? Busy working, I see?"

She whipped the ledger book shut, the deep tones of his voice further weakening her knees. "I am well, thank you. What brings you to Willowbridge today? And how did you manage to get in here unannounced?"

He grinned. "Andrews was detained shortly after my arrival. I thought I would save him the trouble and find you myself." He frowned. "I hope you don't mind?"

She shook her head, hiding a smile. "And your reason for visiting?"

He opened his mouth to speak, then closed it again with a shrug. "I wanted to see you," he said at last.

Her stomach fluttered madly. "You did?"

"And I er… wanted to see if there is anything I could do to assist you," he added, gesturing towards the book.

"Oh. Well…" Her impulse was to refuse his offer as she would have with anyone since becoming mistress of the estate. But she did, in point of fact, need help. And surely, she could trust her neighbour with financial information…

"Privett has gone to visit with family," she explained, sighing on the words. "I cannot get these wretched figures to balance. I do not know what I could be missing. Do you think you could help?"

He took a breath, but she waved her hands self-consciously. "I'm sure I will figure it out eventually."

"Nonsense, I would be only too pleased to take a look." He reached for the ledger. "Not that I would assume I can do a better job," he added hastily.

She showed him the monthly accounts, with all the incomings and outgoings. He understood rapidly and took up her pen.

"May I?"

She nodded. "Of course."

He dipped the pen in the inkwell and began to take down figures on the opposite page, making a note beside each or performing a calculation. He was so thorough that she began to lose track, her attention drifting to the sunny gardens beyond the window. *It's a lovely day for riding… maybe soon.*

When she brought her focus back to his workings, she found his eyes not on the book, but on her.

"You were missing the amount for coal," he murmured.

She was lost in his intense stare. "Coal?"

"Yes, to fuel your fireplaces. I cross-checked with the previous two months, and there is a fixed sum spent on coal. I have added that in and now everything is in order." The pen fell from his hand, the remaining ink splashing from the nib across the paper. He didn't seem to notice, rising from the chair and standing before her at quite an improper distance.

"I am ever so thankful," she said softly, pushing off from her own chair and bracing herself against the table. "I would have been at that for hours more."

He smiled at her, and she felt his affection all the way down to her toes. "I can think of other things I would rather you were doing."

She gasped. "Really, Mr Barrington!" But she also could not stop herself from smiling, too.

His countenance was all innocence, but his eyes sparkled. "Lady Helena, I cannot think why you should censure me. *I* only meant I would rather your gelding could keep my mare company today. She could use a friend, I think."

"How selfless you are, sir. Only thinking of your horse's interest." Had he read her mind?

He offered her his arm. "To be sure. There is nothing at all for me to gain from the plan." As she looped her arm through his, he laid his hand over hers and gazed deeply into her eyes. "Nothing at all," he whispered.

❧

John whistled a cheery tune as he descended the stairs, ready for the new day.

Tom appeared in the vestibule and regarded him with amusement. "A good morning, sir?"

John grinned at him. "Every morning is a blessing, is it not?"

"If you say so, sir." Tom chuckled.

John strode to the dining room and tucked into his breakfast with relish. Just as he was finishing his coffee, Tom came in with some letters. "Looks like one from your sister," he said with a wink.

"Ah. Thank you!" John waited until he was alone, then immediately sifted through the mail until he came to Catherine's handwriting. Soon he was deep in descriptions of her life in town, from shopping expeditions to balls to nights at the theatre. How strange it was to not be there with her, keeping her safe. He missed her giggle and the way her words tumbled from her mouth when she was excited. He even missed the way she teased him. The words scrawled on the page were only an approximation. Still, in a few short months she would be with him, here in Mulberry.

Towards the end of the missive, Catherine wrote:

> It seems likely Louisa will be engaged before the year is out. I
> daresay once she reaches an understanding, I will become the

project.

John sighed. Louisa had had time enough to make a match, but could Catherine remain with the family for a while longer yet? What if she married a man who lived in the north country, or worse yet, Scotland?

He read her letter again, then set about crafting a reply. He began with the usual good wishes and pleasantries, before detailing his adventures over the past weeks. Well, not all the details.

> I have latterly been assisting the mistress of Willowbridge, while her steward is away. It is quite a surprise to discover one is in possession of some useful talents, when one has the opportunity to exploit them. And Lady Helena is

"Helena." John sighed on the word as if it were poetry personified. How could he describe her without giving away his feelings? He finally settled on:

> Lady Helena is a benevolent patroness.

His pen stilled and he sat back in his chair, his heart swelling. He recalled the feeling of her arms encircling him on Thora, and his pride in bringing her home safe. He touched his cheek, his eyes closing. His skin was still afire from her kiss. It had been sweet, but somehow ardent. If it was the only intimate gesture he ever received from her, it would be enough to treasure.

He desired more, but not in the base way he had in the past. He did not want to take her, he wanted to give himself to her... to bring her joy, not take his own pleasure. And he wanted to care for her, to *love* her, more than he had ever wanted anything.

He gulped. Love?

He realised with a start that his longing for Helena did run deeper than what he'd had with Julie. His affections then had been akin to childish innocence. While he had loved her with his whole being, his admiration for her was based on superficial attractions – her beauty, her laughter, the way she danced and the sparkle in her eyes. Had he ever really known the true makeup of her mind, her heart? Was it any wonder she had found him wanting when they had never truly connected at a deeper level?

Now, with Helena, he understood the value and meaning of a truer appreciation. He felt as if he were a different man, with a greater capacity for love which had only been realised in her presence. But he could not escape who he was only months before, on that torrid night. The knowledge of it, and his remorse, hung upon him like the shackles of a man incarcerated. He may not be in prison, but he was not free to seek that which he longed for the most... a requited, lasting love.

Chapter Twenty-One

Helena smiled at the sight of Mr Barrington and Thora approaching from her position at the drawing room window. She pushed her needle into her pin cushion and set aside the dress she was mending. She instead attempted to improve her appearance, tucking stray tendrils into her bun, and pinching her cheeks. Then she shook her head and scolded herself. "Silly woman. He's here to help you pay your creditors in the village – nothing more." Still, one must be presentable.

It would be all too easy to get used to having such a man in her life every day. To loosen her grip on every small detail of both Willowbridge and the lives of all her tenants, and trust someone to share her authority. Of course, she had Privett, but she was reluctant to let him see her weaknesses, and one day he would want to retire. She knew she lacked skills in arithmetic, negotiation, and the ability to make quick decisions. She masked these as best she could, but in his short time aiding her Mr Barrington had already relieved her of several burdens, all while maintaining a level of deference and respect. How could it be that only months before she had accused him of selfishness and indifference?

Of course, it was very pleasant having him about. His striking stature, masculine scent and admiring glances had her flustered at every turn. He stirred in her feelings she thought she'd never have, and her ego was naturally bolstered by his attention.

There were three weeks of this comfortable arrangement before her steward returned home. She was reluctant to no longer have an excuse to have her neighbour around, but she knew she could not keep distracting him from the management of his own estate.

Helena received Privett warmly as he stepped down from his carriage, then embraced his wife.

The steward bowed over her hand. "My lady. I hope my absence has not been too inconvenient."

"Not at all." She smiled. "I've had help when I needed it."

"Indeed?" He quirked an eyebrow. "Jolly good."

They settled into the drawing room and Privett regaled Helena with stories about his family over a cup of tea. Then she updated him on developments at Willowbridge.

He listened with concern as she described the spring blizzard. "Yes, it snowed in Northamptonshire as well, but I had no idea it was that bad this far south. Is there any property damage?"

"None that I am aware of thus far." A pang of disconcertment struck Helena's stomach. It should have occurred to her to having the buildings checked. What with the rain that had settled in after the snow, and her rather distracting assistant, sloshing about in the mud surrounding the outbuildings was the last thing on her mind. She still had so much to learn; perhaps she was not fit to be in control of so much.

Privett polished off the last of his shortbread biscuit and dusted the crumbs from his lap. "Well. Once I complete my usual rounds among the tenants over the next few days, I shall ensure a rigorous inspection of the estate."

Helena rose. "Thank you, Privett. I am eternally in your debt."

"Nonsense, my dear girl." He stood and gave her a friendly pat on the shoulder. "It is my pleasure to be of service."

❧

It was four days later when Privett came to give his report. As they took their places in her study, Helena couldn't fail to notice the dark circles under his eyes, and the slump of his shoulders.

"Are you well?" she enquired anxiously.

"Oh yes, quite well," he replied, flashing a smile. "Willowbridge on the other hand…"

"*Willowbridge?*" Helena had been expecting a list of repairs to tenant property, perhaps some restoration of roads or drains. "Is it the home farm?"

"Oh, there's some work to be done there, and on other property," Privett said, as if these were mere trifles. "But I must tell you, Lady Helena." He paused, watching her, his breath quickening.

"Yes? What is it?"

He sighed. "There is a large crack in the exterior of the east wall, that now runs all the way from the roof to the ground."

"Of this house?" There was suddenly not enough air in the room.

"Yes. We suspect a different event started the weakness, possibly that storm we endured in the autumn. It is clear the damage has recently accelerated."

"The storm…" Helena recalled that horrid night, and the awful sound she had heard from her bed. Had that been the wall splitting apart? "Can anything be done?"

"If we do nothing, my lady, the very foundations could become undone… We could lose the wall entirely."

She gaped at him. "Pardon?"

It was as if Helena's foundations were cracking. Her very home could crumble before her eyes.

"I have taken the liberty of obtaining some preliminary quotations," Privett continued. He withdrew a paper from his satchel and passed it across the deck to Helena.

With shaking fingers, she looked down at the rows of numbers and descriptions. At the bottom there was a total figure, so vast she gasped.

She raised her eyes to Privett's, unable to speak.

"We must raise our rents at Midsummer's Day, and possibly again at Michaelmas."

Helena felt herself nodding, but she had the horrible sensation of being disconnected from her body. A darkness began seeping into her soul, a ghastly awareness that no matter how hard she tried, she would fail. All her father's hopes in her would have been in vain.

Perhaps her doubters were correct; this was too much for a woman. Maybe she *should* just go to town at the height of the Season and find a suitable husband who would see to her material security, and that of Willowbridge… if nothing else.

Privett continued. "And we will need to look to other avenues as well."

I cannot break up the estate. But neither can I dismiss any staff. She couldn't live with herself if she was the cause of someone else's degradation. And if Sinclair got his hands on the estate, there was no telling what cuts he would make to increase profits. No doubt the carriage would need to be sold, along with the horses... and whatever valuable art was left in the house. Still there would likely be a deficit.

She found her voice, hollow though it sounded. "If I have to take out a loan, would that void the conditions of the will?"

Ever prepared, Privett also had a copy of the document in question to hand. "The provisions state that the property cannot be mortgaged or held as security for a loan at the time the inheritance would be confirmed."

"I see. We are able to borrow funds, but they must be repaid by December."

Privett nodded, his eyes kindly. Then he gathered up his papers. "Take some time to think on it, my lady. I'll return in a few days to see if you are ready to engage in the work."

"Thank you, Privett," Helena whispered. She barely noticed his exit from the room.

As she considered what lay before her, her temples began to throb. Her income came in lumps. The quarterly rent payments made up the bulk of it, and throughout summer there was revenue from the sale of products from the home farm. Then of course there was the large amount she was hoping for with the sales of her livestock this autumn. But none of these would allow large scale remedial work on the house to be carried out right away. There were also smaller sums to pay for other damages which Privett hadn't even detailed yet. If her tenant houses needed fixing, she would not delay. Their welfare was of the utmost import.

Helena opened a drawer and pulled out some paper, then began to prepare a pen. She must contact her solicitor, and through him the counting house. A loan was the only way, but if there were no means to pay it back before her deadline, Willowbridge would be lost.

She dipped her pen in the inkwell and brought it to her paper, but tears fell on the page instead. Whatever was she going to do?

∾

By mid-May, spring was well and truly established, and the ground of the woodland firm once more. John strolled along through the undergrowth, admiring the bright green leaves above him. It had been days since he'd seen Lady Helena, and he hadn't even bothered to think of an excuse as to why he was trespassing on her property. He only knew that, once the duties of his day were done, there was nothing he wanted to do except find her.

Upon emerging from the trees, his breath hitched as a noise reached his ears. He frowned, then broke into a jog.

It was someone crying. A woman crying. Was it *her*?

And then, he saw it. The chestnut tree – her father's tree – was irrevocably damaged. The mighty trunk had snapped almost right through and had collapsed on the ground next to the lake in a tangle of limbs and leaves. And there, amongst the branches, was Helena. She was kneeling on the ground, her cream dress pooling around her, and she was hunched over, her body shaking with sobs.

John rushed over, negotiating his way through the ruined giant until he was at her side.

"Helena!" He sank to the ground before her and held out his arms.

She raised her face to him, and his heart constricted at the sight of the desolation in her translucent eyes, her pale cheeks awash in tears. She fell into his embrace, grasping at his coat and continuing to weep on his shoulder.

"I'm so sorry," he whispered near her ear, stroking her head. "It is a great loss."

When at last she was able to speak, Helena's voice came in fits and starts. "I saw it this morning – they say it was the snow – weakened the trunk – rotten inside…"

She sat up straight again and accepted his handkerchief. He kept on of her hands in his.

"I thought it would be here forever," she said. "I feel as it any strength I have has fallen with it."

He squeezed her hand. "No, no. Your father's strength lives within you. Nothing can take it away."

She smiled at him weakly, dabbing at her face.

John looked about him at all the broken wood and sensed the irony. Surely it was he who was like that unlucky specimen. He had rotten from the inside out, and he had fallen. There was no way to mend the damage.

"It is not only the tree," Helena said, drawing his attention back to her.

"Oh?" He reached out and caught a stray tear with his finger, caressing her soft, smooth cheek as he wiped it away.

"It is… too much." She breathed deeply, taking a moment before meeting his eyes again. Then she told him of what had befallen her home, and what she must do to have it repaired. She was the very picture of desolation.

"Oh, Helena." He moved closer and stroked the sides of her arms. "How can I help? I wish I could give you the funds you need, but we have no cash at the ready and practically nothing to sell."

She shook her head. "I couldn't, John."

"Is there something practical I can do?"

She considered, chewing on her lip. At length, she said, "We need to sell… a great many things. Precious items belonging to my parents or many generations before. And… the horses. I simply cannot bear to orchestrate it all myself. Jane will make as many arrangements as she can, but…"

"Say no more. I will speak to Miss Godwin forthwith and make plans. You need not think on it again." He gave her arms a little reassuring squeeze.

She gave him a tremulous smile. "Th – thank you."

As her chin wobbled, John pulled her back into his arms. "No, no. Shh." He held her more tightly to stave off more tears. Would that he could take all her burdens away.

❧

Summer came to Mulberry with a blooming of the flowers in the trees lining the village's high street. Helena could not help smiling as she strolled down the road beneath the pink blossoms, the filtered sunlight warm on her skin. She'd just delivered some food and kindness to a family whose mother was unwell. Now she was on her way to visit the widow Kendall, who was becoming a good friend.

Her regular charitable duties were a welcome distraction from the measures she'd had to take to keep Willowbridge intact. The threat of losing it for good loomed larger than ever.

But the greatest comfort came from her burgeoning relationship with John Barrington. For she had to acknowledge that was what it was – more than a neighbourly acquaintance, more than friendly companionship – her heart was now inextricably linked with this man who she trusted with her secrets, her fears, her vulnerabilities. He supported her at every turn with humour, practical assistance, and restrained physical affection. He was so restrained, in fact, that she yearned for more. A day without him seemed like a week. It was the way his eyes lit up on seeing her, the way his hands fit around her waist as he helped her dismount, the way her pulse set to pounding when he gave her his lopsided grin. Her made her feel like the most special woman in the world.

After luncheon, Helena changed into her riding habit and descended the stairs, giddy with anticipation. What had started as chance encounters with John had now become regular meetings, most often beginning with a gallop across her pastures. She could not remember feeling more exhilarated, the thrill of the chase only matched by the sight of his powerful figure and graceful horsemanship.

On this occasion, Jane crossed the foyer just as Helena stepped down to the floor.

Jane took in her attire. "Out riding again, dear?"

Helena blushed, attempting to conceal this fact with a nonchalant countenance. "Cornelius is yearning to stretch his legs. I must oblige him, of course."

Jane only gave her a knowing smile. "Do give him my regards, won't you?"

"Him? I – that is –"

Jane disappeared into the drawing room, as Helena's cheeks flushed scarlet. The male to which Jane referred was clearly not Helena's horse. Of course Jane knew; she was a clever woman. Helena thought she'd been discreet, but her companion knew her so intimately, and was so familiar with her habits and manners, that the change in her must be obvious. She wondered who else suspected, and then began to wish for a day when discretion was no longer required.

Half an hour later, Helena floated across pastures on Cornelius, her heart likewise aloft as Mr Barrington – John – cantered alongside her. They weaved around trees and jumped fences until they came to a large oak tree near the crest of a hill with a view back to the house.

Helena savoured the dismount, as John set her down on the ground with strength and care. Was it her imagination, or did his hands linger about her waist a little longer each time? There was a water trough nearby for the horses, and John sat on the ground with his back against the oak.

He held out his hand with his lopsided smile. "Will you join me?"

Helena pretended to consider his offer for a few moments, then dropped to the ground eagerly. He laughed as she took her place next to him, allowing him to put his arm around her shoulders.

"Are you comfortable?" he murmured into her ear.

The combination of his touch and his voice sent shivers up her spine. "Perfectly," she replied, before nestling into his shoulder contentedly. They were silent for some time in repose. Helena could not remember the last time she had felt so relaxed and happy. For so long, she had derived all her satisfaction from serving others. For all the good her works did, being cared for in this way was a tonic for her soul. Perhaps it would give her the fortitude she needed for the battles ahead.

"It is a sublime aspect," John said, interrupting her thoughts. "I can see why you are so attached to this place."

She followed his gaze out across the rolling hills, to the gardens, lawns, and the great house itself. "'Tis true: I have such a sense of belonging here. I am sure I could never live anywhere else – not without breaking my heart."

John reached for her hand, gently taking it up. After a moment, he said quietly, "I am not sure I have ever belonged anywhere."

Helena frowned and tilted her head back to see his face. "Not even your family seat in Shropshire?"

He shrugged. "I am comfortable there, but I know it will belong to my brother. I have not that deep sense of attachment that you have."

"I see." Helena settled back onto his chest. "You have your family about you, which is something of inestimable value that I can no longer claim."

He squeezed her hand. "You are right, my dear. We each have our blessings." With his other hand, he rubbed the top of her shoulder in a gesture of fond affection that warmed her from the inside out.

Suddenly, a treacherous thought invaded Helena's conscience. Did he envy her inheriting a large estate? He wanted the autonomy his brother would have. Had he suddenly metamorphosed into her ideal man solely to win not only her heart, but her property?

Does he want me, or Willowbridge? The same question that had been present in her every interaction with gentlemen during her seasons.

Another strange little thought popped into her head as she retraced the past several months in her mind. Had all her troubles begun after John's arrival?

A change in John's demeanour distracted her from her qualms. His hands were tense, and his breathing was shallow and unsteady. She sat up and moved around to better face him, catching the emotion welling in his eyes, and the rapid movement of his Adam's apple.

"John? What is it?"

His gaze flicked to hers and away again, and he drew a hand across his eyes. "You were right, you know."

Her heart wrenched at the raw sound of his voice. She sat up on her knees and put her hands on his bent knee. "How so? I feel I have misjudged so many things."

He shook his head. "No, indeed. I believe your wisdom to be... I should defer to you in all things. You were correct when you observed that I do not conduct myself as a gentleman."

It pained Helena that her words had caused him grief. She knew so much more of him now. "You may have had your reasons for representing yourself in such a manner."

"No, I did not know. I was not sensible. That is, you have opened my eyes to how selfish I have been. I want to be better, Helena. I *want* to be a gentleman... for you." The use of her name without her title was an intimacy, but she had long since given him leave to do so, and now it sounded as music to her ears.

He regarded her with such deep sincerity that any doubt as to his intentions flew from Helena's mind. Her earlier notions had been absurd, ridiculous... perhaps the inventions of an inexperienced maiden afraid of falling in love. And she was falling.

He reached out and cupped her jaw with one hand, caressing her cheek with his thumb. If she had not already been on the ground, she may have swooned. His eyes were like fire on hers: the heat of love. She was certain of it.

He bent towards her, a tender smile on his lips. Was he going to kiss her? She leaned nearer to him and held her breath.

Chapter Twenty-Two

John's heart was full. Overflowing with adoration, appreciation, and gratitude towards the precious creature before him. As he touched her face, so silky and smooth, he drank in the ardour in her eyes, and the fullness of her lips. He yearned to show her how cherished she was, and as she raised her face to his, it seemed now was the moment to begin a sweet union.

Heart pounding, he closed the distance between them and dropped his head to hers. In a blinding flash, he remembered the last woman he'd kissed, and what he'd done to her. Helena may never have been kissed. Dare he sully her lips with his own, so impure? No, he dare not.

Halting with his mouth only an inch from hers, he moved to the side and instead placed a soft kiss on her cheek, lingering with his face touching hers for longer than he should. "Oh, Helena," he whispered near her ear. "You are so very, very dear to me."

He pulled back and watched her eyes flutter open, taking up her hand. "It is an honour to be in your company."

She stared at him for a long moment, and he could read the confusion and – disappointment? – in her expression. In that exquisite moment, he had failed her, and he couldn't tell her why.

"Thank you, John," she said eventually, and then she looked back towards the house, the spell quite broken. "Will you escort me home, please?"

"Certainly, my lady."

During the ride back, John cursed his past for now imposing on his hopes for the future. Why had he been so reckless? For the hundredth time, he wished he could have his time over. It was a nightmare of his own making.

There was a week or two when things were somewhat uneasy between them. Their interactions at church and the vestry lacked the secret spark he'd enjoyed. But, slowly, with his quiet but steadfast attention, their intimacy returned. John discovered that without the expectation of physical escalation, there was the time and space for deeper sharing of themselves.

Helena began to tell him of her dreams for the future – her aspirations for Willowbridge and Mulberry, and her latent longing for a family of her own. As for John, he allowed himself to dream for the first time since his youth. His wretched heart began to hope.

He continued to offer her support with her tasks, feeling uncharacteristically included, needed, useful. He admired her as she made decisions, carefully weighing up the options. He took her guidance on who to visit and how to help. He volunteered to manage matters at vestry meetings. He was so changed from the shadowy existence of his past, he almost began to like himself.

What with managing his own property, assisting with Willowbridge, and helping with village affairs, he hardly had a moment to himself from dawn to dusk. And it was wonderful… so refreshing not to be a prisoner in his own mind all day long. And then of course, there was his time with Helena, when he was so absorbed in her loveliness that nothing else could possibly intrude in those moments of sweet perfection.

She was becoming such an integral, euphoric part of his life, that he wondered how he would ever do without her. The thought was painful, in fact. He knew that whatever happened between them, he would always look out for her best interest. He would protect and encourage her, even if from afar. Her happiness was all that mattered.

೭∘⊸

On the morning of his sister's arrival, some weeks later, John rose early. His intention was to take care of any business first thing so that most of the day was clear for Catherine. After breakfast, he answered correspondence in the parlour, barely noticing when Tom came in.

"D'you want me to put in an order for some more liquor, Mr B?"

John swivelled in his seat and then eyed the liquor cabinet, now completely empty. It must have been so for several weeks – since he polished off the last of Sinclair's brandy. Strangely, he hadn't been craving alcohol as he usually would. His desperate need to escape himself must have waned.

"No, I thank you, that will not be necessary." He turned to Tom. "Is the bedchamber in order for Lady Catherine?"

"Aye, sir. My Betty and Rosie have taken care of it."

"And the bed for her maid?"

"Made up ready, sir."

"Very good."

Turning back to the desk, a rising emotion surged in John. To think, he would soon be enjoying the company of *both* ladies most dear to him in the world. Could that feeling be… happiness? He couldn't be sure, so alien was the sensation to him.

He positively beamed when he ran outside to meet the arriving post chaise. As the coachman opened the door, John reached out and grasped his sister's hand. The sight of Catherine's face sent his thoughts into a whirl. She was so changed, and yet the same. Would she be happy to see him, and would she find his modest accommodation suitable?

She stepped down to the ground, shielding her eyes from the autumn sun.

John swallowed back his brotherly pride, finding his voice. "Catherine! Welcome." He embraced her. "How well you look, dear sister. I hope the journey was not too taxing."

"Not at all." She smiled and regarded him appraisingly. "And you, John, look as well as I have ever seen you! It seems being a country squire quite agrees with you."

He laughed. How he'd missed their gentle teasing. "You can be the judge of that." He offered her his arm and led her inside, while Rosie greeted the maid she'd brought from Amberley. John took her on a tour of his cottage ornée, ending with the room she would call hers for the duration of her stay.

"Oh, John, the house is simply charming!" Catherine removed her wrap and sat on the bed, adjusting the pins in her auburn hair.

John pulled up a chair opposite. "Do you really think so?"

Catherine nodded. "Of course, it needs a woman's touch. It's quite obvious there has been no lady of the manor for many years."

"Ah yes, quite." His sister's seemingly innocuous observation had a profound effect on John. A woman... touch... "How does she get on?" he blurted out.

Catherine frowned. "She... oh, you mean Amy Miller?"

He flinched. The sound of her name was like daggers in his ears. A reminder of the monster he really was.

"Yes," he croaked.

Catherine ruminated for several moments, as if weighing up what to say. "Amy is safe and well. She seems to be enjoying motherhood. I met the babe not long after we returned to Amberley. A bonny little thing. He has your –"

"And her material situation is acceptable?" John could not stand to hear about the baby, or what they might have in common. The child should not exist.

"Oh, I believe so. The Fortescues are taking care of her, bless them."

John nodded. "Yes." Bless them indeed. They had taken up the mantle where he should have done.

There was a long silence, and then Catherine launched into a long exposition of her time in London. John enjoyed her colourful accounts immensely, and while he still felt some regret at not being able to share those experiences with her, he would not have missed his time with Helena for the world.

❧◦❧

Helena anticipated the arrival of Lady Catherine Barrington with immense curiosity and debilitating nerves. She was the first person she would meet with any connection to John, and he was apparently closer to her than anyone. Would she be like John in female form, with the same intense dark eyes and initial reserve? And what would she think of Helena? It scared Helena to realise how desperate she was for this lady to like her.

As soon as she received word of Lady Catherine's arrival, Helena penned an invitation to tea the following morning. She rang for a footman, hastily sealing the letter.

"Will you please deliver this to Mulberry Manor?"

The footman took the missive, bowing. "Right away, my lady."

Helena busied herself with charitable work for the rest of the day, her mind and heart in a state of agitation. After breakfasting the next day, she donned a pale green gown and a soft grey wrap, then tried to imitate the hairstyles of the ladies she'd seen in London.

Taking in her reflection, Helena sighed. "She is sure to be a lady of fashion," she murmured to herself. "And I am not." Her jitters increased as feminine inferiority settled upon her. Would she be deemed good enough for Lady Catherine's beloved brother?

There was a knock upon her door, and Andrews came to announce that the Barringtons were in the drawing room with Miss Godwin. Helena rushed from the room, but then slowed her steps upon the stairs, trying to adopt a regal air. This was her home, her element. She must not be intimidated.

As she entered the drawing room, the three gathered stood to greet her. She nodded to Jane, before curtseying to her guests.

"Mr Barrington, Lady Catherine, welcome."

They bowed and curtseyed respectively, and John said, "Thank you for your gracious invitation."

As Lady Catherine straightened, Helena had the leisure to scrutinise her appearance.

Helena knew the lady to be about three years her junior, but she was quite tall, sharing her brother's stature. She was indeed clad in a fashionable, yet demure, ensemble. Helena's gaze caught the richness of the fabrics before taking in pale skin and shining copper-coloured hair. And when their eyes met, Helena noticed Lady Catherine's were a much lighter brown than her brother's, and they seemed to sparkle somehow.

"Lady Helena," the girl greeted her with a smile, which extended to those same eyes.

Helena smiled back. "It is an honour to meet you, my dear. Do sit down."

John and his sister settled onto the sofa, and Helena took up the chair beside it, which placed her right next to Lady Catherine.

"I hope you left your family in good health?" Helena enquired of the lady.

"All in excellent health, I thank you," Lady Catherine replied, her tone matching her engaging appearance. She leaned towards Helena, lowering her voice a little. "I have been so looking forward to meeting you, my lady."

Helena held her breath. "Oh?"

"To be sure. My brother speaks so highly of you."

Helena exhaled and cast a sideways glance at John. "Does he? I'm flattered."

Jane made some sort of squeak from across the room, and Helena glared at her. Her companion seemed to be holding back laughter, or something equally mischievous. She sent an apologetic glance back to Helena.

"He has likewise told us many complimentary things about you, and how much he depends on you."

Lady Catherine laughed. "Perhaps that may be so, but I have been fairly lost without him."

The siblings exchanged a loving glance, and Helena suffered a pang of envy for their familial bond. There was no denying its authenticity.

"You have a lovely home, Lady Helena," Lady Catherine said after a moment.

Helena smiled an acknowledgement, secretly wishing that Willowbridge had not been lately stripped of so many of its treasures. She supposed Ashworth Hall was far more elaborately and elegantly decorated.

The tea service arrived, and Helena set about pouring. "You have four other brothers and sisters, is that correct? Are they all still at home?"

Helena already knew the answers to these questions, thanks to her intimacy with John. But she rather enjoyed his sister's vivid descriptions of their siblings and their life in Amberley and London.

When the need for a new subject arose, Helena wished she could likewise expound upon family connections. Instead, with Jane's assistance, she told Lady Catherine about the characters who peppered their village and some of their recent antics.

Lady Catherine listened attentively, her laugh ringing out on occasion. She had a youthful, carefree demeanour, which must be common for a young lady newly enjoying the delights of the world… and without the weight of the world on her shoulders.

Helena felt so serious and downtrodden in comparison. Perhaps some of this lady's exuberance might rub off on her. She had seen glimpses of it in John during their private moments, when he was relaxed and at ease.

The visit flew by, and it was soon the polite time for the Barringtons to take their leave. While Jane helped Lady Catherine retrieve her pelisse, John came alongside Helena in the foyer, and she drank in the affection in his countenance.

He raised his brows. "Well?" he whispered.

"She's lovely, John," Helena told him. "I can see why you adore her."

He gave her an appreciative smile. "I'm so glad you think so."

Helena's heart lifted. Had he been worried that she might not like his sister? He must have considered that Helena might be part of his family one day.

"I'm ready, John." Lady Catherine turned to them as she tied her bonnet in place. "Thank you again, Lady Helena."

The ladies curtsied to one another, and John took Helena's hand, bowing deeply over it and dropping a kiss on her fingers. "How fortunate I am to have such a kind neighbour," he murmured as he straightened, his eyes never leaving Helena's.

She shivered in response to the husky timbre of his voice and the fire in his eyes. When he let go of her hand, she was quite bereft.

As he and Jane waved goodbye to their guests, it belatedly occurred to Helena that she would not see John as much now that his sister was here. They would certainly not have the privilege of private conversation.

As she laid in bed that night, a beastly voice nagged at her, whispering that their best times together were over. She tried to push it to the side – after all, John lived here now. They had time on their side… unless she was to be cast out of Willowbridge in a few short months… or he grew tired of their limited society once he was permitted to return to his family. Surely their attachment would not prove so fickle?

⁊≈⁊

Later that week, Betty helped John put a basket of leftover foods together to take to the orphanage. Then he found Catherine engaged in needlework in the parlour.

"Will you join me for a long walk?" he asked her. "I have a task to undertake, and I should be glad of your company."

She laid her work down. "Of course, John. Do I need to change?"

John chuckled. "No, no. You're fine as you are. And it is quite mild this afternoon."

They strolled together along the road out of town, enjoying bantering conservation in the old way. Catherine twirled her parasol gaily and enquired as to their destination.

John glanced at her self-consciously. "It's an orphanage for foundlings in the district."

"Is it now?" Catherine took a moment to absorb this information. "And the basket of food is for the children? Silly me, thinking you were taking me out for a picnic."

John chuckled. "My apologies. Perhaps we can have such an outing tomorrow."

"It was my mistake. You see, while you have always been more than kind to me, I am not used to my brother carrying out selfless deeds for strangers… especially the poor."

"You are right, of course." John sighed. "You may find me changed, and for the better, I hope. Living in Mulberry has opened my eyes to the rewards of helping other people."

"How happy an alteration! I am so pleased for you, John. Perhaps this accounts for your general air of contentment since I arrived."

John smiled. "Perhaps it does."

Catherine smiled back, with a devious twinkle in her eye, as if she thought there might be another reason entirely for the change in his disposition.

He cleared his throat and pointed down the road. "It is just around that corner."

Once inside the orphanage, the Barringtons were greeted with the usual enthusiasm from the children and their carers. Catherine seemed a little overwhelmed at first, but soon warmed to the scene and began talking to each child in turn. John took the basket down to the kitchen and unpacked its contents.

On his return to the main hall, he paused in the doorway on noticing Catherine conversing with Grace, the older girl. He watched and waited until there seemed a natural conclusion to the exchange. Then he laid the empty basket on a table and went to his sister.

"Charming, are they not?"

"Oh yes, the poor dears." Catherine regarded the children with sympathy. "One hopes they are all able to find good situations when they are older."

"Ah, yes. About that. Catherine, I have a proposal for you."

She smiled. "Do you now, brother?"

"Is the maid you've brought permanently appointed to the position?"

Catherine shook her head. "Why, no. She is an upper housemaid who was selected to help me for this visit. As a rule, I have been sharing Annabel with Louisa."

"I see." He lowered his voice. "And... how did you like this girl, Grace?" He titled his head in the girl's direction.

"I liked her very well. She is polite and articulate."

John took a deep breath. "What would you say to having her as your lady's maid?"

Understandably, Catherine seemed surprised. "Oh, I..." She looked back at Grace and toyed with the necklace at her throat as she considered John's suggestion.

"I believe she will find it a challenge to secure a genteel and – safe – situation."

Catherine met John's eyes. "Yes. Undoubtedly."

"But I would not want to coerce you. Take some time to think on it, unless you are quite sure it is a terrible idea."

"Do you think Mama approve?"

A fair question. "I am sure she would, given the circumstances – but if she does not, there would surely be a position for her somewhere in the household."

"But has she a suitable wardrobe in which to present herself to Mama?"

John nodded. "Indeed, she has. Lady Helena has seen to that."

Catherine smiled. "I need not think further. It does my heart good to see *you* thinking of others in this manner. I shall take her back to Amberley with me, if she is agreeable, and I should know by the end of the journey if she is suitable to be my lady's maid."

"Capital! Let's have a word with the matron."

A little weight lifted from John as the arrangements were discussed. He had brought about ruin to one lady, but if he could save this one, might that be a small atonement?

Chapter Twenty-Three

"This morning's letters, my lady."

Andrews laid a salver on the low table next to Helena in the drawing room, where she was engaged in mending some baby clothes for a heavily pregnant tenant. "Thank you, Andrews," she said, glancing at the pile of correspondence before taking up her needle again.

But she immediately set eyes upon the letters again, with one catching her eye. "Could that be… it is!"

She clutched at the paper, addressed to her in John's own hand. She checked that Andrews had closed the door behind him, then broke the seal.

It was an invitation from he and Catherine for a walk and a picnic. They hoped that others in their Mulberry circle would also join them.

"How delightful!" The date was set for three days' time. How could she contain her excitement until then?

Never before had it been seemly for John to openly write to her. But with his sister there, it was quite appropriate that he should do so. She set about replying at once, her shaking pen betraying her discomposure on the page. She was careful not to say anything personal to him – surely Catherine would read her missive, too.

❧

The day of the picnic was fair, if windy. The ground was rather muddy from recent rains, but nothing would deter Helena from joining the picnic party.

They were to meet at the manor and then set out for the valley on John's land. Helena and Jane arrived at the house at the same time as Mr Pike and Mrs Kendall, along with her children. They had driven over in Mr Pike's sociable phaeton, and the children now chased each other round it, laughing and shrieking.

"I am not sure I should have come," said Mrs Kendall above the noise. "The party must be hoping for a serene stroll, and I fear we will put paid to that."

"I do wish you would hire a governess," her brother said, with the irked tone of one who has frequently uttered such a phrase.

"No governess?" Jane said. "How ever do you manage?"

"Well… there are other servants, of course, and I wanted my children to know me. But sometimes…"

Helena took her by the arm. "Nonsense, they are simply charming." She was genuinely enjoying the free-spirited fun of the children, until a flying rock narrowly missed her.

"Bertie! We do not throw things at ladies! You almost injured poor Lady Helena."

The little boy paused momentarily, giving Helena an apologetic look so pathetic she couldn't help but say, "It is no matter, you are forgiven."

Then she turned to regard the house, impatient to see John. The front door opened, and she held her breath. But it was only Tom Morgan, setting two picnic baskets down. The ladies went over and added the various provisions they had brought with them, to add to John's offerings.

"Good afternoon, Lady Helena."

At the sound of the male voice, she whirled around, but it was only Mr Harding. "Good day to you," she replied. "What a merry outing this shall be."

Finally, the Barringtons emerged from the house and the party of nine set off with Tom following. Harding offered Helena his arm, and they fell into step behind John and Catherine. As the doctor informed her of his latest discoveries in the settings of broken bones, she watched the siblings intently.

John took great care in guiding Catherine through the small wood to the east of the manor. He pointed out rocks and roots she might trip on, and gently directed her with a hand at her elbow. All the while they chatted and laughed. Helena supposed they must still have a lot to catch up on.

The group emerged into open fields, and the children rolled and tumbled down the hill towards the valley floor. As the party crossed through paddocks, they had to negotiate a stile. John hopped over it with ease, then reached to assist Catherine. When she was safely on the ground, he remained next to the stile to ensure the rest of the party crossed over without incident.

Helena gestured to Harding to go before her, and then she pulled herself up to the step and hitched her skirts a little in order to pivot over the top. She turned to face John, his hand outstretched to her. His countenance was a study in neutrality, but she could not miss the secret shine in his eyes.

She reached for his hand but lost her footing on the step and fell. John swooped in and caught her, clasping her to him before setting her firmly on the ground.

"Are you all right, Lady Helena?" he asked, his hands still on her shoulders.

She gently shrugged them away, not daring to meet his gaze. "Quite all right, thank you, Mr Barrington," she said stoically, but a blush stained her cheeks. The feeling of his arms around her, his care and concern, had thrown her off her equilibrium more than her stumble off the stile. To regain her composure, she looked for Harding, taking his arm when offered.

As they waited for the Pikes and Jane to cross the stile, Helena caught Lady Catherine's eye. The young lady was staring at her curiously, a half-smile on her lips. This only served to deepen the shade of Helena's skin, all the way to the roots of her hair.

"Shall we?" Harding asked, apparently oblivious to her embarrassment.

Helena nodded. "Do let's."

The walkers made their way down to a spot at a bend in the river, where a mat was laid out ready to receive them. Tom set the picnic baskets in the centre, and Harding took a position next to Mr Pike. Jane appeared deep in conversation with Mrs Kendall, so Helena sat at the opposite side.

As the children opened the baskets and exclaimed over the contents, the Barringtons took the remaining space, which somehow ended with John sitting next to Helena.

"Did you enjoy the walk, my lady?" he enquired as he arranged his long legs.

"Very much, thank you. This was a lovely idea."

"It was Catherine's," he said, turning to his sister.

She nodded with a smile. "John is not as social as he ought to be. I thought it was high time he issued an invitation to his neighbours."

Helena returned her smile, then asked playfully, "And what else do you find lacking in your brother's character?"

"Well!" John huffed at her indignantly, while Catherine giggled.

The young lady then regarded her brother thoughtfully. "I think perhaps he does not have confidence in his abilities, or his nature," she said quietly. "That is likely why he has not been so forthcoming in the past. He thinks himself unworthy of affection or admiration."

John observed the ground, wide eyed, and Helena ached for him.

"How insightful you are," she said to the lady. "I agree; in my observation he has underestimated his capacity to be a force for good."

"That is quite enough, thank you ladies," John said, with a tight smile. "Next time we shall analyse your characters?"

Lady Catherine patted his hand. "Do not fly into the boughs, brother dear. It was kindly meant. Shall I make you up a plate?"

The picnic luncheon then progressed in earnest. Helena hardly knew what food she ate, so aware was she of the man next to her. At one point they both reached for a bowl of strawberries at the same moment, and their bare hands brushed against one another. Even this light touch sent sparks shooting through Helena, and the look in John's eyes betrayed a similar sensation.

A period of affable group conversation followed, before it was declared time to return to the manor. Helena stood awkwardly, half hoping that John would offer her his arm.

"Would you mind terribly if I accompanied you?" It was Lady Catherine at her side.

"Of course I would not mind," Helena said, offering her arm. "I should love to."

The ladies linked arms and began the walk. They passed by John, who was conferring with Tom Morgan. He broke into a grin when he saw them together.

At first, they exchanged observations regarding the food and the weather, but then Lady Catherine's tone became more serious.

"John took me to the orphanage the other day," she began.

Helena turned to her. "Oh, did he?"

"Yes, we must have been there for above an hour with those tragic, darling children. John had a particular interest in an older foundling. Grace, I believe she was called."

"Yes, poor dear. I do wonder what will become of her."

"Wonder no more, my lady. John has convinced me to take her under my wing, as my lady's maid."

Helena's mouth dropped open. "You mean to say you will take her back to Amberley with you?"

Catherine nodded. "She will need to meet with my mother's approval, of course, but I am sure there will be some sort of employment for her at the very least."

Helena was without the power of speech for some moments, before breaking into a smile. "How wonderful. Such a weight off my mind."

"Oh? Do you consider the fate of all the local downtrodden individuals to be your personal responsibility, my lady?"

Helena nodded. "In a way. When they are within my parish, I do."

"What a kind-hearted creature you are." She paused. "I do hope we shall spend a great deal of time together in the future."

Helena studied her, sure the lady knew exactly what was afoot. "As do I."

At present there was no greater pleasure for John than seeing the two ladies most dear to him strolling arm in arm. As he walked back to the house with Miss Godwin, his heart swelled to nearly bursting, and his mind filled with visions of how their future might be. If he could only let himself believe it was possible… but, he could not change who he was. Or rather, who he had been.

As the walkers all returned to his lawn, the group continued in amiable chatter. John took in the smiling faces, wondering if perhaps he might begin to belong with these people? For surely he was more himself than he had ever been.

"Mr Barrington, may I have a word with you?"

He whipped around to see Helena, taken by surprise. Her tone was not accusing. In fact, her gaze was tinged with wonder. "Of course, my lady."

His spirits aflutter, John led her to the mulberry tree next to the house. It was still in view of the party but out of earshot.

Keeping his yearning arms pinned at his sides, John searched for the words to express all that he was feeling, but Helena came straight to her object.

"John, dear John." Her countenance admiring, and he felt another little piece of his heart giving way to her. "You've found a place for Grace?"

He nodded, smiling. He'd pleased her.

"And within your own family?"

"Well… within the household, I hope."

She smiled back. "It is too good of you."

"Nonsense." He shook his head. "It was a solution to two problems. My sister is well satisfied with the arrangement."

"I hope she continues to be. Grace is a wonderful girl – so earnest and eager to please." Behind the folds of her dress, she took his hand. "It is a great relief to me. Thank you."

He squeezed her fingers, unable to find any words. He only wished that she would look at him like that – so trusting, pure, accepting – for all his days. She seemed to rub the tarnish off his soul.

Horses were brought round, and farewells made. After they'd waved off the last of the party, John led Catherine back into the house and they collapsed onto the sofa in the parlour.

Rosie brought tea and they drank, celebrating the success of the picnic.

"Well!" Catherine said. "I expect I'll need to do some shopping soon, brother mine."

He glanced over at her. "For anything in particular?"

"Why, yes. I shall need a new dress to wear to your wedding."

John choked on his tea. "My wedding?"

Catherine laughed. "Come now, John. Do not pretend you are not absolutely besotted with Lady Helena Davenport, and she with you."

John flushed scarlet and blew out a breath. "To you, I shall not attempt to deny my feelings. But do you really think she…"

She grinned. "I really do."

His heart began to pound. "Did she say as much?"

"Not in as many words. But it was quite obvious to me from watching you together. Could it be, brother dearest, you have finally met your match?"

John leaned forward, propping his elbows on his knees. "I pray that I have. For she is the best lady in the world."

Catherine feigned indignance. "Excepting your darling sister, of course."

John laughed. "Of course."

"Why do you not declare yourself forthwith?"

John sighed and pressed a hand to his temple, squeezing his eyes closed. "She does not know."

"Know? Ah. I see." She put a comforting hand on his back.

"She is all that is good and virtuous. Once she knows the truth about me, it will surely destroy all that we have built."

"When will you tell her?"

"I cannot bear to. We've been so happy…" John broke down into aching, rasping sobs. "Why must I have been so despicable? I could never be deserving of her love!"

Catherine tightened her arm about him, holding him as his emotion poured forth. "My dear John. I can see how you are changed, your efforts to better yourself. You have caused irreparable damage, that much is true. But now, do you have the strength to attempts amends?"

He turned to her. "Amends?"

She nodded. "When you return to Amberley. You must do what is right."

"Yes." He grasped her hand. "I must. Regardless of whether I am able to win Lady Helena's hand, I must face up to what I have done."

∞

About a week after the picnic, Helena was in Allen's shop when she happened upon Lady Catherine. After concluding their respective business, they agreed to visit the tea rooms together. Once their beverages and cakes had been served, Lady Catherine smiled at Helena over her cup.

"I must say, you've worked wonders with our John."

"Oh! I…" Helena demurred, self-consciously stirring sugar into her tea. There was no point in denying all knowledge. "If he is changed," she said at last, "I am sure I cannot claim any credit."

"La, I think you can! I do not know if I have ever met someone so selfless, and now my brother is going out of his way to help others. It is my opinion, dear lady, that you have been a shining influence on him."

"Well." Helena blushed and hid her face behind her cup. "I may have pointed out his lack of altruism."

Lady Catherine laughed. "Indeed? I would not have thought his pride could have borne it."

"Ah, yes." Helena looked at her wryly. "It could not."

"And yet… his character has been propelled to this new sphere… into your sphere." Lady Catherine toyed with her cake fork. "I am not so naïve as to think his motivation to impress you is merely because you outrank him." She grinned.

Helena couldn't help herself. She smiled back. How much to reveal? And without John's permission? She certainly didn't want to lie.

"I will acknowledge we have been enjoying each other's company, particularly over the summer," she said at last. "But… I do wonder if he considers me as anything more than a friend, or another sister. He has not expressed, or demonstrated…" She blushed to the roots of her hair.

"Oh, my dear lady." Lady Catherine reached across and laid her hand on Helena's. "You need have no doubts on that score. I have *never* seen him look at anyone the way he looks at you."

Helena frowned. "Even that lady from his past?"

Lady Catherine nodded. "To be sure. He idolised her, as one admires a gem or a trinket. But you… he adores you completely – because you truly know each other, I think?"

Another weight lifted from Helena's heart, taking her another step closer to falling in love. "Yes, you are right," she replied. "I hope you are."

Lady Catherine grew pensive. "John's heart has been at sea for the longest time. But now…" – she gave Helena's hand a squeeze – "now, it might have found its home at last."

"There is one thing I might ask you."

"Yes, my lady?"

"Why is he bound to stay in Mulberry for a year?"

Lady Catherine's countenance clouded over in an instant, and she withdrew her hand. "I am not… that is…" She sighed, her eyes betraying sadness – or was it pain? "It is best that you ask him," she said finally.

"I have tried to steer conversations in that direction, but it is clear he is very sensitive about it," Helena said. "I do not wish to cause him distress, but I feel it is important to know."

Lady Catherine nodded, clearly unwilling to discuss it further. Helena thought quickly, seeking to change the subject.

"You are quite wrong about me, you know, with regards to selfless intentions."

"Oh?"

"I am desperate to keep Willowbridge for myself."

"And why should you not keep it?"

"I need to earn it, as per the conditions of my father's will."

"I see. Well, I can understand why you would want to retain the home where you parents lived. I wish you success in meeting those conditions."

"Thank you. My future is hanging in the balance. That is, unless I…"

"Yes?"

Helena's cheeks coloured again. "Nothing."

❧

For John, the following weeks passed in increasing contentment. He and Catherine cohabited comfortably, whether enjoying conversation at home or trips to Walford. She accompanied him as he visited his tenants and other Mulberry folk. They had weekly invitations to Willowbridge for tea and walks. When it rained, they would join Helena and Jane in her library to read. With such delightful company, John almost forgot his banishment.

But Helena still had the worry creases about her eyes, and though he tried to cheer her, he knew she would never be at ease until Willowbridge was safe. The sale of her purebred sheep loomed on the calendar. It was unclear whether even a good profit would be enough.

Another shadow loomed over his mind: his intention to humble himself in Amberley, to make clear his regrets and work to make amends. He could not declare himself to Helena until he'd done his utmost. He had fallen, and he must try to claw himself out of the hole.

In mid-October, an interesting card appeared in the afternoon post. It caught Catherine's eye as John sifted through the letters.

"What is that?"

John took it up and scanned it, then smiled and handed it to his sister. "See for yourself."

Catherine read the card and then squealed with excitement. "A ball!"

"Just so. Shall we go, do you think?"

She batted his arm. "I shall never forgive you if we don't. It would be a slight to Lady Helena in the extreme."

"I suppose you are right. But you will have no ballgown."

"Will I not?" She grinned. "You underestimate me, brother."

He laughed. "Touché. I had best send a reply, then. Only Catherine…"

"Yes?"

"This will be nothing like your London balls. We are a small society."

"We, John? Do you consider yourself part of Mulberry now?"

He swallowed, embarrassed by the slip of the tongue. It had revealed more than he had acknowledged to himself. He met Catherine's teasing eyes. "Perhaps I do."

<h1 align="center">Chapter Twenty-Four</h1>

A week before the ball, with preparations in full swing, a package arrived for Helena. The return address was a familiar location in London. An unfamiliar excitement began to stir within her. She was not accustomed to receiving gifts.

Tearing off the brown paper wrapping, she revealed a pristine white rectangular box, with the emblem of a dressmaker on the top.

"Whoever would have..." she murmured to herself. Then she lifted the lid from the box, and was greeted with a cloud of gauze, silver and pink. She gasped. "It cannot be!"

She hastily picked up the note sitting atop the fabric.

Dear Helena,

I hope you are well, and your mind more at ease than when we last spoke. On that occasion, I could not fail to notice your appreciation of a particular gown. As you were unable to bid, I determined to buy it for you. Perhaps you might have reason to wear it soon. Please forgive the delay in my sending it to you – I contrived to acquire one of your mother's dresses and have this altered to her measurements. I am sure it will suit you perfectly and can only hope it might play a role in the determination of your future.

With all my love,
Lady Lockhart

"Goodness gracious me!" Helena cried as she scooped up the dress and held it to herself, almost in an embrace. It felt as if this was a gift from her mother, like she was somehow reaching out to Helena from beyond the grave.

She walked to her mirror and arranged the dress so that it hugged her figure. The silver embroidery glittered in the sun, and the sheer gauze floated to the ground over the pale pink silk beneath.

How thoughtful of Lady Lockhart. She'd had no idea of being observed when she had admired this gown. And how kind she was to have it altered in order to save Helena the expense.

"When we last spoke…" That conversation came back to Helena with perfect clarity.

I think it will be a long and lonely road if you do not have someone to share it with. Your Mama would have wanted you to be happy… Will keeping a tight grip on Willowbridge keep you content in all the years to come? Or is there a deeper felicity to be found?

Helena's mind filled with a singular image. "A deeper felicity…"

"Oh, my dear, wherever did you get that?"

Jane's voice broke into her reverie, and she whirled around in surprise.

"I did knock. Three times. I began to worry and decided to enter. Upon my troth, what a handsome gown!"

Helena nodded, swiping at the tears in her eyes. "Lady Lockhart sent it to me. It's from the –"

"The auction in London! I remember!"

Helena nodded. "The very one."

"Do not let us delay, dear girl. Try it on!"

Jane helped Helena into the appropriate under garments, and then the dress itself. They were both rendered speechless by her image in the mirror. Jane hugged her warmly. "It serves to make you even lovelier, if that were possible."

"Oh, hush!" Helena scolded, returning the embrace. "I am determined not to cry. It would not do to stain the silk."

It was very nearly a perfect fit, and Helena again felt the presence of her mother in the delicate fabric about her. Jane rushed off to get her sewing kit, promising to complete the small adjustments required before the ball.

One week later, Helena stood in exactly the same spot, wearing the exquisite gown, now fitted to her precisely. Both Jane and her maid fussed about her, seeing to her hair, her jewellery, her gloves. Helena was such a bundle of nerves that she could hardly string a sentence together. Hopes and fears danced about in her stomach. Would her appearance please John? Would she dance gracefully? Would they have a chance to, perhaps, solidify their connection?

Whatever happened, she had a profound sense that this night was to be of great significance to them both.

❧

"Do you think there will be a waltz?" Catherine directed the question at John from where she sat at the edge of his bed in a luminous cream gown. She'd been ready for the ball for above a quarter of an hour, but her brother still fussed with his hair, his whiskers, his neckcloth.

"I – I couldn't possibly say," he said, his voice shaking as he fumbled with the buttons of his waistcoat.

"Here, let me," Catherine said, coming over to him. She glanced up at him as she worked on the buttons. "You do know how to waltz, don't you?"

"Of course!" John scoffed. "I first encountered it during my Tour. Although I cannot say I approve of *you* dancing it."

Catherine laughed. "How silly you are! It was quite the thing in London this season."

John halted as he pulled on his jacket. "Do you mean to say that you have danced it? With more than one gentleman?"

Catherine nodded. "To be sure."

"And your reputation was not sullied?" He reached for her hand. "Dear Catherine, you must be careful."

Her countenance softened. "Worry not, brother mine. Nothing improper has transpired." She helped him into his jacket, smoothing out the shoulders. "Now, let me look at you."

John turned and gave a little bow. "Do I pass muster?"

Catherine surveyed him and tutted. "Your neckcloth is a shambles. A pity you have no man to tie it for you."

"A pity indeed." John remembered a similar observation from a different lady, and the delightful moments that ensued thereafter. "Can you fix it?"

"I will try."

John's nerves only increased as Tom drove them over to Willowbridge on the home farm's wagon. He so wanted to give Helena a memorable night, to see her happy. And, perhaps, to give her his heart.

⁂

"Mr John Barrington and Lady Catherine Barrington," Andrews boomed.

John brought Catherine across the threshold and into the ballroom, although it was he who clung to her hand for support.

"Oh, how charming," Catherine breathed as they took in the sight of a myriad of candles, greenery, and flowers in the grand room. Elegant music drifted to them from a small orchestra at the far end, and an assortment of Mulberry's great and good intermingled in their finest apparel, filling the air with excited chatter.

And then, as the couple before them joined the crowd, John saw Helena… or was she a goddess? A vision in pale pink, her very skin seemed to glow in ethereal beauty. Her golden hair was luminous and graced with ribbons in the same colour as her gown, and her clear blue eyes shone as if every candle in the room were reflected in them. And they were on him, and she smiled.

And he knew. He knew he wanted to make her his wife.

"Mr Barrington, Lady Catherine," she said, dropping into a curtsey along with Miss Godwin, who stood with her.

John and Catherine bowed and curtsied, and John approached his hostess. "Lady Helena, how happy we are to be here tonight," he said, grinning at her helplessly. He barely noticed his sister moving forward to talk to Miss Godwin.

A tiny flush lit the buds of Helena's cheeks, and she offered her hand to him. He took it up and bent to kiss her gloved fingers, taking his time. His raised his eyes to his face from this position.

"You are surely the most beautiful woman in the world," he said, *sotto voce*. "That dress is… perfection."

"Thank you." Her blush deepened, and she gently took her hand from his grasp. "It was a gift from a family friend in London."

His heart melted a little more for her, recognising she wanted to assure him that she hadn't wasted money on new clothes.

Keeping his voice low, John said, "Helena, I am worried for you. Can you afford to host such an evening?"

"Oh, dear John." She gave him a small, private smile. "Is it little expense, really. The flowers are from the garden, and the players are friends from Walford and don't charge much…"

"And the food, the beverages, the candles?"

She shook her head. "I wouldn't deny the townspeople this event. It's how we celebrate the end of the harvest, and a ritual they look forward to the whole year. 'Tis the only ball many of them will ever attend."

"Mr and Mrs Powell," Andrews announced.

Helena's smile changed back to a polished one. "I hope to speak with you later, Mr Barrington," she said in a formal tone.

"Oh yes, and may I request the honour of a dance…"

But Helena had already been sequestered by Mrs Powell and didn't hear his request. He gave his regards to Miss Godwin and escorted Catherine further into the room, where they greeted all manner of local people. John wouldn't remember who they spoke to. Helena's presence at the end of the room was like a beacon to him, and she was all he could think on. When all had gathered, and dancing was announced, he turned to go to her, but she had already joined the throng. He moved with Catherine to the side as pairs of dancers began to assemble.

A pointed throat-clearing brought his attention back to his sibling, who was staring at him in expectation.

"Oh, do forgive me, sister mine. Will you do me the honour of this dance?"

She feigned surprise. "I should be delighted. Thank you for asking."

As they joined the dancers, it was then that Helena appeared at the head of the pairs on the arm of Harding. He willed himself not to gawk at her as the music began. This was her night, after all. He would be privileged to enjoy her company, but it was not a given. He concentrated on keeping his feet in the correct places so as not to embarrass his sister.

As the ball continued, John watched her with increasing frustration. She danced with Pike, she danced with Privett. She even danced with a gentleman farmer. Each time a dance concluded, he was thwarted in his attempts to be next.

Catherine urged him to find other partners, as she was a popular choice and hardly ever at his side. He agreed begrudgingly, acknowledging it would be rude not to. He stood up with Mrs Kendall, with Miss Godwin, and another local girl who was alone and clearly keen to dance. Any attempts at conversation were perfunctory at best.

When there was an interlude for refreshments, Helena was instantly surrounded by a gaggle of females. It would be unseemly to interrupt. He feigned interest in a dialogue with Pike and Harding while failing to quench his heated impatience with iced punch.

When the music began again, the introductory bars were in an unmistakably lilting rhythm unlike any English country dance.

"Excuse me, sir, but do you know how to waltz?"

John started in surprise and whirled around to find none other than his lady love. "Helena!" He cleared his throat. "Lady Helena," he intoned more deeply.

Her eyes sparkled with mischief, as if she were quite enjoying a game of pretending they were mere acquaintances. She raised her brows, demanding an answer to her question.

"Why, yes, my lady. I have often danced the waltz in the past."

"Oh, that is a relief. You see, I am familiar with the steps, but I have never had the good fortune of being able to dance it with a… er, male partner. I am afraid I will not be proficient."

Something about the way she said "male partner" sent a bolt of fire through him. He fought to keep his breath even. "I cannot promise perfection, but I would endeavour to do my very best. Would you allow me to dance it with you, my lady?"

She smiled and extended her hand. "I would, indeed."

❧❦

Was the room spinning, or was it Helena? She knew not. Were her feet even touching the ground? They seemed to move of their own volition, in perfect time with John's as he led her confidently, yet reverently, around the floor. Her attention was fully rapt on his face, his eyes locked on hers, admiration and joy shining from their depths, making her feel like the only woman in his world. She trusted him to guide her, absolutely.

She'd not been allowed to dance the waltz at balls in London, but had watched it done on a few occasions, transfixed by the rhythm and the grace of it. Her father would never permit her to dance so close to a man, and in a hold which was almost an embrace. But now, as a grown independent woman, when asked if she wanted a waltz played, she readily gave her approval. The few practises she and Jane had done should be enough to keep her in time, if not in step. And she knew exactly who she wanted to dance it with.

Helena's heart soared higher and higher as she swayed and twirled in his arms. Since her father died, she'd been so caught up in helping others, and keeping Willowbridge profitable, that she almost forgot who she was – who she really was – a woman who deserved to be loved.

She'd been feeling lost, overwhelmed, alone. And now, was he finding her? His was a quiet strength that offered calm reassurance just when she needed it… the feeling that he would pick her up if she should fall.

She wanted John as more than her partner for only this dance, but for all the dances of her life. She loved him.

As the music concluded, Helena was vaguely sensible of other eyes upon them, but she no longer cared who knew how she felt about John. There was simply no point in trying to deny it.

After they bowed and curtseyed to each other, he looped her arm through his and strode purposefully from the room.

"John!" she cried breathlessly. "Where are you taking me?"

"I hardly know." He grinned at her. "But I am not ready to lose your company just yet."

His words set Helena aglow. She'd been wanting to be with him the entire evening.

They found their way to the library, leaving the door ajar as they wandered over to the window and settled next to each other on a chaise longue.

"I must thank you," Helena said, suddenly unable to meet his eyes. "The waltz was… exhilarating."

"On the contrary, I was honoured to have the loveliest woman in England as my partner."

She blushed, and her colour only deepened as he took her hand to his lips and grazed it with a kiss.

"Tell me again," he murmured, "why you have not allowed another man to claim you? They must have been beating down your door."

She laughed softly. "Hardly. Perhaps I was not as forthcoming as the other ladies. I have been reluctant to give up my control… to submit to a man's dominion. I may have been too forthright in my opinions."

John frowned, his eyebrows knitting together. "Helena," he said, wrapping her hand in his. The warmth and tenderness of his touch sent shivers racing up and down her arm. "Do you feel exploited in my presence? Am I at all controlling, or have I ever pressured you into doing something you do not want?"

Her heart pounding, she met his eyes and found a desperate intensity there. "No," she said softly. Indeed, she had never felt more free or content than when in his company. She had never wanted more to yield everything to him. Everything.

She reached up with her other hand and brushed her fingers over the soft bristles on his cheek. His eyes closed as he sucked in a breath, and when he opened them again, fire burned in them. He caught her hand and turned it over, pressing a slow kiss into her palm, all the while maintaining heated eye contact with her.

She sighed at the caress of his lips. Every fibre of her being longed to be close to him, to have him love her, cherish her. She did not know until this moment how much she yearned to be loved, to belong to someone. And she could no longer resist this magnetic attraction to him.

She slid her arm up around his neck, pulling herself closer. He smiled at her tenderly and slipped his own arm around her waist in a motion as gentle as it was bold. She pulled her face up to his, then over to his ear.

"Love," she whispered. "What I feel in your presence is love."

His breath hitched, and his hands quivered. Was he happy?

She pulled back to read his expression and discovered not only a tremulous smile on his mouth, but a tear gathered at the corner of one eye. "Oh, my dear, my very dear" he said, his voice splintering. "How I have dreamed of a moment like this." He slowly brought a hand up to her face and slid his finger along her jaw, before cupping her face and throat tenderly. "For all of my heart – all that I am – is yours, if you will have it."

His words, his touch, sent Helena's senses into raptures. Tears pricked at her own eyes, and her heart was so full she thought it might burst at any moment. He asked not to take her hand, but instead to give of himself. It was the perfect proposition, a selfless spirit to unite with her own.

Helena could not find words, but she smiled and nodded, tilting her head closer to his as her emotions spilled over into a physical need. But surprisingly, John did not drop his mouth towards hers.

Instead, he released her hand and drew his thumb across her lips. A tremor went through her, only serving to increase her longing. There was a clear yearning in his eyes, but there was something holding him back.

"Do you not think, Lady Helena, that I am a gentleman now?"

In that moment, she wished he were not.

She briefly wondered if he was teasing or flirting with her, but his countenance was quite serious. It must be that her harsh words several months before still played on his mind. It seemed like a lifetime ago.

"My darling," she said, stroking the curls of his hair. "In my eyes you have become the perfect gentleman."

The crease between his brows instantly disappeared, and he relaxed into her touch. "Helena?"

"Yes?"

"May I kiss you?"

Her heart fluttered with pleasure. It was a sweet gesture, though hardly necessary when she felt she could not go on until she knew what it was to be connected with him. She brushed her fingers through his hair to the back of his head. "You may."

He smiled and let her pull his face towards hers. He caressed her cheek and then moved to now hold her head in both of his hands, as if she were exquisite and fragile.

Her eyes slid shut, and she held her breath. On the meeting of their skin, a spark ignited between them. But then, as he took her lips with gentle pressure, a delicious warmth began to spread through her whole body.

Everything else in her world – all her worries, struggles, wants – fell away as he kissed her. She wanted to scold herself for being so ridiculously feminine, so overpowered – and yet the sensation was sweeter than anything she had ever known. His lips were soft, and yet he showed her how much he wanted her too, in a caress which ended all too soon.

She opened her eyes in wonder and found him gazing back at her, his expression questioning… Did she enjoy it? She smiled at him again and this time she pressed her lips to his, slowly exploring the shapes of his mouth. She wanted to claim all of him… his heart, his mind, his soul.

Chapter Twenty-Five

How was it that John Barrington came to be alone in the library with Lady Helena Davenport? How could it be that she was speaking words of love in his ear, and stroking his face with featherlight fingertips? Was it all a beautiful dream?

But he touched her, cradled her precious face, and she was real. He'd declared his own feelings, and she'd leaned into him, her eyes on his mouth. He'd held back his own desire to kiss her for so long, terrified of taking more than she was willing to give.

Did she truly think him honourable? On his enquiry, she'd assured him she thought him a proper gentleman now. Had he done enough?

He must be sure she wanted this. He could never be guilty of taking liberties again. And the only way he could be sure was to ask her.

With her consent, he finally gave himself permission to express his love for her. He took her lips in a kiss so pure, so sweet, that his wretched, aching heart broke free of the chains he'd bound it in. She was heavenly.

He made himself stop, anxious to check on her. Was she pleased? Offended? Her response was to kiss him with delightful eagerness. His world spun off its axis and, wonderfully, he was without the power of sensible thought or sense of time. There was nothing but her.

At length, he sighed into her embrace. "Oh, my Helena." His happiness was beyond belief... but it was not complete. He was ready, more than ready, to declare himself and ask for her hand. But he could never do that until she knew all of him. And the last part of him was the worst. To tell her the awful truth was to risk everything.

As much as he wanted to retain her good opinion, it was unsupportable to speak of marriage when she did not know the whole. She was so near to being his, but now his past actions may have ended their union before it even began. It was a risk he had to take.

He owed her the truth. He owed her everything. But how to begin?

He took in a shuddery breath against her shoulder, and murmured, "I do not deserve you."

"Come now, John," she said, easing back from him. "Let us have no more of that kind of talk."

He forced himself to meet her kindly eyes, and her smile faded. "John?" She tentatively laid her hand on his. "What could you have done that is so horrible?"

John fought to keep his welling emotions from overwhelming him as his mind swum with images of the past. The feelings of desperation and guilt churned in his gut. He squeezed his eyes shut against them, his breaths coming quick and shallow.

Helena entwined her fingers with his, which was enough to open his eyes, although now he could not see her, only the horrible series of events that led to his downfall.

"You – you will recall… I once told you of…" He gulped in some air. "My, er, association with a certain young lady. Her name was Miss Julie Stone." On those three words, he faltered, and buried his face in his hands.

"Yes," Helena whispered. "The lady you once loved."

John swallowed as he nodded, hating himself for doing this to her, to them. "Well, it came to pass, years later, that…" John fought for control, trying to get the words in the right order, but struggling for breath. His heart beat so hard it was as if someone was pounding his chest. He pressed his fingers into his eyes and discovered he was already crying.

"John, you're scaring me." Helena's voice wobbled. "Speak, for heaven's sake. Please."

He opened his mouth, trying to focus on her eyes. But the room began to spin in a blurry haze, and he simply could not get enough air.

"There you are!"

They both jumped in their seat, then turned to find Catherine in the doorway.

"I thought you might like to know the party is missing you," she said with a smile as she walked toward them. On looking more closely at John, she halted. "Is anything the matter?"

John shook his head – not to deny the seriousness of the situation, but to ask his sister to stop any questioning.

Catherine approached gingerly, coming to his side. "John, I think it best you return to the ballroom if you want to maintain any honour at all. If you care about Lady Helena's reputation."

A fresh horror overtook John. He had no wish to ruin her... quite the opposite. "Of course I care," he mumbled, gently taking his hand from Helena's and telling her he was sorry with his eyes. What more could he say now?

He took his leave.

∂∾∽

"Lady Helena, are you quite well?"

Lady Catherine sat next to her, in the space John had vacated. No, she was not well. In one moment, she'd been deliriously happy, wrapped in her suitor's arms. The next, the same man had crumbled before her very eyes.

"You must tell me what he did."

Lady Catherine blinked. "My lady?"

"John was on the cusp of telling me the reason he was sent here, the circumstance which seems to be holding him to ransom."

The younger lady's eyes widened. "Just now? What did he divulge?"

"That it relates to a Miss Stone, his former... friend. And that they'd been separated for many years before this thing happened."

Lady Catherine nodded gravely. "And then I came in?"

"Well, when you came in it looked as if John was about to swoon. The effort of recalling his past had a profound effect on him."

"I see. I am sure you know I hold you in the highest regard. But it is not my place to speak for him."

Helena took up the lady's hands, pleading with her eyes. "Oh, but you must. I begin to wonder if he is able to speak of it at all. And we were so close to... that is, I think he was of a mind to..."

"Ask for your hand?"

Helena nodded, tears welling in her eyes. "I beg you. I must know. As a friend – as a woman – please tell me the truth."

Lady Catherine frowned, looking away. "I only hope he won't consider it a betrayal." She shifted on the seat and regarded Helena again. "Very well, I shall tell you. It will serve you both well in the end – though he may not see it in that light."

Helena exhaled. "Thank you."

"Prepare yourself, my lady, for it is an ugly story."

She gasped. "What is it? Has he killed someone?"

"No, it is not as bad as *that*. Or perhaps… you may think it is."

"Dear God," Helena whispered. She gripped the edges of the chair, willing herself to be strong.

❧

It had been above fifteen minutes since John had re-entered the ballroom, and he grew increasingly uneasy. He pretended to attend to conversations, while constantly scanning the room. Had the ladies left the library?

When he could no longer stand the suspense, he left the room through another door, leaving his conversant to think he needed to relieve himself. He found his way back to the library, then knocked upon the door.

There was no response. He knocked again, and waited, and then pushed the door open.

The ladies were indeed still in the room, still on the chaise in fact. He realised in horror that Helena was quietly sobbing onto Catherine's shoulder.

His sister eyed him warily, then said something to Helena before rising and coming to him.

"What has transpired?" he asked her, dreading the answer.

"I have told her, John," she said softly.

"Told her?"

"Yes. Everything."

Comprehension hit John suddenly, and he looked over at his beloved. Her face was so pale, and when she returned his stare, her red eyes were lifeless.

"I hope you do not mind," Catherine said. "Only she told me you were finding it difficult."

John glanced back at her. "It is of no consequence, sister," he said. "It is done now."

She nodded. "I'll get my things."

John turned back to Helena, slowly approaching. "I am sorry I was not able to tell you," he began. "I'm sorry for so many things."

She did not move or speak, and he closed the gap between them. His heart hurt as he took in her face, blotchy and tear-stained. He reached out to soothe her.

She sprang up off the chaise. "Do not *presume* to touch me!" she shrieked.

He stepped back. "My apologies."

"Stop apologising! Saying sorry will not make it go away!" She paused and lowered her tone to one of utter despair. "How could you do such a thing? That poor woman!"

"I don't know, Helena, I don't know! It was despicable. Shame doesn't begin to describe my feelings. That is what held me back from revealing this to you."

She shook her head in an incredulous fashion. "All these months you've been keeping *this* from me!"

"Helena, please." He hovered about, desperate to hold her. "Do you not see how I've changed? How *you've* changed me?"

She sniffed. "Do you really expect me to call you a gentleman *now*? After this?"

"I am no longer that man, that hideous man, whoever he was. You have brought out the true John Barrington, the man I always should have been."

"I'll acknowledge you play the part well enough." Her voice was low and hard and uncompromising. "But you clearly do not possess the *heart* of a gentleman. That is something you cannot fabricate."

The disgust in her eyes was excruciating. He knelt before her. "I have never pretended with you," he said earnestly. "I love you!"

"Do you know what love is?" She stared at him with something akin to pity. "I wish you had never come to Mulberry, that I had never known you."

A shard of broken glass pierced his heart, a heart that had only just become whole again. The pain was too great to allow for words. He rose to standing, hanging his head.

Helena headed towards the door, and he followed her lamely.

"I blame myself for letting you fool me," she said with a horrible sadness. "I assume you will leave Mulberry as soon as you're able and return to your life of distractions elsewhere. Until that time, I beg of you to stay away from Willowbridge, from me. I cannot bear the sight of you."

And without looking back, she left the room.

John began to tremble violently, his mouth hanging open and his eyes wild. His heart had gone with her, and he would never get it back.

He'd had a glimpse of what a future of happiness could have looked like. One with love and a purpose and hope. He should have known that type of contentment was not meant for him. His past actions would always catch up with him, would they not?

He could never escape this evil shadow he had cast over himself.

❧❦

It took all of Helena's courage to stalk from the library with her head held high, but as soon as she was out of sight her shoulders slumped, and she stumbled to the foyer as her head began to throb dreadfully. She stopped to squeeze her eyes shut against the pain, rubbing her temples.

"Oh no, no, no," she moaned.

"Can I get you anything, my lady?"

"Ah!" Helena opened her eyes with a start, having been unaware of anyone approaching. "Oh, 'tis just you, Ethel." She took a deep breath, trying to regain some composure in front of the maid. "Pray find Miss Godwin and send her to my chamber."

"Of course, my lady." She curtsied and hurried off.

Helena dragged her feet across the foyer to the stairs and clutched at the banister as she trudged up each step. In her mind she replayed the words Lady Catherine had spoken, and the accompanying images she conjured made her want to retch. How could she unite herself with a man who was capable of such an act? It was unsupportable, unthinkable, unpardonable.

She was not so naïve as to think that things like that never happened. Men had long exerted their dominance over women in many ways. She'd been justified in her quest to exist without allowing the same.

But then, she recalled the precious moments she'd relished only minutes before that revelation. John's embrace, his kiss, his sweet words of adoration and dedication. Her spirits had soared to the stars. How could it be the same man? Had it all been a charade?

With tears streaming down her cheeks, she collapsed onto the second step from the top. How could she believe it of him? He, who had been so gentle with her. He, who had taken her heart so completely that now she could not imagine her life without him.

"Helena! Are you ill?"

Jane rushed to her side, dropping onto the steps and folding her in a secure embrace.

Helena's body shuddered as she sobbed. "Jane, oh Jane!"

"What is it? Bad news about the estate?"

Helena shook her head. She gulped out, "No, no. It is my heart I have risked, and I have lost it."

"Oh, my dear. Come. Let me take you to your chamber and then you can tell me all." She helped Helena to stand.

"But Jane, what will we say to my guests?"

"I'll see to it. They can wait."

Once in Helena's room, Jane helped her out of her dress. The beautiful gown, which had seemed like a promise of love, seemed to mock her now.

"I knew there was a secret from his past," Helena said as she slipped out of her stays. "But it is so much worse than I could have imagined!"

They settled on the bed, and Helena divulged the whole through angry tears. "Why did I let myself love him? My instincts from the beginning were not to trust him. His true character was revealed at the start."

"Do not blame yourself, my sweet. There are very few who have not been led astray by love... Mr Barrington included, I think."

"What do you mean?"

"We can discuss it another day, perhaps. I will stay with you tonight. Make yourself comfortable, and I shall return before long."

"Bless you, Jane."

In the morning, some of Helena's customary strength and pragmatism returned. She would endure any emotional turmoil by putting her focus where it needed to be – on Willowbridge. Today she would consult with Adams and Privett to ascertain the day the finished sheep would be auctioned at the market. The prices they fetched would determine what measures she would need to take to achieve the terms of her father's will.

Lady Catherine had confirmed that John's mandated year in Mulberry was a punishment for his crime. It would be a matter of weeks before he was free to leave… and surely, he would. She had given him no reason to hope.

After Jane awoke, they exchanged stories of the night before, carefully avoiding any mention of sensitive subjects. Jane even made Helena laugh as she reenacted the tuneless singing of an inebriated elderly tenant.

Mrs Mead came in with a breakfast tray for Helena, followed by a maid bearing Jane's food.

"Good morning, Mrs Mead. You needn't have taken the trouble to bring my tray yourself."

"Nonsense, child. I wanted to see how you are. We are all concerned for you."

Helena smiled at her fondly. "As you see, I am quite well. I was only tired last night, and I suppose I hadn't eaten enough yesterday."

Mrs Mead grinned. "Ah! Well, I have brought you a feast! Tuck in, m'dear. You'll be right as rain."

Helena glanced down at the mounds of eggs, kidneys, chops, and liver, and her stomach quivered. "Could you please have some toast and butter sent up, as well?"

"Certainly, my lady." Mrs Mead curtsied and bustled from the room.

The second tray, which appeared shortly thereafter, also bore a pile of letters. After polishing off a thick slice of buttered bread, Helena began to sift through them.

On seeing the fourth letter, she froze. Darkness returned to the pit of her stomach.

"What is it?" Jane enquired around a mouthful of ham.

Helena held up the letter so Jane could see the handwriting.

"Sinclair."

Chapter Twenty-Six

In the aftermath of the revelations at the ball, John considered returning to his old ways: to drown himself in drink, to wallow in his wretchedness, perhaps find a pretty young thing to make him forget.

But he could not. The very idea of returning to that sort of existence was repugnant to him. He was forever changed, a man restored. And even without a desire to prove himself to a lady, he would continue to live in this new, nobler way. There was no going back.

In the days that followed, the confrontation with Helena haunted him. Was it the last time he would ever speak to her? Deep in his heart, he'd known what the intelligence of his past would do. Her reaction was precisely what he deserved. No more, no less. He would forever keep sacred the exquisite memory of their kiss, a reminder that true beauty and happiness do exist in the world… although, not for him.

He remained at home or on his estate, so as to avoid any uncomfortable questions or, at worst, an encounter with *her*. He sat far away from her at church and decided to step down from the parish vestry. It reminded him of his early days in Mulberry, but this time, he could not remain idle. His spirit was now infused with the need to do something, to help in some way. He wished he could be by Helena's side as she navigated these final few months before her fate was decided.

This was more akin to real imprisonment, worse than anything his family had imposed. He ached to be with her, so close as she was, but he could not. So, instead, he made it his goal to continue his deeds about the village, as discreetly as possible.

One afternoon, he sat at the desk in the parlour, reviewing the notes Mr Wilson had left him.

Catherine hovered about, apparently unable to find an occupation.

He turned to her. "You must be bored, Catherine. I must apologise, for I am not inclined to seek out company at present."

"I quite understand. Have no care on my account. It is *you* I worry about. To have so completely given yourself over to someone, and now…"

John shook his head. "There is no dwelling on it, sister dear. I will move forward as best I can. Would that we could return to Amberley immediately, for her sake. But I dare not defy our father's orders."

"Do you wish *me* to leave, John?"

"No… but you are free to go, of course, if you wish."

She came closer and laid a hand on his shoulder. "No."

He smiled at her. "Are you still of a mind to have Grace accompany us back?"

"To be sure. It is the right thing to do."

"Then let us visit with her and make the final arrangements."

They made up a basket for the orphans: preserves, jam, fruits, cheese, and a stack of writing paper. Catherine also put in some ribbons and other hair accessories, some handkerchiefs, and some stockings she'd been mending for the girls since their last visit.

On their arrival at the orphanage, Grace greeted them with hopeful enthusiasm, and they exchanged gratified smiles. They spent the whole afternoon with the children: playing, drawing, and singing songs.

A few days later, John collected a package from Allen's and then headed to Longdale Farm. After giving Mrs Granger her own basket of goods and consulting with her husband on the health of his animals, he beckoned to Bart, the little boy he'd played with in the summer. Taking the boy outside, he gave him the package and watched with delight as he tore it open and found a bat and ball inside. Bart nearly knocked him over in a fierce hug, and the whole family joined in a game of cricket.

Meanwhile, Catherine visited with Mrs Kendall. The children put on a show, and then she helped them practise their French.

Soon, the winds turned northerly, and the first frosts descended on the ground. The fiery colours in the trees faded until only brittle, brown leaves remained. The very landscape seemed to signal a bleak future… or at least, an uncertain one.

It was a dull and drizzly day when, as the Barringtons concluded their breakfast, there was a knock at the front door. John opened it to find a footman from Willowbridge.

The young man addressed him. "Mr Barrington?"

"Yes. What is it? Is there something wrong?"

John's mind raced. Did she need him? He mentally prepared himself to ride over with haste. Whatever she needed.

"No, sir. I am instructed to deliver this to your hand." He withdrew a folded paper from his coat pocket and held it out.

John snatched it up and his heart sank as he saw the style of handwriting.

Catherine appeared at his side, taking in the sight of the footman shifting his weight on the doorstep. "Is it from her?" she whispered.

John shook his head, reading the words of the note again in disbelief. "It is from her cousin, Mr Sinclair. He invites me to visit him at the house tomorrow."

"Is he a friend?"

John met her eyes. "I would not put it quite that way."

ॐ✦

The Sinclairs arrived late in the afternoon in the third week of October, and Helena steeled herself as she watched her cousin step down from the hackney coach. Her focus was on the livestock auction which would take place the following Friday, and she would not allow herself to be intimated by him.

She came down for dinner and found the man and his wife already seated at the dining table with Jane.

"I do hope I'm not late," she said as she slid into her chair.

Sinclair opened his mouth, but Jane quickly said, "Not at all, Helena."

Helena picked up her napkin and flashed a smile at the Sinclairs as she laid it in her lap. "What brings you back to Willowbridge, cousins?"

Sinclair smiled back, his beady eyes glinting. "Because I want to be here, my dear, when you fail."

Jane and Mrs Sinclair gasped, and Helena's mouth dropped open. "How dare you!" she exclaimed. The door opened, and footmen arrived bearing the first courses. A thick silence hung over the dining table as the dishes were laid out, and Helena worked to control her breathing.

"Thank you," she said to her staff as they left the room.

Then she turned to Sinclair. "I will succeed. You shall see!"

Her nemesis took up a ladle and dished himself a large quantity – never mind that he was supposed to serve the adjacent ladies first. His wife exchanged a glance with Helena, clearly uncomfortable.

Sinclair fixed her with an expression which was, one assumed, supposed to be kindly. "My dear Lady Helena, when I take over the estate, you may rest assured you can stay under this roof for as long as you need... until you establish a new situation. I could never push you out on to the street, cousin."

Helena choked on her soup, and her skin crawled. What did he mean by "when"? As if her defeat were a forgone conclusion? Why was he so confident, so smug?

She narrowed her eyes at him. "What is it that you think you know?"

He laughed. "All in good time, m'dear."

～∽

Helena studiously avoided her cousins thenceforth. Upon hearing voices in the drawing room two days after their arrival, she entered without knocking. Within she found the Sinclairs facing two people seated on the sofa.

"Sinclair, what is the meaning –" The two gentlemen stood, the other man turning to face her. Her steps halted and her heart skipped a beat. It was John. "Oh! What are *you* doing here?"

"Lady Helena," he said quietly, bending into a low bow.

She could not curtsey to him. She could not move at all. The deep tones of his voice set her nerves to fizzing. His sister turned to give her a polite nod, her eyes all apprehension.

"I invited him," Sinclair said smoothly. "Will you join us?"

"You..." He had invited them without asking her permission? The man was already acting as if he owned her property. And to add to the insult, these were the guests he had chosen! Conflicting emotions danced about inside her.

"I do apologise," John said, and on meeting his eyes Helena was impacted anew by their intensity. "I assumed you would be aware of the engagement."

"Helena? What..." Jane entered the room, quickly assessing the situation. She took Helena by the elbow and whispered in her ear. "What is the nature of this meeting?"

"I know not," Helena whispered back. She did know, however, that she would not be browbeaten in her own home. She raised her chin. "I should be delighted to join you," she said with as much enthusiasm as she could muster. She and Jane made their way to a settee at right angles to both couples. Helena folded her hands in her lap and stared at the flower arrangement on the low table between them.

Sinclair jumped up and made his way to a decanter and glasses. The vessel was only topped up when her cousin was visiting, as she seldom offered liquor to her guests.

"A drink, Barrington," Sinclair said, as a statement, not a question. "Single or double?"

Helena heard John clear his throat. "Neither."

"What?" Sinclair guffawed. "Are you ill?"

"No, sir. In fact, you could say I was ill before, when I wanted to lose myself in drink. I have given it up, you see."

Helena looked up to find John's eyes upon her, beseeching.

"I did not like the man I was when I'd imbibed."

This declaration was clearly directed at her – an attempt to illustrate how he had changed. She stubbornly kept her countenance stoic, but inside she was melting.

The urge to go to him, to be enclosed in his arms, was so strong she tore her gaze away. Why did he have to be so unbearably handsome, so hopelessly charismatic?

"Very well." Sinclair poured himself a glass and settled back on his chair. He took a gulp of brandy and his lips puckered as he swallowed it. He gestured around the room. "Perhaps you ladies would enjoy a turn about the garden?"

Helena let out an involuntarily squeak of indignance. Was she being dismissed in her own house? The gall of that man! The ladies all looked to her to respond, not likewise daring to overstep the mark.

She took in a breath. A walk would mean she wouldn't have to suffer through another insulting conversation with Sinclair, but it would also require her to be in the awkward company of Mrs Sinclair, who aspired to be mistress of Willowbridge, and Lady Catherine, who she had until recently considered as nearly a sister.

Removing herself from the tormenting presence of her former suitor became her top priority. She stood. "It is a fine afternoon," she said with forced brightness. "Some fresh air would be just the thing, I think." The other ladies rose, murmuring their agreement.

As she crossed in front of him, John said, "Good day, Lady Helena." She shrugged off the spark of fire his voice, so close, sent racing through her.

"Oh, er, good day," she stuttered, not daring to look back.

❧

Sinclair polished off his brandy and leaned forward in his chair. "So, my good man. How have you been faring? Not too stifled by the mistress of the house?"

"Stifled?" John held back his urge to laugh incredulously. He had never felt more liberated, more himself, than with Helena. And now, knowing full well what this man hoped to achieve, his skin crawled with abhorrence. He would do whatever he could to protect her from Sinclair, and whatever the man's plans were to derail her success with Willowbridge.

"I have settled in tolerably," he replied at last.

"Capital. I daresay she hasn't allowed you to have any sport this season?"

John shook his head. "I have not requested to partake in any." For how could he think of partridges or pheasant when his lady love was near?

Sinclair laughed. "Too much of an ogre, is she?"

"Mind how you speak of her, sir," John snapped.

Sinclair's eyebrows shot up. He pushed himself off his chair and headed back to the decanter. "Well, then. Let us come to the heart of the matter. Will you have a drink now?"

John shook his head. "What is your business?"

Returning with another full glass, Sinclair smiled. "I need some more information."

More. John cringed inwardly as he remembered he'd previously revealed something to the man. Why had he been so weak?

"Oh?"

"Yes. I want to know where and when she is selling those precious sheep of hers. Lord knows her staff have been no help to me at all. I hope you may know something about it? Are they to be sold at Smithfield?"

"She has not discussed it with me," John said honestly. As far as he knew, the finer details of how to auction off the sheep had not been finalised prior to the ball.

"Blast!" Sinclair took some brandy. "But surely you have your own livestock? Could you enquire with your farming people as to the best market for such a breed?"

John's patience was beginning to wear thin. "I think not."

Sinclair shifted in his seat, his smile wavering. "But, my dear fellow, we were on such good terms during my last visit."

"And I should like us to remain so," John said. "However – I am now loyal to Lady Helena."

The man's face crumpled, revealing his true ugliness. "Ah, so it's like that, is it? Worked her feminine charms on you, I suppose?"

John tried to suppress the blush that began creeping up his neck. "It is more that I came to admire her altruistic tendencies. She works very hard for Willowbridge – for everyone."

After a tense moment, Sinclair abruptly stood. "I quite understand your position. And it is of no use to me. I shall remember this when I am installed as the owner of this estate. Mark my words!"

John rose, towering over the little man. "Yes, I should like to be remembered for honourable actions. And I pray your dishonourable deeds do not come to fruition. If that is all, I shall see myself out."

Chapter Twenty-Seven

Cornelius cantered along the Hampshire roads with urgency, as if he knew how important this day was. Helena was on her way to the Weyhill Fair, where her Southdown ewes and lambs would be sold. The prices they fetched would determine how much she would need sacrifice to retain ownership of Willowbridge. An excellent result would all but guarantee her future.

The journey had taken the beasts themselves five days, but for Helena and her groom it was a half day's ride. They'd set off at sunrise on the rather impromptu journey – for it was only the day before that Helena had decided she couldn't possibly wait for her farmers to return before discovering the outcome of the day's trading. Being under Sinclair's ever closer watch certainly hadn't helped her nerves.

The length of the ride gave her ample time to think – too much time. Various scenarios of her future days played out in her mind. How different her recent imaginings had been before the revelation at the ball. Now, as before, love played no part in her aspirations. She'd been reckless, foolish, gambling with her very heart. No more.

Even as she told herself this, her thoughts strayed to John. Ridiculous though it was, she wished he was there, riding next to her. To calm her, reassure her, and hold her hand as she learned what was to become of her. Her frailty and dependence on him brought hot tears to her eyes.

They could hear the market before it came within view. A cacophony of bellows, barking, and bleats mingled with human cries and the ringing of bells. Then the fair revealed itself as a city of pens, rings, buildings, and tents, bursting with the assortment of livestock, traders, and customers. Down amongst them were her people, her animals and, she hoped, her buyers.

Helena and Cornelius approached the administration office, whereupon she dismounted and gave her horse to the groom. Knowing this would be the domain of men, she held her head high as she pushed through the main doors, projecting a confidence she did not feel.

The interior was crowded, with rows of desks and clerks surrounded by milling farmers and tradespeople. Helena searched for a friendly face, someone who might be able to tell her which direction to go in. And then, she found the friendliest face of all.

"Privett!"

Her faithful steward turned at the sound of his name and rushed over to her.

"Oh, my lady." He took her hands as if they had not seen each other in years. The lines between his brows seemed deeper. "I am glad you are here. I must speak with you. Come."

He led her to a bench by the far wall and bid her sit down. Helena's heart set to pounding. "What is it, Privett? What news?"

He took in a large breath. "We have not received any offers close to what we are asking. Thus far, we have not struck a single bargain."

She gaped at him. "Not one?"

"I'm afraid not."

"But…" This was most unexpected. The Southdown breed had only been in Hampshire for a short time and was much admired for its qualities. The ewes had been procured from a well renowned breeder. Why would they and their offspring attract low offers?

"Now," the steward went on, "if our fortunes do not improve today, we could travel to another nearby fair within the next week or two."

"Is there likely to be higher prices at another fair?"

Privett frowned. "This is the largest fair in the county. It is unlikely we will find farmers with deeper pockets elsewhere."

"I see." Suddenly Helena felt herself on the precipice of a deep, dark hole.

"So, I must ask you, my lady, if you would prefer us to sell your stock today, no matter the price? Or shall we hold and try again in the spring, when we may fetch more favourable offers?"

"Spring?" Her exclamation drew stares from those standing nearby, and she lowered her voice. "No, no, that is too late. You know this, Privett. Willowbridge may well wait until April, but I cannot. We must sell today."

Privett held her eyes in a kindly way, as if he wanted to savour the moment. Was it to be one of the last times he took her orders? "Very good, my lady," he said, his voice faltering. And then he stood, beckoning her to join him as he threaded his way through the crowds to where her livestock was penned. The smell of animal waste overpowered her senses, and she drew her handkerchief to her nose. Before long, her boots and petticoat were caked in mud.

As they walked, he said, "I was lately talking to another farmer about the prices for Southdown sheep, and he too was surprised by the lack of interest in our flock."

"Oh?"

"He wondered if there is some sort of defect among them."

"Among my sheep?" she asked incredulously.

"Yes, my lady."

"Impossible." She'd inspected them with Adams herself.

Privett sighed. "Just over there." He paused and pointed to a large pen towards the middle of the next row, and there was Adams, engaging with another man who gestured towards her animals.

Helena watched as Adams became very animated and shouted something, before folding his arms across his chest and turning away. Another rejected offer.

"Hmph!" Helena marched over to the pen and addressed the farmer.

"Lady Helena!" he cried, losing his balance.

"How much?" she asked.

"I beg your pardon?"

"How much did he offer you?"

"Twenty shillings for the ewes, and twelve for the lambs."

"What? But they're worth twice that!"

Adams went red in the face. "Yes, my lady. I assure you I'm doing my very best."

"I have no doubt of that, Adams. Where did that fellow go?"

She looked about and saw the man sauntering off down the row of pens. He wore a distinctive cap with a feather in it. Without any further thought, she hurried after him.

"Lady Helena?"

Ignoring Privett's call, she followed as the man went around a tent, running to keep sight of him. She also pretended not to see the startled looks of all the men about her.

Without warning, the man stopped and began to speak with another man who wore a hat with a wide brim that shielded his face. This man nodded, and gave something to the man with the feathered cap. They shook hands, and the first man went on his way.

What was afoot?

Helena retreated to a space between tents where she was partially obscured, continuing to watch the man in the large hat. After a few minutes, he was approached by two men, and they conversed for a time before shaking hands. The two men then came towards Helena, and she shrank further into the folds of a tent to avoid being seen. On emerging she could hardly believe what she saw. The men walked directly to her flock, whereupon they spent some time examining the beasts before addressing Adams. The same unsatisfactory exchange took place, whereupon the men returned to again converse with the man bearing the wide straw hat. This time, she clearly saw him give them paper notes, and she gasped.

Who was this man, and what was he playing at?

She jumped back behind the tent as the man turned in her direction and removed his hat before wiping his brow. She gasped, dropping her reticule. It was Sinclair's man!

Helena clutched at the tent's fabric as her world began to spin.

"Lady Helena! Are you well?"

She made out the shape of Privett. "No, no I am not. For I know now why we are being offered such low prices. Sinclair is behind it! Look!" She pointed. "There's his valet, and he's bribing everyone to come to us and put forth insulting figures!"

Privett squinted in that direction. "By Jove, it's him, to be sure! And you have seen cash exchanged?"

Helena nodded, struggling for breath.

"'Tis unpardonable! Devious in the extreme. But there must be some other genuine buyers among those gathered."

"I suppose time will tell."

They returned to the pens, and it was some time before another farmer approached the Willowbridge flock. As he inspected the animals, a man approached him and drew him into conversation. Helena thought it might be one of the same men she'd seen earlier. After he withdrew, the farmer entered into negotiations with Adams, and a deal was struck. The farmer left to complete the necessary paperwork, and Helena approached Adams.

"Well?" she asked, knowing her voice was laced with hope.

Adams shook his head. "I talked him up a bit, but it's still far below market rates. Privett told me I am to accept all offers from now on."

Beginning to feel quite desperate, Helena chased after the farmer.

"Excuse me! You there!"

He turned around. "Yes, miss?"

"That man, the one who talked to you in the Southdown pen. What did he say to you?"

The farmer grinned. "He said that the owner of that flock was desperate to be rid of them, so I was likely to get them for a fraction of their worth."

A stone settled in the pit of Helena's stomach. "And… did you?"

"Aye. Can't believe my luck! Are you looking to buy, miss?"

"I, er… thank you. Good day."

The farmer tipped his hat to her and went on his way. Privett appeared at her side.

"Well?"

"He was told to buy low. I daresay the same thing will happen to anyone who shows an interest in our animals."

Privett whistled under his breath. "Well, I never! And the reprobate himself dares not to show his own face while the mischief is carried out."

Helena chewed her lip. "Can something be done?"

"To be sure. He'll desist forthwith or be taken to the Court."

Before Helena could reply, Privett marched off towards Sinclair's man.

"Wait!" she called, starting after him. She did not wish Privett to come to any harm. The valet was clearly without morals.

Instead of dealing a blow to Privett, the man took flight as soon as he saw the steward approaching. He darted into the crowd and disappeared.

Helena caught up with Privett, who said, ""I imagine he'll be back before too long, in a less conspicuous location."

She nodded. "And who knows how many other minions are concealed within the crowds. He could simply nominate someone else to carry out the unscrupulous transactions." She wrung her hands. "If we go to another fair, surely they will follow us. I think – dear Privett – it pains me to say… we have lost."

🙠🙢

John woke in a frenzied sweat. His nightmares had returned since parting ways with Helena. The grief, the desperation, the remorse of that torrid night broke over him in relentless waves. The reality of what he'd done was worse than any dream could be. He rolled out of bed and stripped out of his nightdress, picking up the jug of water at his nightstand and pouring it straight over his head. Shaking the water from his eyes, he still felt less than a human being. His body was naked, his soul raw.

Two hours later, he'd dressed and breakfasted, and resumed the mask he wore in company to conceal his regrets. There was a knock at the door, and John answered it himself.

"Good morning," the visitor greeted him.

"Why, Doctor Harding! Good morning. What brings you to my house? Will you come in?"

John procured two cups of coffee and the gentlemen settled into the parlour.

"What can I do for you, my good man?" John asked. "Not a medical problem, I hope?"

Harding chuckled. "Fortunately, no. I rather hoped I might help *you*, or perhaps our benefactress."

John was immediately serious. "Helena? Lady Helena?"

"Yes." Harding took a gulp of his coffee before laying his cup down on the table. "You see, after your sudden exit from the ball, tongues set to wagging."

"Oh, did they?"

"Indeed. Not helped by the fact that you had escorted Lady Helena from the room earlier. It is none of my business, of course, but I thought you should know there are questions being asked about what transpired between you, and why you are now estranged."

John pulled at his cravat. "It is *nobody's* business."

"Quite so, but it doesn't take much to ruin a lady's reputation – and her future prospects. The gossip mill is gaining momentum, and I thought I should get the story from the horse's mouth, so to speak, before

Lady Helena gets hurt."

John stared at him, aghast. He had already dragged one woman's name through the mud. He would not have that happen to someone else, especially someone he loved.

"Quite right," he said at length. "I should have said something… only I thought it would hurt her less if I spoke to no one."

Harding sat back in his chair and assumed a quiet air of patience. John was glad of the space to gather his thoughts.

"When I took Helena to the library, I declared my feelings to her. And while we were… affectionate, I assure you nothing scandalous transpired. In fact, when my sister came into the room, Helena and I were in the middle of a discussion." Crimson stained his cheeks, and he could not meet the doctor's eyes.

The man cleared his throat. "A discussion?"

"Yes. There was something in particular I needed to tell her, and once she discovered the whole, she… well, that is the reason I left abruptly."

"Er, what is the reason?"

John's breach quickened, and he raised wary eyes to Harding.

"You are under no compulsion to explain, of course, but I can assure it will go no further."

John sighed. "I am soon to be returning to Shropshire, and I assume I won't be back, so I may as well confess the whole."

His anxiety returned, and the words came in fits and starts. But now that he had already lost his lady love, the stakes were no longer heightened, and he managed to communicate his folly.

Harding's countenance grew more incredulous as the story went on. At its conclusion, he uttered an oath. "I am privy to many secrets," he said. "That one is, I grant you, very salacious. And… you did not offer the girl anything?"

"I had nothing to offer." John hung his head.

"Even so. Did you give your sincere apologies, your deepest regrets – your concern for her welfare?"

John forced himself to look Harding in the eye. "I did not. I could not face up to what I'd done."

There was an awful silence, saying more than the doctor ever could. Harding rose from his chair, and went to the window, staring out in the direction of Willowbridge. "Terrible business," he muttered.

"Terrible man," John whispered, sinking his head into his hands. The clock on the mantlepiece seemed to tick with increasing force.

After some minutes, Harding turned back to face him. "Well, Barrington, I can see there has been a change in you over the last year – many changes. I hope that you are now stronger, and able to put things right – at least, as much as you can. You said you are leaving. What do you intend to do?"

John swallowed. "I will visit her – I will visit Amy. I'll do what I should have done and say what I should have said." He frowned. "I cannot ask for her forgiveness – I know that is impossible.

Instead, I shall beg to assist her and the child however I can. I will dedicate myself to the task."

Harding nodded, and came to stand beside John, grasping his shoulder. "You cannot torture yourself forever, John. Everyone deserves some happiness."

"How I curse the man I was before." John blinked back tears.

Harding shook his head. "If that man is gone, then pay him no mind."

John stood. "Will you watch over Helena for me?"

"You have my word. Shall I write to you?"

"Please do."

☙❧

As the sun hit the horizon a day after the humiliating livestock fair, Helena charged into her house without even removing her coat.

Andrews came running into the foyer. "My lady! I hope your journey was –"

"Where is Sinclair?"

"Pardon? Oh, er, he's in the library, my lady. May I –"

Helena marched down the hall and burst into the library, where she found Sinclair smoking a pipe in the armchair while reading the newspaper, and his wife dozing on the chaise longue with a book in her lap.

Sinclair had the decency to look up as she stalked over to him.

"How did you find out?" she demanded. "About the auction?"

Mrs Sinclair suddenly woke with a snort, before muttering to herself and falling back to sleep.

Sinclair smiled at Helena, his eyes glinting in triumph. "It was a challenge, I grant you. Your own people are watertight." He sucked on his pipe and blew a cloud of smoke in her direction. "So, I had to ask

285

around among the rural folk, those who don't know me from Adam. Eventually I happened upon a farmer who knew about your premium breed, and where would be the best place to sell it. Though he took some, er, persuading!"

"Bribing," Helena corrected, from between her teeth. "Let us not be coy, sir."

Sinclair laughed. "As you say, my dear. Of course, I wouldn't have known what information to ask for if it hadn't been for the tip off from Barrington."

Helena's eyes flashed, and her heart froze. "John Barrington?"

"Oh, yes." Sinclair smirked. "When I went to see him last Christmas. Naturally, I had to ply him with ample, er, lubrication. And then he willingly obliged the intelligence about your precious sheep, and your hope for them as your saviour."

She stared at him in horror as she recalled the day last autumn. Her first ride with John. It had been thrilling, enchanting… and she'd shown him her Southdown flock. It had never occurred to her that he would betray her that way. What a gullible fool she'd been.

Unable to stand in her cousin's presence a moment longer, Helena fled from the room, with Sinclair's laughter echoing down the hall.

I did not like the man I was when I'd imbibed.

John…

That night, Helena endured a fitful sleep. The truth and nightmares blurred into a horrible turmoil of emotions. She breakfasted early, dressed in her riding habit, and had Cornelius tacked. Stepping outside, she gasped at the cold and pulled her scarf tighter about her.

Shortly thereafter, she pounded upon the door of Mulberry Manor with righteous indignation. Several moments later the door was thrown open and she was met by a soured-faced Tom Morgan.

"What the devil d'ye think… Oh, my lady! Begging your pardon!" Tom bowed awkwardly. "Come in, do!"

He stepped aside, but Helena did not move. "That will not be necessary. I do not need admittance to the house; I only request a word with Mr Barrington." Her breath hitched on the name, as the man himself filled the doorway.

"Thank you, Tom," John addressed his servant. "I'll not keep you any longer." As Tom scurried away, John turned to her. "It is cold, my lady, with the sun barely up. Will you not come inside?"

She heard the kindness in his voice, choosing to avoid his eyes. Instead, she stared at his chin, noticing he had not shaved yet. Then, remembering her object, she advanced on him. She had rehearsed a speech over and over again, but all those words abandoned her in the heat of her feelings.

"You!" she cried. "You told him! And now I am ruined!"

"Helena? I mean –"

"About the Southdown sheep. My intention to sell them to save the estate. He knew because of you!"

"What? Your sheep? I never…" He sounded genuinely puzzled, but then after a moment said, "Oh, there was that night. Sinclair?"

"Yes! He conspired to spoil any chance we had of selling the flock at a profit. We failed. And now, I will never pay back the loan I took out for the repairs. I will forfeit the terms of Papa's will. I shall lose Willowbridge. How could you?" In a fit of rage, she bashed her fists against his chest repeatedly. "Why?"

He remained stoic, letting her strike him. "My lady, I did not intend to –"

"Oh, a mistake, was it? Just the same as when you attacked that girl?"

He flinched. Her words had wounded him where her fists had not. She stepped back. "You are only out to raise your own position. You thought you would side with Sinclair, until it proved easier to influence me. All the better to take the property yourself?"

"No! Do not think that!"

"It's not me you wanted," she went on, voicing the thought that had tortured her during the night. "It was Willowbridge." And with that, her anger dissipated, and to her chagrin, she began to cry.

He came closer. "Oh, Helena." The tenderness in his voice unravelled her further. "I never meant to hurt you. All those months ago when Sinclair wanted information… I didn't know you. I didn't know what was at stake. And I didn't tell him anything until he'd poured a bottle of brandy down my throat. I'd forgotten all about it, so muddled is the memory."

She sniffed, remembering her first impressions of him, and how correct they had been. His weaknesses had now become part of her own downfall.

"Now I do know you, and I would never be disloyal again. That is, if I had the chance…"

"Do you not see, John, what your carelessness has cost me?"

A sob shook her, and in one swift motion he cupped her head in his hands, dropping his face near her own.

"Yes, I see it and I am mortified beyond words." His voice cracked, and she saw a tear roll down his cheek. "I am so, so sorry. About everything."

She took his wrists to pull his hands away, but didn't have the strength, or perhaps the will, to do so. So, they stayed there, each weeping, until Helena fell forward onto his chest, completely spent. She clung to his shoulders, as if he could save her from sinking. But no one could.

His arms went around her back, at first tentative, and then stronger, supporting her. Oh, how she longed to receive his support… his love.

He spoke softly against her ear. "I want nothing more than to stay and help you – to be with you. But I know you would rather I leave."

She choked out a shuddering sob, not knowing what she wanted. "I wish…"

That her precious home was not falling apart, that it would be hers forever. That her parents were still here to guide her, so that the burden was not hers alone. And that John had never been lost and tempted into wrongdoings. "Oh, how I wish," she whispered.

But she could not change her circumstances. And he could not change the things he had done.

She forced herself to push away from his embrace. "I must go." Before she succumbed to her yearnings… before she let him love her.

He nodded, and she caught the dreadful pain and resignation in his eyes. "God bless you, Lady Helena," he said.

And she turned away.

⌘

John remained in the open doorway long after Helena's mount had galloped away with her. His arms had never felt emptier. Oh, the agony of having her so close and yet not his. If only he could have kissed the tears away from her cheeks, and whispered words of his undying love into her ear. He'd ached to hold her closer, to tell her everything would work out. They could make a plan and see it through together. She need not navigate the world alone any longer.

But instead, it was his lack of character that had scuppered their happiness once again. He'd betrayed her and hurt her, though she clearly retained some connection to him. It was folly to remain here when his very existence was causing her anguish.

Catherine alerted him to her presence with a gentle hand on his shoulder.

John sighed. "We must prepare to go home at once."

"To Amberley? Now? But isn't it a few weeks until…"

He turned to face her. "It is unfair on her for me to stay. Surely our sire cannot quibble over a few days."

Catherine nodded. "I shall ask Grace to ready herself."

"Thank you. I shall make enquiries into the earliest availability of a stagecoach."

As John gathered up his belongings in anticipation of the journey, he regarded his house fondly. That which had seemed so foreign and inadequate to begin with, was now cosy and familiar. How different he was now, his perspective of himself and the world around him so changed. He recognised how fortunate he was to be in possession of such a property.

Everyone deserves some happiness…

That may be so. What he didn't deserve, and never would, was the love of a fine woman like Helena. She was everything he could never be. And he would taunt her with his nearness no longer.

He needed to go back to Amberley and face up to what he had done. He couldn't undo the past, but he would not run from it any longer. If he could do anything to live up to Helena's lofty goals for him, the least would be to admit he'd been wicked, and to do whatever he could to set things right. He owed it to Amy, to Helena, and to Julie. But mostly to himself.

PART THREE: THE RETURN

Chapter Twenty-Eight

Privett spent the entire afternoon with Helena in her study, looking at the situation this way and that. Helena's deadline was looming – if the estate was not in the black by her, she would lose it forever. She had less than three weeks.

"Is there nothing else?" Helena asked at length.

Privett removed his glasses and mopped his brow with his handkerchief. "To sum up, the only ways you *might* be able to pay the loans are to double rents before Christmas Day, auction the entire contents of this house, or to find a willing benefactor to credit you. As you are unable to sell off any part of the properties, I cannot think of any other avenues."

"The first is inconceivable, the last highly improbable. As for the other, we have already sold the most valuable pieces I had in my possession. Are you confident emptying Willowbridge of all beds, chairs and tables would generate enough cash?"

"Sadly, I am not."

"It is also unlikely that such an auction could be conducted in so short a time. And with Sinclair here... well, I doubt he would allow any buyer onto the property."

Privett closed his books. "I must tell you that your cousin has already asked me for a statement of the accounts, in order to verify your position – and his. I was without power to refuse him."

Helena nodded, sinking back in her chair. "The worst of it is that I have failed Papa.”

“Dear child, do not blame yourself. It was none of your doing. I am sorry you will need to pay the price for this unfortunate series of events.”

She smiled at him tremulously. “I appreciate your service… and your friendship.”

He stood. “It has been my honour to watch you grow into a wonderful young woman, my lady. I wish you all the best for whatever your future holds.”

That evening when Helena came down for dinner, she found Sinclair in her chair at the head of the dining table. She gaped at him.

“Good evening, Helena,” he greeted her, unable to contain his grin. “Join us, won’t you?”

First, he takes my place, then he refuses to address me properly, and now he invites me to my own table? It is too much.

Mrs Sinclair sat at the other end of the table, so Helena sat in the middle on one side, opposite Jane. Her companion sent her a sympathetic look.

Seething, Helena turned to her cousin. “May I remind you, sir, that I am still in possession of Willowbridge until the fourth of December.”

Sinclair filled his glass with wine. “That should be ample time for you to vacate the main apartments.”

“Do let me know if you need any help packing your things,” Mrs Sinclair said sweetly.

Helena gritted her teeth. “You are too kind.”

The dinner courses were served, and Helena sat in sullen silence for some time. Was this to be her life now, subjugated in her own home? It could not be borne.

Pushing slices of beef around her plate, she said, “I expect I will relocate to the London townhouse.”

Sinclair spoke around a mouthful of potato. “Of course I shall allow you to stay, my dear, but do see you are gone by Christmas. I like to bring in the new year in town, and it wouldn’t do to be getting under each other’s feet in a smaller house, would it?”

“No,” Helena agreed coldly. “No, it wouldn’t do.”

Later, Jane sat with Helena in the drawing room’s window seat. “I suppose I shall go back to my family.”

Helena nodded. “For Christmas?”

“No, dear. As a permanent arrangement. I do not want you to have the burden of housing me, as well."

"Oh." A desperate forlornity came over Helena. "Jane, I would not stop you from being with your loved ones for the world. And I will not be able to pay your wages any longer. But…"

Jane's mouth twitched. "Yes?"

"You will think me very selfish." She took up Jane's hand. "I do not know how I could endure on my own, without your company."

"Then it's settled," Jane said firmly. "I shall stay with you, until you find a… suitable situation."

❧

"What do you say, Mama?"

John leaned forward in anticipation of his mother's answer to Catherine's question.

It was the morning after their return to Amberley, and a nervous Grace waited out in the hallway after her interview with Lady Ashworth.

The matriarch of Amberley was an inscrutable, regal woman, the beauty of her youth still apparent. She'd welcomed her children home in her own unique style.

John had stepped down from the carriage and reached for his sister's hand.

"Could you not have taken the courtesy to send a letter in advance of your arrival?"

John ensured Catherine was safely down before turning around. "Hello, Mama. There wasn't the time to write. Circumstances necessitated an expedient departure."

Her eyes slid shut as if she were in pain. "What have you done now, John?"

He sighed heavily before approaching her. "Nothing for you to worry about, Mama." He placed a kiss on her cheek, then walked past her into the house.

Now, she had the power to determine an ill-fated girl's future. She spoke at last.

"I have no objection to her being your maid, Catherine, if the arrangement is acceptable to you. I will offer her a two-week trial. If you and I are satisfied at the end of that term, we shall have a contract drawn up."

John smiled broadly, with relief and gratification. "Thank you,

Mama," he said earnestly. He was immediately possessed of a desire to write to Helena with the good news… but of course, he could not.

Lady Ashworth nodded her acknowledgement to him, regarding him thoughtfully.

"And my thanks to you too, sister mine," he said, turning his smile to Catherine. "I hope she is an asset to you."

"I have a notion she will be," she replied, "for she was an angel on the journey home."

Shortly afterwards, John readied Thora for the short ride to the village. He could have sent a servant to procure what he needed – a new razor, writing paper, and a fob chain – but he was in the habit of doing his own shopping since residing in Mulberry, and he wanted to reacquaint himself with his surroundings.

He was uneasy about being seen in public in Amberley, as if he were a marked man. He'd never been nervous about venturing into the village before. His pride had overcome any sense of responsibility. But now, he saw the main street with new eyes. He noticed the barefoot children sharing scraps of bread. He saw the widow in a chair outside her rooms, basking in the pale winter sun. As he dismounted and tethered Thora to a hitching post outside the public house, he heard the boisterous shouts of the men gathered inside.

Then he took a deep breath and walked in the direction of Jones' shop, conscious of barely-concealed stares and whispers in his wake. He tipped his hat to a group of gentry acquaintances, and the men in the group hastily returned the greeting. Were they his friends, he wondered, or did they secretly despise him?

In front of Jones', there was a baby bundled up in a perambulator, another sight he would usually ignore. But something drew him nearer. He looked about and saw what must be the nursemaid close by, chatting to a farm girl. He crept closer to the tiny creature until he could see its plump little face. In slumber, it was as innocent and peaceful as an angel. He gasped as the baby stirred and gurgled sweetly. Then, he opened his eyes.

For there was no question it was a boy. It was *John's* boy: his own flesh and blood. The eyes looking back at him were exactly like his own. The same large dark orbs he had come to despise in the mirror. These were new and fresh and free from his soiling influence. As they would ever be.

Something shifted within John, deep and irrevocable. He swallowed against the lump rising in his throat. Then his heart began to pound as he realised the boy's mother might be nearby.

The baby wriggled in his wrappings, pulling an arm free. He cooed at John, the corners of his mouth bending into a handsome toothless smile.

"Hello there," John whispered, "my boy."

The baby reached out with both chubby arms, and John was powerless to resist the strong paternal urge. He reached into the perambulator purely on instinct, having no idea how to handle an infant, no idea what he would do.

"Get back!"

At the sound of the scream, John jerked upright then whirled towards the sound, meeting pure hatred in the eyes of Miss Amy Miller.

"Get away from my child!" She ran at him and shoved him away from the pram.

The force of her blow sent him reeling backwards. His mind spun from his hostile victim to their baby. "He's my son," he murmured, still shocked and awed.

"No!" she shrieked. "He's not yours, and he never will be!"

A crowd was gathering. Amy exchanged heated words with her maid, before charging back at John.

He held up his palms in a placatory gesture. She was quite correct – he had no claim on his own son, no right to touch him. It was a love he would never know. "Enough," he said, unable to give voice to his thoughts. "Enough." There was nothing for either of them to gain from such a public confrontation. With a last glance at the infant, he pivoted and headed back down the road. His errands would have to wait.

John's emotions overwhelmed him as he made his way back to Thora. The most powerful were the ever-pervasive regret and guilt, made infinitely more real by Amy's unbridled loathing of him. She was not alone in her assessment. His own utter revulsion towards his past behaviour made the bile rise from his stomach. He'd seen it in Helena's eyes, too.

On reaching Thora, he stroked the length of her nose and then rested his cheek against the whiskers on her muzzle. She nickered softly, and he said, "We need to go home again, girl."

As he began to untie her, he heard footsteps behind him. Glancing behind, he saw a local man approach, then he brought Thora's reins over her head and reached for the saddle.

"I'll have a word," a voice said behind him, and not in a congenial manner.

Barrington turned to see the same man, his curiosity piqued. "Who are you? I know I've seen your face."

The man sighed. "I'm Henry Russell. The son of–"

"Oh yes, the farmer. I remember. What can you have to say to me?"

Russell took a step closer. "It's about Amy Miller."

Another dagger of remorse stabbed at John's heart. "Oh?"

"Yes. You scared her half to death just now. And I for one am not going to let you get away without you knowing how much you've hurt her."

He'd frightened her with his very presence, as if he was a monster she needed to ward off. Well, he was, wasn't he?

This man clearly needed to say his piece. John would hear it. He forced himself to look Russell square in the eyes, determined to no longer run from the truth.

"Do you realise what you did to her? You took her innocence. You made her unable to trust or love anyone again. She'll never be happy because of you!"

Dagger after dagger, and he deserved them all. He blew out a breath and blinked hard to keep tears at bay. There was no defence.

He ran a hand over his face, searching for words. His mind filled with the image of Amy charging at him with rage and indignation. "I admit I was surprised to see her in the village," he said. Then he recalled the baby, with its smile and small arms reaching for him. "And the child…"

"Surprised? Inconvenient for you, is it? I'll have you know you left her destitute, on the verge of life in the workhouse. She was taken in by good people, but that's no thanks to you. You used her and then deserted her." He paused. "I know what you people think. Those of the lower classes don't deserve your pity or your help. We exist simply to serve you. Well, you have to know that we hurt just as much as any lord or lady – we have feelings and rights. And what you did to Amy is just plain evil."

The barrage of words cascaded over John, pushing him under the waters of his guilt so far that he fought for breath. Desperately he asked, "Are you finished, sir?"

"Yes, I suppose I am. What do you have to say for yourself?"

He had rehearsed the words he would say to Amy, refining and repeating them for the whole journey back to Shropshire. For this man, all he had was the raw truth. He shook his head, knowing there was nothing that would satisfy him. "I was a fool. I was the bloody devil. I wish it could be undone."

He studied Russell. For a man who wasn't Amy's relative, he was incredibly defensive of her. He must be in love with her. John admired his gumption and could only hope he had good intentions. "Are you going to look after her?"

"What?"

"A man does not challenge another man unless there is a significant degree of feeling in the case. You love her, do you not?"

Russell nodded.

"And you intend to do the decent thing by her?"

"I hope to, if she will have me."

A sense of relief washed over John. He could sense the man's integrity. "You are a better man than I am. My good wishes to you both. I will try to stay out of the way."

His emotions now threatening to spill over, he turned and mounted Thora, riding away from the village without looking back.

He would face his past head on. He'd return home, attempt to eat some luncheon, and confirm the directions to where Amy now resided. He must convey his feelings to her. Where once pride and cowardice had prevented him from speaking, now conscience and rectitude demanded it. He would not know it, but Henry Russell had given him some more words to say.

❧

Helena spent the week on a farewell tour of sorts. First, she visited the Powells and conveyed the sad news that she was to no longer be mistress of Willowbridge.

She attempted a smile as she announced, "The Sinclairs will be your new patrons."

The vicar and his wife exchanged a glance. "I do hope they share your enthusiasm for serving our community."

"So I do," Helena said doubtfully.

Each day, she loaded a basket with food provisions and other household items, and distributed gifts to her tenants and friends as she said goodbye. She left the most difficult farewells for last: Mr Harding and Mrs Kendall. The former enclosed her in a fatherly hug, and the latter shed a tear.

"I've come to rely on you as a true friend," the widow said.

"Oh!" Helena sniffed, quite overcome. "I shall be able to visit from time to time."

She held her composure until leaving the house and quitting the village, whereupon she began to sob violently, and wish for a certain pair of strong and loving arms to comfort her. How could she turn her back on everyone and everything she held dear, and forge a new path, alone?

Upon returning home she found Jane in her chamber, packing clothes into her trunk. She relayed the day's difficult conversations.

Jane sat next to her on the bed. "I am in the same boat, my love. It is very, very sad."

They embraced each other in shared sorrow.

"I do not know if I shall ever return to Mulberry," Jane said on a sigh. "You may return for a visit, of course."

"You are right, dear Jane. Although I may not have the funds to travel in future… and I do wonder if I can bear Sinclair's condescension."

"I was hoping it wouldn't come to this." Jane shook her head. "I didn't quite believe you would lose it."

Helena took her hand. "I suppose I'd been secretly wishing that John's affections had come at just the right time, that a union with him would ensure Willowbridge was safe."

"Yes. But you did love him as well, did you not?"

"Yes," Helena whispered. "Yes."

That undeniable truth stayed with her as she continued to pack her own belongings. The ache over John's absence from her life was as strong as ever.

But she could not overlook his past actions, or align herself with someone capable of such behaviour… could she? To put her trust and faith in such a man was a monumental risk – but what was the alternative? Now that she had known the wonder and joy of his attentions, his understanding, could she endure a life alone? He'd comprehended aspects of her that no other man had. He'd wanted to know her thoroughly and completely. And now, as she ventured forth into the world, she would be unknown.

As her things were brought down to the waiting stagecoach, Helena sat in her parents' sitting room. Hanging above the fireplace was a portrait of them both, commissioned shortly after their marriage. Arm in arm, they radiated love, joy, and hope. Surely, they had looked forward to many happy years together, with a large family about them, and Willowbridge secure for future generations.

Helena stood and went to stand under the painting. "I'm sorry," she said to the image of her parents, and then she turned away to leave the only home she'd ever known.

Chapter Twenty-Nine

Despite his desperation to address Amy Miller, John made himself wait for nearly three hours before setting out again. He wanted to make sure she'd had time to return home again and, hopefully, regain some equilibrium. As for John, he was a bundle of nerves.

As he perched on a chair in the drawing room, attempting to read the newspaper, he was joined by his father. They exchanged pleasantries, discussed the news of the day, and then Lord Ashworth paused.

"You were prompt in your return here, John. I thought you might grow to like living in Mulberry, and the independence it affords."

John stifled a sigh. "Your suppositions were not entirely inaccurate. But developments of a rather personal nature obliged me to leave."

Lord Ashworth blinked. "Ah."

Silence descended upon them, perhaps an invitation for John to elaborate – but he had no intention of doing so.

At length the older man enquired, "When do you intend to go back to Hampshire?"

"Er… I cannot say." For now, John could only focus on this day, this task. Shortly thereafter he had Thora readied, and his mind was in tumult as he cantered back to the village.

Would Amy hear him out as he expressed his regrets? Would she see how much his heart towards her had changed? Would she let him beg to help her and the child in practical service, in any way she saw fit?

His hand shook as he rapped upon the door of Harcourt Lodge, the residence of the gentry couple the Fortescues and now, Miss Miller and her baby. The door was opened in short order by an austere-looking butler who enquired as to his business there.

He cleared his throat. "I am John Barrington, and I wish to speak with Amy Miller."

The butler looked him up and down, then gave a brief nod. "Come in, please."

He was shown to a withdrawing room and asked to wait while the butler ascertained the lady's availability. He tried to sit on the seat he'd been offered, but he began to pace about the room before the butler had even left. He muttered his rehearsed phrases as he trod this way and that.

Then, through the room's open door he heard a noise which stilled his steps and his voice. A sudden pounding, which began loudly and then faded away. Footsteps. Someone running?

Next there was the sound of knocking, and Amy's name being called... repeatedly. Nausea began to stir in John's gut, which only increased as he heard the butler move to other parts of the house in his search.

Finally, the servant reappeared, his colour heightened. "It appears, sir, that Miss Miller is no longer home."

"I see." John wiped the sweat from his upper lip with the back of his hand, considering his options. "I expect there is no point in waiting for her," he said, trying to conceal his disillusionment. "Thank you for your time. I'll see myself out."

John's limbs felt numb as he went around the house to retrieve Thora. Of course she would not see him. Why should she grant him the courtesy of an audience? Why would she risk exposing herself to more hurt?

Had she run away from him just now? Had she seen his approach and decided to flee rather than face him? She could have simply told the butler to lie, to say that she was not at home. But no, he'd said she was 'no *longer* home', when he'd clearly expected her to be there.

Amy, his victim, was terrified of him, as she had every right to be. With every beat of Thora's hooves on the return journey, he descended further and further into self-loathing.

...you do not possess the heart of a gentleman...

...just plain evil...

His pulse throbbed in his ears as he dismounted and handed Thora to a stablehand. He paused before heading to the house. Catherine had gone to visit nearby relatives with their sister Louise, so there was no one there he could talk to. She didn't deserve to be burdened with this in any case. He turned and headed towards the woods, trudging through the mud and slushy snow as darkness began to descend.

He could never begin to fathom the depth of the suffering he'd imposed upon Amy Miller. The abhorrence in her eyes went some way to showing him. She'd looked at him as if he were worse than the very lowest insect which crawled the earth – and he quite agreed with her.

At the same time, there was his son, his own flesh and blood. John would never know the joy of receiving the boy's love, or of even holding him. He'd wouldn't dream of denying the baby his mother or poisoning the child with his influence. No, his son was in the best place… although he shouldn't exist at all.

He came to a river and was reminded of Cecilia Grant, whom he knew often sketched or painted near here. Thank goodness she hadn't accepted his marriage proposal. He would have ruined her life, too. At least William Brook had strength of character enough to overcome John's stupid schemes against him.

He began to walk alongside the river's dark rushing waters, and visions of Helena ambushed his mind. How was she faring in the light of her uncertain future? Did she regularly curse his name, or not think of him at all? He would never forgive himself for his part in her undoing. She, above anyone, merited a secure and happy life. Would that he could have given that to her, but he was doomed to destroy, not cherish. For a few precious months, he'd thought he could live a satisfying life of dedication to others, but he was surely better off alone… or not here at all.

He was so, so tired. Tired of running from himself and his nefarious nature. A life without love was not worth living. And he could never redeem himself now. Who would miss him if he were gone? All those years he had thought he didn't need the world, but perhaps the world didn't need him.

He raised his gaze, through tears he hadn't noticed falling, and made out the silhouette of a bridge. At this point the river grew narrow and deep, and it seemed beckon John to disappear into its inky blackness.

With each step his feet grew heavier and heavier, until he could barely walk. He hauled himself to the crest of the bridge and peered down at the rushing waters below, as soft flakes of snow began to drift down from the sky.

…I wish that I had never known you…

…I cannot bear the sight of you…

After tonight, no one would have to see him again. It was time to get his feet off the ground.

This was for Helena, for Amy, for Catherine. Even for his mother. Women who had put their faith in him, and who he'd failed miserably.

His sobs subsided and an eery sense of calm descended on him. A resolve, a purpose. He stepped up onto the bridge's wall and ran a finger over his signet ring. This was for Julie, too; God rest her soul.

He jumped.

At first, there was the icy shock of the water's surface. Then when he hit the riverbed, pain cascaded through him: a welcome pain. He deserved it… and so much more. It staved off his numbness and desperate emptiness. His body instinctively fought to break above the water, but a torrent gushed over him, and he choked blindly. Flailing as he bumped over jagged rocks, his sensations started to weaken and he finally gave up and surrendered himself to this, his final journey. After his head collided with a large boulder, a bolt of agony shot down his neck and along his limbs, and then there was no more feeling, only darkness.

Unbeknownst to John, there was someone else perilously close to death that night.

❧

Helena woke gasping for breath. "John! John?"

Her cheeks were soaked in tears, her heart pounding. In that state where dreams are still reality, fear for the man she loved gripped her. He was not only gone from her world, but from the wider world too. The feeling of losing him forever was too painful to withstand.

It was just a dream, Helena, she chided herself. Still, the strength of her emotions toward him, even now, surprised her. The sensation that something was wrong was overwhelming. She wished she could write to him, but then, what could she say?

She sat up and reacquainted herself with where she was. She was in her room in London, and even in what must be very early morning there was noise outside, with light shining through the gap in her curtains. She pushed the bedclothes aside, padding to the nightstand in stockinged feet. She poured water into the bowl there, moistened a cloth, and wiped at the sweat on her forehead. Did John need her?

"Don't be silly," she said to herself aloud. He was at home, with his friends and family. He'd be too busy to be thinking about her.

Sighing, she tiptoed to the window and pulled the curtain back to see the activity in the street below. The pale light of the streetlamps illuminated thick yellow fog which swirled about the few people in the street. A horse and cart went by laden with goods. From the other direction came a farmhand, driving half a dozen cattle along the road. Light flickered in the baker's shop on the corner as the day's bread was made, and a boy came whistling up the street as he delivered copies of *The Times*. It was so very different from the early morning chorus of birds in the country.

Helena picked up the cloth again and sat on the edge of the bed. She washed her face and neck, accepted she would have no more sleep this night. Her real worries would keep her awake until the sun rose.

She had ten days. Ten days to find somewhere to live, and consider how she might pay her way, for the short term at least. The most obvious solution would be to seek employment as a governess, or perhaps a secretary. She would visit in person as many agencies as she could, but until the Season began many would be closed.

Today, though, she had other plans. She and Jane would visit with Laura Montgomery. Helena was desperate to see a friend before beginning her mission in earnest. The city seemed larger and more hostile than ever, and she sorely needed some reassurance.

The first thing Laura did upon welcoming Helena in was to offer her a room in their house. She held her little baby close, while Agnes ran around them in circles in the drawing room.

"I couldn't possibly impose," Helena protested. "You have your hands full."

"Nonsense, I would welcome your help," Laura said as she motioned for them to sit.

Helena exchanged a glanced with Jane. "I did not come here to beg for your hospitality," she said, hoping her friend knew she valued her more highly than that. She also knew that even if she could bring herself to accept this offer, it must only be for a short time. She had no intention of being a third wheel to a young married couple.

"I know you didn't, dear," said Laura, shifting the baby onto her shoulder.

Agnes plopped down onto the couch between Helena and Jane, then kicked each of her feet in turn. Helena admired her shining gold curls, and wondered what colour hair her children with John would have. Treacherous heart!

"Have you discussed this with your husband?" Jane asked.

Laura nodded with a smile. "He'd be delighted for me to have some consistent company. It might mean my mother would be a less frequent visitor."

Helena laughed. "I will consider it. You are really too good. But I must find a way to contribute to your outgoings."

Before Laura could reply, Agnes jumped up and announced she would give a concert. Standing before them, she began to tunelessly sing possibly every nursery rhyme she knew. Helena applauded wildly at the end of each song, her enthusiasm bolstered by the relief of knowing she would not necessarily be homeless at Christmas. Beyond that, who could say.

❧❧

Light penetrated John's eyelids, and his mind began to stir. Was this heaven or hell?

Pain flooded his body, like a hundred shards of glass stabbing him. Hell. Of course, hell.

Next, he was aware of the sounds of water running, a bird chirping, and a low voice. Where was he? He forced his eyes open, his temples pounding like a sinister drum. He blinked, adjusting to the light.

A man was bent over him, frowning though his eyes were closed, and muttering words. Surely it could not be…

"Brook?" His voice was thick and gravelly.

The man's eyes flew open. "Ah, praise the Lord!" It was indeed William Brook, Amberley's vicar. "I thought you were slipping away from us."

That was my intention. But I seem to have failed at that, too.

John tried to look about, though the hurt that consumed his head limited his range. He was lying on a grassy bank next to the river, though he did not recognise this stretch of it.

"You're near the vicarage," Brook told him. "I found you face down in the river. You were… not in a good way."

Comprehension dawned. "You saved my life," he croaked.

Brook met his eyes. "Perhaps."

"Why would you, when I tried to ruin you?"

"Well, I didn't see who it was at first." Brook smiled. "Do you think I could let another man die, regardless of what he has done?"

There was a clarity and steadiness in Brook's eyes that John wanted to cling to. "No, I suppose you could not."

"Am I able to leave you to summon assistance?"

John nodded, then winced as the cloudiness threatened to consume him again. As the vicar stood, he noticed the man was clad only in shirtsleeves. He looked down and realised that Brook's greatcoat, jacket, and scarf were wrapped around him instead.

"Brook, you must be freezing!"

The vicar smiled again. "You have the greater need." Then he turned and ran up towards the row of buildings at the top of the hill.

John tried to move his hands, but they were so cold he couldn't feel them. His feet were also numb. He was completely immobile for the first time in his life. Then something moved on his forehead, slowly coming down and across one eyebrow. The thing trickled into his eye, and as his vision was obscured in a red blur, he realised it was blood. He dropped his head back down to the ground and cried out in agony.

The next time he woke, it was to find the burgundy velvet of a bed canopy. *His* bed at Ashworth Hall. He tried to take a deep breath, but his chest contracted in pain. This time when he wiggled his fingers, he could feel them. Relieved, he tried moving his arms, but one of them was too sore, and now that he raised his head, he saw it neatly bandaged – surely the work of a physician. With his free hand he tentatively reached up to touch his face. There were cuts and probably bruises, and he felt bandages just above his eyeline. Then he tried moving his legs, but instantly regretted the attempt, his head hitting the pillow once more. Why did he not remember a doctor's visit?

When he'd calmed his own breathing, he became aware of the sound of someone else's. His gaze followed the sound, and found his mother, asleep in a chair a few feet from the bed.

"Mama?" His voice was thin, his throat thick.

Lady Ashworth murmured something in her sleep and then woke with a start. She rubbed her eyes, yawning, then saw him and blinked several times. "John? Oh, John, you're awake! You're alive!"

She rushed to his side and took his hand in both her own. She examined his face as if he were a precious heirloom. "Dear child, I thought I might never see those eyes again."

Were those tears forming in her eyes? John swallowed back his own emotion, suddenly shy and confused.

He tilted his head toward the chair. "Why… why were you sleeping there?"

She gave him a wry smile. "I was here with you all last night. I must have nodded off."

"Last night?"

"Yes, John. This is your second day abed." She released his hand and got up from the bed. "Will you take some water?"

"I – er, yes."

Lady Ashworth moved to the nightstand and took up the pitcher, half-filling a drinking glass. Returning next to John, she put one hand behind his neck and gently pulled his head up, before putting the glass to his bottom lip and carefully tipping water into his mouth.

John watched her in awe. He was almost sure he could have held the glass himself, but the care and attention of his mother was a balm to his soul.

"Thank you, Mama," he said after several small mouthfuls. "Can you not send someone to look after me? Even one of my sisters?"

She frowned. "Despite what you may think, I do care about you. You are badly injured and have lost a lot of blood. The doctor was not sure if you would wake again. I would not have left you for the world."

John did not have any words, so full was his heart. She really cared for him? He thought he'd lost that privilege long ago.

"John," she said softly, "did you mean to leave us?"

He took a slow breath. There was no point hiding anything now. He nodded.

She squeezed her eyes shut. "It seemed the only explanation," she whispered, "but I did not want to believe it."

"I'm sorry," he said, and he was.

Chapter Thirty

Helena and Jane took tea in her sitting room, collating a list of the agencies in London who placed servants among the upper classes, including governesses.

Helena sighed as she set her teacup down on its saucer. "I do not have high hopes, Jane. I have no references, no experience, and not even the knowledge required to teach and care for children. Why would any respectable person engage me in employment?"

Jane regarded her seriously, as if carefully selecting her words. "My dear, I believe in these matters that character is considered of the utmost importance. You are beyond reproach."

"Still, I –"

Helena was interrupted by the sound of knocking upon the front door. A few minutes later, the butler appeared in her doorway.

"It's Lady Lockhart, my lady. Are you at home?"

Helena smiled. "Yes. Please inform her ladyship that I shall be down presently." She went to the mirror in her room to tidy her hair, then draped a shawl around her shoulders. As she stepped into the drawing room, with Jane in attendance, Lady Lockhart rose to embrace her.

"Dear girl," said her ladyship as she pressed her cheek to Helena's. "I wish you had told me!"

"Do sit down," Helena said. "What is your meaning?"

"Good day, Miss Godwin," Lady Lockhart exchanged a smile with Jane. "Helena, your poor thing! I am just arrived in town, and I heard that you have been cast out of your home by that degenerate uncle of yours! I am quite distraught. It is too shocking."

"Your information is correct." Helena sighed. "I have not fulfilled the terms of my father's will, and therefore ownership of Willowbridge passes to Mr Sinclair."

"But is there nothing to be done? When do the deeds change into his name?"

"On my birthday, which is this next Thursday. And I am unable to accept any, er, charitable donations to save the estate. It would be too great an obligation."

Jane eyed the other ladies and rose from her seat. "If you will excuse me, I shall attend to my own correspondence."

Helena nodded her acknowledgement, and once Jane had closed the door behind her, Lady Lockhart moved to sit in the chair adjacent to her young friend.

"Now, my dear. You must tell me what your plans are."

Helena shook her head. "I have no concrete plans, save for temporary accommodation with a friend once Sinclair comes up to town. My hopes are pinned on finding a post as a governess, a companion, or... something."

"And who is helping you?"

"Miss Godwin, of course. I will apply to all the available agencies in London."

"Oh, no, that simply will not do! You may be placed somewhere quite unsuitable. No, you must be referred to an appropriate situation by your network of friends and acquaintances."

Helena took a shuddering breath. "But my lady, I have no others to speak of. I shall be quite alone."

"Nonsense! I should be only too pleased to be your conduit. It is the least I can do to honour the memory of your poor mother."

Helena stared at her. "Are you quite sure? I have no wish to –"

"Quite sure. And we shall have no more talk of loneliness. You have more friends than you realise. You must simply overcome your inflated sense of independence and reach for help. You will find it is all around you."

"Thank you." Helena smiled into the older woman's eyes, which were crinkled with kindness. "And I must thank you again for sending me that gown. I have never felt more beautiful than the night I wore it."

"I am so glad. Were you admired?"

Helena blushed, her memory filling with the sight of John's countenance when he saw her. "I believe so." She looked down at her hands, unable to stop recalling the feeling of his lips on hers.

All of my heart is yours, if you will have it.

"How lovely," Lady Lockhart said, and when Helena met her eyes there was an unmistakable sparkle in them. "There is someone, then?"

Helena nodded, then swiped at her eyes with the back of one hand. "But he has done something unspeakably horrid."

"Ah. I see. Many of us have, my dear. And yet, life must go on."

"I don't know how it can. It is unforgivable."

Her ladyship frowned. "Has he injured you, my dear?"

"No." Helena shook her head. "Someone else."

"And do you believe him capable of such deeds in the future? Your future?"

Helena shrugged helplessly. "I would not have believed him capable at all. The man I came to know… was so gentle and kind. He treated me with the utmost respect. It is all too confusing. I – I must put him behind me."

"Hmm. The look on your face just now showed me that he is still very much in your heart. I think he has made you very happy."

The hint of a smile tugged at Helena's lips. "Perhaps."

Lady Lockhart reached over and took one of Helena's hands. "I'm afraid there is no such thing as a perfect love, or indeed a perfect person. We must take the good with the bad – we must at least come to terms with it."

"That is not an easy task. I know not if I can trust him."

"Nothing worth possessing is easy, Helena. The choice is entirely yours. If you have faith in this man, you have the choice to be brave and accept his past as well as his future. Or, you can decide to face life, at least for now, on your own, which would take perhaps even more courage."

Helena nodded, her mind and heart racing. "This is all theoretical, of course. I told him I wished we had never met. And I had humbled him before. Can the male ego overcome such sentiments?"

Lady Lockhart smiled wryly. "A good test of character, is it not?"

☜❦❦

Three days later, John was propped up on a couch in the drawing room, sitting almost comfortably. His left arm was still almost useless, but his head no longer throbbed constantly.

Lady Ashworth entered with a tray, then held a bowl of chicken and cabbage soup steady as he spooned it into his mouth. Her devoted attention gave him far more healing than the broth.

"John," she began as she buttered him a slice of toasted bread, "there is something I think you should know."

He surveyed her demeanour anxiously. She was very serious. He drew in a breath. "What is it, Mama?"

"On the night of your... accident, Miss Miller took her baby through some snowy pastures and suffered an injury."

"She..." John frowned. That was the night after they'd met in the street, and he'd tried to visit with her. He remembered the sound of hurried footsteps, the confused butler, the coming snowstorm. She'd fled from him without any regard for her safety – or that of their child. He dropped his spoon as his stomach plummeted. "Dear God, are they both well?"

Lady Ashworth nodded. "They were found the following morning, the baby miraculously unharmed. Miss Miller was in a sorry state, I believe, but is beginning to come to rights."

John fell back onto his mound of cushions in relief. Still, the situation was far from ideal. He'd come to offer her help, but he'd only traumatised her further.

"I only received the news this morning," Lady Ashworth added.

If only he could ask his sister to wait upon Amy. "Will you write to Catherine, and ask her to return early? She may be able to offer Miss Miller some cheer... and perhaps some gifts to occupy her while she recovers?"

Lady Ashworth smiled. "That is a considerate notion, John. I have in fact already dispatched a missive to Catherine, as I too thought she would want to know the information."

John lurched upright again. "Did you tell her about my... er..."

"No. It is your decision how much you divulge, and I would urge you to treat the subject with extreme delicacy. She is still very young."

John nodded. "Yes, I would not trouble her unnecessarily." He was also ashamed to admit his own weakness to her.

Lady Ashworth handed him the toast, and he dunked it in the soup before taking a bite. "John," she said in quite a different tone, "you are changed – for the better. It is quite remarkable. Who is she?"

John hastily swallowed the chunk of bread which almost became lodged in his throat. "She?"

His mother just looked at him knowingly. With their new level of transparency, he had no wish to demur.

"There is – was – someone, but I am not… of good enough character for her."

Lady Ashworth raised an eyebrow. "Did she tell you that?"

He shrugged. "She knows the truth." The disappointment in Helena's eyes was all still fresh in his mind.

"Do you love her?"

He shrugged again, but tears welled in his eyes as he looked away helplessly. His regard for her was as strong as ever.

"Does she love you?"

"Not anymore." He sighed. "Because of what I did, I will never be acceptable to any lady of good moral character."

"Oh, John." She took his good hand and pressed it to her cheek, her own eyes misty. "I do wish to see you happy. When – if – you have met the right person, the love will be too great to deny. It will endure any trial."

∽∾

"Brook, good of you to come."

John pushed himself to stand on unsteady legs in order to greet the vicar properly, with a handshake. It was a gesture he never would have considered in prior circumstances.

Brook gripped his hand firmly, the warmth in his eyes seeming to acknowledge a truce between them.

"You must be pleased to be on your feet."

Once they were both seated, John was compelled to address the trauma he'd learned the Brooks had recently suffered through: the death of a newborn child.

Looking the vicar in the eye, he said, "Please allow me to offer my sincere condolences to you and your wife for your loss."

Brook stared at him for a few moments, before blinking hard. Then he nodded in response.

"How is Mrs Brook?" John asked gently.

"As well as can be expected, I think."

"Is there anything you need? Not presuming that I am equipped to assist you…"

Brook shook his head and smiled. "I can see your intentions are genuine, and I thank you."

John had had a lot of time to think over the past few days. There was so much he needed to say to this man, and much he needed to hear.

He took a breath. "I must express my gratitude to you for pulling me from the river – for saving my life."

Brook tilted his head in acknowledgement. "Every life is precious, John. I hope you know that."

"Yes, now more than ever. I know I have not been respectful of others' lives. I know I have been spiteful, vindictive, and careless… and cowardly. And as I *am* still alive, it is my intention to make amends as well as I can… to build some bridges, at least. I know it is impossible to change my past behaviour, though I wish I could. So much will *never* be righted."

He shook his head and sighed, then gestured toward Brook.

"At least you were able to rise above my machinations. Please know I am sorry, truly sorry, for everything I did. To you, Mrs Brook, and especially Miss Miller, of course. My actions will haunt me forever."

Brook held his eyes. "There is no greater breach of trust," he said quietly. "It is a relief to know you feel remorse. Your actions, or lack thereof, following the attack were also deplorable."

John nodded, readily accepting the censure. "I know, I know. She begged me for help. I had nothing to give her – no material support. And I was too proud to admit it. I hate myself for the way I behaved."

"Yes, guilt is a heavy burden to shoulder. If you should want to speak to someone about it, you know where I am."

"Thank you." Perhaps he would take up the offer, one day. "I suppose you know I went to see Amy? She will not see me – quite understandable, of course – so I am unable to offer my apologies or my help. What can I do for her if I cannot be in her presence? What can I give?"

Brook raised an eyebrow. "What do you have?"

John considered this, the answer suddenly obvious. "I have the manor. My lands in Hampshire."

"That you do." Brook shifted in his seat. "I admit I am curious. What transpired during your stay there? You are not the same man as before."

"Oh, well…" Visions of the past year whirled through John's mind, with feelings and hopes so tender he'd been certain he would never share them. But the vicar's countenance was nothing but open and earnest, and before he could stop himself John began to talk about all that had happened during his time in Mulberry, and how it had changed him. He spoke of his love for Helena and how he'd wronged her. The words tumbled out of him, much the same way his bruised body had tumbled helplessly over the rocks in the river. Once he had started revealing himself, it seemed he did not know how to stop. Brook only murmured occasional encouragement as he went on with ruthless honesty.

"I cannot drive her face from my mind," he said brokenly, in conclusion. "I would do anything – anything – to have her think well of me. But it is hopeless." He gazed down at his hands, realising he'd removed his signet ring during his speech, and now he'd crushed it so hard into one palm that it ached. He opened his fingers and placed it down on the side table next to him.

"We all make mistakes, every one of us," Brook said, "though they vary by degree. We live in a constant state of redemption. But if one's intentions are good, one's motives pure, there is no end to the forgiveness and patience of those who love us."

A lump formed in John's throat. He willed himself not to hope.

"Give it time, John. The story may not be over just yet." He stood and crossed the room, taking John's shoulder in a reassuring grip. "I believe you can be a force for good. My prayers will be with you."

"Thank you," John said, again. "If I may ask one more thing… would you ask my father to come to me, please?"

"Certainly."

A few minutes later, Lord Ashworth entered the room, taking the seat opposite John and crossing one leg over the other. "What is it? Anything amiss?"

John shook his head, a broad smile taking over his face. "No, indeed. May I ask permission to send for the solicitor in Walford? I have some instructions for him."

"Oh?" The elder man scratched the beard on his cheek. "What are your plans?"

❧

Helena accompanied Jane to the mews behind the Davenport townhouse. There waited the hired carriage that would take Miss Godwin to her brother's house in Lancashire. Helena had insisted she make the journey while the roads were dry, in plenty of time for Christmas.

The coachman was at the rear, loading the last of her possessions. There had been many tears from both women over the last few days as they'd prepared for Jane's departure and reminisced about many special times in their shared past. Helena's governess-turned-companion had been the most constant presence in her life, and a future without her was beyond comprehension. And yet, here it was.

Now, at the moment of parting, there were no more tears left. Helena supposed Jane wanted to be brave to spare her feelings, as she was employing the same tactic. The tension was evident in the tight hold of both their hands.

"I pray you have a swift and uneventful journey, dearest," Helena said in scarcely more than a whisper.

"And I wish you all the luck in the world in finding a suitable post. Do take care of yourself, darling Helena."

The ladies embraced, and then with a last affectionate look, Jane stepped up into the carriage and took her seat. The coachman leapt onto the box seat, took the reins, and set the horses into motion. As Jane waved from the window, the reality of their parting stung in Helena's chest. She waved the carriage from sight, and then she was alone – quite alone – for the first time in her life.

She returned to the townhouse. Her solitary footsteps echoed in the entrance hall, hers the only hats and scarves that hung on the hooks by the door. She glanced at the stairs down to the basement, where the servants dwelled. That would likely be her place in a different house once she found a position. She hoped that Jane would find a permanent place soon, too.

She went upstairs and found herself entering her mother's room, which Mrs Sinclair would no doubt soon claim. This was her last chance to preserve the memories of the late Lady Davenport, and it was a task for Helena alone.

With a resigned sense of purpose, Helena opened her mother's trunk and began filling it with precious items. She emptied the wardrobe of clothes, then ran her fingers over the rings and necklaces in the jewellery box before placing it, too, in the trunk. In the drawers of Lady Davenport's dresser were hair accessories, corsets, petticoats, and the like, as well as hundreds of letters. One of the bottom drawers held a box full of treasures: gifts from her husband too precious to put on display. A beautiful lace shawl lay on top. Helena held an emerald brooch up to the light and green shards pierced the room. There was a dried floral corsage, a cameo of her ladyship's likeness, and a bottle of French perfume. At the bottom lay a book of poems with handwritten notes from both of Helena's parents. She hugged it to her chest before carefully laying it back in the box, along with all the other items.

The final items to inspect were contained in two boxes at the bottom of the wardrobe. The contents were a mystery to Helena. Upon opening the first, she discovered a great many drawings, undoubtedly by the lady herself. While Helena had been aware that her mother had such a talent, Lady Davenport was very self-conscious about it, preferring to keep her sketches private.

Helena sat on the floor and began to sift through them. Immediately emotion swelled in her chest, for her mother's subjects were confined to only those she loved.

While there were drawings of her ladyship's closest friends (including Lady Lockhart), her parents and siblings, the majority of the pictures were of Lord Davenport and their daughter. Scenes from Helena's early years were documented, from her christening to the last days they had together. Her attention was particularly captured by a sketch of herself on a rocking horse, lovingly done. The eyes of the little girl in the picture were on the artist, the face glowing with a wide grin. She could almost remember being there, and the affection they had shared.

Oh, Mama.

The most complete sketch was of her father, reading in the library. The most striking aspect was the style in which Lord Davenport had been depicted. The sinuous lines and delicate curves which marked out his face, his hair, his fingers, left no doubt of the artist's regard for her subject. Helena's heart ached for the absence of her father, and she cried for the missing years with her mother. She mourned for the loss of their great love, and the siblings she might have known.

Helena withdrew the last picture, and gasped as she found her mother looking back at her. Recovering from her shock, she choked on a sob as she reached out a shaking finger and lightly stroked one of the cheeks, then ran her finger over the curls of hair. Then, Helena pressed two fingers to her own lips, and placed a 'kiss' on her mother's.

Taking a deep breath, she opened the other box, and temporarily forgot how to breathe. Lying atop fabric of creamy white satin, was a pair of white slippers, a tiara, long gloves, and silk stockings.

"Her wedding attire," Helena whispered reverently, carefully putting each item aside. And then, she withdrew the gown beneath, standing to let the dress fall to its full height. Fine lace adorned the bodice, sleeves and hem, and a delicate pattern of flowers and leaves was embroidered on the skirt. An elegant pelisse in golden satin was the last item in the box.

Helena was unable to resist the temptation to walk with the dress to the mirror that sat atop the dresser. As she moulded the dress to her figure, fresh tears pricked her eyes. *Was she keeping it for me to wear?*

She closed her eyes, and immediately a vision of herself in the dress consumed her imagination. She walked down the aisle at a church on her father's arm, feeling the warmth of his love. And who was waiting for her at the altar? None other than John Barrington – of course. No other man had ever laid claim to her heart.

Could she make peace with the horrendous sins in his past? She recalled Lady Lockhart's words.

Nothing worth possessing is easy, Helena... you have the choice to be brave and accept his past as well as his future.

She could no longer deny that this union was the desire of her heart. To be with him, to know him deeply and be cared for by him, to share everything they had. To rest in his strength – physically and emotionally. To be his.

She opened her eyes. She might never see him again. And then, she would have lost not only her home, but the chance for a life as a cherished wife, perhaps an adored mother. In four days, she would be twenty-one, and she must accept a life of uncertainty and dependence.

Helena packed the wedding things away and set the two boxes down beside the trunk. The last item to collect was a bottle of her mother's favourite fragrance from a bedside table. She picked it up and sprayed the perfume into the air. Walking through the gardenia mist, she made a promise.

I'll be brave for you, Mama.

Chapter Thirty-One

"Are you quite sure you want to do this, young Barrington?"

The solicitor, Mr Bancroft, laid his pen down upon the desk and then paused, scrutinising John over his glasses.

"Yes," John replied. "Quite sure."

Mr Bancroft's gaze flicked to Lord Ashworth and back. "But what will you do?"

Barrington shrugged. "I rather think I shall beg my father to purchase a commission in the army for me. Perhaps I may join a regiment engaged in battle with the French."

"Surely you'd be much safer on home soil, sir."

"I daresay you are correct." His safety and comfort were not the priority.

"Well, if you are determined…" Mr Bancroft gathered up the papers in front of him and laid them before John, pointing to all the places he needed to sign or initial. Lord Ashworth added his own moniker as the witness, and it was done. And with it, some of the weight lifted from John's shoulders.

He followed his father to where most of the family were assembled, in the drawing room. Three of his siblings were playing cards, and his mother was engaged with a book. John shifted his weight from foot to foot, wondering how to begin.

During the night, he had come to a startling realisation. He must leave Amberley for the long term. While reluctant to turn his back on his home, after Amy's dramatic reaction to his presence he knew it must be hers instead.

In his past life, he would have baulked – what right did a farmer's daughter have to supplant him from his home territory? But after what he'd done to her, she had every right – and then some. He must leave her to live in peace and find as much happiness as she could for herself and for their son. He was to become Russell's son by the looks of things. And although John would make sure the boy was taken care of financially and would always want to know how he was doing, he wouldn't interfere further. He owed her that much and so much more besides.

It was fitting, in a way. He had refused to speak to her when she needed him the most, and now she could not speak to him when he needed to make his peace with her – to try. He would leave her be, but at some stage in the distant future when her hurt was not so raw, he would come back to Amberley and apologise to her face to face. He must. For now, a letter would have to do.

At the sound of crunching gravel on the driveway, John went to the window to watch the arriving carriage. Catherine was assisted to alight, and he rushed to the foyer to meet her.

"My darling sister!" he greeted her, crushing her in a fond embrace.

"I have only been away for a week, brother dear," she said with a laugh. She pulled back and frowned. "You're hurt."

He shook his head. "Only a little. Dearest, will you do me a favour?"

"Such as?" She arched a brow.

He reached into his jacket pocket. "Will you please give this letter to Amy?"

She took the folded paper and regarded it warily. "It will not cause her further alarm? I'm led to believe she is in low spirits as it is."

"I would not trouble her further for the world. Please trust me."

She nodded. "I do."

John smiled and offered his arm. "Come."

He led her to the drawing room, asking her to sit down. Then, he announced his plans to the gathered family. After his explanation, he concluded, "And that is why I must give up Amberley, for good."

His elder brother stood. "Steady on, old chap. A trifle histrionic, don't you think? Surely you cannot allow a little country miss to make you to abandon your own home. Not Ashworth."

John fixed him with a cold stare. "It is not her doing, George. It is mine."

George gaped at him but resumed his seat without another word.

"I am proud of him, for I think his motives are selfless," Lady Ashworth said to the group. "Although I will miss him, of course." She and John shared a look of newfound understanding.

There was a knock at the door, and a footman entered with letters on a salver. Lord Ashworth took up the mail and sifted through it, handing various pieces to members of his family. "John." He passed one letter across, and John took it up curiously. Who knew he was here now?

When he read the return address, all breath left his body.

Mr Privett, of Willowbridge, Mulberry, Hampshire

He took the letter to a chair in the far corner of the room, broke the seal, and consumed its contents.

Mr Barrington,

I hope you will forgive me the presumption of writing to you. I fear Miss Davenport will not.

In her words – all is lost. She has forfeited the estate and everything she holds dear. She is fled to London and knows not how she will manage.

I gather you are somehow responsible – at least partly – for her demise. However, you may also be her saviour, if you'll permit my intrusion.

I know not if you are familiar with the full terms of Miss Davenport's right to inherit Willowbridge. There were two paths by which she could become the legal owner by her twenty-first birthday. One, I presume you know, was continuing to turn over a certain sum in profit. The other path is by matrimony.

If she is not only betrothed, but legally married, by the fourth of December, all of her uncle's devious efforts would have been in vain, and she can turn him out. She would be the rightful lady of Willowbridge, alongside her husband. I suppose it was her father's way of ensuring she was successful in one way or another… assuming the man would bring his own fortune to bear.

I take a great risk in acquainting you with this information, knowing you will need to make the correct choice of action in good conscience. It is my lady's greatest fear that a gentleman will take her hand in marriage solely to gain her property. However, if I am not mistaken, a union would be a love match as well.

My sincere apologies if my words have been impertinent or unwelcome. They are meant with the greatest of concern for Lady Helena.

Yours, etc
Gerald Privett

John's heartbeat accelerated rapidly. He'd completely forgotten that there was another way to secure Helena's future. Sinclair's words at their shoot all those months ago now, unheeded at the time, came back to him with blinding clarity.

If she marries before she is one-and-twenty she will keep the estate regardless of the profits.

The words rung in his ears like the tolling of bells. If she marries... if she marries…

Dare he try?

John swallowed. He had only minutes before signed away all his assets and future income. If he united with Helena, he would be saving her in name and title only – hardly an attractive proposition by the standards of the *ton*. But he could bring her something none other could – a love he would die for. A heart willing to do whatever it took to make her happy. A man ready to walk away from everything he had ever been, in order to be the person she rightly deserved. Her lover, in every sense of the word, for the rest of his life… whether she took his hand or not.

She had said and done enough to give him confidence in her affections. But the main hurdle to their future together lay in his past. Could she come to terms with it? Or would he simply hurt her more by reminding her of what could have been? If she still wanted him gone from her life, he would abide by her wishes. But he would never forgive himself if he didn't try in time to save her legacy.

What was the date? The first? By Jove, he only had three days.

Catherine approached, just as the wheels of his mind began to turn into a frenzy of plans.

"What is it, John? News from Mulberry?"

He stood. "I must leave at once."

"At once?" Her mouth dropped open.

He nodded. "If you would be so good as to help me gather up my things, I will apprise you of the situation."

"Of course, John. I do hope all is well."

He took her hand and squeezed it. "I hope so, too."

He hurried across the room, to where his father was still occupied with his own correspondence.

"Papa, may I trouble you to help me with one more thing?"

Lord Ashworth laid his looking glass down with a sigh. "What is it you intend to do *now*, John?"

"I need to procure a special license."

"A special *marriage* license?"

"Yes, sir."

"Good God, I thought you were set on joining the army!"

John grinned. "I shall write to you from London in three days, and then you will know my course."

☙❧

John woke early on the day he was to ride into London, at an inn in High Wycombe. Snow fell softly on the ground as he led Thora from the stables. Swinging into the saddle, he buried his nose and mouth in his greatcoat and gave the horse an encouraging pat on the neck before nudging her with his heels. "Almost there, girl."

He should be nervous, apprehensive at the uncertainty of how his advances would be received. Instead, he proceeded with an unfathomable tranquillity. Could it be that for once in his life, he was exactly where he should be, with precisely the right intent?

Not long after setting off, they came to a bridge over the River Wye. John was conscious of another burden he could be liberated from, and he pulled Thora to a stop near the riverbank.

He dismounted and pulled the leather glove from his right hand, then twisted the signet ring from his little finger. The onyx was dark as ever in the cold grey light. And now, that darkness was to John all the afflictions and mistakes of the past. It was time to move on. It was time to be free.

He tossed the ring into the slow-moving waters. It breached the surface cleanly, but created ripples that almost reached the banks on either side.

When all was still again, John slipped his glove back on with ease.

"Goodbye, Julie. May you rest in peace. And farewell, John of old."

❧❧

Helena sat with her embroidery in her lap, her needle long since abandoned. She was in the drawing room at the Montgomery townhouse, wherein the family were all on the floor in front of the fire. Laura occupied her baby's attention with a game of peek-a-boo, while her husband read a story to Agnes. It was a delightful, idyllic scene of family life, and Helena's heart ached.

She forced her eyes down to her needlework, trying not to think of what Sinclair would do to Willowbridge, trying not to miss Jane, and trying not to imagine that it was she and John playing with their own children.

There was a knock on the drawing room door, and the butler entered with a visitor's card.

"I have a Mr John Barrington here, your lord and ladyship."

Puzzled looks were exchanged between the adults on the floor, while Helena's heart threatened to burst through her chest.

"He says he is acquainted with Lady Davenport," the butler intoned.

Laura's eyes flew to Helena, and then she raised her eyebrows in a silent question.

Helena nodded.

Breaking into a broad smile, Laura addressed the butler. "You may show him in."

In increasing agitation, Helena laid her embroidery aside and smoothed her hair away from her face. She straightened her dress and pinched her cheeks, then cast sheepish eyes at Laura, who regarded her in amusement.

The door opened again, and a tall man with dark hair and eyes strode in. His earnest gaze roved the room before settling on her, and then his eyes brimmed with love and hope. There was no doubt as to his purpose. There would never be a doubt again.

Introductions were made. Had she curtseyed? She knew not.

He said words she barely heard – please forgive the lateness of the hour… took some time to discover your direction… a particular matter to attend…

Her emotions threatened to spill over into tears. The time without him had only made her feelings for him deeper, and now it was all she could do not to throw herself in his arms. As he exchanged pleasantries with the Montgomerys their eyes remained locked on each other.

A pointed throat-clearing drew Helena's attention to Laura.

"What do you say, dear husband, to taking the children up for their supper?"

He stared at her. "It's very early for that, my love."

"Yes, but I think that Helena and her guest may need to, er, exchange some information in *private*."

"Ah. Yes. Quite." He scooped the baby up. "Right you are."

As she took her daughter's hand, Laura gave Helena a meaningful look. "I shall return on the hour to learn of your news," she said with a smile.

Helena nodded in appreciation. "Thank you." She glanced at the clock on the mantel. They would have nigh on fifteen minutes alone.

With the family safely gone, John closed the distance between them and reached for her hands. His countenance spoke of uncertainty, a question of whether she would accept him.

She immediately placed her hands in his, and her insides were lit aglow with the warmth and gentleness of his touch. "You came," she said in wonder.

He'd passed the test of character. She'd pushed him away – quite justifiably – and now he was pursuing her, nonetheless. The strength of his affection, the strength of his disposition, had overcome her reticence. A man with that kind of determination was what she wanted in her life – nay, what she needed.

He ran a thumb over her fingers, setting them to tingling. A frown creased his forehead. "How are you?"

His genuine care and concern touched her heart. "I am displaced, and I will admit somewhat disheartened. But I am glad to see you."

He broke into a tremulous smile. "You are?"

She nodded, slipping her hands along the length of his forearms and grasping his elbows, unable to stop herself from drawing nearer to him.

"I had every intention of leaving you in peace," he said, his fingers brushing the undersides of her arms. "But I have learned that time is of the essence."

"You know about my father's provision?"

"Yes. Privett wrote to me."

Privett. Still looking after her even though he no longer needed to do so. She must remember to thank him.

"I know these circumstances may make me appear mercenary," he went on, "but please know it is only your happiness I care for. I want you, with or without Willowbridge. All the grand houses and lands in the world would be nothing to me without you."

His eyes were desperately seeking affirmation. But she already knew that he was not here out of pity or to usurp her. She smiled. "I feel the same way."

"Oh! My Helena," he said fondly, and he ran his hands up her arms to take her gently by the shoulders. "There is something else you should know."

She frowned. Was there another surprise from his past?

He continued quickly. "I must disclose to you that I am no longer a man of property. I come to you penniless – but again, this has no bearing on my proposal."

How could that be? "What about the manor and your lands?"

John shook his head. "I have signed them over to… the child."

"The child?" Helena could not make sense of this at first, but then realisation dawned. "The child that is yours and…"

He nodded. "I am sorry to raise the subject. This is my attempt to make amends, to provide a secure future for him and his mother. Helena, please believe me, I did this before I was aware of the marriage proviso."

Helena's head spun with this new information. By making such a grand gesture, he was drawing a veil of finality over the situation. And she could see his motives were pure, especially if, as he said, there was no chance of getting Willowbridge when he made the decision. Then something important dropped into *her* mind.

"There is one thing *you* should know, John."

His eyebrows lifted. "Yes?"

"There is another condition, which applies when a gentleman acquires Willowbridge by marriage. They must take the name of Davenport."

He considered this, and then his lips spread in a broad grin. "I cannot think of a better arrangement." He slid his hands around behind her, resting one at her waist and one between her shoulders. In response to the comfort and delight of his hold, she moved in to hold him across the shoulders, near his neck. They were now joined from the waist down. Her head now spun for quite another reason.

"John?" she asked softly.

"Yes?"

"I need to be not only engaged but married by tomorrow. We would be too late to secure the estate once the banns are read."

His smiled remained in place. "It can be done. My business today was obtaining a special license for us."

"Oh!" He had thought of everything. Her spirits lifted.

"But I regret there is no time for you to choose some wedding attire. I know that is special to a lady. I wish I had realised earlier."

"It is no matter," she replied confidently. "I already have the perfect thing."

All worry evaporated from his face. "In that case, I have something in particular I should like to ask you."

Helena's pulse began to race. "Oh, yes?"

Keeping one arm about her waist, John caressed her cheek, his fingertips leaving a trail of fire. The admiration in his eyes sent a delicious shiver down her spine.

"My darling lady, I love you. It is a deep and abiding love that will not fade through difficulties. A love I know eclipses all the wicked things I have done. Please know that I am so, so sorry for the part I played in your ruin. If you condescend to take my hand, I vow to spend the rest of our lives proving my worth. Already, you have made me a nobler man. I will never equal your goodness, your sweetness, or your compassion, but it will be my ambition to do so. Your happiness is all I desire. Please allow me to take you as my wife."

Helena began to tremble all over as the enormity of the situation overwhelmed her. This was a moment she thought would never come, and now it was here it seemed like a wonderful dream. And yet, the depths of sincerity and adoration in his eyes confirmed this was real, and she would no longer have to be alone in the world. Absorbing his words, she struggled to find her own at first.

John tenderly claimed a loose tendril of her hair and tucked it behind her ear, before slipping his hand around to rest at the nape of her neck. Her breaths became quick and shallow.

"What is your answer, dearest Helena?" He searched her eyes. "Is your heart my own? Will you allow me to love you forever?"

"Yes!" She broke into an elated muddle of laughter and crying. "Yes, I will." She pulled herself up and into his embrace, nestling into his shoulder. "I love you too," she whispered into his ear. "In spite of everything... in spite of myself. There is something in you that draws me in, that pulls my heart towards yours."

She drew back to look into his eyes. "You have proven yourself to be capable of achieving a great many things for good." She smiled tremulously. "I could not have asked for a better gentleman to have by my side."

John moved his hands to cup her face, his countenance a study in pure joy. "You know my heart, Helena, and it is yours."

He bent down and touched his lips to hers, a caress so light Helena felt as if she was floating on clouds of ecstasy. How he cherished her. To show him how much he was wanted, she pulled herself up and into him, kissing him with euphoric eagerness. At length, she assured him, "I am yours, too."

And so it was that John and Helena pledged their troth to each other, as snow washed the city white. John wore a suit of blue, and Helena glowed in her gown of cream and gold. There to witness their commitment were three of John's bachelor friends, and the Montgomerys and Lady Lockhart on Helena's side... though the bridal couple hardly noticed the company. Directly thereafter, they visited Helena's solicitor and requested that he write to Sinclair with the happy news.

There was another surprise waiting for them upon their return to Willowbridge. John's maternal grandmother had settled a legacy upon him for the occasion of his marriage. The sum would more than cover the debts on the property and allow the Davenports to make several improvements which would shore up the estate's future.

It seemed the entire society of Mulberry had turned out to celebrate their arrival. After they descended from the carriage to cheers and applause, Helena turned to her new husband. "Welcome home," she said with a sparkling smile. "I love you, John."

*E*pilogue

Six months later

"There." John turned over his spade and put the last load of soil around their sapling.

Helena patted the soil down with her hands, then stood back to admire the new tree. "That should do nicely." It was near to the spot where her father's tree had been, and it marked their new life together.

John watered around the trunk, then put his arm around Helena's shoulders. "I hope one day we will see our children swinging from its branches."

Helena looked at him with a twinkle in her eye, beginning to colour.

He regarded her with curious amusement. "What is it, my dear?"

She grinned. "That day may be coming sooner than you think."

He gasped, turning to face her. "No, do you really mean…" He placed one hand lightly on her stomach. "A child?"

She nodded, tears gathering in her eyes. "Our child."

"Oh! My wonderful wife." He lifted her up and whirled her around as he laughed with delight. Setting her down gently, he said, "I am surely the most blessed man in the kingdom. And I shall love you both more than any man has ever loved."

"We shall treasure your love," she said breathlessly, "and I shall do my best to concede to your opinions as head of the household." She winked at him, and he laughed again.

"You are not fooling anyone, my love. I am entirely ruled by you, and always shall be… with pleasure."

She circled her arms around his waist. "Hush now, let us not talk of ruling – but I am all for pleasure."

He raised an eyebrow. "Why Lady Helena, such saucy talk!"

She giggled. "You have corrupted me, John Davenport." She reached up for an adoring kiss.

"My darling Helena," he whispered.

As they strolled back to Willowbridge, arm in arm, John's heart was so full he thought it might explode at any moment. He knew himself to be the luckiest man alive. He had turned the page on the old John, who took from the world with nary a care, to a new story of a man who would spend his days giving to others.

A new name, a new beginning. While he could never truly atone for his past actions, with Helena by his side he would forge a new existence as a kind, patient, and loving man. The man he always wanted to be... the man he truly was.

The End

Author's Note: Thank You

Thank you for reading *Heart of a Gentleman*. I very much hope you enjoyed it.

I would greatly appreciate it if you would leave a review for this book at Goodreads or Amazon.

Visit my website www.charlottebrentwood.com to sign up for my email newsletter to find out about my next releases and other news about my books.

Ways to connect with Charlotte:

Email:	charlotte.brentwood@gmail.com
Facebook:	www.facebook.com/charbrentwood
Twitter:	www.twitter.com/charbrentwood
Pinterest:	www.pinterest.com/charbrentwood
BookBub:	www.bookbub.com/authors/charlotte-brentwood

About the Author

A bookworm and scribbler for as long as she can remember, Charlotte always dreamed of sharing her stories with the world.

She lives in Auckland, New Zealand and loves exploring her beautiful surroundings. Her "day job" is in digital marketing. She is mother to two tiny tyrants and married to her real-life hero.

9 781738 616114